EXPEDITION TO EARTH

BOOKS BY ARTHUR C. CLARKE

EXPEDITION
TO EARTH

Arthur C. Clarke

BALLANTINE BOOKS • NEW YORK

A Del Rey® Book
Published by The Ballantine Publishing Group

Preface to the 1998 edition copyright © 1998 by Arthur C. Clarke
Copyright © 1953 by Arthur C. Clarke
Copyright renewed 1981 by Arthur C. Clarke

The story "Expedition to Earth" appeared in *Amazing Stories* under the title "Encounter in the Dawn," Copyright 1953 by Ziff-Davis Publishing Company; "Second Dawn" appeared in *Science Fiction Quarterly* and " 'If I Forget Thee, Oh, Earth' " appeared in *Future combined with Science Fiction Stories*, both Copyright 1951 by Columbia Publications, Inc.; "Breaking Strain" appeared in *Thrilling Wonder Stories* under the title "Thirty Seconds—Thirty Days," Copyright 1949 by Standard Magazines, Inc.; "History Lesson" appeared in *Startling Stories*, Copyright 1949 by Better Publications, Inc.; "*Superiority*" appeared in *The Magazine of Fantasy and Science Fiction*, Copyright 1951 by Fantasy House, Inc.; "Loophole," "Inheritance," and "Hide and Seek" appeared in *Astounding Science Fiction*, Copyright 1946, 1948, and 1949 respectively by Street & Smith Publications, Inc.; "Exile of the Eons" appeared in *Super Science*, Copyright 1950 by Popular Publications, Inc.; "The Sentinel" appeared in *The Avon Science Fiction and Fantasy Reader*, Copyright 1951 by Avon Periodicals, Inc.

http://www.randomhouse.com

Library of Congress Catalog Card Number: 98-96306

ISBN: 0-345-43073-5

Cover design by Min Choi
Cover photos: background © Tony Stone Images; Pyramid © Peter A. Simon/Phototake NYC
Text design by Jie Yang

Manufactured in the United States of America

First Mass Market Edition: December 1953
First Ballantine Books Trade Edition: October 1998
10 9 8 7 6 5 4 3 2 1

To Walter Gillings
—*who must share much of the blame.*

Contents

Preface to the 1998 Edition

I have a particular affection for *Expedition to Earth*, as it was the first collection of my short stories ever put between hard covers: the U.S. edition appeared in 1953 and the British one in 1954.

It also gives me great pleasure to reprint the dedication "To Walter Gillings, who must share much of the blame." Walter was the first editor of the pioneering British science fiction magazine *Tales of Wonder*, and my debt to him is incalculable. He gave me my very first typewriter—a monstrous machine that I can remember carrying back to my residence in a London bus. (It must now be a valuable antique, and I trust is duly cataloged in the "Clarkives.") Walter was the only editor who ever returned a story of mine saying, "It's too good for me—send it to the U.S. market." I did just that, and the legendary John W. Campbell promptly bought it for *Astounding*.

Since all the tales in this book were written between 1944 and 1948, several of them have inevitably dated. Thus, the title story put the first landing on the Moon in 1985: I am sure I thought this was wildly optimistic when I wrote it in 1945.

"Expedition to Earth" was originally called "History Lesson," and it was one of two stories I have written about the return of the glaciers (the other is "The Forgotten Enemy," reprinted in *Reach for Tomorrow*). Many years later, I came across a (almost literally!) chilling phrase in Will and Ariel Durant's *Story of Civilization*: "Civilization is an interlude between Ice Ages." Well, the next one is already overdue; perhaps global warming has arrived just in time to save us.

"Superiority" was inspired—if that is not too pretentious a word—by the German V2 rocket program. With 20-20 hindsight, it is now clear that the Third Reich's efforts to develop an intercontinental ballistic missile, which was too late to have any major influence on World War II, sapped its resources and contributed to the Allied victory.

Soon after publication, "Superiority" was inserted into the Engineering curriculum of M.I.T.—to warn future graduates that the Better is often the enemy of the Good—and the Best can be the enemy of both, as it is always too late.

And I must confess that the two characters in this little squib were based on Dr. Wernher von Braun and General Walter Dornberger, both of whom later became good friends. To set the record straight, may I say that Wernher was nothing like the Dr. Strangelove image many people have of him: He had a wonderful sense of humor and was greatly liked by all those who worked under him—Germans and Americans.

The most important story in this volume is undoubtedly "The Sentinel," which was written over Christmas 1948 for a BBC competition. (It wasn't even placed—I have often wondered what did win.) I am amused to see that I put the exploration of the Mare Crisium in "the late Summer of 1996." Well, we missed that date, but I hope we'll get there early in the next century.

The idea that extraterrestrial artifacts might be found on the Moon—or elsewhere in the Solar System—is now taken quite seriously, and a number of papers have been written on that subject; see, for example, "Small, Smart Interstellar Probes" and "The Possibility of Finding Traces of Extra-terrestrial Intelligence on Asteroids" in the *British Interplanetary Society's Journal* for May 1998. I cannot, alas, claim that it was an original idea: one of the most striking fictional treatments is still Jack London's "The Red One" (1918). And here are the subsequent adventures of "The Sentinel," after I met Stanley Kubrick at Trader Vic's in May 1964:

After various false starts and twelve-hour talkathons, by early May 1964, Stanley agreed that "The Sentinel" would provide good story material. But our first concept—and it is hard now for me to focus on such an idea, though it would have been perfectly viable—involved working up to the discovery of an extraterrestrial artifact as the climax, not the beginning, of the story. Before that, we would have a series of incidents or adventures devoted to the exploration of the Moon and Planets. For this Mark I version, our private title (never, of course, intended for public use) was "How the Solar System Was Won."

So once more I went back to my stockpile of short stories to find material that would fit into this pattern. I returned with five: "Breaking Strain" (from *Expedition to Earth*); "Out of the Cradle, Endlessly Orbiting . . . ," "Who's There?," "Into the Comet," and "Before Eden" (all from *Tales of Ten Worlds*). On May 28, 1964, I sold the lot to Stanley and signed an agreement to work on the projected movie. Our initial schedule was hilariously optimistic: working script, twelve weeks; discussing it, two weeks; revising, four weeks; fixing deal, four weeks; visuals, art, twenty weeks; shooting, twenty weeks; cutting, editing, twenty weeks—a total of eighty-two weeks. Allowing another twelve weeks before release, this added up to ninety-two weeks, or the better part of two years. I was very depressed by this staggering period of time, since I was (as always) in a hurry to get back to Ceylon. It was just as well that neither of us could have guessed the project's ultimate duration—four years.

The rest of 1964 was spent brainstorming. As we developed new ideas, so the original conception slowly changed. "The Sentinel" became the opening, not the finale; one by one, the other five stories were discarded. A year later, deciding (not necessarily in this order) that (a) it wasn't fair to Stanley to make him pay for something he didn't need and (b) these stories might make a pretty good movie someday, I bought them back from him.

The announced title of the project, when Stanley gave his intentions to the press, was *Journey Beyond the Stars*. I never liked this, because there had been far too many science fictional journeys and voyages. (Indeed, the inner space epic *Fantastic Voyage*, featuring Raquel Welch and a supporting cast of ten thousand blood corpuscles, was also going into production about this time.) Other titles that we ran up and failed to salute were *Universe, Tunnel to the Stars,* and *Planetfall.* It was not until eleven months after we started—April 1965—that Stanley selected *2001: A Space Odyssey.* As far as I can recall, it was entirely his idea.

The Lost Worlds of 2001

Well, it is hard to believe that more than thirty years later I was to embark on the *Final Odyssey,* and it is with great pleasure that I now relaunch this volume to join it.

Sir Arthur C. Clarke
June 10, 1998

Second Dawn

"Here they come," said Eris, rising to his forefeet and turning to look down the long valley. For a moment the pain and bitterness had left his thoughts, so that even Jeryl, whose mind was more closely tuned to his than to any other, could scarcely detect it. There was even an undertone of softness that recalled poignantly the Eris she had known in the days before the War—the old Eris who now seemed almost as remote and as lost as if he were lying with all the others out there on the plain.

A dark tide was flowing up the valley, advancing with a curious, hesitant motion, making odd pauses and little bounds forward. It was flanked with gold—the thin line of the Atheleni guards, so terrifyingly few compared with the black mass of the prisoners. But they were enough: indeed, they were only needed to guide that aimless river on its faltering way. Yet at the sight of so many thousands of the enemy, Jeryl found herself trembling and instinctively moved toward her mate, silver pelt resting against gold. Eris gave no sign that he had understood or even noticed the action.

The fear vanished as Jeryl saw how slowly the dark flood was moving forward. She had been told what to expect, but the reality was even worse than she had imagined. As the prisoners came nearer, all the hate and bitterness ebbed from her mind, to be replaced by a sick compassion. No one of her race need evermore fear the aimless, idiot horde that was being shepherded through the pass into the valley it would never leave again.

The guards were doing little more than urge the prisoners on with meaningless but encouraging cries, like nurses calling to infants too young to sense their thoughts. Strain as she might, Jeryl could detect no vestige of reason in any of those thousands of minds passing so near at hand. That brought home to her, more vividly than could anything else, the magnitude of the victory—and of the defeat. Her mind was sensitive enough to detect the first faint thoughts of children, hovering on the verge of consciousness. The defeated enemy had become not even children, but babies with the bodies of adults.

The tide was passing within a few feet of them now. For the first time, Jeryl realized how much larger than her own people the Mithraneans were, and how beautifully the light of the twin suns gleamed on the dark satin of their bodies. Once a magnificent specimen, towering a full head above Eris, broke loose from the main body and came blundering toward them, halting a few paces away. Then it crouched down like a lost and frightened child, the splendid head moving uncertainly from side to side as if seeking it knew not what. For a moment the great, empty eyes fell full upon Jeryl's face. She was as beautiful, she knew, to the Mithraneans as to her own race— but there was no flicker of emotion on the blank features, and no pause in the aimless movement of the questing head. Then an exasperated guard drove the prisoner back to his fellows.

"Come away," Jeryl pleaded. "I don't want to see any more. Why did you ever bring me here?" The last thought was heavy with reproach.

Eris began to move away over the grassy slopes in great bounds that she could not hope to match, but as he went his mind threw its message back to hers. His thoughts were still gentle, though the pain beneath them was too deep to be concealed.

"I wanted everyone—even you—to see what we had to to do to win the War. Then, perhaps, we will have no more in our lifetimes."

He was waiting for her on the brow of the hill, undistressed by the mad violence of his climb. The stream of prisoners was now too far below for them to see the details of its painful progress. Jeryl crouched down beside Eris and began to browse on the sparse vegetation that had been exiled from the fertile valley. She was slowly beginning to recover from the shock.

"But what will happen to them?" she asked presently, still haunted by the memory of that splendid, mindless giant going into a captivity it could never understand.

"They can be taught how to eat," said Eris. "There is food in the valley for half a year, and then we'll move them on. It will be a heavy strain on our own resources, but we're under a moral obligation—and we've put it in the peace treaty.

"They can never be cured?"

"No. Their minds have been totally destroyed. They'll be like that until they die."

There was a long silence. Jeryl let her gaze wander across the hills, falling in gentle undulations to the edge of the ocean. She could just make out, beyond a gap in the hills, the distant lines of blue that marked the sea—the mysterious, impassable sea. Its blue would soon be deepening into darkness, for the fierce white sun was setting and presently there would only be the red disk—hundreds of times larger but giving far less light—of its pale companion.

"I suppose we had to do it," Jeryl said at last. She was

thinking almost to herself, but she let enough of her thoughts escape for Eris to overhear.

"You've seen them," he answered briefly. "They were bigger and stronger than we. Though we outnumbered them, it was a stalemate: in the end, I think they would have won. By doing what we did, we saved thousands from death—or mutilation."

The bitterness came back into his thoughts, and Jeryl dared not look at him. He had screened the depths of his mind, but she knew that he was thinking of the shattered ivory stump upon his forehead. The War had been fought, except at the very end, with two weapons only—the razor-sharp hoofs of the little, almost useless forepaws, and the unicorn-like horns. With one of these, Eris could never fight again, and from the loss stemmed much of the embittered harshness that sometimes made him hurt even those who loved him.

Eris was waiting for someone, though who it was Jeryl could not guess. She knew better than to interrupt his thoughts while he was in his present mood, and so remained silently beside him, her shadow merging with his as it stretched far along the hilltop.

Jeryl and Eris came of a race which, in Nature's lottery, had been luckier than most—and yet had missed one of the greatest prizes of all. They had powerful bodies and powerful minds, and they lived in a world which was both temperate and fertile. By human standards, they would have seemed strange but by no means repulsive. Their sleek, fur-covered bodies tapered to a single giant rear-limb that could send them leaping over the ground in thirty-foot bounds. The two forelimbs were much smaller, and served merely for support and steadying. They ended in pointed hoofs that could be deadly in combat, but had no other useful purpose.

Both the Atheleni and their cousins, the Mithraneans, possessed mental powers that had enabled them to develop a very advanced mathematics and philosophy: but over the physical world they had no control at all. Houses, tools, clothes—indeed, artifacts of any kind—were utterly unknown to them. To races which possessed hands, tentacles, or other means of manipulation, their culture would have seemed incredibly limited: yet such is the adaptability of the mind, and the power of the commonplace, that they seldom realized their handicaps and could image no other way of life. It was natural to wander in great herds over the fertile plains, pausing where food was plentiful and moving on again when it was exhausted. This nomadic life had given them enough leisure for philosophy and even for certain arts. Their telepathic powers had not yet robbed them of their voices and they had developed a complex vocal music and an even more complex choreography. But they took the greatest pride of all in the range of their thoughts: for thousands of generations they had sent their minds roving through the misty infinities of metaphysics. Of *physics*, and indeed of all the sciences of matter, they knew nothing—not even that they existed.

"Someone's coming," said Jeryl suddenly. "Who is it?"

Eris did not bother to look, but there was a sense of strain in his reply.

"It's Aretenon. I agreed to meet him here."

"I'm so glad. You were such good friends once—it upset me when you quarreled."

Eris pawed fretfully at the turf, as he did when he was embarrassed or annoyed.

"I lost my temper with him when he left me during the fifth battle of the Plain. Of course I didn't know then why he had to go."

Jeryl's eyes widened in sudden amazement and understanding.

"You mean—he had something to do with the Madness, and the way the War ended?"

"Yes. There were very few people who knew more about the mind than he did. I don't know what part he played, but it must have been an important one. I don't suppose he'll ever be able to tell us much about it."

Still a considerable distance below them, Aretenon was zigzagging up the hillside in great leaps. A little later he had reached them, and instinctively bent his head to touch horns with Eris in the universal gesture of greeting. Then he stopped, horribly embarrassed, and there was an awkward pause until Jeryl came to the rescue with some conventional remarks.

When Eris spoke, Jeryl was relieved to sense his obvious pleasure at meeting his friend again, for the first time since their angry parting at the height of the War. It had been longer still since her last meeting with Aretenon, and she was surprised to see how much he had changed. He was considerably younger than Eris—but no one would have guessed it now. Some of his once-golden pelt was turning black with age, and with a flash of his old humor Eris remarked that soon no one would be able to tell him from a Mithranean.

Aretenon smiled.

"That would have been useful in the last few weeks. I've just come through their country, helping to round up the wanderers. We weren't very popular, as you might expect. If they'd known who I was, I don't suppose I'd have got back alive—armistice or no armistice."

"You weren't actually in charge of the Madness, were you?" asked Jeryl, unable to control her curiosity.

She had a momentary impression of thick, defensive mists forming around Aretenon's mind, shielding all his thoughts from the outer world. Then the reply came, curiously muffled, and with a sense of distance that was very rare in telepathic contact.

"No: I wasn't in supreme charge. But there were only two others between myself and—the top."

"Of course," said Eris, rather petulantly, "I'm only an ordinary soldier and don't understand these things. But I'd like to know just how you did it. Naturally," he added, "neither Jeryl nor myself would talk to anyone else."

Again that veil seemed to descend over Aretenon's thoughts. Then it lifted, ever so slightly.

"There's very little I'm allowed to tell. As you know, Eris, I was always interested in the mind and its workings. Do you remember the games we used to play, when I tried to uncover your thoughts, and you did your best to stop me? And how I sometimes made you carry out acts against your will?"

"I still think," said Eris, "that you couldn't have done that to a stranger, and that I was really unconsciously co-operating."

"That was true then—but it isn't any longer. The proof lies down there in the valley." He gestured toward the last stragglers who were being rounded up by the guards. The dark tide had almost passed, and soon the entrance to the valley would be closed.

"When I grew older," continued Aretenon, "I spent more and more of my time probing into the ways of the mind, and trying to discover why some of us can share our thoughts so easily, while others can never do so but must remain always isolated and alone, forced to communicate by sounds or gestures. And I became fascinated by those rare minds that are completely deranged, so that those who possess them seem less than children.

"I had to abandon these studies when the War began. Then, as you know, they called for me one day during the fifth battle. Even now, I'm not quite sure who was responsible for that. I was taken to a place a long way from here, where I found a little group of thinkers, many of whom I already knew.

"The plan was simple—and tremendous. From the dawn of our race we've known that two or three minds, linked together, could be used to control another mind, *if it were willing,* in the way that I used to control yours. We've employed this power for healing since ancient times. Now we planned to use it for destruction.

"There were two main difficulties. One was bound up with that curious limitation of our normal telepathic powers—the fact that, except in rare cases, we can only have contact over a distance *with someone we already know*, and can communicate with strangers only when we are actually in their presence.

"The second, and greater problem, was that the massed power of many minds would be needed, and never before had it been possible to link together more than two or three. How we succeeded is our main secret: like all such things, it seems easy now it has been done. And once we had started, it was simpler than we had expected. Two minds are more than twice as powerful as one, and three are much more than thrice as powerful as a single will. The exact mathematical relationship is an interesting one. You know how very rapidly the number of ways a group of objects may be arranged increases with the size of the group? Well, a similar relationship holds in this case.

"So in the end we had our Composite Mind. At first it was unstable, and we could hold it together for only a few seconds. It's still a tremendous strain on our mental resources, and even now we can only do it for—well, for long enough.

"All these experiments, of course, were carried out in great secrecy. If we could do this, so could the Mithraneans, for their minds are as good as ours. We had a number of their prisoners, and we used them as subjects."

For a moment the veil that hid Aretenon's inner thoughts seemed to tremble and dissolve: then he regained control.

"That was the worst part. It was bad enough to send madness into a far land, but it was infinitely worse when you could watch with your own eyes the effects of what you did.

"When we had perfected our technique, we made the first long-distance test. Our victim was someone so well-known to one of our prisoners—whose mind we had taken over—that we could identify him completely and thus the distance between us was no objection. The experiment worked, but of course no one suspected that we were responsible.

"We did not operate again until we were certain that our attack would be so overwhelming that it would end the War. From the minds of our prisoners we had identified about a score of Mithraneans—their friends and kindred—in such detail that we could pick them out and destroy them. As each mind fell beneath our attack, it gave up to us the knowledge of others, and so our power increased. We could have done far more damage than we did, for we took only the males."

"Was that," asked Jeryl bitterly, "so very merciful?"

"Perhaps not: but it should be remembered to our credit. We stopped as soon as the enemy sued for peace, and, as we alone knew what had happened, we went into their country to undo what damage we could. It was little enough."

There was a long silence. The valley was deserted now, and the white sun had set. A cold wind was blowing over the hills, passing, where none could follow it, out across the empty and untraveled sea. Then Eris spoke his thoughts almost whispering to Aretenon's mind.

"You did not come to tell me this, did you? There is something more." It was a statement rather than a query.

"Yes," replied Aretenon. "I have a message for you—one that will surprise you a good deal. It's from Therodimus."

"Therodimus! I thought—"

"You thought he was dead, or worse still, a traitor. He's neither, although he's lived in enemy territory for the last twenty years. The Mithraneans treated him as we did, and gave him everything he needed. They recognized his mind for what it was, and even during the War no one touched him. Now he wants to see you again."

Whatever emotions Eris was feeling at this news of his old teacher, he gave no sign of them. Perhaps he was recalling his youth, remembering now that Therodimus had played a greater part in the shaping of his mind than had any other single influence. But his thoughts were barred to Aretenon and even to Jeryl.

"What's he been doing all this time?" Eris asked at length. "And why does he want to see me now?"

"It's a long and complicated story," said Aretenon, "but Therodimus has made a discovery quite as remarkable as ours, and one that may have even greater consequences."

"Discovery? What sort of discovery?"

Aretenon paused, looking thoughtfully along the valley. The guards were returning, leaving behind only the few who would be needed to deal with any wandering prisoners.

"You know as much of our history as I do, Eris," he began. "It took, we believe, something like a million generations for us to reach our present level of development—and that's a tremendous length of time! Almost all the progress we've made has been due to our telepathic powers: without them we'd be little different from all those other animals that show such puzzling resemblances to us. We're very proud of our philosophy and our mathematics, of our music and dancing—but have you ever thought, Eris, that there might be other lines of cultural development which we've never even dreamed of? *That there might be other forces in the Universe besides mental ones?*"

"I don't know what you mean," said Eris flatly.

"It's hard to explain, and I won't try—except to say this. Do you realize just how pitiably feeble is our control over the external world, and how useless these limbs of ours really are? No—you can't, for you won't have seen what I have. But perhaps this will make you understand.

The pattern of Aretenon's thoughts modulated suddenly into a minor key.

"I remember once coming upon a bank of beautiful and curiously complicated flowers. I wanted to see what they were like inside, so I tried to open one, steadying it between my hoofs and picking it apart with my teeth. I tried again and again—and failed. In the end, half mad with rage, I trampled all those flowers into the dirt."

Jeryl could detect the perplexity in Eris's mind, but she could see that he was interested and curious to know more.

"I have had that sort of feeling, too," he admitted. "But what can one do about it? And after all, is it really important? There are a good many things in this universe which are not exactly as we should like them."

Aretenon smiled.

"That's true enough. But Therodimus has found out how to do something about it. Will you come and see him?"

"It must be a long journey."

"About twenty days from here, and we have to go across a river."

Jeryl felt Eris give a little shudder. The Atheleni hated water, for the excellent and sufficient reason that they were too heavy-boned to swim, and promptly drowned if they fell into it.

"It's in enemy territory: they won't like me."

"They respect you, and it might be a good idea for you to go—a friendly gesture, as it were."

"But I'm wanted here."

"You can take my word that nothing you do here is as important as the message Therodimus has for you—and for the whole world."

Eris veiled his thoughts for a moment, then uncovered them briefly.

"I'll think about it," he said.

* * *

It was surprising how little Aretenon managed to say on the many days of the journey. From time to time Eris would challenge the defenses of his mind with half-playful thrusts, but always they were parried with an effortless skill. About the ultimate weapon that had ended the War he would say nothing, but Eris knew that those who had wielded it had not yet disbanded and were still at their secret hiding place. Yet though he would not talk about the past, Aretenon often spoke of the future, and with the urgent anxiety of one who had helped to shape it and was not sure if he had acted aright. Like many others of his race, he was haunted by what he had done, and the sense of guilt sometimes overwhelmed him. Often he made remarks which puzzled Eris at the time, but which he was to remember more and more vividly in the years ahead.

"We've come to a turning-point in our history, Eris. The powers we've uncovered will soon be shared by the Mithraneans, and another war will mean destruction for us both. All my life I've worked to increase our knowledge of the mind, but now I wonder if I've brought something into the world that is too powerful, and too dangerous, for us to handle. Yet it's too late, now, to retrace our footsteps: sooner or later our culture was bound to come to this point, and to discover what we have found.

"It's a terrible dilemma: and there's only one solution. We cannot go back, and if we go forward we may meet disaster. So we must change the very nature of our civilization, and break completely with the million generations behind us. You can't imagine how that could be done: nor could I, until I met Therodimus and he told me of his dream.

"The mind is a wonderful thing, Eris—but by itself it is helpless in the universe of matter. We know now how to multiply the power of our brains by an enormous factor: we can solve, perhaps, the great problems of mathematics that have baffled us for ages. But neither our unaided minds, nor the group-mind we've now created, can alter in the slightest the one fact that all through history has brought us and the Mithraneans into conflict—the fact that the food supply is fixed, and our populations are not."

Jeryl would watch them, taking little part in their thoughts, as they argued these matters. Most of their discussions took place while they were browsing, for like all active ruminants they had to spend a considerable part of each day searching for food. Fortunately the land through which they were passing was extremely fertile—indeed, its fertility had been one of the causes of the War. Eris, Jeryl was glad to see, was becoming something of his old self again. The feeling of frustrated bitterness that had filled his mind for so many months had not lifted, but it was no longer as all-pervading as it had been.

They left the open plain on the twenty-second day of their journey. For a long time they had been traveling through Mithranean territory, but those few of their ex-enemies they had seen had been inquisitive rather than hostile. Now the grasslands were coming to an end, and the forest with all its primeval terrors lay ahead.

"Only one carnivore lives in this region," Aretenon reassured them, "and it's no match for the three of us. We'll be past the trees in a day and a night."

"A night—in the forest!" gasped Jeryl, half petrified with terror at the very thought.

Aretenon was obviously a little ashamed of himself.

"I didn't like to mention it before," he apologized, "but there's really no danger. I've done it by myself, several times. After all, none of the great flesh-eaters of ancient times still exists—and it won't be really dark, even in the woods. The red sun will still be up."

Jeryl was still trembling slightly. She came of a race which, for thousands of generations, had lived on the high hills and the open plains, relying on speed to escape from danger. The thought of going among trees—and in the dim red twilight while the primary sun was down—filled her with panic. And of the three of them, only Aretenon possessed a horn with which to fight. (It was nothing like so long or sharp, thought Jeryl, as Eris's had been.)

She was still not at all happy even when they had spent a completely uneventful day moving through the woods. The only animals they saw were tiny, long-tailed creatures that ran up and down the tree-trunks with amazing speed, gibbering with anger as the intruders passed. It was entertaining to watch them, but Jeryl did not think that the forest would be quite so amusing in the night.

Her fears were well founded. When the fierce white sun passed below the trees, and the crimson shadows of the red giant lay everywhere, a change seemed to come over the world. A sudden silence swept across the forest—a silence abruptly broken by a very distant wail toward which the three of them turned instinctively, ancestral warnings shrieking in their minds.

"What was that?" gasped Jeryl.

Aretenon was breathing swiftly, but his reply was calm enough.

"Never mind," he said. "It was a long way off. I don't know what it was."

And Jeryl knew that he was lying.

They took turns keeping guard, and the long night wore slowly away. From time to time Jeryl would awaken from troubled dreams into the nightmare reality of the strange, distorted trees gathered threateningly around her. Once, when she was on guard, she heard the sound of a heavy body moving through the woods very far away—but it came no nearer and she did not disturb the others. So at last the longed-for brilliance of the white sun began to flood the sky, and the day had come again.

Aretenon, Jeryl thought, was probably more relieved than he pretended to be. He was almost boyish as he frisked around in the morning sunlight, snatching an occasional mouthful of foliage from an overhanging branch.

"We've only half a day to go now," he said cheerfully. "We'll be out of the forest by noon."

There was a mischievous undertone to his thoughts that puzzled Jeryl. It seemed as if Aretenon was keeping still another secret from them, and Jeryl wondered what further obstacles they would have to overcome. By midday she knew, for their way was barred by a great river flowing slowly past them as if in no haste to meet the sea.

Eris looked at it with some annoyance, measuring it with a practiced eye.

"It's much too deep to ford here. We'll have to go a long way upstream before we can cross."

Aretenon smiled.

"On the contrary," he said cheerfully, "we're going *downstream*."

Eris and Jeryl looked at him in amazement.

"Are you mad?" Eris cried.

"You'll soon see. We've not far to go now—you've come all this way, so you might as well trust me for the rest of the journey."

The river slowly widened and deepened. If it had been impassable before, it was doubly so now. Sometimes, Eris knew, one came upon a stream across which a tree had fallen, so that one could walk over on the trunk—though it was a risky thing to do. But this river was the width of many trees, and was growing no narrower.

"We're nearly there," said Aretenon at last. "I recognize the place. Someone should be coming out of those woods at any moment." He gestured with his horn to the trees on the far side of the river, and almost as he did so three figures came bounding out on to the bank. Two of them, Jeryl saw, were Atheleni: the third was a Mithranean.

They were now nearing a great tree, standing by the water's edge, but Jeryl had paid it little attention: she was too interested in the figures on the distant bank, wondering what they were going to do next. So when Eris's amazement exploded like a thunderclap in the depths of her own mind, she was too confused for a moment to realize its cause. Then she turned toward the tree, and saw what Eris had seen.

To some minds and some races, few things could have been more natural or more commonplace than a thick rope tied round a tree trunk, and floating out across the waters of a river to another tree on the far bank. Yet it filled both Jeryl and Eris with the terror of the unknown, and for one awful moment Jeryl thought that a gigantic snake was emerging from the water. Then she saw that it was not alive, but her fear remained. For it was the first artificial object that she had ever seen.

"Don't worry about *what* it is, or how it was put there," counseled Aretenon. "It's going to carry you across, and that's all that matters for the moment. Look—there's someone coming over now!"

One of the figures on the far bank had lowered itself into the water, and was working its way with its forelimbs along the rope. As it came nearer—it was the Mithranean, and a female—Jeryl saw that it was carrying a second and much smaller rope looped round the upper part of its body.

With the skill of long practice, the stranger made her way across the floating cable, and emerged dripping from the river. She seemed to know Aretenon, but Jeryl could not intercept their thoughts.

"I can go across without any help," said Aretenon, "but I'll show you the easy way."

He slipped the loop over his shoulder and, dropping into the water, hooked his fore-limbs over the fixed cable. A moment later he was being dragged across at a great speed by the two others on the far bank where, after much trepidation, Eris and Jeryl presently joined him.

It was not the sort of bridge one would expect from a race which could quite easily have dealt with the mathematics of a reinforced concrete arch—if the possibility of such an object had ever occurred to it. But it served its purpose, and once it had been made, they could use it readily enough.

Once it had been made. But—who had made it?

When their dripping guides had rejoined them, Aretenon gave his friends a warning.

"I'm afraid you're going to have a good many shocks while you're here. You'll see some very strange sights, but when you understand them, they'll cease to puzzle you in the slightest. In fact, you will soon come to take them for granted."

One of the strangers, whose thoughts neither Eris nor Jeryl could intercept, was giving him a message.

"Therodimus is waiting for us," said Aretenon. "He's very anxious to see you."

"I've been trying to contact him," complained Eris. "But I've not succeeded."

Aretenon seemed a little troubled.

"You'll find he's changed," he said. "After all, you've not seen each other for many years. It may be some time before you can make full contact again."

Their road was a winding one through the forest, and from time to time curiously narrow paths branched off in various directions. Therodimus, thought Eris, must have changed indeed for him to have taken up permanent residence among trees. Presently the track opened out into a large, semicircular clearing with a low white cliff lying along its diameter. At the foot of the cliff were several dark holes of varying sizes—obviously the openings of caves.

It was the first time that either Eris or Jeryl had ever entered a cave, and they did not greatly look forward to the experience. They were relieved when Aretenon told them to wait just outside the opening, and went on alone toward the puzzling yellow light that glowed in the depths. A moment later, dim memories began to pulse in Eris's mind, and he knew that his old teacher was coming, even though he could no longer fully share his thoughts.

Something stirred in the gloom, and then Therodimus came out into the sunlight. At the sight of him, Jeryl screamed once and buried her head in Eris's mane, but Eris stood firm, though he was trembling as he had never done before battle. For Therodimus blazed with a magnificence that none of his race had ever known since history began. Around his neck hung a band of glittering objects that caught and refracted the sunlight in myriad colors, while covering his body was a sheet of some thick, many-hued material that rustled softly as he walked. And his horn was no longer the yellow of ivory: some magic had changed it to the most wonderful purple that Jeryl had ever seen.

Therodimus stood motionless for a moment, savoring their amazement to the full. Then his rich laugh echoed in their minds, and he reared up upon his hind limb. The colored garment fell whispering to the ground, and at a toss of his head the glittering necklace arched like a rainbow into a corner of the cave. But the purple horn remained unchanged.

It seemed to Eris that he stood at the brink of a great chasm, with Therodimus beckoning to him on the far side. Their thoughts struggled to form a bridge, but could make no contact. Between them was the gulf of half a lifetime and many battles, of myriad unshared experiences—Therodimus' years in this strange land, his own mating with Jeryl and the memory of their lost children. Though they stood face to face, a few feet only between them, their thoughts could never meet again.

Then Aretenon, with all the power and authority of his unsurpassed skill, did something to his mind that Eris was never quite able to recall. He only knew that the years seemed to have rolled back, that he was once more the eager, anxious pupil—and that he could speak to Therodimus again.

It was strange to sleep underground, but less unpleasant than spending the night amid the unknown terrors of the forest. As she watched the crimson shadows deepening beyond the entrance to the little cave, Jeryl tried to collect her scattered thoughts. She had understood only a small part of what had passed between Eris and Therodimus, but she knew that something incredible was taking place. The evidence of her eyes was enough to prove that: today she had seen things for which there were no words in her language.

She had heard things, too. As they had passed one of the cave-mouths, there had come from it a rhythmic, "whirring" sound, unlike that made by any animal she knew. It had continued steadily without pause or break as long as she could hear it, and even now its unhurried rhythm had not left her mind. Aretenon, she believed, had also noticed it, though without any surprise: Eris had been too engrossed with Therodimus.

The old philosopher had told them very little, preferring, as he said, to show them his empire when they had had a good night's rest. Nearly all their talk had been concerned with the events of their own land during the last few years, and Jeryl found it somewhat boring. Only one thing had interested her, and she had eyes for little else. That was the wonderful chain of colored crystals that Therodimus had worn around his neck. What it was, or how it had been created, she could not imagine: but she coveted it. As she fell asleep, she found herself thinking idly, but more than half seriously, of the sensation it would cause if she returned to her people with such a marvel gleaming against her own pelt. It would look so much better there than upon old Therodimus.

Aretenon and Therodimus met them at the cave soon after dawn. The philosopher had discarded his regalia—which he had obviously worn only to impress his guests—and his horn had returned to its normal yellow. That was one thing Jeryl thought she could understand, for she had come across fruits whose juices could cause such color changes.

Therodimus settled himself at the mouth of the cave. He began his narration without preliminaries, and Eris guessed that he must have told it many times before to earlier visitors.

"I came to this place, Eris, about five years after leaving our country. As you know, I was always interested in strange lands, and from the Mithraneans I'd heard rumors that intrigued me very much. How I traced them to their source is a long story that doesn't matter now. I crossed the river far upstream one summer, when the water was very low. There's only one place where it can be done, and then only in the driest years. Higher still the river loses itself in the mountains, and I don't think there's any way through them. So this is virtually an island— almost completely cut off from Mithranean territory.

"It's an island, but it's not uninhabited. The people who live here are called the Phileni, and they have a very remarkable culture—one entirely different from our own. Some of the products of that culture you've already seen.

"As you know, there are many different races on our world, and quite a few of them have some sort of intelligence. But there is a great gulf between us and all other creatures. As far as we know, we are the only beings capable of abstract thought and complex logical processes.

"The Phileni are a much younger race than ours, and they are intermediate between us and the other animals. They've lived here on this rather large island for several thousand generations—but their rate of development has been many, many times swifter than ours. They neither possess nor understand our telepathic powers, but they have something else which we may well envy—something which is responsible for the whole of their civilization and its incredibly rapid progress."

Therodimus paused, then rose slowly to his feet.

"Follow me," he said. "I'll take you to see the Phileni."

He led them back to the caves from which they had come the night before, pausing at the entrance from which Jeryl had heard that strange, rhythmic whirring. It was clearer and louder now, and she saw Eris start as though he had noticed it for the first time. Then Therodimus uttered a high-pitched whistle, and at once the whirring slackened, falling octave by octave until it had ebbed into silence. A moment later something came toward them out of the semigloom.

It was a little creature, scarcely half their height, and it did not hop, but walked upon two jointed limbs that seemed very thin and feeble. Its large spherical head was dominated by three huge eyes, set far apart and capable of independent movement. With the best will in the world, Jeryl did not think it was very attractive.

Then Therodimus uttered another whistle, and the creature raised its fore-limbs toward them.

"Look closely," said Therodimus, very gently, "and you will see the answer to many of your questions."

For the first time, Jeryl saw that the creature's fore-limbs did not end in hoofs, or indeed after the fashion of any animal with which she was acquainted. Instead, they divided into a least a dozen thin, flexible tentacles and two hooked claws.

"Go toward it, Jeryl," commanded Therodimus. "It has something for you."

Hesitantly, Jeryl moved forward. She noticed that the creature's body was crossed with bands of some dark material, to which were attached unidentifiable objects. It dropped a forelimb to one of these, and a cover opened to reveal a cavity, inside which something glittered. Then the little tentacles were clutching that marvelous crystal necklace, and with a movement so swift and dexterous that Jeryl could scarcely follow it, the Phileni moved forward and clasped it round her neck.

Therodimus brushed aside her confusion and gratitude, but his shrewd old mind was well pleased. Jeryl would be his ally now in whatever he planned to do. But Eris's emotions might not be so easily swayed, and in this matter mere logic was not enough. His old pupil had changed so much, had been so deeply wounded by the past, that Therodimus could not be certain of success. Yet he had a plan that could turn even these difficulties to his advantage.

He gave another whistle, and the Phileni made a curious waving gesture with its hands and disappeared into the cave. A moment later that strange whirring ascended once more from the silence, but Jeryl's curiosity was now quite overshadowed by her delight in her new possession.

"We'll go through the woods," said Therodimus "to the nearest settlement—it's only a little way from here. The Phileni don't live in the open, as we do. In fact, they differ from us in almost every conceivable way. I'm even afraid," he added ruefully, "that they're much better natured than we are, and I believe that one day they'll be more intelligent. But first of all, let me tell you what I've learned about them, so that you can understand what I'm planning to do."

* * *

The mental evolution of any race is conditioned, even dominated, by physical factors which that race almost invariably takes for granted as part of the natural order of things. The wonderfully sensitive hands of the Phileni had enabled them to find by experiment and trial facts which had taken the planet's only other intelligent species a thousand times as long to discover by pure deduction. Quite early in their history, the Phileni had invented simple tools. From these they had proceeded to fabrics, pottery, and the use of fire. When Therodimus had discovered them, they had already invented the lathe and the potter's wheel, and were about to move into their first Metal Age—with all that that implied.

On the purely intellectual plane, their progress had been less rapid. They were clever and skillful, but they had a dislike of abstract thought and their mathematics was purely empirical. They knew, for example, that a triangle with sides in the ratio three-four-five was right-angled, but had not suspected that this was only a special case of a much more general law. Their knowledge was full of such yawning gaps which, despite the help of Therodimus and his several-score disciples, they seemed in no great hurry to fill.

Therodimus they worshipped as a god, and for two whole generations of their short-lived race they had obeyed him in everything, giving him all the products of their skill that he needed, and making at his suggestion the new tools and devices that had occurred to him. The partnership had been incredibly fertile, for it was as if both races had suddenly been released from their shackles. Great manual skill and great intellectual powers had fused in a fruitful union probably unique in all the universe—and progress that would normally have taken millennia had been achieved in less than a decade.

As Aretenon had promised them, though Eris and Jeryl saw many marvels, they came across nothing that they could not understand once they had watched the little Phileni craftsmen at work and had seen with what magic their hands shaped natural materials into lovely or useful forms. Even their tiny towns and primitive farms soon lost their wonder and became part of the accepted order of things.

Therodimus let them look their fill, until they had seen every aspect of this strangely sophisticated Stone Age culture. Because they knew no different, they found nothing incongruous in the sight of a Phileni potter—who could scarcely count beyond ten—shaping a series of complex algebraic surfaces under the guidance of a young Mithranean mathematician. Like all his race, Eris possessed tremendous powers of mental visualization, but he realized how much easier geometry would be if one could actually *see* the shapes one was considering. From this beginning (though he could not guess it) would one day evolve the idea of a written language.

Jeryl was fascinated above all things by the sight of the little Phileni women weaving fabrics upon their primitive looms. She could sit for hours watching the flying shuttles and wishing that she could use them. Once one had seen it done, it seemed so simple and obvious—and so utterly beyond the power of the clumsy, useless limbs of her own people.

They grew very fond of the Phileni, who seemed eager to please and were pathetically proud of all their manual skills. In these new and novel surroundings, meeting fresh wonders every day, Eris seemed to be recovering from some of the scars which the War had left upon his mind. Jeryl knew, however, that there was still much damage to be undone. Sometimes, before he could hide them, she would come across raw, angry wounds in the depths of Eris's mind, and she feared that many of them—like the broken stump of his horn—would never heal. Eris had hated the War, and the manner of its ending still oppressed him. Beyond this, Jeryl knew, he was haunted by the fear that it might come again.

These troubles she often discussed with Therodimus, of

whom she had now grown very fond. She still did not fully understand why he had brought them here, or what he and his followers were planning to do. Therodimus was in no hurry to explain his actions, for he wished Jeryl and Eris to draw their own conclusions as far as possible. But at last, five days after their arrival, he called them to his cave.

"You've now seen," he began, "most of the things we have to show you here. You know what the Phileni can do, and perhaps you have thought how much our own lives will be enriched once we can use the products of their skill. That was my first thought when I came here, all those years ago.

"It was an obvious and rather naïve idea, but it led to a much greater one. As I grew to know the Phileni, and found how swiftly their minds had advanced in so short a time, I realized what a fearful disadvantage our own race had always labored under. I began to wonder how much further forward *we* would have been had we the Phileni's control over the physical world. It is not a question of mere convenience, or the ability to make beautiful things like that necklace of yours, Jeryl, but something much more profound. It is the difference between ignorance and knowledge, between weakness and power.

"We have developed our minds, and our minds alone, until we can go no further. As Aretenon has told you, we have now come to a danger that threatens our entire race. We are under the shadow of the irresistible weapon against which there can be no defense.

"The solution is, quite literally, in the hands of the Phileni. We must use their skills to reshape our world, and so remove the cause of all our wars. We must go back to the beginning and re-lay the foundations of our culture. It won't be *our* culture alone, though, for we shall share it with the Phileni. They will be the hands—we the brains. Oh, I have dreamed of the world that may come, ages ahead, when even the marvels you see around you now will be considered childish toys! But not many are philosophers, and I need an argument more substantial than dreams. That final argument I believe I may have found, though I cannot yet be certain.

"I have asked you here, Eris, partly because I wanted to renew our old friendship, and partly because your word will now have far greater influence than mine. You are a hero among your own people, and the Mithraneans also will listen to you. I want you to return, taking with you some of the Phileni and their products. Show them to your people, and ask them to send their young men here to help us with our work."

There was a pause during which Jeryl could gather no hints of Eris's thoughts. Then he replied hesitantly:

"But I still don't understand. These things that the Phileni make are very pretty, and some of them may be useful to us. But how can they change us as profoundly as you seem to think?"

Therodimus sighed. Eris could not see past the present into the future that was yet to be. He had not caught, as Therodimus had done, the promise that lay beyond the busy hands and tools of the Phileni—the first faint intimations of the Machine. Perhaps he would never understand: but he could still be convinced.

Veiling his deeper thoughts, Therodimus continued:

"Perhaps some of these things are toys, Eris—but they may be more powerful than you think. Jeryl, I know, would be loath to part with hers . . . and perhaps I can find one that would convince you."

Eris was skeptical, and Jeryl could see that he was in one of his darker moods.

"I doubt it very much," he said.

"Well, I can try." Therodimus gave a whistle, and one of the Phileni came running up. There was a short exchange of conversation.

"Would you come with me, Eris? It will take some time."

Eris followed him, the others, at Therodimus' request, remaining behind. They left the large cave and went toward the row of smaller ones which the Phileni used for their various trades.

The strange whirring was sounding loudly in Eris's ears, but for a moment he could not see its cause, the light of the crude-oil lamps being too faint for his eyes. Then he made out one of the Phileni bending over a wooden table upon which something was spinning rapidly, driven by a belt from a treadle operated by another of the little creatures. He had seen the potters using a similar device, but this was different. It was shaping wood, not clay, and the potter's fingers had been replaced by a sharp metal blade from which long, thin shavings were curling out in fascinating spirals. With their huge eyes, the Phileni, who disliked full sunlight, could see perfectly in the gloom, but it was some time before Eris could discover just what was happening. Then, suddenly, he understood.

"Aretenon," said Jeryl when the others had left them, "why should the Phileni do all these things for us? Surely they're quite happy as they are?"

The question, Aretenon thought, was typical of Jeryl and would never have been asked by Eris.

"They will do anything that Therodimus says," he answered, "but even apart from that there's so much we can give them as well. When we turn our minds to their problems, we can see how to solve them in ways that would never have occurred to them. They're very eager to learn, and already we must have advanced their culture by hundreds of generations. Also, they're physically very feeble. Although we don't possess their dexterity, our strength makes possible tasks they could never attempt."

They had wandered to the edge of the river, and stood

for a moment watching the unhurried waters moving down to the sea. They Jeryl turned to go upstream, but Aretenon stopped her.

"Therodimus doesn't want us to go that way, yet," he explained. "It's just another of his little secrets. He never likes to reveal his plans until they're ready."

Slightly piqued, and distinctly curious, Jeryl obediently turned back. She would, of course, come this way again as soon as there was no one else about.

It was very peaceful here in the warm sunlight, among the pools of heat trapped by the trees. Jeryl had almost lost her fear of the forest, though she knew she would never be quite happy there.

Aretenon seemed very abstracted, and Jeryl knew that he wished to say something and was marshaling his thoughts. Presently he began to speak, with the freedom that is possible only between two people who are fond of each other but have no emotional ties.

"It is very hard, Jeryl," he began, "to turn one's back on the work of a lifetime. Once I had hoped that the great new forces we have discovered could be safely used, but now I know that is impossible, at least for many ages. Therodimus was right—we can go no further with our minds alone. Our culture has been hopelessly one-sided, though through no fault of ours. We cannot solve the fundamental problem of peace and war without a command over the physical world such as the Phileni possess—and which we hope to borrow from them.

"Perhaps there will be other great adventures here for our minds, to make us forget what we will have to abandon. We shall be able to learn something from Nature at last. What is the difference between fire and water, between wood and stone? What are the suns, and what are those millions of faint lights we see in the sky when both the suns are down? Perhaps the answers to all these questions may lie at the end of the new road along which we must travel."

He paused.

"New knowledge—new wisdom—in realms we have never dreamed of before. It may lure us away from the dangers we have encountered: for certainly nothing we can learn from Nature will ever be as great a threat as the peril we have uncovered in our own minds."

The flow of Aretenon's thoughts was suddenly interrupted. Then he said: "I think that Eris wants to see you."

Jeryl wondered why Eris had not sent the message to her: she wondered, too, at the undertone of amusement—or was it something else?—in Aretenon's mind.

There was no sign of Eris as they approached the caves, but he was waiting for them and came bounding out into the sunlight before they could reach the entrance. Then Jeryl gave an involuntary cry, and retreated a pace or two as her mate came toward her.

For Eris was whole again. Gone was the shattered stump on his forehead: it had been replaced by a new, gleaming horn no less splendid than the one that he had lost.

In a belated gesture of greeting, Eris touched horns with Aretenon. Then he was gone into the forest in great joyous leaps—but not before his mind had met Jeryl's as it had seldom done since the days before the War.

"Let him go," said Therodimus softly. "He would rather be alone. When he returns I think you will find him—different." He gave a little laugh. "The Phileni are clever, are they not? Now, perhaps, Eris will be more appreciative of their 'toys.' "

"I know I am impatient," said Therodimus, "but I am old now, and I want to see the changes begin in my own lifetime.

That is why I am starting so many schemes in the hope that some at least will succeed. But this is the one, above all, in which I have put most faith."

For a moment he lost himself in his thoughts. Not one in a hundred of his own race could fully share his dream. Even Eris, though he now believed in it, did so with his heart rather than his mind. Perhaps Aretenon—the brilliant and subtle Aretenon, so desperately anxious to neutralize the powers he had brought into the world—might have glimpsed the reality. But his was of all minds the most impenetrable, save when he wished otherwise.

"You know as well as I do," continued Therodimus, as they walked upstream, "that our wars have only one cause—Food. We and the Mithraneans are trapped on this continent of ours with its limited resources, which we can do nothing to increase. Ahead of us we have always the nightmare of starvation, and for all our vaunted intelligence there has been nothing we can do about it. Oh yes, we have scraped some laborious irrigation ditches with our fore-hoofs, but how slight their help has been!

"The Phileni have discovered how to grow crops that increase the fertility of the ground many-fold. I believe that we can do the same—once we have adapted their tools for our own use. That is our first and most important task, but it is not the one on which I have set my heart. The final solution to our problem, Eris, *must be the discovery of new, virgin lands into which our people can migrate.*"

He smiled at the other's amazement.

"No, don't think I'm mad. Such lands do exist, I'm sure of it. Once I stood at the edge of the ocean and watched a great flight of birds coming inland from far out at sea. I have seen them flying outward, too, so purposefully that I was certain they were going to some other country. And I have followed them with my thoughts."

"Even if your theory is true, which it probably is," said Eris, "what use is it to us?" He gestured to the river flowing beside them. "We drown in the water, and you cannot build a rope to support us—" His thoughts suddenly faded out into a jumbled chaos of ideas.

Therodimus smiled.

"So you have guessed what I hope to do. Well, now you can see if you are right."

They had come to a level stretch of bank, upon which a group of Phileni were busily at work, under the supervision of some of Therodimus' assistants. Lying at the water's edge was a strange object which, Eris realized, was made of many tree-trunks joined together by ropes.

They watched in fascination as the orderly tumult reached its climax. There was a great pulling and pushing, and the raft moved ponderously into the water with a mighty splash. The spray had scarcely ceased to fall when a young Mithranean leaped from the bank and began to dance gleefully upon the logs, which were now tugging at the moorings as if eager to break away and follow the river down to the sea. A moment later he had been joined by others, rejoicing in their mastery of a new element. The little Phileni, unable to make the leap, stood watching patiently on the bank while their masters enjoyed themselves.

There was an exhilaration about the scene that no one could miss, though perhaps few of those present realized that they were at a turning point in history. Only Therodimus stood a little apart from the rest, lost in his own thoughts. This primitive raft, he knew, was merely a beginning. It must be tested upon the river, then along the shores of the ocean. The work would take years, and he was never likely to see the first voyagers returning from those fabulous lands whose existence was still no more than a guess. But what had been begun, others would finish.

Overhead, a flight of birds was passing across the forest. Therodimus watched them go, envying their freedom to move at will over land and sea. He had begun the conquest of the water for his race, but that the skies might one day be theirs also was beyond even his imagination.

Aretenon, Jeryl, and the rest of the expedition had already crossed the river when Eris said good-bye to Therodimus. This time they had crossed without a drop of water touching their bodies, for the raft had come downstream and was performing valuable duties as a ferry. A new and much improved model was already under construction, as it was painfully obvious that the prototype was not exactly seaworthy. These initial difficulties would be quickly overcome by designers who, even if they were forced to work with Stone Age tools, could handle with ease the mathematics of metacenters, buoyancies, and advanced hydrodynamics.

"Your task won't be a simple one," said Therodimus, "for you cannot show your people all the things you have seen here. At first you must be content to sow the seed, to arouse interest and curiosity—particularly among the young, who will come here to learn more. Perhaps you will meet opposition: I expect so. But every time you return to us, we shall have new things to show you to strengthen your arguments."

They touched horns: then Eris was gone, taking with him the knowledge that was to change the world—so slowly at first, then ever more swiftly. Once the barriers were down, since the Mithraneans and the Atheleni had been given the simple tools which they could fasten to their fore-limbs and use unaided, progress would be swift. But for the present they must rely on the Phileni for everything: and there were so few of them.

Therodimus was well content. Only in one respect was he

disappointed, for he had hoped that Eris, who had always been his favorite, might also be his successor. The Eris who was now returning to his own people was no longer self-obsessed or em-bittered, for he had a mission and hope for the future. But he lacked the keen, far-ranging vision that was needed here: it would be Aretenon who must continue what he had begun. Still, that could not be helped, and there was no need yet to think of such matters. Therodimus was very old, but he knew that he would be meeting Eris many times again here by the river at the entrance to his land.

The ferry was gone now, and though he had expected it, Eris stopped amazed at the great span of the bridge, swaying sightly in the breeze. Its execution did not quite match its design—a good deal of mathematics had gone into its para-bolic suspension—but it was still the first great engineering feat in history. Constructed entirely of wood and rope though it was, it forecast the shape of the metal giants to come.

Eris paused in the middle. He could see smoke rising from the shipyards facing the ocean, and thought he could just glimpse the masts of some of the new vessels that were being built for coastal trade. It was hard to believe that when he had first crossed this river he had been dragged over, dangling from a rope.

Aretenon was waiting for them on the far bank. He moved rather slowly now, but his eyes were still bright with the old, eager intelligence. He greeted Eris warmly.

"I'm glad you could come now. You're just in time."

That, Eris knew, could mean only one thing.

"The ships are back?"

"Almost: they were sighted an hour ago, out on the horizon. They should be here at any moment, and then we shall know the truth at last, after all these years. If only—"

His thoughts faded out, but Eris could continue them. They had come to the great pyramid of stones beneath which Therodimus lay—Therodimus, whose brain was behind everything they saw, but who could never learn now if his most cherished dream was true or not.

There was a storm coming up from the ocean, and they hurried along the new road that skirted the river's edge. Small boats of a kind that Eris had not seen before went past them occasionally, operated by Atheleni or Mithraneans with wooden paddles strapped to their fore-limbs. It always gave Eris great pleasure to see such new conquests, such new liberations of his people from their age-old chains. Yet sometimes they reminded him of children who had suddenly been let loose into a wonderful new world, full of exciting and interesting things that must be done, whether they were likely to be useful or not. However, anything that promised to make his race into better sailors was more than useful. In the last decade Eris had discovered that pure intelligence was sometimes not enough: there were skills that could not be acquired by any amount of mental effort. Though his people had largely overcome their fear of water, they were still quite incompetent on the ocean, and the Phileni had therefore become the first navigators of the world.

Jeryl looked nervously around her as the first peal of thunder came rolling in from the sea. She was still wearing the necklace that Therodimus had given her so long ago: but it was by no means the only ornament she carried now.

"I hope the ships will be safe," she said anxiously.

"There's not much wind, and they will have ridden out much worse storms than this," Aretenon reassured her, as they entered his cave. Eris and Jeryl looked round with eager interest to see what new wonders the Phileni had made during their absence: but if there were any they had been hidden away, as usual, until Aretenon was ready to show them. He was still rather childishly fond of such little surprises and mysteries.

There was an air of absent-mindedness about the meeting that would have puzzled an onlooker ignorant of its cause. As Eris talked of all the changes in the outer world, of the success of the new Phileni settlements, and of the steady growth of agriculture among his people, Aretenon listened with only half his mind. His thoughts, and those of his friends, were far out at sea, meeting the on-coming ships, which might be bringing the greatest news their world had ever received.

As Eris finished his report, Aretenon rose to his feet and began to move restlessly around the chamber.

"You have done better than we dared to hope at the beginning. At least there has been no war for a generation, and our food supply is ahead of the population for the first time in history—thanks to our new agricultural techniques."

Aretenon glanced at the furnishings of his chamber, recalling with an effort the fact that in his own youth almost everything he saw would have appeared impossible or even meaningless to him. Not even the simplest of tools had existed then, at least in the knowledge of his people. Now there were ships and bridges and houses—and these were only the beginning.

"I am well satisfied," he said. "We have, as we planned, diverted the whole stream of our culture, turning it away from the dangers that lay ahead. The powers that made the Madness possible will soon be forgotten: only a handful of us still know of them, and we will take our secrets with us. Perhaps when our descendants rediscover them they will be wise enough to use them properly. But we have uncovered so many new wonders that it may be a thousand generations before we turn again to look into our own minds and to tamper with the forces locked within them."

The mouth of the cave was illuminated by a sudden flash of

lightning. The storm was coming nearer, though it was still some miles away. Rain was beginning to fall in large, angry drops from the leaden sky.

"While we're waiting for the ships," said Aretenon rather abruptly, "come into the next cave and see some of the new things we have to show you since your last visit."

It was a strange collection. Side by side on the same bench were tools and inventions which in other cultures had been separated by thousands of years of time. The Stone Age was past: bronze and iron had come, and already the first crude scientific instruments had been built for experiments that were driving back the frontiers of the unknown. A primitive retort spoke of the beginnings of chemistry, and by its side were the first lenses that the world had seen—waiting to reveal the unsuspected universes of the infinitely small and the infinitely great.

The storm was upon them as Aretenon's description of these new wonders drew to a close. From time to time he had glanced nervously at the mouth of the cave, as if awaiting a messenger from the harbor, but they had remained undisturbed save by the occasional crash of thunder.

"I've shown you everything of importance," he said, "but here's something that may amuse you while we're waiting. As I said, we've sent expeditions everywhere to collect and classify all the rocks they can, in the hope of finding useful minerals. One of them brought back this."

He extinguished the lights and the cave became completely dark.

"It will be some time before your eyes grow sensitive enough to see it," Aretenon warned. "Just look over there in that corner."

Eris strained his eyes into the darkness. At first he could see nothing: then, slowly, a glimmering blue light became faintly visible. It was so vague and diffuse that he could not focus his eyes upon it, and he automatically moved forward.

"I shouldn't go too near," advised Aretenon. "It seems to be a perfectly ordinary mineral, but the Phileni who found it and carried it here got some very strange burns from handling it. Yet it's quite cold to the touch. One day we'll learn its secret: but I don't suppose it's anything at all important."

A vast curtain of sheet-lightning split the sky, and for a moment the reflected glare lighted up the cave, pinning weird shadows against the walls. At the same moment one of the Phileni staggered into the entrance and called something to Aretenon in this thin, reedy voice. He gave a great shout of triumph, as one of his ancestors might have done on some ancient battlefield: then his thoughts came crashing into Eris's mind.

"Land! They've found land—a whole new continent waiting for us!"

Eris felt the sense of triumph and victory well up within him like water bursting from a spring. Clear ahead now into the future lay the new, the glorious road along which their children would travel, mastering the world and all its secrets as they went. The vision of Therodimus was at last sharp and brilliant before his eyes.

He felt for the mind of Jeryl, so that she could share his joy—and found that it was closed to him. Leaning toward her in the darkness, he could sense that she was still staring into the depths of the cave, as if she had never heard the wonderful news, and could not tear her eyes away from the enigmatic glow.

Out of the night came the roar of the belated thunder as it raced across the sky. Eris felt Jeryl tremble beside him, and sent out his thoughts to comfort her.

"Don't let the thunder frighten you," he said gently. "What is there to fear now?"

"I do not know," replied Jeryl. "I am frightened—but not of the thunder. Oh, Eris, it is a wonderful thing we have done, and I wish that Therodimus could be here to see it. But where will it lead in the end—this new road of ours?"

Out of the past, the words that Aretenon had once spoken had risen up to haunt her. She remembered their walk by the river, long ago, when he had talked of his hopes and had asked: "Certainly nothing we can learn from Nature will ever be as great a threat as the peril we have uncovered in our own minds." Now the words seemed to mock her and to cast a shadow over the golden future: but why, she could not say.

Alone, perhaps, of all the races in the Universe, her people had reached the second crossroads—and had never passed the first. Now they must go along the road that they had missed, and must face the challenge at its end—the challenge from which, this time, they could not escape.

In the darkness, the faint glow of dying atoms burned unwavering in the rock. It would still be burning there, scarcely dimmed, when Jeryl and Eris had been dust for centuries. It would be only a little fainter when the civilization they were building had at last unlocked its secrets.

"If I Forget Thee,
Oh Earth . . ."

When Marvin was ten years old, his father took him through the long, echoing corridors that led up through Administration and Power, until at last they came to the uppermost levels of all and were among the swiftly growing vegetation of the Farmlands. Marvin liked it here: it was fun watching the great, slender plants creeping with almost visible eagerness toward the sunlight as it filtered down through the plastic domes to meet them. The smell of life was everywhere, awakening inexpressible longings in his heart: no longer was he breathing the dry, cool air of the residential levels, purged of all smells but the faint tang of ozone. He wished he could stay here for a little while, but Father would not let him. They went onward until they had reached the entrance to the Observatory, which he had never visited: but they did not stop, and Marvin knew with a sense of rising excitement that there could be only one goal left. For the first time in his life, he was going Outside.

There were a dozen of the surface vehicles, with their wide balloon tires and pressurized cabins, in the great servicing chamber. His father must have been expected, for they were led at once to the little scout car waiting by the huge circular door of the airlock. Tense with expectancy, Marvin settled himself down in the cramped cabin while his father started the motor and checked the controls. The inner door of the lock slid open and then closed behind them: he heard the roar of the great air pumps fade slowly away as the pressure dropped to zero. Then the "Vacuum" sign flashed on, the outer door parted, and before Marvin lay the land which he had never yet entered.

He had seen it in photographs, of course: he had watched it imaged on television screens a hundred times. But now it was lying all around him, burning beneath the fierce sun that crawled so slowly across the jet-black sky. He stared into the west, away from the blinding splendor of the sun—and there were the stars, as he had been told but had never quite believed. He gazed at them for a long time, marveling that anything could be so bright and yet so tiny. They were intense unscintillating points, and suddenly he remembered a rhyme he had once read in one of his father's books:

> Twinkle, twinkle, little star,
> How I wonder what you are.

Well, *he* knew what the stars were. Whoever asked that question must have been very stupid. And what did they mean by "twinkle"? You could see at a glance that all the stars shone with the same steady, unwavering light. He abandoned the puzzle and turned his attention to the landscape around him.

They were racing across a level plain at almost a hundred miles an hour, the great balloon tires sending up little spurts of dust behind them. There was no sign of the Colony: in the few minutes while he had been gazing at the stars, its domes and radio towers had fallen below the horizon. Yet there were other indications of man's presence, for about a mile ahead Marvin could see the curiously shaped structures clustering round the head of a mine. Now and then a puff of vapor would emerge from a squat smokestack and would instantly disperse.

They were past the mine in a moment: Father was driving with a reckless and exhilarating skill as if—it was a strange thought to come into a child's mind—he were trying to escape from something. In a few minutes they had reached the edge of the plateau on which the Colony had been built. The ground fell sharply away beneath them in a dizzying slope whose lower stretches were lost in shadow. Ahead, as far as the eye could reach, was a jumbled wasteland of craters, mountain ranges, and ravines. The crests of the mountains, catching the low sun, burned like islands of fire in a sea of darkness: and above them the stars still shone as steadfastly as ever.

There could be no way forward—yet there was. Marvin clenched his fists as the car edged over the slope and started the long descent. Then he saw the barely visible track leading down the mountainside, and relaxed a little. Other men, it seemed, had gone this way before.

Night fell with a shocking abruptness as they crossed the shadow line and the sun dropped below the crest of the plateau. The twin searchlights sprang into life, casting blue-white bands on the rocks ahead, so that there was scarcely need to check their speed. For hours they drove through valleys and past the foot of mountains whose peaks seemed to comb the stars, and sometimes they emerged for a moment into the sunlight as they climbed over higher ground.

And now on the right was a wrinkled, dusty plain, and on the left, its ramparts and terraces rising mile after mile into the sky, was a wall of mountains that marched into the distance until its peaks sank from sight below the rim of the world. There was no sign that men had ever explored this land, but once they passed the skeleton of a crashed rocket, and beside it a stone cairn surmounted by a metal cross.

It seemed to Marvin that the mountains stretched on

forever: but at last, many hours later, the range ended in a towering, precipitous headland that rose steeply from a cluster of little hills. They drove down into a shallow valley that curved in a great arc toward the far side of the mountains: and as they did so, Marvin slowly realized that something very strange was happening in the land ahead.

The sun was now low behind the hills on the right: the valley before them should be in total darkness. Yet it was awash with a cold white radiance that came spilling over the crags beneath which they were driving. Then, suddenly, they were out in the open plain, and the source of the light lay before them in all its glory.

It was very quiet in the little cabin now that the motors had stopped. The only sound was the faint whisper of the oxygen feed and an occasional metallic crepitation as the outer walls of the vehicle radiated away their heat. For no warmth at all came from the great silver crescent that floated low above the far horizon and flooded all this land with pearly light. It was so brilliant that minutes passed before Marvin could accept its challenge and look steadfastly into its glare, but at last he could discern the outlines of continents, the hazy border of the atmosphere, and the white islands of cloud. And even at this distance, he could see the glitter of sunlight on the polar ice.

It was beautiful, and it called to his heart across the abyss of space. There in that shining crescent were all the wonders that he had never known—the hues of sunset skies, the moaning of the sea on pebbled shores, the patter of falling rain, the unhurried benison of snow. These and a thousand others should have been his rightful heritage, but he knew them only from the books and ancient records, and the thought filled him with the anguish of exile.

Why could they not return? It seemed so peaceful beneath those lines of marching cloud. Then Marvin, his eyes no longer blinded by the glare, saw that the portion of the disk that should have been in darkness was gleaming faintly with an evil phosphorescence: and he remembered. He was looking upon the funeral pyre of a world—upon the radioactive aftermath of Armageddon. Across a quarter of a million miles of space, the glow of dying atoms was still visible, a perennial reminder of the ruinous past. It would be centuries yet before that deadly glow died from the rocks and life could return again to fill that silent, empty world.

And now Father began to speak, telling Marvin the story which until this moment had meant no more to him than the fairy tales he had once been told. There were many things he could not understand: it was impossible for him to picture the glowing, multicolored pattern of life on the planet he had never seen. Nor could he comprehend the forces that had destroyed it in the end, leaving the Colony, preserved by its isolation, as the sole survivor. Yet he could share the agony of those final days, when the Colony had learned at last that never again would the supply ships come flaming down through the stars with gifts from home. One by one the radio stations had ceased to call: on the shadowed globe the lights of the cities had dimmed and died, and they were alone at last, as no men had ever been alone before, carrying in their hands the future of the race.

Then had followed the years of despair, and the long-drawn battle for survival in this fierce and hostile world. That battle had been won, though barely: this little oasis of life was safe against the worst that Nature could do. But unless there was a goal, a future toward which it could work, the Colony would lose the will to live, and neither machines nor skill nor science could save it then.

So, at last, Marvin understood the purpose of this pilgrimage. He would never walk beside the rivers of that lost and legendary world, or listen to the thunder raging above its softly rounded hills. Yet one day—how far ahead?—his children's children would return to claim their heritage. The winds and the rains would scour the poisons from the burning lands and carry them to the sea, and in the depths of the sea they would waste their venom until they could harm no living things. Then the great ships that were still waiting here on the silent, dusty plains could lift once more into space, along the road that led to home.

That was the dream: and one day, Marvin knew with a sudden flash of insight, he would pass it on to his own son, here at this same spot with the mountains behind him and the silver light from the sky streaming into his face.

He did not look back as they began the homeward journey. He could not bear to see the cold glory of the crescent Earth fade from the rocks around him, as he went to rejoin his people in their long exile.

Breaking Strain

Grant was writing up the *Star Queen*'s log when he heard the cabin door opening behind him. He didn't bother to look round—it was hardly necessary for there was only one other man aboard the ship. But when nothing happened, and when McNeil neither spoke nor came into the room, the long silence finally roused Grant's curiosity and he swung the seat round in its gimbals.

McNeil was just standing in the doorway, looking as if he had seen a ghost. The trite metaphor flashed into Grant's mind instantly. He did not know for a moment how near the truth it was. In a sense McNeil *had* seen a ghost—the most terrifying of all ghosts—his own.

"What's the matter?" said Grant angrily. "You sick or something?"

The engineer shook his head. Grant noticed the little beads of sweat that broke away from his forehead and went glittering across the room on their perfectly straight trajectories. His throat muscles moved, but for a while no sound came. It looked as though he was going to cry.

"We're done for," he whispered at last. "Oxygen reserve's gone."

Then he did cry. He looked like a flabby doll, slowly collapsing on itself. He couldn't fall, for there was no gravity, so he just folded up in mid-air.

Grant said nothing. Quite unconsciously he rammed his smoldering cigarette into the ash tray, grinding it viciously until the last tiny spark had died. Already the air seemed to be thickening around him as the oldest terror of the spaceways gripped him by the throat.

He slowly loosed the elastic straps which, while he was seated, gave some illusion of weight, and with an automatic skill launched himself toward the doorway. NcNeil did not offer to follow. Even making every allowance for the shock he had undergone, Grant felt that he was behaving very badly. He gave the engineer an angry cuff as he passed and told him to snap out of it.

The hold was a large hemispherical room with a thick central column which carried the controls and cabling to the other half of the dumb-bell-shaped spaceship a hundred meters away. It was packed with crates and boxes arranged in a surrealistic three-dimensional array that made very few concessions to gravity.

But even if the cargo had suddenly vanished Grant would scarcely have noticed. He had eyes only for the big oxygen tank, taller than himself, which was bolted against the wall near the inner door of the airlock.

It was just as he had last seen it, gleaming with aluminum paint, and the metal sides still held the faint touch of coldness that gave the only hint of the contents. All the piping seemed in perfect condition. There was no sign of anything wrong apart from one minor detail. The needle of the contents gauge lay mutely against the zero stop.

Grant gazed at that silent symbol as a man in ancient London, returning home one evening at the time of the Plague, might have stared at a rough cross newly scrawled upon his door. Then he banged half a dozen times on the glass in the futile hope that the needle had stuck—though he never really doubted its message. News that is sufficiently bad somehow carries its own guarantee of truth. Only good reports need confirmation.

When Grant got back to the control room, McNeil was himself again. A glance at the opened medicine chest showed the reason for the engineer's rapid recovery. He even assayed a faint attempt at humor.

"It was a meteor," he said. "They tell us a ship this size should get hit once a century. We seem to have jumped the gun with ninety-five years still to go."

"But what about the alarms? The air pressure's normal—how could we have been holed?"

"We weren't," McNeil replied. "You know how the oxygen circulates night-side through the refrigerating coils to keep it liquid? The meteor must have smashed them and the stuff simply boiled away."

Grant was silent, collecting his thoughts. What had happened was serious—deadly serious—but it need not be fatal. After all, the voyage was more than three quarters over.

"Surely the regenerator can keep the air breathable, even if it does get pretty thick?" he asked hopefully.

McNeil shook his head. "I've not worked it out in detail, but I know the answer. When the carbon dioxide is broken down and the free oxygen gets cycled back there's a loss of about ten per cent. That's why we have to carry a reserve."

"The space suits!" cried Grant in sudden excitement. "What about their tanks?"

He had spoken without thinking, and the immediate realization of his mistake left him feeling worse than before.

"We can't keep oxygen in them—it would boil off in a few

days. There's enough compressed gas there for about thirty minutes—merely long enough for you to get to the main tank in an emergency."

"There must be a way out—even if we have to jettison cargo and run for it. Let's stop guessing and work out exactly where we are."

Grant was as much angry as frightened. He was angry with McNeil for breaking down. He was angry with the designers of the ship for not having foreseen this God-knew-how-many-million-to-one-chance. The deadline might be a couple of weeks away and a lot could happen before then. The thought helped for a moment to keep his fears at arm's length.

This was an emergency, beyond doubt, but it was one of those peculiarly protracted emergencies that seem to happen only in space. There was plenty of time to think—perhaps too much time.

Grant strapped himself in the pilot's seat and pulled out a writing-pad.

"Let's get the facts right," he said with artificial calmness. "We've got the air that's still circulating in the ship and we lose ten per cent of the oxygen every time it goes through the generator. Chuck me over the Manual, will you? I can never remember how many cubic meters we use a day."

In saying that the *Star Queen* might expect to be hit by a meteor once every century, McNeil had grossly but unavoidably oversimplified the problem. For the answer depended on so many factors that three generations of statisticians had done little but lay down rules so vague that the insurance companies still shivered with apprehension when the great meteor showers went sweeping like a gale through the orbits of the inner worlds.

Everything depends, of course, on what one means by the word meteor. Each lump of cosmic slag that reaches the surface of the Earth has a million smaller brethren that perish utterly in the no-man's-land where the atmosphere has not quite ended and space has yet to begin—that ghostly region where the weird Aurora sometimes walks by night.

These are the familiar shooting stars, seldom larger than a pin's head, and these in turn are outnumbered a millionfold again by particles too small to leave any visible trace of their dying as they drift down from the sky. All of them, the count-less specks of dust, the rare boulders and even the wandering mountains that Earth encounters perhaps once every million years—all of them are meteors.

For the purposes of space-flight, a meteor is only of interest if, on penetrating the hull of a ship, it leaves a hole large enough to be dangerous. This is a matter of relative speeds as well as size. Tables have been prepared showing approximate collision times for various parts of the Solar System—and for various sizes of meteors down to masses of a few milligrams.

That which had struck the *Star Queen* was a giant, being nearly a centimeter across and weighing all of ten grams. Ac-cording to the table the waiting-time for collision with such a monster was of the order of ten to the ninth days—say three million years. The virtual certainty that such an occurrence would not happen again in the course of human history gave Grant and McNeil very little consolation.

However, things might have been worse. The *Star Queen* was 115 days on her orbit and had only 30 still to go. She was traveling, as did all freighters, on the long tangential ellipse kissing the orbits of Earth and Venus on opposite sides of the Sun. The fast liners could cut across from planet to planet at three times her speed—and ten times her fuel consumption—but she must plod along her predetermined track like a street-car, taking 145 days, more or less, for each journey.

Anything more unlike the early-twentieth-century idea of a spaceship than the *Star Queen* would be hard to imagine. She consisted of two spheres, one fifty and the other twenty meters in diameter, joined by a cylinder about a hundred meters long. The whole structure looked like a match-stick-and-Plasticine model of a hydrogen atom. Crew, cargo, and controls were in the larger sphere, while the smaller one held the atomic motors and was—to put it mildly—out of bounds to living matter.

The *Star Queen* had been built in space and could never have lifted herself even from the surface of the Moon. Under full power her ion drive could produce an acceleration of a twentieth of a gravity, which in an hour would give her all the velocity she needed to change from a satellite of the Earth to one of Venus.

Hauling cargo up from the planets was the job of the powerful little chemical rockets. In a month the tugs would be climbing up from Venus to meet her, but the *Star Queen* would not be stopping for there would be no one at the controls. She would continue blindly on her orbit, speeding past Venus at miles a second—and five months later she would be back at the orbit of the Earth, though Earth itself would then be far away.

It is surprising how long it takes to do a simple addition when your life depends on the answer. Grant ran down the short column of figures half a dozen times before he finally gave up hope that the total would change. Then he sat doodling nervously on the white plastic of the pilot's desk.

"With all possible economies," he said, "we can last about twenty days. That means we'll be ten days out of Venus when. . . ." His voice trailed off into silence.

Ten days didn't sound much—but it might just as well have been ten years. Grant thought sardonically of all the hack adventure writers who had used just this situation in their stories and radio serials. In these circumstances, according to the carbon-copy experts—few of whom had ever gone beyond the Moon—there were three things that could happen.

The popular solution—which had become almost a cliché—was to turn the ship into a glorified greenhouse or a hydroponic farm and let photosynthesis do the rest. Alternatively one could perform prodigies of chemical or atomic engineering—explained in tedious technical detail—and build an oxygen manufacturing plant which would not only save your life—and of course the heroine's—but also make you the owner of fabulously valuable patents. The third or *deus ex machina* solution was the arrival of a convenient spaceship which happened to be matching your course and velocity exactly.

But that was fiction and things were different in real life. Although the first idea was sound in theory there wasn't even a packet of grass seed aboard the *Star Queen*. As for feats of inventive engineering, two men—however brilliant and however desperate—were not likely to improve in a few days on the work of scores of great industrial research organizations over a full century.

The spaceship that "happened to be passing" was, almost be definition, impossible. Even if other freighters had been coasting on the same elliptic path—and Grant knew there were none—then by the very laws that governed their movements they would always keep their original separations. It was not quite impossible that a liner, racing on its hyperbolic orbit, might pass within a few hundred thousand kilometers of them—but at a speed so great that it would be as inaccessible as Pluto.

"If we threw out the cargo," said McNeil at last, "would we have a chance of changing our orbit?"

Grant shook his head.

"I'd hoped so," he replied, "but it won't work. We could reach Venus in a week if we wished—but we'd have no fuel for braking and nothing from the planet could catch us as we went past."

"Not even a liner?"

"According to Lloyd's Register Venus has only a couple of freighters at the moment. In any case it would be a practically impossible maneuver. Even if it could match our speed how would the rescue ship get back? It would need about fifty kilometers a second for the whole job!"

"If we can't figure a way out," said McNeil, "maybe someone on Venus can. We'd better talk to them."

"I'm going to," Grant replied, "as soon as I've decided what to say. Go and get the transmitter aligned, will you?"

He watched McNeil as he floated out of the room. The engineer was probably going to give trouble in the days that lay ahead. Until now they had got on well enough—like most stout men McNeil was good-natured and easy-going. But now Grant realized that he lacked fiber. He had become flabby—physically and mentally—living too long in space.

A buzzer sounded on the transmitter switchboard. The parabolic mirror out on the hull was aimed at the gleaming arc-lamp of Venus, only ten million kilometers away and moving on an almost parallel path. The three-millimeter waves from the ship's transmitter would make the trip in little more than half a minute. There was bitterness in the knowledge that they were only thirty seconds from safety.

The automatic monitor on Venus gave its impersonal Go ahead signal and Grant began to talk steadily, and he hoped, quite dispassionately. He gave a careful analysis of the situation and ended with a request for advice. His fears concerning McNeil he left unspoken. For one thing he knew that the engineer would be monitoring him at the transmitter.

As yet no one on Venus would have heard the message, even though the transmission time-lag was over. It would still be coiled up in the recorder spools, but in a few minutes an unsuspecting signal officer would arrive to play it over.

He would have no idea of the bombshell that was about to burst, triggering trains of sympathetic ripples on all the inhabited worlds as television and newssheet took up the refrain. An accident in space has a dramatic quality that crowds all other items from the headlines.

Until now Grant had been too preoccupied with his own safety to give much thought to the cargo in his charge. A sea captain of ancient times, whose first thought was for his ship, might have been shocked by this attitude. Grant, however, had reason on his side.

The *Star Queen* could never founder, could never run upon uncharted rocks or pass silently, as so many ships have passed, forever from the knowledge of man. She was safe, whatever might befall her crew. If she was undisturbed she would continue to retrace her orbit with such precision that men might set their calendars by her for centuries to come.

The cargo, Grant suddenly remembered, was insured for over twenty million dollars. There were not many goods valuable enough to be shipped from world to world and most of the crates in the hold were worth more than their weight—or rather their mass—in gold. Perhaps some items might be useful in this emergency and Grant went to the safe to find the loading schedule.

He was sorting the thin, tough sheets when McNeil came back into the cabin.

"I've been reducing the air pressure," he said. "The hull shows some leaks that wouldn't have mattered in the usual way."

Grant nodded absently as he passed a bundle of sheets over to McNeil.

"Here's our loading schedule. I suggest we both run through it in case there's anything in the cargo that may help."

If it did nothing else, he might have added, it would at least give them something to occupy their minds.

As he ran down the long columns of numbered items—a complete cross-section of interplanetary commerce—Grant found himself wondering what lay behind these inanimate symbols. *Item 347 - 1 book - 4 kilos gross.*

He whistled as he noticed that it was a starred item, insured for a hundred thousand dollars, and he suddenly remembered hearing on the radio that the Hesperian Museum had just bought a first edition *Seven Pillars of Wisdom*.

A few sheets later was a very contrasting item, *Miscellaneous books—25 kilos—no intrinsic value.*

It had cost a small fortune to ship those books to Venus, yet they were of "no intrinsic value." Grant let his imagination loose on the problem. Perhaps someone who was leaving Earth forever was taking with him to a new world his most cherished treasures—the dozen or so volumes that above all others had most shaped his mind.

Item 564 - 12 reels film.

That, of course, would be the Neronian super-epic, *While Rome Burns*, which had left Earth just one jump ahead of the censor. Venus was waiting for it with considerable impatience.

Medical supplies - 50 kilos. Case of cigars - 1 kilo. Precision instruments - 75 kilos. So the list went on. Each item was something rare or something which the industry and science of a younger civilization could not yet produce.

The cargo was sharply divided into two classes—blatant luxury or sheer necessity. There was little in between. And there was nothing, nothing at all, which gave Grant the slightest hope. He did not see how it could have been otherwise, but that did not prevent him from feeling a quite unreasonable disappointment.

The reply from Venus, when it came at last, took nearly an hour to run through the recorder. It was a questionnaire so detailed that Grant wondered morosely if he'd live long enough to answer it. Most of the queries were technical ones concerning the ship. The experts on two planets were pooling their brains in the attempt to save the *Star Queen* and her cargo.

"Well, what do you think of it?" Grant asked McNeil when the other had finished running through the message. He was watching the engineer carefully for any further sign of strain.

There was a long pause before McNeil spoke. Then he shrugged his shoulders and his first words were an echo of Grant's own thoughts.

"It will certainly keep us busy. I won't be able to do all these tests in under a day. I can see what they're driving at most of the time, but some of the questions are just plain crazy."

Grant had suspected that, but said nothing as the other continued.

"Rate of hull leakage—that's sensible enough, but why should anyone want to know the efficiency of our radiation screening? I think they're trying to keep up our morale by pretending they have some bright ideas—or else they want to keep us too busy to worry."

Grant was relieved and yet annoyed by McNeil's calmness—relieved because he had been afraid of another scene and annoyed because McNeil was not fitting at all neatly into the mental category he had prepared for him. Was that first momentary lapse typical of the man or might it have happened to anyone?

Grant, to whom the world was very much a place of blacks and whites, felt angry at being unable to decide whether McNeil was cowardly or courageous. That he might be both was a possibility that never occurred to him.

There is a timelessness about space-flight that is unmatched by any other experience of man. Even on the Moon there are shadows that creep sluggishly from crag to crag as the sun makes its slow march across the sky. Earthward there is always the great clock of the spinning globe, marking the hours with continents for hands. But on a long voyage in a gyro-stabilized ship the same patterns of sunlight lie unmoving on wall or floor as the chronometer ticks off its meaningless hours and days.

Grant and McNeil had long since learned to regulate their lives accordingly. In deep space they moved and thought with a leisureliness that would vanish quickly enough when a voyage was nearing its end and the time for braking maneuvers had arrived. Though they were now under sentence of death, they continued along the well-worn grooves of habit.

Every day Grant carefully wrote up the log, checked the ship's position and carried out his various routine duties. Mc-Neil was also behaving normally as far as could be told, though Grant suspected that some of the technical maintenance was being carried out with a very light hand.

It was now three days since the meteor had struck. For the last twenty-four hours Earth and Venus had been in conference and Grant wondered when he would hear the result of their deliberations. He did not believe that the finest technical brains in the Solar System could save them now, but it was hard to abandon hope when everything still seemed so normal and the air was still clean and fresh.

On the fourth day Venus spoke again. Shorn of its technicalities, the message was nothing more or less than a funeral oration. Grant and McNeil had been written off, but they were given elaborate instructions concerning the safety of the cargo.

Back on Earth the astronomers were computing all the possible rescue orbits that might make contact with the *Star Queen* in the next few years. There was even a chance that she might be reached from Earth six or seven months later, when she was back at aphelion, but the maneuver could be carried out only by a fast liner with no payload and would cost a fortune in fuel.

McNeil vanished soon after this message came through. At first Grant was a little relieved. If McNeil chose to look after himself that was his own affair. Besides there were various letters to write—though the last-will-and-testament business could come later.

It was McNeil's turn to prepare the "evening" meal, a duty he enjoyed for he took good care of his stomach. When the usual sounds from the galley were not forthcoming Grant went in search of his crew.

He found McNeil lying in his bunk, very much at peace with the universe. Hanging in the air beside him was a large metal crate which had been roughly forced open. Grant had no need to examine it closely to guess its contents. A glance at McNeil was enough.

"It's a dirty shame," said the engineer without a trace of embarrassment, "to suck this stuff up through a tube. Can't you put on some 'g' so that we can drink it properly?"

Grant stared at him with angry contempt, but McNeil returned his gaze unabashed.

Oh, don't be a sourpuss! Have some yourself—what does it matter now?

He pushed across a bottle and Grant fielded it deftly as it floated by. It was a fabulously valuable wine—he remembered the consignment now—and the contents of that small crate must be worth thousands.

"I don't think there's any need," said Grant severely, "to behave like a pig—even in these circumstances."

McNeil wasn't drunk yet. He had only reached the brightly lighted anteroom of intoxication and had not lost all contact with the drab outer world.

"I am prepared," he said with great solemnity, "to listen to any good argument against my present course of action—a course which seems eminently sensible to me. But you'd better convince me quickly while I'm still amenable to reason."

He pressed the plastic bulb again and a purple jet shot into his mouth.

"Apart from the fact that you're stealing Company property which will certainly be salvaged sooner or later—you can hardly stay drunk for several weeks."

"That," said McNeil thoughtfully, "remains to be seen."

"I don't think so," retorted Grant. Bracing himself against the wall, he gave the crate a vicious shove that sent it flying through the open doorway.

As he dived after it and slammed the door he heard McNeil shout, "Well, of all the dirty tricks!"

It would take the engineer some time—particularly in his present condition—to unbuckle himself and follow. Grant steered the crate back to the hold and locked the door. As there was never any need to lock the hold when the ship was in space McNeil wouldn't have a key for it himself and Grant could hide the duplicate that was kept in the control cabin.

McNeil was singing when, some time later, Grant went back past his room. He still had a couple of bottles for company and was shouting:

"We don't care *where* the oxygen goes
If it doesn't get into the wine. . . ."

Grant, whose education had been severely technical, couldn't place the quotation. As he paused to listen he suddenly found himself shaken by an emotion which, to do him justice, he did not for a moment recognize.

It passed as swiftly as it had come, leaving him sick and trembling. For the first time, he realized that his dislike of McNeil was slowly turning to hatred.

* * *

It is a fundamental rule of space-flight that, for sound psychological reasons, the minimum crew on a long journey shall consist of not less than three men.

But rules are made to be broken and the *Star Queen*'s owners had obtained full authority from the Board of Space Control and the insurance companies when the freighter set off for Venus without her regular captain.

At the last moment he had been taken ill and there was no replacement. Since the planets are disinclined to wait upon man and his affairs, if she did not sail on time she would not sail at all.

Millions of dollars were involved—so she sailed. Grant and McNeil were both highly capable men and they had no objection at all to earning double their normal pay for very little extra work. Despite fundamental differences in temperament, they got on well enough in ordinary circumstances. It was nobody's fault that circumstances were now very far from ordinary.

Three days without food, it is said, is long enough to remove most of the subtle differences between a civilized man and a savage. Grant and McNeil were still in no physical discomfort. But their imaginations had been only too active and they now had more in common with two hungry Pacific Islanders in a lost canoe than either would have cared to admit.

For there was one aspect of the situation, and that the most important of all, which had never been mentioned. When the last figures on Grant's writing-pad had been checked and rechecked, the calculation was still not quite complete. Instantly each man had made the one further step, each had arrived simultaneously at the same unspoken result.

It was terribly simple—a macabre parody of those problems in first-year arithmetic that begin, "If six men take two days to assemble five helicopters, how long . . ."

The oxygen would last *two* men for about twenty days, and Venus was thirty days away. One did not have to be a calculating prodigy to see at once that one man, and one man only, might yet live to walk the metal streets of Port Hesperus.

The acknowledged deadline was twenty days ahead, but the unmentioned one was only ten days off. Until that time there would still be enough air for two men—and thereafter for one man only for the rest of the voyage. To a sufficiently detached observer the situation would have been very entertaining.

It was obvious that the conspiracy of silence could not last much longer. But it is not easy, even at the best of times, for two people to decide amicably which one of them shall commit suicide. It is still more difficult when they are no longer on speaking terms.

Grant wished to be perfectly fair. Therefore the only thing to do was to wait until McNeil sobered up and then to put the question to him frankly. He could think best at his desk, so he went to the control cabin and strapped himself down in the pilot's chair.

For a while he stared thoughtfully into nothingness. It would be better, he decided, to broach the matter by correspondence, especially while diplomatic relations were in their present state. He clipped a sheet of notepaper on the writing-pad and began, "Dear McNeil . . ." Then he tore it out and started again, "McNeil . . ."

It took him the best part of three hours and even then he wasn't wholly satisfied. There were some things it was so darned difficult to put down on paper. But at last he managed to finish. He sealed the letter and locked it away in his safe. It could wait for a day or two.

Few of the waiting millions on Earth and Venus could have any idea of the tensions that were slowly building up aboard the *Star Queen*. For days press and radio had been full of fantastic rescue schemes. On three worlds there was hardly any other topic of conversation. But only the faintest echo of the planet-wide tumult reached the two men who were its cause.

At any time the station on Venus could speak to the *Star Queen*, but there was so little that could be said. One could not with any decency give words of encouragement to men in the condemned cell, even when there was some slight uncertainty about the actual date of execution.

So Venus contented itself with a few routine messages every day and blocked the steady stream of exhortations and newspaper offers that came pouring in from Earth. As a result private radio companies on Earth made frantic attempts to contact the *Star Queen* directly. They failed, simply because it never occurred to Grant and McNeil to focus their receiver anywhere except on Venus, now so tantalizingly near at hand.

There had been an embarrassing interlude when McNeil emerged from his cabin, but though relations were not particularly cordial, life aboard the *Star Queen* continued much as before.

Grant spent most of his waking hours in the pilot's position, calculating approach maneuvers and writing interminable letters to his wife. He could have spoken to her had he wished, but the thought of all those millions of waiting ears had prevented him from doing so. Interplanetary speech circuits were supposed to be private—but too many people would be interested in this one.

In a couple of days, Grant assured himself, he would hand his letter to McNeil and they could decide what was to be done. Such a delay would also give McNeil a chance of raising the subject himself. That he might have other reasons for his hesitation was something Grant's conscious mind still refused to admit.

He often wondered how McNeil was spending his time. The engineer had a large library of microfilm books, for he read widely and his range of interests was unusual. His favorite book, Grant knew, was *Jurgen* and perhaps even now he was trying to forget his doom by losing himself in its strange magic. Others of McNeil's books were less respectable and not a few were of the class curiously described as "curious."

The truth of the matter was that McNeil was far too subtle and complicated a personality for Grant to understand. He was a hedonist and enjoyed the pleasures of life all the more for being cut off from them for months at a time. But he was by no means the moral weakling that the unimaginative and somewhat puritanical Grant had supposed.

It was true that he had collapsed completely under the initial shock and that his behavior over the wine was—by Grant's standards—reprehensible. But McNeil had had his breakdown and had recovered. Therein lay the difference between him and the hard but brittle Grant.

Though the normal routine of duties had been resumed by tacit consent, it did little to reduce the sense of strain. Grant and McNeil avoided each other as much as possible except when mealtimes brought them together. When they did meet, they behaved with an exaggerated politeness as if each were striving to be perfectly normal—and inexplicably failing.

Grant had hoped that McNeil would himself broach the subject of suicide, thus sparing him a very awkward duty. When the engineer stubbornly refused to do anything of the sort it added to Grant's resentment and contempt. To make matters worse he was now suffering from nightmares and sleeping very badly.

The nightmare was always the same. When he was a child it had often happened that at bedtime he had been reading a story far too exciting to be left until morning. To avoid detection he had continued reading under the bedclothes by flashlight, curled up in a snug white-walled cocoon. Every ten minutes or so the air had become too stifling to breathe and his emergence into the delicious cool air had been a major part of the fun.

Now, thirty years later, these innocent childhood hours returned to haunt him. He was dreaming that he could not escape from the suffocating sheets while the air was steadily and remorselessly thickening around him

He had intended to give McNeil the letter after two days, yet somehow he put it off again. This procrastination was very unlike Grant, but he managed to persuade himself that it was a perfectly reasonable thing to do.

He was giving McNeil a chance to redeem himself—to prove that he wasn't a coward by raising the matter himself. That McNeil might be waiting for him to do exactly the same thing somehow never occurred to Grant.

The all-too-literal deadline was only five days off when, for the first time, Grant's mind brushed lightly against the thought of murder. He had been sitting after the "evening" meal, trying to relax as McNeil clattered around in the galley with, he considered, quite unnecessary noise.

What use, he asked himself, was the engineer to the world? He had no responsibilities and no family—no one would be any the worse off for his death. Grant, on the other hand, had a wife and three children of whom he was moderately fond, though for some obscure reason they responded with little more than dutiful affection.

Any impartial judge would have no difficulty in deciding which of them should survive. If McNeil had a spark of decency in him he would have come to the same conclusion already. Since he appeared to have done nothing of the sort he had forfeited all further claims to consideration.

Such was the elemental logic of Grant's subconscious mind, which had arrived at its answer days before but had only now succeeded in attracting the attention for which it had been clamoring. To Grant's credit he at once rejected the thought with horror.

He was an upright and honorable person with a very strict code of behavior. Even the vagrant homicidal impulses of what is misleadingly called "normal" man had seldom ruffled his mind. But in the days—the very few days—left to him, they would come more and more often.

The air had now become noticeably fouler. Though there was still no real difficulty in breathing, it was a constant reminder of what lay ahead, and Grant found that it was keeping him from sleep. This was not pure loss, as it helped to break the power of his nightmares, but he was becoming physically run down.

His nerve was also rapidly deteriorating, a state of affairs accentuated by the fact that McNeil seemed to be behaving with unexpected and annoying calmness. Grant realized that he had come to the stage when it would be dangerous to delay the showdown any longer.

McNeil was in his room as usual when Grant went up to the control cabin to collect the letter he had locked away in the safe—it seemed a lifetime ago. He wondered if he need add anything more to it. Then he realized that this was only another excuse for delay. Resolutely he made his way toward McNeil's cabin.

A single neutron begins the chain-reaction that in an instant can destroy a million lives and the toil of generations. Equally insignificant and unimportant are the trigger-events which can sometimes change a man's course of action and so alter the whole pattern of his future.

Nothing could have been more trivial than that which made Grant pause in the corridor outside McNeil's room. In the ordinary way he would not even have noticed it. It was the smell of smoke—tobacco smoke.

The thought that the sybaritic engineer had so little self-control that he was squandering the last precious liters of oxygen in such a manner filled Grant with blinding fury. He stood for a moment quite paralyzed with the intensity of his emotion.

Then slowly, he crumpled the letter in his hand. The thought which had first been an unwelcome intruder, then a casual speculation, was at last fully accepted. McNeil had had his chance and had proved, by his unbelievable selfishness, unworthy of it. Very well—he could die.

The speed with which Grant had arrived at this conclusion would not have deceived the most amateurish of psychologists. It was relief as much as hatred that drove him away from McNeil's room. He had wanted to convince himself that there would be no need to do the honorable thing, to suggest some game of chance that would give them each an equal probability of life.

This was the excuse he needed, and he had seized upon it to salve his conscience. For though he might plan and even carry out a murder, Grant was the sort of person who would have to do it according to his own particular moral code.

As it happened he was—not for the first time—badly misjudging McNeil. The engineer was a heavy smoker and tobacco was quite essential to his mental well-being even in normal circumstances. How much more essential it was now, Grant, who only smoked occasionally and without much enjoyment, could never have appreciated.

McNeil had satisfied himself by careful calculation that four cigarettes a day would make no measurable difference whatsoever to the ship's oxygen endurance, whereas they would make all the difference in the world to his own nerves and hence indirectly to Grant's.

But it was no use explaining this to Grant. So he had smoked in private and with a self-control he found agreeably, almost voluptuously, surprising. It was sheer bad luck that Grant had detected one of the day's four cigarettes.

For a man who had only at that moment talked himself into murder, Grant's actions were remarkably methodical. Without hesitation, he hurried back to the control room and opened the medicine chest with its neatly labeled compartments, designed for almost every emergency that could occur in space.

Even the ultimate emergency had been considered, for there behind its retaining elastic bands was the tiny bottle he had been seeking, the image of which had been lying hidden far down in the unknown depths of his mind through all these days. It bore a white label carrying a skull-and-crossbones, and beneath them the words: *Approx. one-half gram will cause painless and almost instantaneous death.*

The poison was painless and instantaneous— that was good. But even more important was a fact unmentioned on the label. It was also tasteless.

The contrast between the meals prepared by Grant and those organized with considerable skill and care by McNeil was striking. Anyone who was fond of food and who spent a good deal of his life in space usually learned the art of cooking in self-defense. McNeil had done this long ago.

To Grant, on the other hand, eating was one of those necessary but annoying jobs which had to be got through as quickly as possible. His cooking reflected this opinion,. McNeil had ceased to grumble about it, but he would have been very interested in the trouble Grant was taking over this particular meal.

If he noticed any increasing nervousness on Grant's part as the meal progressed, he said nothing. They ate almost in silence, but that was not unusual for they had long since exhausted most of the possibilities of light conversation. When the last dishes—deep bowls with inturned rims to prevent the contents drifting out—had been cleared away, Grant went into the galley to prepare the coffee.

He took rather a long time, for at the last moment something quite maddening and quite ridiculous happened. He suddenly recalled one of the film classics of the last century in which the fabulous Charlie Chaplin tried to poison an unwanted wife—and then accidentally changed the glasses.

No memory could have been more unwelcome, for it left him shaken with a gust of silent hysteria. Poe's *Imp of the Perverse*, that demon who delights in defying the careful canons of self-preservation, was at work and it was a good minute before Grant could regain his self-control.

He was sure that, outwardly at least, he was quite calm as he carried in the two plastic containers and their drinking-tubes. There was no danger of confusing them, for the engineer's had the letters MAC painted boldly across it.

At the thought Grant nearly relapsed into psychopathic giggles but just managed to regain control with the somber reflection that his nerves must be in even worse condition than he had imagined.

He watched, fascinated, though without appearing to do so, as McNeil toyed with his cup. The engineer seemed in no great hurry and was staring moodily into space. Then he put his lips to the drinking tube and sipped.

A moment later he spluttered slightly—and an icy hand seemed to seize Grant's heart and hold it tight. Then McNeil turned to him and said evenly, "You've made it properly for once. It's quite hot."

Slowly, Grant's heart resumed its interrupted work. He did not trust himself to speak, but managed a noncommittal nod. McNeil parked the cup carefully in the air, a few inches away from his face.

He seemed very thoughtful, as if weighing his words for some important remark. Grant cursed himself for having made the drink so hot—that was just the sort of detail that hanged murderers. If McNeil waited much longer he would probably betray himself through nervousness.

"I suppose," said McNeil in a quietly conversational sort of way, "it has occurred to you that there's still enough air to last one of us to Venus?"

Grant forced his jangling nerves under control and tore his eyes away from that hypnotic cup. His throat seemed very dry as he answered, "It—it had crossed my mind."

McNeil touched his cup, found it still too hot and continued throughtfully, "Then wouldn't it be more sensible if one of us decided to walk out of the airlock, say—or to take some of the poison in there?" He jerked his thumb toward the medicine chest, just visible from where they were sitting.

Grant nodded.

"The only trouble, of course," added the engineer, "is to decide which of us will be the unlucky one. I suppose it would have to be by picking a card or in some other quite arbitrary way."

Grant stared at McNeil with a fascination that almost outweighed his mounting nervousness. He had never believed that the engineer could discuss the subject so calmly. Grant was sure he suspected nothing. Obviously McNeil's thoughts had been running on parallel lines to his own and it was scarcely even a coincidence that he had chosen this time, of all times, to raise the matter.

McNeil was watching him intently, as if judging his reactions.

"You're right," Grant heard himself say. "We must talk it over."

"Yes," said McNeil quite impassively. "We must." Then he reached for his cup again, put the drinking tube to his lips and sucked slowly.

Grant could not wait until he had finished. To his surprise the relief he had been expecting did not come. He even felt a stab of regret, though it was not quite remorse. It was a little late to think of it now, but he suddenly remembered that he would be alone in the *Star Queen*, haunted by his thoughts, for more than three weeks before rescue came.

He did not wish to see McNeil die, and he felt rather sick. Without another glance at his victim he launched himself toward the exit.

Immovably fixed, the fierce sun and the unwinking stars looked down upon the *Star Queen*, which seemed as motionless as they. There was no way of telling that the tiny dumbbell of the ship had now almost reached her maximum speed and that millions of horsepower were chained within the smaller sphere, waiting for the moment of its release. There was no way of telling, indeed, that she carried any life at all.

An airlock on the night-side of the ship slowly opened, letting a blaze of light escape from the interior. The brilliant circle looked very strange hanging there in the darkness. Then it was abruptly eclipsed as two figures floated out of the ship.

One was much bulkier than the other, and for a rather important reason—it was wearing a space-suit. Now there are some forms of apparel that may be worn or discarded as the fancy pleases with no other ill-effects than a possible loss of social prestige. But space-suits are not among them.

Something not easy to follow was happening in the darkness. Then the smaller figure began to move, slowly at first but with rapidly mounting speed. It swept out of the shadow of the ship into the full blast of the sun, and now one could see that strapped to its back was a small gas-cylinder from which a fine mist was jetting to vanish almost instantly into space.

It was a crude but effective rocket. There was no danger that the ship's minute gravitational pull would drag the body back to it again.

Rotating slightly, the corpse dwindled against the stars and vanished from sight in less than a minute. Quite motionless, the figure in the airlock watched it go. Then the outer door swung shut, the circle of brilliance vanished and only the pale Earthlight still glinted on the shadowed wall of the ship.

Nothing else whatsoever happened for twenty-three days.

The captain of the *Hercules* turned to his mate with a sigh of relief.

"I was afraid he couldn't do it. It must have been a colossal job to break his orbit single-handed—and with the air as thick as it must be by now. How soon can we get to him?"

"It will take about an hour. He's still got quite a bit of eccentricity but we can correct that."

"Good. Signal the *Leviathan* and *Titan* that we can make contact and ask them to take off, will you? But I wouldn't drop any tips to your news commentator friends until we're safely locked."

The mate had the grace to blush. "I don't intend to," he said in a slightly hurt voice as he pecked delicately at the keys of his calculator. The answer that flashed instantly on the screen seemed to displease him.

"We'd better board and bring the *Queen* down to circular speed ourselves before we call the other tugs," he said, "otherwise we'll be wasting a lot of fuel. She's still got a velocity excess of nearly a kilometer a second."

"Good idea—tell *Leviathan* and *Titan* to stand by but not to blast until we give them the new orbit."

While the message was on its way down through the unbroken cloudbanks that covered half the sky below, the mate remarked thoughtfully, "I wonder what he's feeling like now?"

"I can tell you. He's so pleased to be alive that he doesn't give a hoot about anything else."

"Still, I'm not sure I'd like to have left my shipmate in space so that I could get home."

"It's not the sort of thing that anyone would like to do. But you heard the broadcast—they'd talked it over calmly and the loser went out of the airlock. It was the only sensible way."

"Sensible, perhaps—but it's pretty horrible to let someone else sacrifice himself in such a cold-blooded way so that you can live."

"Don't be a ruddy sentimentalist. I'll bet that if it happened to us you'd push me out before I could even say my prayers."

"Unless you did it to me first. Still, I don't think it's ever likely to happen to the *Hercules*. Five days out of port's the longest we've ever been, isn't it? Talk about the romance of the spaceways?"

The captain didn't reply. He was peering into the eyepiece of the navigating telescope, for the *Star Queen* should now be within optical range. There was a long pause while he adjusted the vernier controls. Then he gave a little sigh of satisfaction.

"There she is—about nine-fifty kilometers away. Tell the crew to stand by—and send a message to cheer him up. Say we'll be there in thirty minutes even if it isn't quite true."

Slowly the thousand-meter nylon ropes yielded beneath the strain as they absorbed the relative momentum of the ships, then slackened again as the *Star Queen* and the *Hercules* rebounded toward each other. The electric winches began to turn and, like a spider crawling up its thread, the *Hercules* drew alongside the freighter.

Men in space-suits sweated with heavy reaction units—tricky work, this—until the airlocks had registered and could be coupled together. The outer doors slid aside and the air in the locks mingled, fresh with foul. As the mate of the *Hercules* waited, oxygen cylinder in hand, he wondered what condition the survivor would be in. Then the *Star Queen*'s inner door slid open.

For a moment, the two men stood looking at each other

across the short corridor that now connected the two airlocks. The mate was surprised and a little disappointed to find that he felt no particular sense of drama.

So much had happened to make this moment possible that its actual achievement was almost an anticlimax, even in the instant when it was slipping into the past. He wished—for he was an incurable romantic—that he could think of something memorable to say, some "Doctor Livingstone, I presume?" phrase that would pass into history.

But all he actually said was, "Well, McNeil, I'm pleased to see you."

Though he was considerably thinner and somewhat haggard, McNeil had stood the ordeal well. He breathed gratefully the blast of raw oxygen and rejected the idea that he might like to lie down and sleep. As he explained, he had done very little but sleep for the last week to conserve air. The first mate looked relieved. He had been afraid he might have to wait for the story.

The cargo was being trans-shipped and the other two tugs were climbing up from the great blinding crescent of Venus while McNeil retraced the events of the last few weeks and the mate made surreptitious notes.

He spoke quite calmly and impersonally, as if he were relating some adventure that had happened to another person, or indeed had never happened at all. Which was, of course, to some extent the case, though it would be unfair to suggest that McNeil was telling any lies.

He invented nothing, but he omitted a good deal. He had had three weeks in which to prepare his narrative and he did not think it had any flaws. . . .

Grant had already reached the door when McNeil called softly after him, "What's the hurry? I thought we had something to discuss."

Grant grabbed at the doorway to halt his headlong flight. He turned slowly and stared unbelievingly at the engineer. McNeil should be already dead—but he was sitting quite comfortably, looking at him with a most peculiar expression.

"Sit down," he said sharply—and in that moment it suddenly seemed that all authority had passed to him. Grant did so, quite without volition. Something had gone wrong, though what it was he could not imagine.

The silence in the control room seemed to last for ages. Then McNeil said rather sadly, "I'd hoped better of you, Grant."

At last Grant found his voice, though he could barely recognize it.

"What do you mean?" he whispered.

"What do you think I mean?" replied McNeil, with what seemed no more than mild irritation. "This little attempt of yours to poison me, of course."

Grant's tottering world collapsed at last, but he no longer cared greatly one way or the other. McNeil began to examine his beautifully kept fingernails with some attention.

"As a matter of interest," he said, in the way that one might ask the time, "when did you decide to kill me?"

The sense of unreality was so overwhelming that Grant felt he was acting a part, that this had nothing to do with real life at all.

"Only this morning," he said, and believed it.

"Hmm," remarked McNeil, obviously without much conviction. He rose to his feet and moved over to the medicine chest. Grant's eyes followed him as he fumbled in the compartment and came back with the little poison bottle. It still appeared to be full. Grant had been careful about that.

"I suppose I should get pretty mad about this whole business," McNeil continued conversationally, holding the bottle between thumb and forefinger. "But somehow I'm not. Maybe it's because I never had many illusions about human nature. And, of course, I saw it coming a long time ago."

Only the last phrase really reached Grant's consciousness.

"You—saw it coming?"

"Heavens, yes! You're too transparent to make a good criminal, I'm afraid. And now that your little plot's failed it leaves us both in an embarrassing position, doesn't it?"

To this masterly understatement there seemed no possible reply.

"By rights," continued the engineer thoughtfully, "I should now work myself into a good temper, call Venus Central, and denounce you to the authorities. But it would be a rather pointless thing to do, and I've never been much good at losing my temper anyway. Of course, you'll say that's because I'm too lazy—but I don't think so."

He gave Grant a twisted smile.

"Oh, I know what you think about me—you've got me neatly classified in that orderly mind of yours, haven't you? I'm soft and self-indulgent, I haven't any moral courage—or any morals for that matter—and I don't give a damn for anyone but myself. Well, I'm not denying it. Maybe it's ninety per cent true. But the odd ten per cent is mighty important, Grant!"

Grant felt in no condition to indulge in psychological analysis, and this seemed hardly the time for anything of the sort. Besides, he was still obsessed with the problem of his failure and the mystery of McNeil's continued existence. McNeil, who knew this perfectly well, seemed in no hurry to satisfy his curiosity.

"Well, what do you intend to do now?" Grant asked, anxious to get it over.

"I would like," said McNeil calmly, "to carry on our discussion where it was interrupted by the coffee."

"You don't mean—"

"But I do. Just as if nothing had happened."

"That doesn't make sense. You've got something up your sleeve!" cried Grant.

McNeil sighed. He put down the poison bottle and looked firmly at Grant.

"*You're* in no position to accuse me of plotting anything. To repeat my earlier remarks, I am suggesting that we decide which one of us shall take poison—only we don't want any more unilateral decisions. Also"—he picked up the bottle again—"it will be the real thing this time. The stuff in here merely leaves a bad taste in the mouth."

A light was beginning to dawn in Grant's mind, "You changed the poison!"

"Naturally. You may think you're a good actor, Grant, but frankly—from the balcony—I thought the performance stank. I could tell you were plotting something, probably before you knew it yourself. In the last few days I've deloused the ship pretty thoroughly. Thinking of all the ways you might have done me in was quite amusing and helped to pass the time. The poison was so obvious that it was the first thing I fixed. But I rather overdid the danger signals and nearly gave myself away when I took the first sip. Salt doesn't go at all well with coffee."

He gave that wry grin again. "Also, I'd hoped for something more subtle. So far I've found fifteen infallible ways of murdering anyone aboard a spaceship. But I don't propose to describe them now."

This was fantastic, Grant thought. He was being treated, not like a criminal, but like a rather stupid schoolboy who hadn't done his homework properly.

"Yet you're still willing," said Grant unbelievingly, "to start all over again? And you'd take the poison yourself if you lost?"

McNeil was silent for a long time. Then he began, slowly, "I can see that you still don't believe me. It doesn't fit at all nicely into your tidy little picture, does it? But perhaps I can make you understand. It's really quite simple.

"I've enjoyed life, Grant, without many scruples or regrets—but the better part of it's over now and I don't cling to what's left as desperately as you might imagine. Yet while I *am* alive I'm rather particular about some things.

"It may surprise you to know that I've got any ideals at all. But I have, Grant—I've always tried to act like a civilized, rational being. I've not always succeeded. When I've failed I've tried to redeem myself."

He paused, and when he resumed it was as though he, and not Grant, was on the defensive. "I've never exactly liked you Grant, but I've often admired you and that's why I'm sorry it's come to this. I admired you most of all the day the ship was holed."

For the first time, McNeil seemed to have some difficulty in choosing his words. When he spoke again he avoided Grant's eyes.

"I didn't behave very well then. Something happened that I thought was impossible. I've always been quite sure that I'd never lose my nerve but—well—it was so sudden it knocked me over."

He attempted to hide his embarrassment by humor. "The same sort of thing happened on my very first trip. I was sure *I'd* never be spacesick—and as a result I was much worse than if I had not been over-confident. But I got over it then—and again this time. It was one of the biggest surprises of my life, Grant, when I saw that you of all people were beginning to crack.

"Oh, yes—the business of the wines! I can see you're thinking about that. Well, that's one thing I *don't* regret. I said I'd always tried to act like a civilized man—and a civilized man should always know when to get drunk. But perhaps you wouldn't understand."

Oddly enough, that was just what Grant was beginning to do. He had caught his first real glimpse of McNeil's intricate and tortuous personality and realized how utterly he had misjudged him. No—misjudged was not the right word. In many ways his judgment had been correct. But it had only touched the surface—he had never suspected the depths that lay beneath.

In a moment of insight that had never come before, and from the nature of things could never come again, Grant understood the reasons behind McNeil's action. This was nothing so simple as a coward trying to reinstate himself in the eyes of the world, for no one need ever know what happened aboard the *Star Queen*.

In any case, McNeil probably cared nothing for the world's opinion, thanks to the sleek self-sufficiency that had so often annoyed Grant. But that very self-sufficiency meant that at all costs he must preserve his own good opinion of himself. Without it life would not be worth living—and McNeil had never accepted life save on his own terms.

The engineer was watching him intently and must have guessed that Grant was coming near the truth, for he suddenly changed his tone as though he was sorry he had revealed so much of his character.

"Don't think I get a quixotic pleasure from turning the other cheek," he said. "Just consider it from the point of view of pure logic. After all, we've got to come to *some* agreement.

"Has it occurred to you that if only one of us survives without a covering message from the other, he'll have a very uncomfortable time explaining just what happened?"

In his blind fury, Grant had completely forgotten this. But he did not believe it bulked at all important in McNeil's own thoughts.

"Yes," he said, "I suppose you're right."

He felt far better now. All the hate had drained out of him

and he was at peace. The truth was known and he accepted it. That it was so different from what he had imagined did not seem to matter now.

"Well, let's get it over," he said unemotionally. "There's a new pack of cards lying around somewhere."

"I think we'd better speak to Venus first—both of us," replied McNeil, with peculiar emphasis. "We want a complete agreement on record in case anyone asks awkward questions later."

Grant nodded absently. He did not mind very much now one way or the other. He even smiled, ten minutes later, as he drew his card from the pack and laid it, face upward, beside McNeil's.

"So that's the whole story, is it?" said the first mate, wondering how soon he could decently get to the transmitter.

"Yes," said McNeil evenly, "that's all there was to it."

The mate bit his pencil, trying to frame the next question. "And I suppose Grant took it all quite calmly?"

The captain gave him a glare, which he avoided, and McNeil looked at him coldly as if he could see through to the sensation-mongering headlines ranged behind. He got to his feet and moved over to the observation port.

"You heard his broadcast, didn't you? Wasn't that calm enough?"

The mate sighed. It still seemed hard to believe that in such circumstances two men could have behaved in so reasonable, so unemotional a manner. He could have pictured all sorts of dramatic possibilities—sudden outbursts of insanity, even attempts at murder. Yet according to McNeil nothing at all had happened. It was too bad.

McNeil was speaking again, as if to himself. "Yes, Grant behaved very well—very well indeed. It was a great pity—"

Then he seemed to lose himself in the ever-fresh, incomparable glory of the approaching planet. Not far beneath, and coming closer by kilometers every second, the snow-white crescent arms of Venus spanned more than half the sky. Down there were life and warmth and civilization—and air.

The future, which not long ago had seemed contracted to a point, had opened out again into all its unknown possibilities and wonders. But behind him McNeil could sense the eyes of his rescuers, probing, questioning—yes, and condemning too.

All his life he would hear whispers. Voices would be saying behind his back, "Isn't that the man who—?"

He did not care. For once in his life at least, he had done something of which he could feel unashamed. Perhaps one day his own pitiless self-analysis would strip bare the motives behind his actions, would whisper in his ear. "Altruism? Don't be a fool! You did it to bolster up your own good opinion of yourself—so much more important than anyone else's!"

But the perverse maddening voices, which all his life had made nothing seem worthwhile, were silent for the moment and he felt content. He had reached the calm at the center of the hurricane. While it lasted he would enjoy it to the full.

History Lesson

No one could remember when the tribe had begun its long journey. The land of great rolling plains that had been its first home was now no more than a half-forgotten dream.

For many years Shann and his people had been fleeing through a country of low hills and sparkling lakes, and now the mountains lay ahead. This summer they must cross them to the southern lands. There was little time to lose. The white terror that had come down from the Poles, grinding continents to dust and freezing the very air before it, was less than a day's march behind.

Shann wondered if the glaciers could climb the mountains ahead, and within his heart he dared to kindle a little flame of hope. This might prove a barrier against which even the remorseless ice would batter in vain. In the southern lands of which the legends spoke, his people might find refuge at last.

It took weeks to discover a pass through which the tribe and the animals could travel. When midsummer came, they had camped in a lonely valley where the air was thin and the stars shone with a brilliance no one had ever seen before.

The summer was waning when Shann took his two sons and

went ahead to explore the way. For three days they climbed, and for three nights slept as best they could on the freezing rocks, and on the fourth morning there was nothing ahead but a gentle rise to a cairn of gray stones built by other travelers, centuries ago.

Shann felt himself trembling, and not with cold, as they walked toward the little pyramid of stones. His sons had fallen behind. No one spoke, for too much was at stake. In a little while they would know if all their hopes had been betrayed.

To east and west, the wall of mountains curved away as if embracing the land beneath. Below lay endless miles of undulating plain, with a great river swinging across it in tremendous loops. It was a fertile land; one in which the tribe could raise crops knowing that there would be no need to flee before the harvest came.

Then Shann lifted his eyes to the south, and saw the doom of all his hopes. For there at the edge of the world glimmered that deadly light he had seen so often to the north—the glint of ice below the horizon.

There was no way forward. Through all the years of flight, the glaciers from the south had been advancing to meet them. Soon they would be crushed beneath the moving walls of ice . . .

Southern glaciers did not reach the mountains until a generation later. In that last summer the sons of Shann carried the sacred treasures of the tribe to the lonely cairn overlooking the plain. The ice that had once gleamed below the horizon was now almost at their feet. By spring it would be splintering against the mountain walls.

No one understood the treasures now. They were from a past too distant for the understanding of any man alive. Their origins were lost in the mists that surrounded the Golden Age, and how they had come at last into the possession of this wandering tribe was a story that now would never be told. For it was the story of a civilization that had passed beyond recall.

Once, all these pitiful relics had been treasured for some good reason, and now they had become sacred though their meaning had long been lost. The print in the old books had faded centuries ago though much of the lettering was still visible—if there had been any to read it. But many generations had passed since anyone had had a use for a set of seven-figure logarithms, an atlas of the world, and the score of Sibelius' Seventh Symphony printed, according to the fly-leaf, by H. K. Chu and Sons, at the City of Pekin in the year 2371 A.D.

The old books were placed reverently in the little crypt that had been made to receive them. There followed a motley collection of fragments—gold and platinum coins, a broken telephoto lens, a watch, a cold-light lamp, a microphone, the cutter from an electric razor, some midget radio tubes, the flotsam that had been left behind when the great tide of civilization had ebbed forever.

All these treasures were carefully stowed away in their resting place. Then came three more relics, the most sacred of all because the least understood.

The first was a strangely shaped piece of metal, showing the coloration of intense heat. It was, in its way, the most pathetic of all these symbols from the past, for it told of man's greatest achievement and of the future he might have known. The mahogany stand on which it was mounted bore a silver plate with the inscription:

> Auxiliary Igniter from Starboard Jet
> Spaceship "Morning Star"
> Earth-Moon, A.D. 1985

Next followed another miracle of the ancient science—a sphere of transparent plastic with strangely shaped pieces of metal imbedded in it. At its center was a tiny capsule of synthetic radio-element, surrounded by the converting screens that shifted its radiation far down the spectrum. As long as the material remained active, the sphere would be a tiny radio transmitter, broadcasting power in all directions. Only a few of these spheres had ever been made. They had been designed as perpetual beacons to mark the orbits of the asteroids. But man had never reached the asteroids and the beacons had never been used.

Last of all was a flat, circular tin, wide in comparison with its depth. It was heavily sealed, and rattled when shaken. The tribal lore predicted that disaster would follow if it was ever opened, and no one knew that it held one of the great works of art of nearly a thousand years before.

The work was finished. The two men rolled the stones back into place and slowly began to descend the mountainside. Even to the last, man had given some thought to the future and had tried to preserve something for posterity.

That winter the great waves of ice began their first assault on the mountains, attacking from north and south. The foothills were overwhelmed in the first onslaught, and the glaciers ground them into dust. But the mountains stood firm, and when the summer came the ice retreated for a while.

So, winter after winter, the battle continued, and the roar of the avalanches, the grinding of rock and the explosions of splintering ice filled the air with tumult. No war of man's had been fiercer than this, and even man's battles had not quite engulfed the globe as this had done.

At last the tidal waves of ice began to subside and to creep slowly down the flanks of the mountains they had never quite subdued. The valleys and passes were still firmly in their grip. It was stalemate. The glaciers had met their match, but their defeat was too late to be of any use to man.

So the centuries passed, and presently there happened

something that must occur once at least in the history of every world in the universe, no matter how remote and lonely it may be.

The ship from Venus came five thousand years too late, but its crew knew nothing of this. While still many millions of miles away, the telescopes had seen the great shroud of ice that made Earth the most brilliant object in the sky next to the sun itself.

Here and there the dazzling sheet was marred by black specks that revealed the presence of almost buried mountains. That was all. The rolling oceans, the plains and forests, the deserts and lakes—all that had been the world of man was sealed beneath the ice, perhaps forever.

The ship closed in to Earth and established an orbit less than a thousand miles away. For five days it circled the planet, while cameras recorded all that was left to see and a hundred instruments gathered information that would give the Venusian scientists many years of work.

An actual landing was not intended. There seemed little purpose in it. But on the sixth day the picture changed. A panoramic monitor, driven to the limit of its amplification, detected the dying radiation of the five-thousand-year-old beacon. Through all the centuries, it had been sending out its signals with ever-failing strength as its radioactive heart steadily weakened.

The monitor locked on the beacon frequency. In the control room, a bell clamored for attention. A little later, the Venusian ship broke free from its orbit and slanted down toward Earth, toward a range of mountains that still towered proudly above the ice, and to a cairn of gray stones that the years had scarcely touched. . . .

The great disk of the sun blazed fiercely in a sky no longer veiled with mist, for the clouds that had once hidden Venus had now completely gone. Whatever force had caused the change in the sun's radiation had doomed one civilization, but had given birth to another. Less than five thousand years before, the half-savage people of Venus had seen sun and stars for the first time. Just as the science of Earth had begun with astronomy, so had that of Venus, and on the warm, rich world that man had never seen progress had been incredibly rapid.

Perhaps the Venusians had been lucky. They never knew the Dark Age that held man enchained for a thousand years. They missed the long detour into chemistry and mechanics but came at once to the more fundamental laws of radiation physics. In the time that man had taken to progress from the Pyramids to the rocket-propelled spaceship, the Venusians had passed from the discovery of agriculture to antigravity itself— the ultimate secret that man had never learned.

The warm ocean that still bore most of the young planet's life rolled its breakers languidly against the sandy shore. So new was this continent that the very sands were coarse and gritty. There had not yet been time enough for the sea to wear them smooth.

The scientists lay half in the water, their beautiful reptilian bodies gleaming in the sunlight. The greatest minds of Venus had gathered on this shore from all the islands of the planet. What they were going to hear they did not know, except that it concerned the Third World and the mysterious race that had peopled it before the coming of the ice.

The Historian was standing on the land, for the instruments he wished to use had no love of water. By his side was a large machine which attracted many curious glances from his colleagues. It was clearly concerned with optics, for a lens system projected from it toward a screen of white material a dozen yards away.

The Historian began to speak. Briefly he recapitulated what

little had been discovered concerning the Third Planet and its people.

He mentioned the centuries of fruitless research that had failed to interpret a single word of the writings of Earth. The planet had been inhabited by a race of great technical ability. That, at least, was proved by the few pieces of machinery that had been found in the cairn upon the mountains.

"We do not know why so advanced a civilization came to an end," he observed. "Almost certainly, it had sufficient knowledge to survive an Ice Age. There must have been some other factor of which we know nothing. Possibly disease or racial degeneration may have been responsible. It has even been suggested that the tribal conflicts endemic to our own species in prehistoric times may have continued on the Third Planet after the coming of technology.

"Some philosophers maintain that knowledge of machinery does not necessarily imply a high degree of civilization, and it is theoretically possible to have wars in a society possessing mechanical power, flight, and even radio. Such a conception is alien to our thoughts, but we must admit its possibility. It would certainly account for the downfall of the lost race.

"It has always been assumed that we should never know anything of the physical form of the creatures who lived on Planet Three. For centuries our artists have been depicting scenes from the history of the dead world, peopling it with all manner of fantastic beings. Most of these creations have resembled us more or less closely, though it had often been pointed out that because we are reptiles it does not follow that all intelligent life must necessarily be reptilian.

"We now know the answer to one of the most baffling problems of history. At last, after hundreds of years of research, we have discovered the exact form and nature of the ruling life on the Third Planet."

There was a murmur of astonishment from the assembled

scientists. Some were so taken aback that they disappeared for a while into the comfort of the ocean, as all Venusians were apt to do in moments of stress. The Historian waited until his colleagues re-emerged into the element they so disliked. He himself was quite comfortable, thanks to the tiny sprays that were continually playing over his body. With their help he could live on land for many hours before having to return to the ocean.

The excitement slowly subsided and the lecturer continued:

"One of the most puzzling of the objects found on Planet Three was a flat metal container holding a great length of transparent plastic material, perforated at the edges and wound tightly into a spool. This transparent tape at first seemed quite featureless, but an examination with the new subelectronic microscope has shown that this is not the case. Along the surface of the material, invisible to our eyes but perfectly clear under the correct radiation, are literally thousands of tiny pictures. It is believed that they were imprinted on the material by some chemical means, and have faded with the passage of time.

"These pictures apparently form a record of life as it was on the Third Planet at the height of its civilization. They are not independent. Consecutive pictures are almost identical, differing only in the detail of movement. The purpose of such a record is obvious. It is only necessary to project the scenes in rapid succession to give an illusion of continuous movement. We have made a machine to do this, and I have here an exact reproduction of the picture sequence.

"The scenes you are now going to witness take us back many thousands of years, to the great days of our sister planet. They show a complex civilization, many of whose activities we can only dimly understand. Life seems to have been very violent and energetic, and much that you will see is quite baffling.

"It is clear that the Third Planet was inhabited by a number of different species, none of them reptilian. That is a blow to our pride, but the conclusion is inescapable. The dominant type of life appears to have been a two-armed biped. It walked upright and covered its body with some flexible material, possibly for protection against the cold, since even before the Ice Age the planet was at a much lower temperature than our own world. But I will not try your patience any further. You will now see the record of which I have been speaking."

A brilliant light flashed from the projector. There was a gentle whirring, and on the screen appeared hundreds of strange beings moving rather jerkily to and fro. The picture expanded to embrace one of the creatures, and the scientists could see that the Historian's description had been correct.

The creature possessed two eyes, set rather close together, but the other facial adornments were a little obscure. There was a large orifice in the lower portion of the head that was continually opening and closing. Possibly it had something to do with the creature's breathing.

The scientists watched spellbound as the strange being became involved in a series of fantastic adventures. There was an incredibly violent conflict with another, slightly different creature. It seemed certain that they must both be killed, but when it was all over neither seemed any the worse.

Then came a furious drive over miles of country in a four-wheeled mechanical device which was capable of extraordinary feats of locomotion. The ride ended in a city packed with other vehicles moving in all directions at breathtaking speeds. No one was surprised to see two of the machines meet head-on with devastating results.

After that, events became even more complicated. It was now quite obvious that it would take many years of research to analyze and understand all that was happening. It was also clear that the record was a work of art, somewhat stylized, rather than an exact reproduction of life as it actually had been on the Third Planet.

Most of the scientists felt themselves completely dazed when the sequence of pictures came to an end. There was a final flurry of motion, in which the creature that had been the center of interest became involved in some tremendous but incomprehensible catastrophe. The picture contracted to a circle, centered on the creature's head.

The last scene of all was an expanded view of its face, obviously expressing some powerful emotion. But whether it was rage, grief, defiance, resignation or some other feeling could not be guessed. The picture vanished. For a moment some lettering appeared on the screen, then it was all over.

For several minutes there was complete silence, save for the lapping of the waves upon the sand. The scientists were too stunned to speak. The fleeting glimpse of Earth's civilization had had a shattering effect on their minds. Then little groups began to start talking together, first in whispers and then more and more loudly as the implications of what they had seen became clearer. Presently the Historian called for attention and addressed the meeting again.

"We are now planning," he said, "a vast program of research to extract all available knowledge from this record. Thousands of copies are being made for distribution to all workers. You will appreciate the problems involved. The psychologists in particular have an immense task confronting them.

"But I do not doubt that we shall succeed. In another generation, who can say what we may not have learned of this wonderful race? Before we leave, let us look again at our remote cousins, whose wisdom may have surpassed our own but of whom so little has survived."

Once more the final picture flashed on the screen, motionless this time, for the projector had been stopped. With something like awe, the scientists gazed at the still figure from the past, while in turn the little biped stared back at them with its characteristic expression of arrogant bad temper.

For the rest of time it would symbolize the human race. The psychologists of Venus would analyze its actions and watch its every movement until they could reconstruct its mind. Thousands of books would be written about it. Intricate philosophies would be contrived to account for its behavior.

But all this labor, all this research, would be utterly in vain. Perhaps the proud and lonely figure on the screen was smiling sardonically at the scientists who were starting on their agelong fruitless quest.

Its secret would be safe as long as the universe endured, for no one now would ever read the lost language of Earth. Millions of times in the ages to come those last few words would flash across the screen, and none could ever guess their meaning:

A Walt Disney Production.

Superiority

In making this statement—which I do of my own free will—I wish first to make it perfectly clear that I am not in any way trying to gain sympathy, nor do I expect any mitigation of whatever sentence the Court may pronounce. I am writing this in an attempt to refute some of the lying reports broadcast over the prison radio and published in the papers I have been allowed to see. These have given an entirely false picture of the true cause of our defeat, and as the leader of my race's armed forces at the cessation of hostilities I feel it my duty to protest against such libels upon those who served under me.

I also hope that this statement may explain the reasons for the application I have twice made to the Court, and will now induce it to grant a favor for which I can see no possible grounds of refusal.

The ultimate cause of our failure was a simple one: despite all statements to the contrary, it was not due to lack of bravery on the part of our men, or to any fault of the Fleet's. We were defeated by one thing only—by the inferior science of our enemies. I repeat—by the *inferior* science of our enemies.

When the war opened we had no doubt of our ultimate

victory. The combined fleets of our allies greatly exceeded in number and armament those which the enemy could muster against us, and in almost all branches of military science we were their superiors. We were sure that we could maintain this superiority. Our belief proved, alas, to be only too well founded.

At the opening of the war our main weapons were the long-range homing torpedo, dirigible ball-lightning and the various modifications of the Klydon beam. Every unit of the Fleet was equipped with these and though the enemy possessed similar weapons their installations were generally of lesser power. Moreover, we had behind us a far greater military Research Organization, and with this initial advantage we could not possibly lose.

The campaign proceeded according to plan until the Battle of the Five Suns. We won this, of course, but the opposition proved stronger than we had expected. It was realized that victory might be more difficult, and more delayed, than had first been imagined. A conference of supreme commanders was therefore called to discuss our future strategy.

Present for the first time at one of our war conferences was Professor-General Norden, the new Chief of the Research Staff, who had just been appointed to fill the gap left by the death of Malvar, our greatest scientist. Malvar's leadership had been responsible, more than any other single factor, for the efficiency and power of our weapons. His loss was a very serious blow, but no one doubted the brilliance of his successor—though many of us disputed the wisdom of appointing a theoretical scientist to fill a post of such vital importance. But we had been overruled.

I can well remember the impression Norden made at that conference. The military advisers were worried, and as usual turned to the scientists for help. Would it be possible to improve our existing weapons, they asked, so that our present advantage could be increased still further?

Norden's reply was quite unexpected. Malvar had often been asked such a question—and he had always done what we requested.

"Frankly, gentlemen," said Norden, "I doubt it. Our existing weapons have practically reached finality. I don't wish to criticize my predecessor, or the excellent work done by the Research Staff in the last few generations, but do you realize that there has been no basic change in armaments for over a century? It is, I am afraid, the result of a tradition that has become conservative. For too long, the Research Staff has devoted itself to perfecting old weapons instead of developing new ones. It is fortunate for us that our opponents have been no wiser: we cannot assume that this will always be so."

Norden's words left an uncomfortable impression, as he had no doubt intended. He quickly pressed home the attack.

"What we want are *new* weapons—weapons totally different from any that have been employed before. Such weapons can be made: it will take time, of course, but since assuming charge I have replaced some of the older scientists by young men and have directed research into several unexplored fields which show great promise. I believe, in fact, that a revolution in warfare may soon be upon us."

We were skeptical. There was a bombastic tone in Norden's voice that made us suspicious of his claims. We did not know, then, that he never promised anything that he had not already almost perfected in the laboratory. *In the laboratory*—that was the operative phrase.

Norden proved his case less than a month later, when he demonstrated the Sphere of Annihilation, which produced complete disintegration of matter over a radius of several hundred meters. We were intoxicated by the power of the new weapon, and were quite prepared to overlook one fundamental defect—the fact that it *was* a sphere and hence destroyed its rather complicated generating equipment at the instant of formation. This meant, of course, that it could not be used on warships but only on guided missiles, and a great program was started to convert all homing torpedoes to carry the new weapon. For the time being all further offensives were suspended.

We realize now that this was our first mistake. I still think that it was a natural one, for it seemed to us then that all our existing weapons had become obsolete overnight, and we already regarded them as almost primitive survivals. What we did not appreciate was the magnitude of the task we were attempting, and the length of time it would take to get the revolutionary super-weapon into battle. Nothing like this had happened for a hundred years and we had no previous experience to guide us.

The conversion problem proved far more difficult than anticipated. A new class of torpedo had to be designed, as the standard model was too small. This meant in turn that only the larger ships could launch the weapon, but we were prepared to accept this penalty. After six months, the heavy units of the Fleet were being equipped with the Sphere. Training maneuvers and tests had shown that it was operating satisfactorily and we were ready to take it into action. Norden was already being hailed as the architect of victory, and had half promised even more spectacular weapons.

Then two things happened. One of our battleships disappeared completely on a training flight, and an investigation showed that under certain conditions the ship's long-range radar could trigger the Sphere immediately it had been launched. The modification needed to overcome this defect was trivial, but it caused a delay of another month and was the source of much bad feeling between the naval staff and the scientists. We were ready for action again—when Norden announced that the radius of effectiveness of the Sphere had now been increased by ten, thus multiplying by a thousand the chances of destroying an enemy ship.

So the modifications started all over again, but everyone agreed that the delay would be worth it. Meanwhile, however, the enemy had been emboldened by the absence of further attacks and had made an unexpected onslaught. Our ships were short of torpedoes, since none had been coming from the factories, and were forced to retire. So we lost the systems of Kyrane and Floranus, and the planetary fortress of Rhamsandron.

It was an annoying but not a serious blow, for the recaptured systems had been unfriendly, and difficult to administer. We had no doubt that we could restore the position in the near future, as soon as the new weapon became operational.

These hopes were only partially fulfilled. When we renewed our offensive, we had to do so with fewer of the Spheres of Annihilation than had been planned, and this was one reason for our limited success. The other reason was more serious.

While we had been equipping as many of our ships as we could with the irresistible weapon, the enemy had been building feverishly. His ships were of the old pattern with the old weapons—but they now outnumbered ours. When we went into action, we found that the numbers ranged against us were often 100 per cent greater than expected, causing target confusion among the automatic weapons and resulting in higher losses than anticipated. The enemy losses were higher still, for once a Sphere had reached its objective, destruction was certain, but the balance had not swung as far in our favor as we had hoped.

Moreover, while the main fleets had been engaged, the

enemy had launched a daring attack on the lightly held systems of Eriston, Duranus, Carmanidora and Pharanidon—
recapturing them all. We were thus faced with a threat only
fifty light-years from our home planets.

There was much recrimination at the next meeting of the
supreme commanders. Most of the complaints were addressed
to Norden—Grand Admiral Taxaris in particular maintaining
that thanks to our admittedly irresistible weapon we were now
considerably worse off than before. We should, he claimed,
have continued to build conventional ships, thus preventing
the loss of our numerical superiority.

Norden was equally angry and called the naval staff ungrate-
ful bunglers. But I could tell that he was worried—as indeed we
all were—by the unexpected turn of events. He hinted that
there might be a speedy way of remedying the situation.

We now know that Research had been working on the
Battle Analyzer for many years, but at the time it came as
a revelation to us and perhaps we were too easily swept off
our feet. Norden's argument, also, was seductively convinc-
ing. What did it matter, he said, if the enemy had twice as
many ships as we—if the efficiency of ours could be doubled or
even trebled? For decades the limiting factor in warfare had
been not mechanical but biological—it had become more and
more difficult for any single mind, or group of minds, to cope
with the rapidly changing complexities of battle in three-
dimensional space. Norden's mathematicians had analyzed some
of the classic engagements of the past, and had shown that
even when we had been victorious we had often operated our
units at much less than half of their theoretical efficiency.

The Battle Analyzer would change all this by replacing the
operations staff with electronic calculators. The idea was not
new, in theory, but until now it had been no more than a
utopian dream. Many of us found it difficult to believe that it

was still anything but a dream: after we had run through several very complex dummy battles, however, we were convinced.

It was decided to install the Analyzer in four of our heaviest ships, so that each of the main fleets could be equipped with one. At this stage, the trouble began—though we did not know it until later.

The Analyzer contained just short of a million vaccum tubes and needed a team of five hundred technicians to maintain and operate it. It was quite impossible to accommodate the extra staff aboard a battleship, so each of the four units had to be accompanied by a converted liner to carry the technicians not on duty. Installation was also a very slow and tedious business, but by gigantic efforts it was completed in six months.

Then, to our dismay, we were confronted by another crisis. Nearly five thousand highly skilled men had been selected to serve the Analyzers and had been given an intensive course at the Technical Training Schools. At the end of seven months, 10 per cent of them had had nervous breakdowns and only 40 per cent had qualified.

Once again, everyone started to blame everyone else. Norden, of course, said that the Research Staff could not be held responsible, and so incurred the enmity of the Personnel and Training Commands. It was finally decided that the only thing to do was to use two instead of four Analyzers and to bring the others into action as soon as men could be trained. There was little time to lose, for the enemy was still on the offensive and his morale was rising.

The first Analyzer fleet was ordered to recapture the system of Eriston. On the way, by one of the hazards of war, the liner carrying the technicians was struck by a roving mine. A warship would have survived, but the liner with its irreplaceable cargo was totally destroyed. So the operation had to be abandoned.

The other expedition was, at first, more successful. There

was no doubt at all that the Analyzer fulfilled its designers' claims, and the enemy was heavily defeated in the first en gagements. He withdrew, leaving us in possession of Saphran, Leucon and Hexanerax. But his Intelligence Staff must have noted the change in our tactics and the inexplicable presence of a liner in the heart of our battle-fleet. It must have noted, also, that our first fleet had been accompanied by a similar ship—and had withdrawn when it had been destroyed.

In the next engagement, the enemy used his superior num bers to launch an overwhelming attack on the Analyzer ship and its unarmed consort. The attack was made without regard to losses—both ships were, of course, very heavily protected— and it succeeded. The result was the virtual decapitation of the Fleet, since an effectual transfer to the old operational methods proved impossible. We disengaged under heavy fire, and so lost all our gains and also the systems of Lormyia, Is marnus, Beronis, Alphanidon and Sideneus.

At this stage, Grand Admiral Taxaris expressed his disap proval of Norden by committing suicide, and I assumed supreme command.

The situation was now both serious and infuriating. With stubborn conservatism and complete lack of imagination, the enemy continued to advance with his old-fashioned and inef ficient but now vastly more numerous ships. It was galling to realize that if we had only continued building, without seeking new weapons, we would have been in a far more advantageous position. There were many acrimonious conferences at which Norden defended the scientists while everyone else blamed them for all that had happened. The difficulty was that Nor den had proved every one of his claims: he had a perfect ex cuse for all the disasters that had occurred. And we could not now turn back—the search for an irresistible weapon must go on. At first it had been a luxury that would shorten the war. Now it was a necessity if we were to end it victoriously.

We were on the defensive, and so was Norden. He was more than ever determined to re-establish his prestige and that of the Research Staff. But we had been twice disappointed, and would not make the same mistake again. No doubt Norden's twenty thousand scientists would produce many further weapons: we would remain unimpressed.

We were wrong. The final weapon was something so fantastic that even now it seems difficult to believe that it ever existed. Its innocent, noncommittal name—The Exponential Field—gave no hint of its real potentialities. Some of Norden's mathematicians had discovered it during a piece of entirely theoretical research into the properties of space, and to everyone's great surprise their results were found to be physically realizable.

It seems very difficult to explain the operation of the Field to the layman. According to the technical description, it "produces an exponential condition of space, so that a finite distance in normal, linear space may become infinite in pseudo-space." Norden gave an analogy which some of us found useful. It was as if one took a flat disk of rubber—representing a region of normal space—and then pulled its center out to infinity. The circumference of the disk would be unaltered—but its "diameter" would be infinite. That was the sort of thing the generator of the Field did to the space around it.

As an example, suppose that a ship carrying the generator was surrounded by a ring of hostile machines. If it switched on the Field, *each* of the enemy ships would think that it—and the ships on the far side of the circle—had suddenly receded into nothingness. Yet the circumference of the circle would be the same as before: only the journey to the center would be of infinite duration, for as one proceeded, distances would appear to become greater and greater as the "scale" of space altered.

It was a nightmare condition, but a very useful one. Nothing could reach a ship carrying the Field: it might be englobed by an enemy fleet yet would be as inaccessible as if it were at the other side of the Universe. Against this, of course, it could not fight back without switching off the Field, but this still left it at a very great advantage, not only in defense but in offense. For a ship fitted with the Field could approach an enemy fleet undetected and suddenly appear in its midst.

This time there seemed to be no flaws in the new weapon. Needless to say, we looked for all the possible objections before we committed ourselves again. Fortunately the equipment was fairly simple and did not require a large operating staff. After much debate, we decided to rush it into production, for we realized that time was running short and the war was going against us. We had now lost about the whole of our initial gains and enemy forces had made several raids into our own solar system.

We managed to hold off the enemy while the Fleet was re-equipped and the new battle techniques were worked out. To use the Field operationally it was necessary to locate an enemy formation, set a course that would intercept it, and then switch on the generator for the calculated period of time. On releasing the Field again—if the calculations had been accurate—one would be in the enemy's midst and could do great damage during the resulting confusion, retreating by the same route when necessary.

The first trial maneuvers proved satisfactory and the equipment seemed quite reliable. Numerous mock attacks were made and the crews became accustomed to the new technique. I was on one of the test flights and can vividly remember my impressions as the Field was switched on. The ships around us seemed to dwindle as if on the surface of an expanding bubble: in an instant they had vanished completely. So had the stars— but presently we could see that the Galaxy was still visible as a faint band of light around the ship. The virtual radius of our pseudo-space was not really infinite, but some hundred thousand light-years, and so the distance to the farthest stars of our system had not been greatly increased—though the nearest had of course totally disappeared.

These training maneuvers, however, had to be cancelled before they were complete owing to a whole flock of minor technical troubles in various pieces of equipment, notably the communications circuits. These were annoying, but not important, though it was thought best to return to Base to clear them up.

At that moment the enemy made what was obviously intended to be a decisive attack against the fortress planet of Iton at the limits of our solar system. The Fleet had to go into battle before repairs could be made.

The enemy must have believed that we had mastered the secret of invisibility—as in a sense we had. Our ships appeared suddenly out of nowhere and inflicted tremendous damage—for a while. And then something quite baffling and inexplicable happened.

I was in command of the flagship *Hircania* when the trouble started. We had been operating as independent units, each against assigned objectives. Our detectors observed an enemy formation at medium range and the navigating officers measured its distance with great accuracy. We set course and switched on the generator.

The Exponential Field was released at the moment when we should have been passing through the center of the enemy group. To our consternation, we emerged into normal space at a distance of many hundred miles—and when we found the enemy, he had already found us. We retreated, and tried again. This time we were so far away from the enemy that he located us first.

Obviously, something was seriously wrong. We broke communicator silence and tried to contact the other ships of the Fleet to see if they had experienced the same trouble.

Once again we failed—and this time the failure was beyond all reason, for the communication equipment appeared to be working perfectly. We could only assume, fantastic though it seemed, that the rest of the Fleet had been destroyed.

I do not wish to describe the scenes when the scattered units of the Fleet struggled back to Base. Our casualties had actually been negligible, but the ships were completely demoralized. Almost all had lost touch with one another and had found that their ranging equipment showed inexplicable errors. It was obvious that the Exponential Field was the cause of the troubles, despite the fact that they were only apparent when it was switched off.

The explanation came too late to do us any good, and Norden's final discomfiture was small consolation for the virtual loss of the war. As I have explained, the Field generators produced a radial distortion of space, distances appearing greater and greater as one approached the center of the artificial pseudo-space. When the Field was switched off, conditions returned to normal.

But not quite. It was never possible to restore the initial state *exactly*. Switching the Field on and off was equivalent to an elongation and contraction of the ship carrying the generator, but there was an hysteretic effect, as it were, and the initial condition was never quite reproducible, owing to all the thousands of electrical changes and movements of mass aboard the ship while the Field was on. These asymmetries and distortions were cumulative, and though they seldom amounted to more than a fraction of one per cent, that was quite enough. It meant that the precision ranging equipment and tuned circuits in the communication apparatus were thrown completely out of adjustment. Any single ship could never detect the change—only when it compared its equipment with that of another vessel, or tried to communicate with it, could it tell what had happened.

It is impossible to describe the resultant chaos. Not a single component of one ship could be expected with certainty to work aboard another. The very nuts and bolts were no longer interchangeable, and the supply position became quite impossible. Given time, we might even have overcome these difficulties, but the enemy ships were already attacking in thousands with weapons which now seemed centuries behind those that we had invented. Our magnificent Fleet, crippled by our own science, fought on as best it could until it was overwhelmed and forced to surrender. The ships fitted with the Field were still invulnerable, but as fighting units they were almost helpless. Every time they switched on their generators to escape from enemy attack, the permanent distortion of their equipment increased. In a month, it was all over.

This is the true story of our defeat, which I give without prejudice to my defense before the Court. I make it, as I have said, to counteract the libels that have been circulating against the men who fought under me, and to show where the true blame for our misfortunes lay.

Finally, my request, which as the Court will now realize, I make in no frivolous manner and which I hope will therefore be granted.

The Court will be aware that the conditions under which we are housed and the constant surveillance to which we are subjected night and day are somewhat distressing. Yet I am not complaining of this: nor do I complain of the fact that shortage of accommodation has made it necessary to house us in pairs.

But I cannot be held responsible for my future actions if I am compelled any longer to share my cell with Professor Norden, late Chief of the Research Staff of my armed forces.

Exile of the Eons

Already the mountains were trembling with the thunder that only man can make. But here the war seemed very far away, for the full moon hung over The Himalayas and the blinding furies of the battle were still hidden below the edge of the world. Not for long would they remain. The Master knew that the last remnants of his fleet were being hurled from the sky as the circle of death closed swiftly on his stronghold.

In a few hours at the most, the Master and his dreams of empire would have vanished into the past. Nations would still curse his name, but they would no longer fear it. Later, even the hatred would be gone and he would mean no more to the world than Hitler or Napoleon or Genghis Khan. Like them he would be a blurred figure far down the infinite corridor of time, dwindling toward oblivion.

Far to the south, a mountain was suddenly edged with the violet flame. Ages later, the balcony on which the Master stood shuddered beneath the impact of the ground wave racing through the rocks below. Later still, the air brought the echo to a mammoth concussion. Surely they could not be so close already! The Master hoped it was no more than a stray torpedo that had swept through the contracting battle line. If it were not, time was even shorter than he feared.

The Chief of Staff walked out from the shadows and joined him by the rail. The Marshal's hard face—the second most hated in all the world—was lined and beaded with sweat. He had not slept for many days and his once gaudy uniform hung limply upon him. Yet his eyes, though unutterably weary, were still resolute even in defeat. he stood in silence, awaiting his last orders. Nothing else was left for him to do.

Thirty miles away, the eternal snow-plume of Everest flamed a lurid red, reflecting the glare of some colossal fire below the horizon. Still the Master neither moved nor gave any sign. Not until a salvo of torpedoes passed high overhead with a demon wail did he turn and, with one backward glance at the world he would see no more, descend into the depths.

The lift dropped a thousand feet and the sound of battle died away. As he stepped out of the shaft, the Master paused for a moment to press a hidden switch. The Marshal smiled when he heard the crash of falling rock far above, and knew that pursuit and escape were equally impossible.

As of old, the handful of generals sprang to their feet when the Master entered the room. He walked to his place in silence, steeling himself for the last and hardest speech he would ever have to make. Burning into his soul he could feel the eyes of the men he had led to ruin. Behind and beyond them he could see the squadrons, the divisions, the armies whose blood was on his hands. And more terrible still were the silent specters of the nations that now could never be born.

At last he began to speak. The hypnosis of his voice was as powerful as ever, and after a few words he became once more the perfect, implacable machine whose destiny was destruction.

"This, gentlemen, is the last of all our meetings. There are no more plans to make, no more maps to study. Somewhere above our heads the fleet we built with such pride and care is fighting to the end. In a few minutes, not one of all those thousands of machines will be left in the sky.

"I know that for all of us here surrender is unthinkable, even if it were possible, so in this room you will shortly have to die. You have served our cause and deserved better, but it was not to be. Yet I do not wish you to think that we have wholly failed. In the past, as you saw many times, my plans were always ready for everything that might arise, no matter how improbable. You should not, therefore, be surprised to learn that I was prepared even for defeat."

Still the same superb orator, he paused for effect, noting with satisfaction the ripple of interest, the sudden alertness on the tired faces of his listeners.

"My secret is safe enough with you," he continued, "for the enemy will never find this place. The entrance is already blocked by many hundreds of feet of rock."

Still there was no movement. Only the Director of Propaganda turned suddenly white, and swiftly recovered—but not swiftly enough to escape the Master's eye. The Master smiled inwardly at this belated confirmation of an old doubt. It mattered little now; true and false, they would all die together.

All but one.

"Two years ago," he went on, "when we lost the battle of Antarctica, I knew that we could no longer be certain of victory. So I made my preparations for this day. The enemy has already sworn to kill me. I could not remain in hiding anywhere on the Earth, still less hope to rebuild our fortunes.

"But there is another way, though a desperate one.

"Five years ago, one of our scientists perfected the technique of suspended animation. He found that by relatively simple means all life processes could be arrested for an indefinite time. I am going to use this discovery to escape from the present into a future which will have forgotten me. There I can begin the struggle again, with the help of certain devices that might yet have won this war had we been granted more time.

"Good-by, gentlemen. And once again, my thanks for your help and my regrets at your ill fortune."

He saluted, turned on his heel, and was gone. The metal door thudded decisively behind him. There was a frozen silence; then the Director of Propaganda rushed to the exit, only to recoil with a startled cry. The steel door was already too hot to touch. It had been welded immovably into the wall.

The Minister for War was the first to draw his automatic.

The Master was in no great hurry now. On leaving the council room he had thrown the secret switch of the welding circuit. The same action had opened a panel in the wall of the corridor, revealing a small circular passage sloping steadily upward. He began to walk slowly along it.

Every few hundred feet the tunnel angled sharply, though still continuing the upward climb. At each turning the Master stopped to throw a switch, and there was the thunder of falling rock as a section of corridor collapsed.

Five times the passageway changed its course before it ended in a spherical, metal-walled room. Multiple doors closed softly on rubber seatings, and the last section of tunnel crashed behind. The Master would not be disturbed by his enemies, nor by his friends.

He looked swiftly around the room to satisfy himself that all was ready. Then he walked to a simple control board and threw, one after another, a set of tiny switches. They had to carry little current—but they had been built to last. So had everything in that strange room. Even the walls were made of metals far less ephemeral than steel.

Pumps started to whine, drawing the air from the chamber and replacing it with sterile nitrogen. Moving more swiftly now, the Master went to the padded couch and lay down. He thought he could feel himself bathed by the bacteria-destroying rays from the lamps above his head, but that of course was fancy. From a recess beneath the couch he drew a hypodermic and injected a milky fluid into his arm.

Then he relaxed and waited.

It was already very cold. Soon the refrigerators would bring the temperature down far below freezing, and would hold it there for many hours. Then it would rise to normal, but by that time the process would be completed, all bacteria would be dead and the Master could sleep, unchanged, forever.

He had planned to wait a hundred years. More than that he dared not delay, for when he awoke he would have to master all the changes in science and society that the passing years had wrought. Even a century might have altered the face of a civilization beyond his understanding, but that was a risk he would have to take. Less than a century would not be safe, for the world would still be full of bitter memories.

Sealed in a vacuum beneath the couch were the electronic counters operated by thermocouples hundreds of feet above, on the eastern face of the mountain where no snow could ever cling. Every day the rising sun would operate them and the counters would add one unit to their store. So the coming of dawn would be noted in the darkness where the Master slept.

When any one of the counters reached the total of thirty-six thousand, a switch would close and oxygen would flow back into the chamber. The temperature would rise, and the automatic hypodermic strapped to the Master's arm would inject the calculated amount of fluid. He would awaken. Then he would press the button which would blast away the mountainside and give him free passage to the outer world.

Everything had been considered. There could be no failure. All the machinery had been triplicated and was as perfect as science could contrive.

The Master's last thought as consciousness ebbed was not of

his past life, nor of the mother whose hopes he had betrayed. Unbidden and unwelcome, there came into his mind the words of an ancient poet:

To sleep, perchance to dream . . .

No, he would not, he dared not dream. He would only sleep . . . sleep . . . sleep . . .

Twenty miles away, the battle was coming to its end. Not a dozen of the Master's ships were left, fighting hopelessly against overwhelming fire. The action would have ended long ago had the attackers not been ordered to risk no ships in unnecessary adventures. The decision was to be left to the long-range artillery. So the great destroyers, the airborne battle-ships of this age, lay with their fighter screens in the shelter of the mountains, pouring salvo after salvo into the doomed formations.

Aboard the flagship, a young Hindu gunnery officer set vernier dials with infinite care and gently pressed a pedal with his foot. There was the faintest of shocks as the dirigible torpe-does left their cradles and hurled themselves at the enemy. The young Indian sat waiting tensely as the chronometer ticked off the seconds. This, he thought, was probably the last salvo he would ever fire. Somehow he felt none of the elation he had expected; indeed, he was surprised to discover a kind of impersonal sympathy for his doomed opponents, whose lives were now ebbing with every passing second.

Far away a sphere of violet fire blossomed above the moun-tains, among the darting specks that were enemy ships. The gunner leaned forward tensely and counted. One-two-three-four-five times came that peculiar explosion. Then the sky cleared. The struggling specks were gone.

In his log, the gunner noted briefly: "0124 hrs. Salvo No. 12

fired. Five torps exploded among enemy ships, which were destroyed. One torp failed to detonate."

He signed the entry with a flourish and laid down his pen. For a while he sat staring at the log's familiar brown cover, with the cigarette burns at the edges and the inevitable stained rings where cups and glasses had been carelessly set down. Idly he thumbed through the leaves, noting once again the handwriting of his many predecessors. And as he had done so often before, he turned to a familiar page where a man who had once been his friend had begun to sign his name but had never lived to complete it.

With a sigh, he closed the book and locked it away. The war was over.

Far away among the mountains, the torpedo that had failed to explode was still gaining speed under the drive of its rockets. Now it was a scarcely visible line of light, racing between the walls of a lonely valley. Already the snows that had been disturbed by the scream of its passage were beginning to rumble down the mountain slopes.

There was no escape from the valley: it was blocked by a sheer wall a thousand feet high. Here the torpedo that had missed its mark found a greater one. The Master's tomb was too deep in the mountain even to be shaken by the explosion but the hundreds of tons of falling rock swept away three tiny instruments and their connections, and a future that might have been went with them into oblivion.

The first rays of the rising sun would still fall on the shattered face of the mountain, but the counters that were waiting for the thirty-six thousandth dawn would still be waiting when dawns and sunsets were no more.

In the silence of the tomb that was not quite a tomb, the Master knew nothing of this. And he slumbered on, until the century was far behind—very far indeed.

After what by some standards would have been a little while, the earth's crust decided it had borne the weight of The Himalayas for long enough. Slowly the mountains dropped, tilting the southern plains of India toward the sky. And presently the plateau of Ceylon was the highest point on the surface of the globe, and the ocean about Everest was five and a half miles deep. Yet the Master's slumber was still dreamless and undisturbed.

Slowly, patiently, the silt drifted down through the towering ocean heights onto the wreck of The Himalayas. The blanket that would one day be chalk began to thicken at the rate of an inch or two every century. If one had returned some time later, one might have found that the sea bed was no longer five miles down, or even four, or three. Then the land tilted again, and a mighty range of limestone mountains towered where once had been the oceans of Tibet. But the Master knew nothing of this, nor was his sleep troubled when it happened again and again and yet again.

Now the rain and the rivers were washing away the chalk and carrying it out to the strange new oceans, and the surface was moving down toward the hidden tomb. Slowly the miles of rock were winnowed away until at last the sphere which housed the Master's body returned to the light of day—though to a day much longer, and much dimmer, than it had been when the Master closed his eyes.

Little did the Master dream of the races that had flowered and died since that early morning of the world when he went to his long sleep. Very far away was that morning now, and the shadows were lengthening to the east; the sun was dying and the world was very old. But still the children of Adam ruled its seas and skies, and filled with their tears and laughter the plains and the valleys and the woods that were older than the shifting hills.

The Master's dreamless sleep was more than half ended when Trevindor the Philosopher was born, between the fall of the Ninety-seventh Dynasty and the rise of the Fifth Galactic Empire. He was born on a world very far from Earth. Few were the men who now set foot on the ancient home of their race, so distant from the throbbing heart of the Universe.

They brought Trevindor to Earth when his brief clash with the Empire had come to its inevitable end. Here he was tried by the men whose ideals he had challenged, and here it was that they pondered long over the manner of his necessary fate.

The case was unique. The gentle, philosophic culture that now ruled the Galaxy had never before met with opposition, even on the level of pure intellect, and the polite but implacable conflict of wills had left it severely shaken. It was typical of the Council's members that, when a decision had proved impossible, they had appealed to Trevindor himself for help.

In the whitely gleaming Hall of Justice, that had not been entered for nigh on a million years, Trevindor stood proudly facing the men who had proved stronger than he. In silence he listened to their request; then he paused in reflection. His judges waited patiently until at last he spoke.

"You suggest that I should promise not to defy you again," he began, "but I shall make no promise that I may be unable to keep. Our views are too divergent and sooner or later we should clash again.

"There was a time when your choice would have been easy. You could have exiled me, or put me to death. But today—where among all the worlds of the Universe is there one planet where you could hide me if I did not choose to stay? Remember, I have many disciples scattered the length and breadth of the Galaxy.

"There remains the other alternative. I shall bear you no malice if you revive the ancient custom of execution to meet my case."

There was a murmur of annoyance from the Council, and the President replied sharply, his color heightening.

"That remark is in questionable taste. We asked for serious

suggestions, not reminders—even if intended humorously—of the barbaric customs of our remote ancestors."

Trevindor accepted the rebuke with a bow. "I was merely mentioning all the possibilities. There are two others that have occurred to me. It would be a simple matter to change my mind pattern to your way of thinking so that no future disagreement can arise."

"We have already considered that. We were forced to reject it, attractive though it is, for the destruction of your personality would be equivalent to murder. There are only fifteen more powerful intellects than yours in the Universe, and we have no right to tamper with it. And your final suggestion?"

"Though you cannot exile me in space, there is still one alternative. The river of Time stretches ahead of us as far as our thoughts can go. Send me down that stream to an age when you are certain this civilization will have passed. That I know you can do with the aid of the Roston time-field."

There was a long pause. In silence the members of the Council were passing their decisions to the complex analysis machine which would weigh them one against the other and arrive at the verdict. At length the President spoke.

"It is agreed. We will send you to an age when the sun is still warm enough for life to exist on the Earth, but so remote that any trace of our civilization is unlikely to survive. We will also provide you with everything necessary for your safety and reasonable comfort. You may leave us now. We will call for you again as soon as all arrangements have been made."

Trevindor bowed, and left the marble hall. No guards followed him. There was nowhere he could flee, even if he wished, in this Universe which the great Galactic liners could span in a single day.

For the first and the last time, Trevindor stood on the shore of what had once been the Pacific, listening to the wind sighing through the leaves of what had once been palms. The few stars of the nearly empty region of space through which the sun was now passing shone with a steady light through the dry air of the aging world. Trevindor wondered bleakly if they would still be shining when he looked again upon the sky, in a future so distant that the sun itself would be sinking to its death.

There was a tinkle from the tiny communicator band upon his wrist. So, the time had come. He turned his back upon the ocean and walked resolutely to meet his fate. Before he had gone a dozen steps, the time-field had seized him and his thoughts froze in an instant that would remain unchanged while the oceans shrank and vanished, the Galactic Empire passed away, and the great star clusters crumbled into nothingness.

But, to Trevindor, no time elapsed at all. He only knew that at one step there had been moist sand beneath his feet, and at the next hard, baked rock. The palms had vanished, the murmur of the sea was stilled. It needed only a glance to show that even the memory of the sea had long since faded from this parched and dying world. To the far horizon, a great desert of red sandstone stretched unbroken and unrelieved by any growing thing. Overhead, the orange disk of a strangely altered sun glowered from a sky so black that many stars were clearly visible.

Yet, it seemed, there was still life on this ancient world. To the north—if that were still the north—the somber light glinted upon some metallic structure. It was a few hundred yards away, and as Trevindor started to walk toward it he was conscious of a curious lightness, as if gravity itself had weakened.

He had not gone far before he saw that he was approaching a low metal building which seemed to have been set down on the plain rather than constructed there, for it tilted slightly with the slope of the land. Trevindor wondered at his incredible good fortune at finding civilization so easily. Another dozen steps, and he realized that not chance but design had so conveniently placed this building here, and that it was as much a stranger to this world as he himself.

There was no hope at all that anyone would come to meet him as he walked toward it.

The metal plaque above the door added little to what he had already surmised. Still new and untarnished as if it had just been engraved—as indeed, in a sense, it had—the lettering brought a message at once of hope and of bitterness.

To Trevindor, the greetings of the Council.

This building, which we have sent after you through the time-field, will supply all your needs for an indefinite period.

We do not know if civilization will still exist in the age in which you find yourself. Man may now be extinct, since the chromosome K Star K will have become dominant and the race may have mutated into something no longer human. That is for you to discover.

You are now in the twilight of the Earth and it is our hope that you are not alone. But if it is your destiny to be the last living creature on this once lovely world, remember that the choice was yours. Farewell.

Twice Trevindor read the message, recognizing with an ache the closing words which could only have been written by his friend, the poet Cintillarne. An overwhelming sense of loneliness and isolation came flooding into his soul. He sat down upon a shelf of rock and buried his face in his hands.

A long time later, he arose to enter the building. He felt more than grateful to the long-dead Council which had treated him so chivalrously. The technical achievement of sending an entire building through time was one he had believed beyond the resources of his age. A sudden thought struck him and he glanced again at the engraved lettering, noticing for the first time the date it bore. It was five thousand years later than the time when he had faced his peers in the Hall of Justice.

Fifty centuries had passed before his judges could redeem their promise to a man as good as dead. Whatever the faults of the Council, its integrity was of an order beyond the comprehension of an earlier age.

Many days passed before Trevindor left the building again. Nothing had been overlooked: even his beloved thought records were there. He could continue to study the nature of reality and to construct philosophies until the end of the Universe, barren though that occupation would be if his were the only mind left on Earth. There was little danger, he thought wryly, that his speculations concerning the purpose of human existence would once again bring him into conflict with society.

Not until he had investigated the building thoroughly did Trevindor turn his attention once more to the outer world. The supreme problem was that of contacting civilization, should such still exist. He had been provided with a powerful receiver, and for hours he wandered up and down the spectrum in the hope of discovering a station. The far-off crackle of static came from the instrument and once there was a burst of what might have been speech in a tongue that was certainly not human. But nothing else rewarded his search. The ether, which had been man's faithful servant for so many ages, was silent at last.

The little automatic flyer was Trevindor's sole remaining hope. He had what was left of eternity before him, and Earth was a small planet. In a few years at the most, he could have explored it all.

So the months passed while the exile began his methodical exploration of the world, returning ever and again to his home in the desert of red sandstone.

Everywhere he found the same picture of desolation and ruin. How long ago the seas had vanished he could not even guess, but in their dying they had left endless wastes of salt, encrusting both plains and mountains with a blanket of dirty gray.

Trevindor felt glad that he had not been born on Earth and so had never known it in the glory of its youth. Stranger though he was, the loneliness and desolation of the world chilled his heart; had he lived here before, its sadness would have been unbearable.

Thousands of square miles of desert passed beneath Trevindor's fleeting ship as he searched the world from pole to pole. Only once did he find any sign that Earth had ever known civilization. In a deep valley near the equator he discovered the ruins of a small city of strange white stone and stranger architecture. The buildings were perfectly preserved, though half buried by the drifting sand, and for a moment Trevindor felt a surge of somber joy at the knowledge that man had, after all, left some traces of his handiwork on the world that had been his first home.

The emotion was short-lived. The buildings were stranger than Trevindor had realized, for no man could ever have entered them. Their only openings were wide, horizontal slots close to the ground; there were no windows of any kind. Trevindor's mind reeled as he tried to imagine the creatures that must have occupied them. In spite of his growing loneliness, he felt glad that the dwellers in his inhuman city had passed away so long before his time. He did not linger here, for the bitter night was almost upon him and the valley filled him with an oppression that was not entirely rational.

And once, he actually discovered life. He was cruising over the bed of one of the lost oceans when a flash of color caught his eye. Upon a knoll which the drifting sand had not yet buried was a thin, wiry covering of grass. That was all, but the sight brought tears to his eyes.

He grounded the machine and stepped out, treading warily lest he destroy even one of the struggling blades. Tenderly he ran his hands over the threadbare carpet which was all the life that Earth now knew. Before he left, he sprinkled the spot with as much water as he could spare. It was a futile gesture, but one which made him feel happier.

The search was now nearly completed. Trevindor had long ago given up all hope, but his indomitable spirit still drove him across the face of the world. He could not rest until he had proved what as yet he only feared. And thus it was that he came at last to the Master's tomb as it lay gleaming dully in the sunlight from which it had been banished so unthinkably long.

The Master's mind awoke before his body. As he lay powerless, unable even to lift his eyelids, memory came flooding back. The hundred years were safely behind him. His gamble, the most desperate that any man had ever made, had succeeded! An immense weariness came over him and for a while consciousness faded once more.

Presently the mists cleared again and he felt stronger, though still too weak to move. He lay in the darkness gathering his strength together. What sort of a world, he wondered, would he find when he stepped forth from the mountainside into the light of day? Would he be able to put his plans into—? What was that? A spasm of sheer terror shook the very foundations of his mind. Something was moving beside him, here in the tomb where nothing should be stirring but himself.

Then, calm and clear, a thought rang through his mind and quelled in an instant the fears that had threatened to overturn it.

"Do not be alarmed. I have come to help you. You are safe, and everything will be well."

The Master was too stunned to make any reply, but his subconscious must have formulated some sort of answer, for the thought came again.

"That is good. I am Trevindor, like yourself an exile in this world. Do not move, but tell me how you came here and what is your race, for I have seen none like it."

And now fear and caution were creeping back into the Master's mind. What manner of creature was this that could read his thoughts, and what was it doing in his secret sphere? Again that clear, cold thought echoed through his brain like the tolling of a bell.

"Once more I tell you that you have nothing to fear. Why are you alarmed because I can see into your mind? Surely there is nothing strange in that."

"Nothing strange!" cried the Master. "Who are you—what are you, for God's sake?"

"A man like yourself. But your race must be primitive indeed if the reading of thoughts is foreign to you."

A terrible suspicion began to dawn in the Master's brain. The answer came even before he consciously framed the question.

"You have slept infinitely longer than a hundred years. The world you knew has ceased to be for longer than you can imagine."

The Master heard no more. Once again the darkness swept over him and he sank down into unconsciousness.

In silence Trevindor stood by the couch on which the Master lay. He was filled with an elation which for the moment outweighed any disappointment he might feel. At least, he would no longer have to face the future alone. All the terror of the Earth's loneliness, that was weighing so heavily upon his soul, had vanished in a moment. *No longer alone . . .* no longer alone!

The Master was beginning to stir once more, and into Trevindor's mind crept broken fragments of thought. Pictures of the world the Master had known began to form. At first Trevindor could make nothing of them; then, suddenly, the jumbled shards fell into place. A wave of horror swept over him at the appalling vista of nation battling against nation, of cities flaming to destruction. What kind of world was this? Could man have sunk so low from the peaceful age Trevindor had known? There had been legends of such things, from times incredibly remote, but man had left them with his childhood. Surely they could never have returned!

The broken thoughts were more vivid now, and even more horrible. It was truly a nightmare age from which this only exile had come—no wonder that he had fled from it!

Suddenly the truth began to dawn in the mind of Trevindor as, sick at heart, he watched the ghastly patterns passing through the Master's brain. This was no exile seeking refuge from an age of horror. This was the very creator of that horror, who had embarked on the river of time with one purpose alone—to spread contagion down to later years.

Passions that Trevindor had never imagined began to parade themselves before his eyes: ambition, the lust for power, cruelty, intolerance, hatred. He tried to close his mind, but found he had lost the power to do so. With a cry of anguish, Trevindor rushed out into the silent desert.

It was night, and very still, for the Earth was now too weary even for winds to blow. The darkness hid everything, but Trevindor knew that it could not hide the thoughts of that other mind with which he now must share the world. Once he had been alone, and he had imagined nothing more dreadful. But now he knew that there were things more fearful even than solitude.

The stillness of the night, and the glory of the stars that had once been his friends, brought calm to the soul of Trevindor. Slowly he turned and retraced his footsteps, walking heavily, for he was about to perform a deed that no man of his kind had ever done before.

The Master was erect when Trevindor re-entered the sphere. Perhaps some hint of the other's purpose dawned upon his mind, for he was very pale. Steadfastly, Trevindor forced himself to look once more into the Master's brain. His mind recoiled at the chaos of conflicting emotions, now shot through with sickening flashes of fear. Out of the maelstrom one coherent thought came timidly quavering.

"What are you going to do? Why do you look at me like that?"

Trevindor made no reply, holding his mind aloof from contamination while he marshaled his resolution and all his strength.

The tumult in the Master's mind was rising to crescendo. For a moment his mounting terror brought something akin to pity to the gentle spirit of Trevindor, and his will faltered. But then there came again the picture of those ruined and burning cities.

With all the power of his intellect, backed by thousands of centuries of mental evolution, he struck at the man before him. Into the Master's mind, obliterating all else, flooded the single thought of—death.

For a moment the Master stood motionless, his eyes staring wildly. His breath froze as his lungs ceased their work; in his veins the pulsing blood, which had been stilled for so long, now congealed forever.

Without a sound, the Master toppled and lay still.

Very slowly Trevindor turned and walked out into the night. Like a shroud the silence and loneliness of the world descended upon him. The sand, thwarted so long, began to drift through the open portals of the Master's tomb.

Hide and Seek

We were walking back through the woods when Kingman saw the gray squirrel. Our bag was a small but varied one—three grouse, four rabbits (one, I am sorry to say, an infant in arms) and a couple of pigeons. And contrary to certain dark forecasts, both the dogs were still alive.

The squirrel saw us at the same moment. It knew that it was marked for immediate execution as a result of the damage it had done to the trees on the estate, and perhaps it had lost close relatives to Kingman's gun. In three leaps it had reached the base of the nearest tree, and vanished behind it in a flicker of gray. We saw its face once more, appearing for a moment round the edge of its shield a dozen feet from the ground; but though we waited, with guns leveled hopefully at various branches, we never saw it again.

Kingman was very thoughtful as we walked back across the lawn to the magnificent old house. He said nothing as we handed our victims to the cook—who received them without much enthusiasm—and only emerged from his reverie when we were sitting in the smoking room and he remembered his duties as a host.

"That tree-rat," he said suddenly (he always called them "tree-rats," on the grounds that people were too sentimental to shoot the dear little squirrels), "it reminded me of a very peculiar experience that happened shortly before I retired. Very shortly indeed, in fact."

"I thought it would," said Carson dryly. I gave him a glare: he'd been in the Navy and had heard Kingman's stories before, but they were still new to me.

"Of course," Kingman remarked, slightly nettled, "if you'd rather I didn't . . ."

"Do go on," I said hastily. "You've made me curious What connection there can possibly be between a gray squirrel and the Second Jovian War I can't imagine."

Kingman seemed mollified.

"I think I'd better change some names," he said thoughtfully, "but I won't alter the places. The story begins about a million kilometers sunward of Mars . . ."

K.15 was a military intelligence operative. It gave him considerable pain when unimaginative people called him a spy, but at the moment he had much more substantial grounds for complaint. For some days now a fast enemy cruiser had been coming up astern, and though it was flattering to have the undivided attention of such a fine ship and so many highly trained men, it was an honor that K.15 would willingly have forgone.

What made the situation doubly annoying was the fact that his friends would be meeting him off Mars in about twelve hours, aboard a ship quite capable of dealing with a mere cruiser—from which you will gather that K.15 was a person of some importance. Unfortunately, the most optimistic calculation showed that the pursuers would be within accurate gun range in six hours. In some six hours five minutes, therefore, K.15 was likely to occupy an extensive and still expanding volume of space.

There might just be time for him to land on Mars, but that would be one of the worst things he could do. It would certainly annoy the aggressively neutral Martians, and the political complications would be frightful. Moreover, if his friends *had* to come down to the planet to rescue him, it would cost them more than ten kilometers a second in fuel—most of their operational reserve.

He had only one advantage, and that a very dubious one. The commander of the cruiser might guess that he was heading for a rendezvous, but he would not know how close it was or how large was the ship that was coming to meet him. If he could keep alive for only twelve hours, he would be safe. The "if" was a somewhat considerable one.

K.15 looked moodily at his charts, wondering if it was worthwhile to burn the rest of his fuel in a final dash. But a dash to where? He would be completely helpless then, and the pursuing ship might still have enough in her tanks to catch him as he flashed outward into the empty darkness, beyond all hope of rescue—passing his friends as they came sunward at a relative speed so great that they could do nothing to save him.

With some people, the shorter the expectation of life, the more sluggish are the mental processes. They seem hypnotized by the approach of death, so resigned to their fate that they do nothing to avoid it. K.15, on the other hand, found that his mind worked better in such a desperate emergency. It began to work now as it had seldom done before.

Commander Smith—the name will do as well as any other—of the cruiser *Doradus* was not unduly surprised when K.15 began to decelerate. He had half expected the spy to land on Mars, on the principle that internment was better than annihilation, but when the plotting room brought the news that the little scout ship was heading for Phobos, he felt completely baffled. The inner moon was nothing but a jumble of rock some twenty kilometers across, and not even the economical Martians had ever found any use for it. K.15 must be pretty desperate if he thought it was going to be of any greater value to him.

The tiny scout had almost come to rest when the radar operator lost it against the mass of Phobos. During the braking maneuver, K.15 had squandered most of his lead and the *Doradus* was now only minutes away—though she was now beginning to decelerate lest she overrun him. The cruiser was scarcely three thousand kilometers from Phobos when she came to a complete halt: of K.15's ship, there was still no sign. It should be easily visible in the telescopes, but it was probably on the far side of the little moon.

It reappeared only a few minutes later, traveling under full thrust on a course directly away from the sun. It was accelerating at almost five gravities—and it had broken its radio silence. An automatic recorder was broadcasting over and over again this interesting message:

"I have landed on Phobos and am being attacked by a Z-class cruiser. Think I can hold out until you come, but hurry."

The message wasn't even in code, and it left Commander Smith a sorely puzzled man. The assumption that K.15 was still aboard the ship and that the whole thing was a ruse was just a little too naïve. But it might be a double-bluff: the message had obviously been left in plain language so that he would receive it and be duly confused. He could afford neither the time nor the fuel to chase the scout if K.15 really had landed. It was clear that reinforcements were on the way, and the sooner he left the vicinity the better. The phrase "Think I can hold out until you come" might be a piece of sheer impertinence, or it might mean that help was very near indeed.

Then K.15's ship stopped blasting. It had obviously exhausted its fuel, and was doing a little better than six kilometers a second away from the sun. K.15 *must* have landed, for his ship was now speeding helplessly out of the solar system. Commander Smith didn't like the message it was broadcasting, and guessed that it was running into the track of an approaching warship at some indefinite distance, but there was nothing to be done about that. The *Doradus* began to move toward Phobos, anxious to waste no time.

On the face of it, Commander Smith seemed the master of the situation. His ship was armed with a dozen heavy guided missiles and two turrets of electro-magnetic guns. Against him was one man in a space-suit, trapped on a moon only twenty kilometers across. It was not until Commander Smith had his first good look at Phobos, from a distance of less than a hundred kilometers, that he began to realize that, after all, K.15 might have a few cards up his sleeve.

To say that Phobos has a diameter of twenty kilometers, as the astronomy books invariably do, is highly misleading. The word "diameter" implies a degree of symmetry which Phobos most certainly lacks. Like those other lumps of cosmic slag, the asteroids, it is a shapeless mass of rock floating in space with, of course, no hint of an atmosphere and not much more gravity. It turns on its axis once every seven hours thirty-nine minutes, thus keeping the same face always to Mars—which is so close that appreciably less than half the planet is visible, the poles being below the curve of the horizon. Beyond this, there is very little more to be said about Phobos.

K.15 had no time to enjoy the beauty of the crescent world filling the sky above him. He had thrown all the equipment he could carry out of the airlock, set the controls, and jumped. As the little ship went flaming out toward the stars he watched it go with feelings he did not care to analyze. He had burned his boats with a vengeance, and he could only hope that the oncoming battleship would intercept the radio message as the empty vessel went racing by into nothingness. There was also a faint possibility that the enemy cruiser might go in pursuit, but that was rather too much to hope for.

He turned to examine his new home. The only light was the ocher radiance of Mars, since the sun was below the horizon, but that was quite sufficient for his purpose and he could see very well. He stood in the center of an irregular plain about two kilometers across, surrounded by low hills over which he could leap rather easily if he wished. There was a story he remembered reading long ago about a man who had accidentally jumped off Phobos: that wasn't quite possible—though it was on Deimos—as the escape velocity was still about ten meters a second. But unless he was carefully, he might easily find himself at such a height that it would take hours to fall back to the surface—and that would be fatal. For K.15's plan was a simple one: he must remain as close to the surface of Phobos as possible—*and diametrically opposite the cruiser.* The *Doradus* could then fire all her armament against the twenty kilometers of rock, and he wouldn't even feel the concussion. There were only two serious dangers, and one of these did not worry him greatly.

To the laymen, knowing nothing of the finer details of astronautics; the plan would have seemed quite suicidal. The *Doradus* was armed with the latest in ultra-scientific weapons: moreover, the twenty kilometers which separated her from her prey represented less than a second's flight at maximum speed. But Commander Smith knew better, and was already feeling rather unhappy. He realized, only too well, that of all the machines of transport man has ever invented, a cruiser of space is far and away the least maneuverable. It was a simple fact that K.15 could make half a dozen circuits of his little world while her commander was persuading the *Doradus* to make even one.

There is no need to go into technical details, but those who are still unconvinced might like to consider these elementary facts. A rocket-driven spaceship can, obviously, only accelerate along its major axis—that is, "forward." Any deviation from a straight course demands a physical turning of the ship, so that the motors can blast in another direction. Everyone knows that this is done by internal gyros or tangential steering jets, but very few people know just how long this simple maneuver takes. The average cruiser, fully fueled, has a mass of two or three thousand tons, which does not make for rapid footwork. But things are even worse than this, for it isn't the mass, but the moment of inertia that matters here—and since a cruiser is a long, thin object, its moment of inertia is slightly colossal. The sad fact remains (though it is seldom mentioned by astronautical engineers) that it takes a good ten minutes to rotate a spaceship through 180 degrees, with gyros of any reasonable size. Control jets aren't much quicker, and in any case their use is restricted because the rotation they produce is permanent and they are liable to leave the ship spinning like a slow-motion pinwheel, to the annoyance of all inside.

In the ordinary way, these disadvantages are not very grave. One has millions of kilometers and hundreds of hours in which to deal with such minor matters as a change in the ship's orientation. It is definitely against the rules to move in ten-kilometer radius circles, and the commander of the *Doradus* felt distinctly aggrieved. K.15 wasn't playing fair.

At the same moment that resourceful individual was taking stock of the situation, which might very well have been worse. He had reached the hills in three jumps and felt less naked than he had out in the open plain. The food and equipment he had taken from the ship he had hidden where he hoped he could find it again, but as his suit could keep him alive for over a day that was the least of his worries. The small packet that was the cause of all the trouble was still with him, in one of those numerous hiding places a well-designed space-suit affords.

There was an exhilarating loneliness about his mountain eyrie, even though he was not quite as lonely as he would have wished. Forever fixed in his sky, Mars was waning almost visibly as Phobos swept above the night side of the planet. He could just make out the lights of some of the Martian cities, gleaming pin-points marking the junctions of the invisible canals. All else was stars and silence and a line of jagged peaks so close it seemed he could almost touch them. Of the *Doradus* there was still no sign. She was presumably carrying out a careful telescopic examination of the sunlighted side of Phobos.

Mars was a very useful clock: when it was half full the sun would rise and, very probably, so would the *Doradus*. But she might approach from some quite unexpected quarter: she might even and this was the one real danger—she might even have landed a search party.

This was the first possibility that had occurred to Commander Smith when he saw just what he was up against. Then he realized that the surface area of Phobos was over a thousand square kilometers and that he could not spare more than ten men from his crew to make a search of that jumbled wilderness. Also, K.15 would certainly be armed.

Considering the weapons which the *Doradus* carried, this last objection might seem singularly pointless. It was very far from being so. In the ordinary course of business, side-arms and other portable weapons are as much use to a space-cruiser as are cutlasses and crossbows. The *Doradus* happened, quite by chance—and against regulations at that—to carry one automatic pistol and a hundred rounds of ammunition. Any search party would therefore consist of a group of unarmed men looking for a well concealed and very desperate individual who could pick them off at his leisure. K.15 was breaking the rules again.

The terminator of Mars was now a perfectly straight line, and at almost the same moment the sun came up, not so much like thunder as like a salvo of atomic bombs. K.15 adjusted the filters of his visor and decided to move. It was safe to stay out of the sunlight, not only because here he was less likely to be detected in the shadow but also because his eyes would be much more sensitive there. He had only a pair of binoculars to help him, whereas the *Doradus* would carry an electronic telescope of twenty centimeters aperture at least.

It would be best, K.15 decided, to locate the cruiser if he could. It might be a rash thing to do, but he would feel much happier when he knew exactly where she was and could watch her movements. He could then keep just below the horizon, and the glare of the rockets would give him ample warning of any impending move. Cautiously launching himself along an almost horizontal trajectory, he began the circumnavigation of his world.

The narrowing crescent of Mars sank below the horizon until only one vast horn reared itself enigmatically against the stars. K.15 began to feel worried: there was still no sign of the *Doradus*. But this was hardly surprising, for she was painted black as night and might be a good hundred kilometers away in space. He stopped, wondering if he had done the right thing after all. Then he noticed that something quite large was eclipsing the stars almost vertically overhead, and was moving swiftly even as he watched. His heart stopped for a moment: then he was himself again, analyzing the situation and trying to discover how he had made so disastrous a mistake.

It was some time before he realized that the black shadow slipping across the sky was not the cruiser at all, but something almost equally deadly. It was far smaller, and far nearer, than he had at first thought. The *Doradus* had sent her television-homing guided missiles to look for him.

This was the second danger he had feared, and there was nothing he could do about it except to remain as inconspicuous as possible. The *Doradus* now had many eyes searching for him, but these auxiliaries had very severe limitations. They had been built to look for sunlit spaceships against a background of stars, not to search for a man hiding in a dark jungle of rock. The definition of their television systems was low, and they could only see in the forward direction.

There were rather more men on the chessboard now, and the game was a little deadlier, but his was still the advantage.

The torpedo vanished into the night sky. As it was traveling on a nearly straight course in this low gravitational field, it would soon be leaving Phobos behind, and K.15 waited for what he knew must happen. A few minutes later, he saw a brief stabbing of rocket exhausts and guessed that the projectile was swinging slowly back on its course. At almost the same moment he saw another flare far away in the opposite quarter of the sky, and wondered just how many of these infernal machines were in action. From what he knew of Z-class cruisers—which was a good deal more than he should—there were four missile-control channels, and they were probably all in use.

He was suddenly struck by an idea so brilliant that he was quite sure it couldn't possibly work. The radio on his suit was a tunable one, covering an unusually wide band, and somewhere not far away the Doradus was pumping out power on everything from a thousand megacycles upward. He switched on the receiver and began to explore.

It came in quickly—the raucous whine of a pulse transmitter not far away. He was probably only picking up a subharmonic, but that was quite good enough. It D/F'ed sharply, and for the first time K.15 allowed himself to make long-range plans about the future. The Doradus had betrayed herself: as long as she operated her missiles, he would know exactly where she was.

He moved cautiously forward toward the transmitter. To his surprise the signal faded, then increased sharply again. This puzzled him until he realized that he must be moving through a diffraction zone. Its width might have told him something useful if he had been a good enough physicist, but he couldn't imagine what.

The *Doradus* was hanging about five kilometers above the surface, in full sunlight. Her "non-reflecting" paint was overdue for renewal, and K.15 could see her clearly. As he was still in darkness, and the shadow line was moving away from him, he decided that he was as safe here as anywhere. He settled down comfortably so that he could just see the cruiser and waited, feeling fairly certain that none of the guided projectiles would come so near the ship. By now, he calculated, the commander of the *Doradus* must be getting pretty mad. He was perfectly correct.

After an hour, the cruiser began to heave herself round with all the grace of a bogged hippopotamus. K.15 guessed what was happening. Commander Smith was going to have a look at the antipodes, and was preparing for the perilous fifty-kilometer journey. He watched very carefully to see the orientation the ship was adopting, and when she came to rest again was relieved to see that she was almost broadside on to him. Then, with a series of jerks that could not have been very enjoyable aboard, the cruiser began to move down to the horizon. K.15 followed her at a comfortable walking pace—if one could use the phrase—reflecting that this was a feat very few people had ever performed. He was particularly careful not to overtake her on one of his kilometer-long glides, and kept a close watch for any missiles that might be coming up astern.

It took the *Doradus* nearly an hour to cover the fifty kilometers. This, as K.15 amused himself by calculating, represented considerably less than a thousandth of her normal speed. Once she found herself going off into space at a tangent, and rather than waste time turning end over end again fired off a salvo of shells to reduce speed. But she made it at last, and K.15 settled down for another vigil, wedged between two rocks where he could just see the cruiser and he was quite sure she couldn't see him. It occurred to him that by this time

Commander Smith might have grave doubts as to whether he really was on Phobos at all, and he felt like firing off a signal flare to reassure him. However, he resisted the temptation.

There would be little point in describing the events of the next ten hours, since they differed in no important detail from those that had gone before. The *Doradus* made three other moves, and K.15 stalked her with the care of a big-game hunter following the spoor of some elephantine beast. Once, when she would have led him out into full sunlight, he let her fall below the horizon until he could only just pick up her signals. But most of the time he kept her just visible, usually low down behind some convenient hill.

Once a torpedo exploded some kilometers away, and K.15 guessed that some exasperated operator had seen a shadow he didn't like—or else that a technician had forgotten to switch off a proximity fuse. Otherwise nothing happened to enliven the proceedings: in fact, the whole affair was becoming rather boring. He almost welcomed the sight of an occasional guided missile drifting inquisitively overhead, for he did not believe that they could see him if he remained motionless and in reasonable cover. If he could have stayed on the part of Phobos exactly opposite the cruiser he would have been safe even from these, he realized, since the ship would have no control there in the moon's radio-shadow. But he could think of no reliable way in which he could be sure of staying in the safety zone if the cruiser moved again.

The end came very abruptly. There was a sudden blast of steering jets, and the cruiser's main drive burst forth in all its power and splendor. In seconds the *Doradus* was shrinking sunward, free at last, thankful to leave, even in defeat, this miserable lump of rock that had so annoyingly balked her of her legitimate prey. K.15 knew what had happened, and a great sense of peace and relaxation swept over him. In the radar room of the cruiser, someone had seen an echo of disconcerting amplitude approaching with altogether excessive speed. K.15 now had only to switch on his suit beacon and to wait. He could even afford the luxury of a cigarette.

"Quite an interesting story," I said, "and I see now how it ties up with that squirrel. But it does raise one or two queries in my mind."

"Indeed?" said Rupert Kingman politely.

I always like to get to the bottom of things, and I knew that my host had played a part in the Jovian War about which he very seldom spoke. I decided to risk a long shot in the dark.

"May I ask how you happen to know so much about this unorthodox military engagement? It isn't possible, is it, that *you* were K.15?"

There was an odd sort of strangling noise from Carson. Then Kingman said, quite calmly: "No, I wasn't."

He got to his feet and went off toward the gun room.

"If you'll excuse me a moment, I'm going to have another shot at that tree-rat. Maybe I'll get him this time." Then he was gone.

Carson looked at me as if to say: "This is another house you'll never be invited to again." When our host was out of earshot he remarked in a coldly cynical voice:

"You've done it. What did you have to say that for?"

"Well, it seemed a safe guess. How else could he have known all that?"

"As a matter of fact, I believe he met K.15 after the War: they must have had an interesting conversation together. But I thought you knew that Rupert was retired from the service with only the rank of lieutenant commander. The Court of Inquiry could never see his point of view. After all, it just wasn't reasonable that the commander of the fastest ship in the Fleet couldn't catch a man in a space-suit."

Expedition to Earth

It was in the last days of the Empire. The tiny ship was far from home, and almost a hundred light-years from the great parent vessel searching through the loosely packed stars at the rim of the Milky Way. But even here it could not escape from the shadow that lay across civilization: beneath that shadow, pausing ever and again in their work to wonder how their distant homes were faring, the scientists of the Galactic Survey still labored at their never-ending task.

The ship held only three occupants, but between them they carried knowledge of many sciences, and the experience of half a lifetime in space. After the long interstellar night, the star ahead was warming their spirits as they dropped down toward its fires. A little more golden, a trifle more brilliant than the sun that now seemed a legend of their childhood. They knew from past experience that the chance of locating planets here was more than ninety per cent, and for the moment they forgot all else in the excitement of discovery.

They found the first planet within minutes of coming to rest. It was a giant, of a familiar type, too cold for protoplasmic life and probably possessing no stable surface. So they turned their search sunward, and presently were rewarded.

It was a world that made their hearts ache for home, a world where everything was hauntingly familiar, yet never quite the same. Two great land masses floated in blue-green seas, capped by ice at either pole. There were some desert regions, but the larger part of the planet was obviously fertile. Even from this distance, the signs of vegetation were unmistakably clear.

They gazed hungrily at the expanding landscape as they fell down into the atmosphere, heading toward noon in the subtropics. The ship plummeted through cloudless skies toward a great river, checked its fall with a surge of soundless power, and came to rest among the long grasses by the water's edge.

No one moved: there was nothing to be done until the automatic instruments had finished their work. Then a bell tinkled softly and the lights on the control board flashed in a pattern of meaningful chaos. Captain Altman rose to his feet with a sigh of relief.

"We're in luck," he said. "We can go outside without protection, if the pathogenic tests are satisfactory. What did you make of the place as we came in, Bertrond?"

"Geologically stable—no active volcanoes, at least. I didn't see any trace of cities, but that proves nothing. If there's a civilization here, it may have passed that stage."

"Or not reached it yet?"

Bertrond shrugged. "Either's just as likely. It may take us some time to find out on a planet this size."

"More time than we've got," said Clindar, glancing at the communications panel that linked them to the mother ship and thence to the Galaxy's threatened heart. For a moment there was a gloomy silence. Then Clindar walked to the control board and pressed a pattern of keys with automatic skill.

With a slight jar, a section of the hull slid aside and the fourth member of the crew stepped out onto the new planet, flexing metal limbs and adjusting servo motors to the unaccustomed gravity. Inside the ship, a television screen glimmered into life, revealing a long vista of waving grasses, some trees in the middle distance, and a glimpse of the great river. Clindar punched a button, and the picture flowed steadily across the screen as the robot turned its head.

"Which way shall we go?" Clindar asked.

"Let's have a look at those trees," Altman replied. "If there's any animal life we'll find it there."

"Look!" cried Bertrond. "A bird!"

Clindar's fingers flew over the keyboard: the picture centered on the tiny speck that had suddenly appeared on the left of the screen, and expanded rapidly as the robot's telephoto lens came into action.

"You're right," he said. "Feathers—beak—well up the evolutionary ladder. This place looks promising. I'll start the camera."

The swaying motion of the picture as the robot walked forward did not distract them: they had grown accustomed to it long ago. But they had never become reconciled to this exploration by proxy when all their impulses cried out to them to leave the ship, to run through the grass and to feel the wind blowing against their faces. Yet it was too great a risk to take, even on a world that seemed as fair as this. There was always a skull hidden behind Nature's most smiling face. Wild beasts, poisonous reptiles, quagmires—death could come to the unwary explorer in a thousand disguises. And worst of all were the invisible enemies, the bacteria and viruses against which the only defense might often be a thousand light-years away.

A robot could laugh at all these dangers and even if, as sometimes happened, it encountered a beast powerful enough to destroy it—well, machines could always be replaced.

They met nothing on the walk across the grasslands. If any small animals were disturbed by the robot's passage, they kept outside its field of vision. Clindar slowed the machine as it approached the trees, and the watchers in the spaceship flinched involuntarily at the branches that appeared to slash across their eyes. The picture dimmed for a moment before the controls readjusted themselves to the weaker illumination; then it came back to normal.

The forest was full of life. It lurked in the undergrowth, clambered among the branches, flew through the air. It fled chattering and gibbering through the trees as the robot advanced. And all the while the automatic cameras were recording the pictures that formed on the screen, gathering material for the biologists to analyze when the ship returned to base.

Clindar breathed a sigh of relief when the trees suddenly thinned. It was exhausting work, keeping the robot from smashing into obstacles as it moved through the forest, but on open ground it could take care of itself. Then the picture trembled as if beneath a hammer-blow, there was a grinding metallic thud, and the whole scene swept vertiginously upward as the robot toppled and fell.

"What's that?" cried Altman. "Did you trip?"

"No," said Clindar grimly, his fingers flying over the keyboard. "Something attacked from the rear. I hope . . . ah . . . I've still got control."

He brought the robot to a sitting position and swiveled its head. It did not take long to find the cause of the trouble. Standing a few feet away, and lashing its tail angrily, was a large quadruped with a most ferocious set of teeth. At the moment it was, fairly obviously, trying to decide whether to attack again.

Slowly, the robot rose to its feet, and as it did so the great beast crouched to spring. A smile flitted across Clindar's face: he knew how to deal with this situation. His thumb felt for the seldom-used key labeled "Siren."

The forest echoed with a hideous undulating scream from the robot's concealed speaker, and the machine advanced to meet its adversary, arms flailing in front of it. The startled beast almost fell over backward in its effort to turn, and in seconds was gone from sight.

"Now I suppose we'll have to wait a couple of hours until everything comes out of hiding again," said Bertrond ruefully.

"I don't know much about animal psychology," interjected Altman, "but is it unusual for them to attack something completely unfamiliar?"

"Some will attack anything that moves, but that's unusual. Normally they attack only for food, or if they've already been threatened. What are you driving at? Do you suggest that there are other robots on this planet?"

"Certainly not. But our carnivorous friend may have mistaken our machine for a more edible biped. Don't you think that this opening in the jungle is rather unnatural? It could easily be a path."

"In that case," said Clindar promptly, "we'll follow it and find out. I'm tired of dodging trees, but I hope nothing jumps on us again: it's bad for my nerves."

"You were right, Altman," said Bertrond a little later. "It's certainly a path. But that doesn't mean intelligence. After all, animals—"

He stopped in mid-sentence, and at the same instant Clindar brought the advancing robot to a halt. The path had suddenly opened out into a wide clearing, almost completely occupied by a village of flimsy huts. It was ringed by a wooden palisade, obviously defense against an enemy who at the moment presented no threat. For the gates were wide open, and beyond them the inhabitants were going peacefully about their ways.

For many minutes the three explorers stared in silence at the screen. Then Clindar shivered a little and remarked: "It's uncanny. It might be our own planet, a hundred thousand years ago. I feel as if I've gone back in time."

"There's nothing weird about it," said the practical Altman. "After all, we've discovered nearly a hundred planets with our type of life on them."

"Yes," retorted Clindar. "A hundred in the whole Galaxy! I still think it's strange it had to happen to us."

"Well, it had to happen to *somebody*," said Bertrond philosophically. "Meanwhile, we must work out our contact procedure. If we send the robot into the village it will start a panic."

"That," said Altman, "is a masterly understatement. What we'll have to do is catch a native by himself and prove that we're friendly. Hide the robot, Clindar. Somewhere in the woods where it can watch the village without being spotted. We've a week's practical anthropology ahead of us!"

It was three days before the biological tests showed that it would be safe to leave the ship. Even then Bertrond insisted on going alone—alone, that is, if one ignored the substantial company of the robot. With such an ally he was not afraid of this planet's larger beasts, and his body's natural defenses could take care of the microorganisms. So, at least, the analyzers had assured him; and considering the complexity of the problem, they made remarkably few mistakes . . .

He stayed outside for an hour, enjoying himself cautiously, while his companions watched with envy. It would be another three days before they could be quite certain that it was safe to follow Bertrond's example. Meanwhile, they kept busy enough watching the village through the lenses of the robot, and recording everything they could with the cameras. They had moved the spaceship at night so that it was hidden in the depths of the forest, for they did not wish to be discovered until they were ready.

And all the while the news from home grew worse. Though their remoteness here at the edge of the Universe deadened its impact, it lay heavily on their minds and sometimes overwhelmed them with a sense of futility. At any moment, they knew, the signal for recall might come as the Empire summoned up its last resources in its extremity. But until then they would continue their work as though pure knowledge were the only thing that mattered.

Seven days after landing, they were ready to make the experiment. They knew now what paths the villagers used when going hunting, and Bertrond chose one of the less frequented ways. Then he placed a chair firmly in the middle of the path and settled down to read a book.

It was not, of course, quite as simple as that: Bertrond had taken all imaginable precautions. Hidden in the undergrowth fifty yards away, the robot was watching through its telescopic lenses, and in its hand it held a small but deadly weapon. Controlling it from the spaceship, his fingers poised over the keyboard, Clindar waited to do what might be necessary.

That was the negative side of the plan: the positive side was more obvious. Lying at Bertrond's feet was the carcass of a small, horned animal which he hoped would be an acceptable gift to any hunter passing this way.

Two hours later the radio in his suit harness whispered a warning. Quite calmly, though the blood was pounding in his veins, Bertrond laid aside his book and looked down the trail. The savage was walking forward confidently enough, swinging a spear in his right hand. He paused for a moment when he saw Bertrond, then advanced more cautiously. He could tell that there was nothing to fear, for the stranger was slightly built and obviously unarmed.

When only twenty feet separated them, Bertrond gave a reassuring smile and rose slowly to his feet. He bent down, picked up the carcass, and carried it forward as an offering. The gesture would have been understood by any creature on any world, and it was understood here. The savage reached forward, took the animal, and threw it effortlessly over his shoulder. For an instant he stared into Bertrond's eyes with a fathomless expression; then he turned and walked back toward the village. Three times he glanced round to see if Bertrond was following, and each time Bertrond smiled and waved reassurance. The whole episode lasted little more than a minute. As the first contact between two races it was completely without drama, though not without dignity.

Bertrond did not move until the other had vanished from sight. Then he relaxed and spoke into his suit microphone.

"That was a pretty good beginning," he said jubilantly. "He wasn't in the least frightened, or even suspicious. I think he'll be back."

"It still seems too good to be true," said Altman's voice in his ear. "I should have thought he'd have been either scared or hostile. "Would *you* have accepted a lavish gift from a peculiar stranger with such little fuss?"

Bertrond was slowly walking back to the ship. The robot had now come out of cover and was keeping guard a few paces behind him.

"*I* wouldn't," he replied, "but I belong to a civilized community. Complete savages may react to strangers in many different ways, according to their past experience. Suppose this tribe has never had any enemies. That's quite possible on a large but sparsely populated planet. Then we may expect curiosity, but no fear at all."

"If these people have no enemies," put in Clindar, no longer fully occupied in controlling the robot, "why have they got a stockade round the village?"

"I meant no *human* enemies," replied Bertrond. "If that's true, it simplifies our task immensely."

"Do you think he'll come back?"

"Of course. If he's as human as I think, curiosity and greed will make him return. In a couple of days we'll be bosom friends."

Looked at dispassionately, it became a fantastic routine. Every morning the robot would go hunting under Clindar's direction, until it was now the deadliest killer in the jungle. Then Bertrond would wait until Yaan—which was the nearest they could get to his name—came striding confidently along the path. He came at the same time every day, and he always came alone. They wondered about this: did he wish to keep his great discovery to himself and thus get all the credit for his hunting prowess? If so, it showed unexpected foresight and cunning.

At first Yaan had departed at once with his prize, as if afraid that the donor of such a generous gift might change his mind. Soon, however, as Bertrond had hoped, he could be induced to stay for a while by simple conjuring tricks and a display of brightly colored fabrics and crystals, in which he took a childlike delight. At last Bertrond was able to engage him in lengthy conversations, all of which were recorded as well as being filmed through the eyes of the hidden robot.

One day the philologists might be able to analyze this material; the best that Bertrond could do was to discover the meanings of a few simple verbs and nouns. This was made more difficult by the fact that Yaan not only used different words for the same thing, but sometimes the same word for different things.

Between these daily interviews, the ship traveled far, surveying the planet from the air and sometimes landing for more detailed examinations. Although several other human settlements were observed, Bertrond made no attempt to get in touch with them, for it was easy to see that they were all at much the same cultural level as Yaan's people.

It was, Bertrond often thought, a particularly bad joke on the part of Fate that one of the Galaxy's very few truly human races should have been discovered at this moment of time. Not long ago this would have been an event of supreme importance; now civilization was too hard-pressed to concern itself with these savage cousins waiting at the dawn of history.

Not until Bertrond was sure he had become part of Yaan's everyday life did he introduce him to the robot. He was showing Yaan the patterns in a kaleidoscope when Clindar brought the machine striding through the grass with its latest victim dangling across one metal arm. For the first time Yaan showed something akin to fear; but he relaxed at Bertrond's soothing words, though he continued to watch the advancing monster. It halted some distance away, and Bertrond walked forward to meet it. As he did so, the robot raised its arms and handed him the dead beast. He took it solemnly and carried it back to Yaan, staggering a little under the unaccustomed load.

Bertrond would have given a great deal to know just what Yaan was thinking as he accepted the gift. Was he trying to decide whether the robot was master or slave? Perhaps such conceptions as this were beyond his grasp: to him the robot might be merely another man, a hunter who was a friend of Bertrond.

Clindar's voice, slightly larger than life, came from the robot's speaker.

"It's astonishing how calmly he accepts us. Won't anything scare him?"

"You will keep judging him by your own standards," replied Bertrond. "Remember, his psychology is completely different, and much simpler Now that he has confidence in me, anything that I accept won't worry him."

"I wonder if that will be true of all his race?" queried Altman. "It's hardly safe to judge by a single specimen. I want to see what happens when we send the robot into the village."

"Hello!" exclaimed Bertrond. "*That* surprised him. He's never met a person who could speak with two voices before."

"Do you think he'll guess the truth when he meets us?" said Clindar.

"No. The robot will be pure magic to him—but it won't be any more wonderful than fire and lightning and all the other forces he must already take for granted."

"Well, what's the next move?" asked Altman, a little impatiently. "Are you going to bring him to the ship, or will you go into the village first?"

Bertrond hesitated. "I'm anxious not to do too much too quickly. You know the accidents that have happened with strange races when that's been tried. I'll let him think this over, and when we get back tomorrow I'll try to persuade him to take the robot back to the village."

In the hidden ship, Clindar reactivated the robot and started it moving again. Like Altman, he was growing a little impatient of this excessive caution, but on all matters relating to alien life-forms Bertrond was the expert, and they had to obey his orders.

There were times now when he almost wished he were a robot himself, devoid of feelings or emotions, able to watch the fall of a leaf or the death agonies of a world with equal detachment . . .

The sun was low when Yaan heard the great voice crying from the jungle. He recognized it at once, despite its inhuman volume: it was the voice of his friend, and it was calling him.

In the echoing silence, the life of the village came to a stop. Even the children ceased their play: the only sound was the thin cry of a baby frightened by the sudden silence.

All eyes were upon Yaan as he walked swiftly to his hut and grasped the spear that lay beside the entrance. The stockade would soon be closed against the prowlers of the night, but he did not hesitate as he stepped out into the lengthening shadows. He was passing through the gates when once again that mighty voice summoned him, and now it held a note of urgency that came clearly across all the barriers of language and culture.

The shining giant who spoke with many voices met him a little way from the village and beckoned him to follow. There was no sign of Bertrond. They walked for almost a mile before they saw him in the distance, standing not far from the river's edge and staring out across the dark, slowly moving waters.

He turned as Yaan approached, yet for a moment seemed unaware of his presence. Then he gave a gesture of dismissal to the shining one, who withdrew into the distance.

Yaan waited. He was patient and, though he could never have expressed it in words, contented. When he was with Bertrond he felt the first intimations of that selfless, utterly irrational devotion his race would not fully achieve for many ages.

It was a strange tableau. Here at the river's brink two men were standing. One was dressed in a closely-fitting uniform equipped with tiny, intricate mechanisms. The other was wearing the skin of an animal and was carrying a flint-tipped spear. Ten thousand generations lay between them, ten thousand generations and an immeasurable gulf of space. Yet they were both human. As she must do often in eternity, Nature had repeated one of her basic patterns.

Presently Bertrond began to speak, walking to and fro in short, quick steps as he did, and in his voice there was a trace of madness.

"It's all over, Yaan. I'd hoped that with our knowledge we could have brought you out of barbarism in a dozen generations, but now you will have to fight your way up from the jungle alone, and it may take you a million years to do so. I'm sorry—there's so much we could have done. Even now I wanted to stay here, but Altman and Clindar talk of duty, and I suppose that they are right. There is little enough that we can do, but our world is calling and we must not forsake it.

"I wish you could understand me, Yaan. I wish you knew what I was saying. I'm leaving you these tools: some of them you will discover how to use, though as likely as not in a generation they'll be lost or forgotten. See how this blade cuts: it will be ages before your world can make its like. And guard this well: when you press the button—look! It you use it sparingly, it will give you light for years, though sooner or later it will die. As for these other things—find what use for them you can.

"Here come the first stars, up there in the east. Do you ever look at the stars, Yaan? I wonder how long it will be before you have discovered what they are, and I wonder what will have happened to us by then. Those stars are our homes, Yaan, and we cannot save them. Many have died already, in explosions so vast that I can imagine them no more than you. In a hundred thousand of your years, the light of those funeral pyres will reach your world and set its peoples wondering. By then, perhaps, your race will be reaching for the stars. I wish I could warn you against the mistakes we made, and which now will cost us all that we have won.

"It is well for your people, Yaan, that your world is here at the frontier of the Universe. You may escape the doom that waits for us. One day, perhaps, your ships will go searching among the stars as we have done, and they may come upon the ruins of our world and wonder who we were. But they will never know that we met here by this river when your race was young.

"Here come my friends; they would give me no more time.

Good-by, Yaan—use well the things I have left you. They are your world's greatest treasures."

Something huge, something that glittered in the starlight, was sliding down from the sky. It did not reach the ground, but came to rest a little way above the surface, and in utter silence a rectangle of light opened in its side. The shining giant appeared out of the night and stepped through the golden door. Bertrond followed, pausing for a moment at the threshold to wave back at Yaan. Then the darkness closed behind him.

No more swiftly than smoke drifts upward from a fire, the ship lifted away. When it was so small that Yaan felt he could hold it in his hands, it seemed to blur into a long line of light slanting upward into the stars. From the empty sky a peal of thunder echoed over the sleeping land; and Yaan knew at last that the gods were gone and would never come again.

For a long time he stood by the gently moving waters, and into his soul there came a sense of loss he was never to forget and never to understand. Then, carefully and reverently, he collected together the gifts that Bertrond had left.

Under the stars, the lonely figure walked homeward across a nameless land. Behind him the river flowed softly to the sea, winding through the fertile plains on which, more than a thousand centuries ahead, Yaan's descendants would build the great city they were to call Babylon.

Loophole

From: President.
To: Secretary, Council of Scientists.

I have been informed that the inhabitants of Earth have succeeded in releasing atomic energy and have been making experiments with rocket propulsion. This is most serious. Let me have a full report immediately. And make it *brief* this time.

K.K. IV.

From: Secretary, Council of Scientists.
To: President.

The facts are as follows: Some months ago our instruments detected intense neutron emission from Earth, but an analysis of radio programs gave no explanation at the time. Three days ago a second emission occurred, and soon afterward all radio transmissions from Earth announced that atomic bombs were in use in the current war. The translators have not completed their interpretation, but it appears that the bombs are of considerable power. Two have so far been used. Some details of their construction have been released, but the elements concerned have not yet been identified. A fuller report will be forwarded as soon as possible. For the moment all that is certain is that the inhabitants of Earth *have* liberated atomic power, so far only explosively.

Very little is known concerning rocket research on Earth. Our astronomers have been observing the planet carefully ever since radio emissions were detected a generation ago. It is certain that long-range rockets of some kind are in existence on Earth, for there have been numerous references to them in recent military broadcasts. However, no serious attempt has been made to reach interplanetary space. When the war ends, it is expected that the inhabitants of the planet may carry out research in this direction. We will pay very careful attention to their broadcasts and the astronomical watch will be rigorously enforced.

From what we have inferred of the planet's technology, it should require about twenty years before Earth develops atomic rockets capable of crossing space. In view of this, it would seem that the time has come to set up a base on the Moon, so that a close scrutiny can be kept on such experiments when they commence.

Trescon.

The war on Earth has now ended, apparently owing to the intervention of the atomic bomb. This will not affect the above arguments but it may mean that the inhabitants of Earth can devote themselves to pure research again more quickly than expected. Some broadcasts have already pointed out the application of atomic power to rocket propulsion.

T.

From: President.
To: Chief of Bureau of Extra-Planetary Security. (C.B.E.P.S.)
    You have seen Trescon's minute.

Equip an expedition to the satellite of Earth immediately. It is to keep a close watch on the planet and to report at once if rocket experiments are in progress.

The greatest care must be taken to keep our presence on the Moon a secret. You are personally responsible for this. Report to me at yearly intervals, or more often if necessary.

K.K. IV.

From: President.
To: C.B.E.P.S.
   Where is the report of Earth?!!

K.K. IV.

From: C.B.E.P.S.
To: President.
   The delay is regretted. It was caused by the breakdown of the ship carrying the report.

There have been no signs of rocket experimenting during the past year, and no reference to it in broadcasts from the planet.

Ranthe.

From: C.B.E.P.S.
To: President.
   You will have seen my yearly reports to your respected father on this subject. There have been no developments of interest for the past fifteen years, but the following message has just been received from our base on the Moon:

> Rocket projectile, apparently atomically propelled, left Earth's atmosphere today from Northern land-mass, traveling into space for one-quarter diameter of planet before returning under control.

Ranthe.

From: President.
To: Chief of State.
   Your comments, please.

K.K. V.

From: Chief of State.
To: President.
   This means the end of our traditional policy.

The only hope of security lies in preventing the Terrestrials from making further advances in this direction. From what we know of them, this will require some overwhelming threat.

Since its high gravity makes it impossible for us to land on the planet, our sphere of action is restricted. The problem was discussed nearly a century ago by Anvar, and I agree with his conclusions. We must act *immediately* along those lines.

F.K.S.

From: President.
To: Secretary of State.
   Inform the Council that an emergency meeting is convened for noon tomorrow.

K.K. V.

From: President.
To: C.B.E.P.S.
   Twenty battleships should be sufficient to put Anvar's plan into operation. Fortunately there is no need to arm them—yet. Report progress of construction to me weekly.

K.K. V.

From: C.B.E.P.S.
To: President.
   Nineteen ships are now completed. The twentieth is still

delayed owing to hull failure and will not be ready for at least a month.

Ranthe.

From: President.
To: C.B.E.P.S.

Nineteen will be sufficient. I will check the operational plan with you tomorrow. Is the draft of our broadcast ready yet?

K.K. V.

From: C.B.E.P.S.
To: President.

Draft herewith:

People of Earth!

We, the inhabitants of the planet you call Mars, have for many years observed your experiments toward achieving inter-planetary travel. *These experiments must cease.* Our study of your race has convinced us that you are not fitted to leave your planet in the present state of your civilization. The ships you now see floating above your cities are capable of destroying them utterly, and will do so unless you discontinue your attempts to cross space.

We have set up an observatory on your Moon and can immediately detect any violation of these orders. If you obey them, we will not interfere with you again. Otherwise, one of your cities will be destroyed every time we observe a rocket leaving the Earth's atmosphere.

By order of the President and Council of Mars.

Ranthe.

From: President.
To: C.B.E.P.S.

I approve. The translation can go ahead.

I will not be sailing with the fleet, after all. Report to me in detail immediately on your return.

K.K. V.

From: C.B.E.P.S.
To: President.

I have the honor to report the successful completion of our mission. The voyage to Earth was uneventful: radio messages from the planet indicated that we were detected at a considerable distance and great excitement had been aroused before our arrival. The fleet was dispersed according to plan and I broadcast the ultimatum. We left immediately and no hostile weapons were brought to bear against us.

I will report in detail within two days.

Ranthe.

From: Secretary, Council of Scientists.
To: President.

The psychologists have completed their report, which is attached herewith.

As might be expected, our demands at first infuriated this stubborn and high-spirited race. The shock to their pride must have been considerable, for they believed themselves to be the only intelligent beings in the Universe.

However, within a few weeks there was a rather unexpected change in the tone of their statements. They had begun to realize that we were intercepting all their radio transmissions, and some messages have been broadcast directly to us. They state that they have agreed to ban all rocket experiments, in accordance with our wishes. This is as unexpected as it is welcome. Even if they are trying to deceive us, we are perfectly safe now that we have established the second station just outside the atmosphere. They cannot possibly develop spaceships without our seeing them or detecting their tube radiation.

The watch on Earth will be continued rigorously, as instructed.

Trescon.

From: C.B.E.P.S.
To: President.

Yes, it is quite true that there have been no further rocket experiments in the last ten years. We certainly did not expect Earth to capitulate so easily!

I agree that the existence of this race now constitutes a permanent threat to our civilization and we are making experiments along the lines you suggest. The problem is a difficult one, owing to the great size of the planet. Explosives would be out of the question, and a radioactive poison of some kind appears to offer the greatest hope of success.

Fortunately, we now have an indefinite time in which to complete this research, and I will report regularly.

Ranthe.

From: Lieutenant Commander Henry Forbes, Intelligence
        Branch, Special Space Corps.
To: Professor S. Maxton, Philological Department, University
  of Oxford.
Route: Transender II (vio Schenectady).

The above papers, with others, were found in the ruins of what is believed to be the capital Martian city. (Mars Grid KL302895.) The frequent use of the ideograph for "Earth" suggests that they may be of special interest and it is hoped that they can be translated. Other papers will be following shortly.

H. Forbes, Lt. Cmdr.

Dear Max:

Sorry I've had no time to contact you before. I'll be seeing you as soon as I get back to Earth.

Gosh! Mars is in a mess! Our co-ordinates were dead

accurate and the bombs materialized right over their cities, just as the Mount Wilson boys predicted.

We're sending a lot of stuff back through the two small machines, but until the big transmitter is materialized we're rather restricted and, of course, none of us can return. So hurry up with it!

I'm glad we can get to work on rockets again. I may be old-fashioned, but being squirted through space at the speed of light doesn't appeal to me!

Yours in haste,

Henry.

Inheritance

As David said, when one falls on Africa from a height of two hundred and fifty kilometers, a broken ankle may be an anti-climax but it is none the less painful. But what hurt him most, he pretended, was the way we had all rushed out into the desert to see what had happened to the A.20 and hadn't come near him until hours later.

"Be logical, David," Jimmy Langford had protested. "We knew that you were O.K. because the base 'copter radioed when it picked you up. But the A.20 might have been a complete write-off."

"There's only one A.20," I said, trying to be helpful, "but rocket test-pilots are—well, if not two a penny, at any rate twelve for a dime."

David glared back at us from beneath his bushy eyebrows and said something in Welsh.

"The Druid's curse," Jimmy remarked to me. "Any moment now you'll turn into a leek or a perspex model of Stonehenge."

You see, we were still pretty light-headed and it wouldn't do to be serious for a while. Even David's iron nerve must have taken a terrific beating, yet somehow he seemed the calmest of us all. I couldn't understand it—then.

The A.20 had come down fifty kilometers from her launching point. We'd followed her by radar for the whole trajectory, so we knew her position to within a few meters—though we didn't know at the time that David had landed ten kilometers farther east.

The first warning of disaster had come seventy seconds after takeoff. The A.20 had reached fifty kilometers and was following the correct trajectory to within a few per cent. As far as the eye could tell, the luminous track on the radar screen had scarcely deviated from the pre-computed path. David was doing two kilometers a second: not much, but the fastest any man had ever traveled up to then. And *Goliath* was just about to be jettisoned.

The A.20 was a two-step rocket. It had to be, for it was using chemical fuels. The upper component, with its tiny cabin, its folded aerofoils and flaps, weighed just under twenty tons when fully fueled. It was to be lifted by a lower two-hundred-ton booster which would take it up to fifty kilometers, after which it could carry on quite happily under its own power. The big fellow would then drop back to Earth by parachute: it wouldn't weigh much when its fuel was burnt. Meanwhile the upper step would have built up enough speed to reach the six-hundred-kilometer level before falling back and going into a glide that would take David halfway round the world if he wished.

I don't remember who called the two rockets *David* and *Goliath* but the names caught on at once. Having two Davids around caused a lot of confusion, not all of it accidental.

Well, that was the theory, but as we watched the tiny green spot on the screen fall away from its calculated course, we knew that something had gone wrong. And we guessed what it was.

At fifty kilometers the spot should have divided in two. The brighter echo should have continued to rise as a free projectile, and then fallen back to Earth. But the other should have gone on, still accelerating, drawing swiftly away from the discarded booster.

There had been no separation. The empty *Goliath* had refused to come free and was dragging *David* back to Earth—helplessly, for *David*'s motors could not be used. Their exhausts were blocked by the machine beneath.

We saw all this in about ten seconds. We waited just long enough to calculate the new trajectory, and then we climbed into the 'copters and set off for the target area.

All we expected to find, of course, was a heap of magnesium looking as if a bulldozer had gone over it. We knew that *Goliath* couldn't eject its parachute while *David* was sitting on top of it, any more than *David* could use its motors while *Goliath* was clinging beneath. I remember wondering who was going to break the news to Mavis, and then realizing that she'd be listening to the radio and would know all about it as soon as anyone.

We could scarcely believe our eyes when we found the two rockets still coupled together, lying undamaged beneath the big parachute. There was no sign of David, but a few minutes later Base called to say that he'd been found. The plotters at Number Two Station had picked up the tiny echo from his parachute and sent a 'copter to collect him. He was in the hospital twenty minutes later, but we stayed out in the desert for several hours checking over the machines and making arrangements to retrieve them.

When at last we got back to Base, we were pleased to see our best-hated science-reporters among the mob being held at bay. We waved aside their protests and sailed on into the ward.

The shock and the subsequent relief had left us all feeling rather irresponsible and perhaps childish. Only David seemed unaffected: the fact that he'd just had one of the most miraculous escapes in human history hadn't made him turn a hair. He sat there in the bed pretending to be annoyed at our gibes until we'd calmed down.

"Well," said Jimmy at last, "what went wrong?"

"That's for you to discover," David replied. "*Goliath* went like a dream until fuel-cutoff point. I waited then for the five-second pause before the explosion bolts detonated and the springs threw it clear, but nothing happened. So I punched the emergency release. The lights dimmed, but the kick I'd expected never came. I tried a couple more times but somehow I knew it was useless. I guessed that something had shorted in the detonator circuit and was earthing the power supply.

"Well, I did some rather rapid calculations from the flight charts and abacs in the cabin. At my present speed I'd continue to rise for another two hundred kilometers and would reach the peak of my trajectory in about three minutes. Then I'd start the two-hundred-and-fifty-kilometer fall and should make a nice hole in the desert four minutes later. All told, I seemed to have a good seven minutes of life left—ignoring air-resistance, to use your favorite phrase. That might add a couple of minutes to my expectation of life.

"I knew that I couldn't get the big parachute out, and *David*'s wings would be useless with the forty-ton mass of *Goliath* on its tail. I'd used up two of my seven minutes before I decided what to do.

"It's a good job I made you widen that airlock. Even so, it was a squeeze to get through it in my space-suit. I tied the end of the safety rope to a locking lever and crawled along the hull until I reached the junction of the two steps.

"The parachute compartment couldn't be opened from the outside, but I'd taken the emergency axe from the pilot's cabin. It didn't take long to get through the magnesium skin: once it had been punctured I could almost tear it apart with my hands. A few seconds later I'd released the 'chute. The silk floated aimlessly around me: I had expected some trace of air-resistance at this speed but there wasn't a sign of it. The canopy simply stayed where it was put. I could only hope that when we reentered atmosphere it would spread itself without fouling the rocket.

"I thought I had a fairly good chance of getting away with it. The additional weight of *David* would increase the loading of the parachute by less than twenty per cent, but there was always the chance that the shrouds would chafe against the broken metal and be worn through before I could reach Earth. In addition the canopy would be distorted when it did open, owing to the unequal lengths of the cords. There was nothing I could do about that.

"When I'd finished, I looked about me for the first time. I couldn't see very well, for perspiration had misted over the glass of my suit. (Someone had better look into that: it can be dangerous.) I was still rising, though very slowly now. To the northeast I could see the whole of Sicily and some of the Italian mainland: farther south I could follow the Libyan coast as far as Bengasi. Spread out beneath me was all the land over which Alexander and Montgomery and Rommel had fought when I was a boy. It seemed rather surprising that anyone had ever made such a fuss about it.

"I didn't stay long: in three minutes I would be entering the atmosphere. I took a last look at the flaccid parachute, straightened some of the shrouds, and climbed back into the cabin. Then I jettisoned *David*'s fuel—first the oxygen, and then, as soon as it had had time to disperse, the alcohol.

"That three minutes seemed an awfully long time. I was just over twenty-five kilometers high when I heard the first sound. It was a very high-pitched whistle, so faint that I could scarcely hear it. Glancing through the portholes, I saw that the parachute shrouds were becoming taut and the canopy was beginning to billow above me. At the same time I felt weight returning and knew that the rocket was beginning to decelerate.

"The calculation wasn't very encouraging. I'd fallen free for over two hundred kilometers and if I was to stop in time I'd need an *average* deceleration of ten gravities. The peaks might be twice that, but I'd stood fifteen *g* before now in a lesser cause. So I gave myself a double shot of dynocaine and uncaged the gimbals of my seat. I remember wondering whether I should let out *David's* little wings, and decided that it wouldn't help. Then I must have blacked out.

"When I came round again it was very hot, and I had normal weight. I felt very stiff and sore, and to make matters worse the cabin was oscillating violently. I struggled to the port and saw that the desert was uncomfortably close. The big parachute had done its work, but I thought that the impact was going to be rather too violent for comfort. So I jumped.

"From what you tell me I'd have done better to have stayed in the ship. But I don't suppose I can grumble."

We sat in silence for a while. Then Jimmy remarked casually:

"The accelerometer shows that you touched twenty-one gravities on the way down. Only for three seconds, though. Most of the time it was between twelve and fifteen."

David didn't seem to hear and presently I said:

"Well, we can't hold the reporters off much longer. Do you feel like seeing them?"

David hesitated.

"No," he answered. "Not now."

He read our faces and shook his head violently.

"No," he said with emphasis, "it's not that at all. I'd be willing to take off again right now. But I want to sit and think things over for a while."

His voice sank, and when he spoke again it was to show the real David behind the perpetual mask of extraversion.

"You think I haven't any nerves," he said, "and that I take risks without bothering about the consequences. Well, that isn't quite true and I'd like you to know why. I've never told anyone this, not even Mavis.

"You know I'm not superstitious," he began, a little apologetically, "but most materialists have some secret reservations, even if they won't admit them.

"Many years ago I had a peculiarly vivid dream. By itself, it wouldn't have meant much, but later I discovered that two other men had put almost identical experiences on record. One you've probably read, for the man was J. W. Dunne.

"In his first book, *An Experiment with Time*, Dunne tells how he once dreamed that he was sitting at the controls of a curious flying machine with swept-back wings, and years later the whole experience came true when he was testing his inherent-stability aeroplane. Remembering my own dreams, which I'd had *before* reading Dunne's book, this made a considerable impression on me. But the second incident I found even more striking.

"You've heard of Igor Sikorsky: he designed some of the first commercial long-distance flying-boats—'Clippers,' they were called. In his autobiography, *The Story of the Winged-S*, he tells us how he had a dream very similar to Dunne's.

"He was walking along a corridor with doors opening on either side and electric lights glowing overhead. There was a slight vibration underfoot and somehow he knew that he was in a flying machine. Yet at that time there were no aeroplanes in the world, and few people believed there ever would be.

"Sikorsky's dream, like Dunne's, came true many years later. He was on the maiden flight of his first Clipper when he found himself walking along that familiar corridor."

David laughed, a little self-consciously.

"You've probably guessed what my dream was about," he continued. "Remember, it would have made no permanent impression if I hadn't come across these parallel cases.

"I was in a small, bare room with no windows. There were two other men with me, and we were all wearing what I thought at the time were diving-suits. I had a curious control panel in front of me, with a circular screen built into it. There was a picture on the screen, but it didn't mean anything to me and I can't recall it now, though I've tried many times since. All I remember is turning to the other two men and saying: 'Five minutes to go, boys'—though I'm not sure if those were the exact words. And then, of course, I woke up.

"That dream has haunted me ever since I became a test pilot. No—haunted isn't the right word. It's given me confidence that in the long run everything would be all right—at least until I'm in that cabin with those other two men. What happens after that I don't know. But now you understand why I felt quite safe when I brought down the A.20, and when I crash-landed the A.15 off Pantelleria.

"So now you know. You can laugh if you please: I sometimes do myself. But even if there's nothing in it, that dream's given my subconscious a boost that's been pretty useful."

We didn't laugh, and presently Jimmy said:

"Those other men—did you recognize them?"

David looked doubtful.

"I've never made up my mind," he answered. "Remember, they were wearing space-suits and I didn't see their faces clearly. But one of them looked rather like you, though he seemed a good deal older than you are now. I'm afraid you weren't here, Arthur. Sorry."

"I'm glad to hear it," I said. "As I've told you before, I'll have to stay behind to explain what went wrong. I'm quite content to wait until the passenger service starts."

Jimmy rose to his feet.

"O.K., David," he said. "I'll deal with the gang outside. Get some sleep now—with or without dreams. And by the way, the A.20 will be ready again in a week. I think she'll be the last of the chemical rockets: they say the atomic drive's nearly ready for us."

We never spoke of David's dream again, but I think it was often in our minds. Three months later he took the A.20 up to six hundred and eighty kilometers, a record which will never be broken by a machine of this type, because no one will ever build a chemical rocket again. David's uneventful landing in the Nile Valley marked the end of an epoch.

It was three years before the A.21 was ready. She looked very small compared with her giant predecessors, and it was hard to believe that she was the nearest thing to a spaceship man had yet built. This time the takeoff was from sea level, and the Atlas Mountains which had witnessed the start of our earlier shots were now merely the distant background to the scene.

By now both Jimmy and I had come to share David's belief in his own destiny. I remember Jimmy's parting words as the airlock closed.

"It won't be long now, David, before we build that three-man ship."

And I knew he was only half joking.

We saw the A.21 climb slowly into the sky in great, widening circles, unlike any rocket the world had ever known before. There was no need to worry about gravitational loss now that we had a built-in fuel supply, and David wasn't in a hurry. The machine was still traveling quite slowly when I lost sight of it and went into the plotting room.

When I got there the signal was just fading from the screen, and the detonation reached me a little later. And that was the end of David and his dreams.

The next I recall of that period is flying down the Conway Valley in Jimmy's 'copter, with Snowdon gleaming far away on our right. We had never been to David's home before and were not looking forward to this visit. But it was the least that we could do.

As the mountains drifted beneath us we talked about the suddenly darkened future and wondered what the next step would be. Apart from the shock of personal loss, we were beginning to realize how much of David's confidence we had come to share ourselves. And now that confidence had been shattered.

We wondered what Mavis would do, and discussed the boy's future. He must be fifteen now, though I hadn't seen him for several years and Jimmy had never met him at all. According to his father he was going to be an architect and already showed considerable promise.

Mavis was quite calm and collected, though she seemed much older than when I had last met her. For a while we talked about business matters and the disposal of David's estate. I'd never been an executor before, but tried to pretend that I knew all about it.

We had just started to discuss the boy when we heard the front door open and he came into the house. Mavis called to him and his footsteps came slowly along the passage. We could tell that he didn't want to meet us, and his eyes were still red when he entered the room.

I had forgotten how much like his father he was, and I heard a little gasp from Jimmy.

"Hello, David," I said.

But he didn't look at me. He was staring at Jimmy, with the puzzled expression of a man who has seen someone before but can't remember where.

And quite suddenly I knew that young David would never be an architect.

The Sentinel

The next time you see the full moon high in the south, look carefully at its right-hand edge and let your eye travel upward along the curve of the disk. Round about two o'clock you will notice a small, dark oval: anyone with normal eyesight can find it quite easily. It is the great walled plain, one of the finest on the Moon, known as the Mare Crisium—the Sea of Crises. Three hundred miles in diameter, and almost completely surrounded by a ring of magnificent mountains, it had never been explored until we entered it in the late summer of 1996.

Our expedition was a large one. We had two heavy freighters which had flown our supplies and equipment from the main lunar base in the Mare Serenitatis, five hundred miles away. There were also three small rockets which were intended for short-range transport over regions which our surface vehicles couldn't cross. Luckily, most of the Mare Crisium is very flat. There are none of the great crevasses so common and so dangerous elsewhere, and very few craters or mountains of any size. As far as we could tell, our powerful caterpillar tractors would have no difficulty in taking us wherever we wished to go.

I was geologist—or selenologist, if you want to be pedantic—in charge of the group exploring the southern region of the Mare. We had crossed a hundred miles of it in a week, skirting the foothills of the mountains along the shore of what was once the ancient sea, some thousand million years before. When life was beginning on Earth, it was already dying here. The waters were retreating down the flanks of those stupendous cliffs, retreating into the empty heart of the Moon. Over the land which we were crossing, the tideless ocean had once been half a mile deep, and now the only trace of moisture was the hoarfrost one could sometimes find in caves which the searing sunlight never penetrated.

We had begun our journey early in the slow lunar dawn, and still had almost a week of Earth-time before nightfall. Half a dozen times a day we would leave our vehicle and go outside in the space-suits to hunt for interesting minerals, or to place markers for the guidance of future travelers. It was an uneventful routine. There is nothing hazardous or even particularly exciting about lunar exploration. We could live comfortably for a month in our pressurized tractors, and if we ran into trouble we could always radio for help and sit tight until one of the spaceships came to our rescue.

I said just now that there was nothing exciting about lunar exploration, but of course that isn't true. One could never grow tired of those incredible mountains, so much more rugged than the gentle hills of Earth. We never knew, as we rounded the capes and promontories of that vanished sea, what new splendors would be revealed to us. The whole southern curve of the Mare Crisium is a vast delta where a score of rivers once found their way into the ocean, fed perhaps by the torrential rains that must have lashed the mountains in the brief volcanic age when the Moon was young. Each of these ancient valleys was an invitation, challenging us to climb into the unknown uplands beyond. But we had a hundred miles still to cover, and could only look longingly at the heights which others must scale.

We kept Earth-time aboard the tractor, and precisely at 22.00 hours the final radio message would be sent out to Base and we would close down for the day. Outside, the rocks would still be burning beneath the almost vertical sun, but to us it was night until we awoke again eight hours later. Then one of us would prepare breakfast, there would be a great buzzing of electric razors, and someone would switch on the short-wave radio from Earth. Indeed, when the smell of frying sausages began to fill the cabin, it was sometimes hard to believe that we were not back on our own world—everything was so normal and homely, apart from the feeling of decreased weight and the unnatural slowness with which objects fell.

It was my turn to prepare breakfast in the corner of the main cabin that served as a galley. I can remember that moment quite vividly after all these years, for the radio had just played one of my favorite melodies, the old Welsh air, "David of the White Rock." Our driver was already outside in his space-suit, inspecting our caterpillar treads. My assistant, Louis Garnett, was up forward in the control position, making some belated entries in yesterday's log.

As I stood by the frying pan waiting, like any terrestrial housewife, for the sausages to brown, I let my gaze wander idly over the mountain walls which covered the whole of the southern horizon, marching out of sight to east and west below the curve of the Moon. They seemed only a mile or two from the tractor, but I knew that the nearest was twenty miles away. On the moon, of course, there is no loss of detail with distance—none of that almost imperceptible haziness which softens and sometimes transfigures all far-off things on Earth.

Those mountains were ten thousand feet high, and they climbed steeply out of the plain as if ages ago some subterranean eruption had smashed them skyward through the molten crust. The base of even the nearest was hidden from sight by the steeply curving surface of the plain, for the Moon is a very little world, and from where I was standing the horizon was only two miles away.

I lifted my eyes toward the peaks which no man had ever climbed, the peaks which, before the coming of terrestrial life, had watched the retreating oceans sink sullenly into their graves, taking with them the hope and the morning promise of a world. The sunlight was beating against those ramparts with a glare that hurt the eyes, yet only a little way above them the stars were shining steadily in a sky blacker than a winter midnight on Earth.

I was turning away when my eye caught a metallic glitter high on the ridge of a great promontory thrusting out into the sea thirty miles to the west. It was a dimensionless point of light, as if a star had been clawed from the sky by one of those cruel peaks, and I imagined that some smooth rock surface was catching the sunlight and heliographing it straight into my eyes. Such things were not uncommon. When the Moon is in her second quarter, observers on Earth can sometimes see the great ranges in the Oceanus Procellarum burning with a blue-white iridescence as the sunlight flashes from their slopes and leaps again from world to world. But I was curious to know what kind of rock could be shining so brightly up there, and I climbed into the observation turret and swung our four-inch telescope round to the west.

I could see just enough to tantalize me. Clear and sharp in the field of vision, the mountain peaks seemed only half a mile away, but whatever was catching the sunlight was still too small to be resolved. Yet it seemed to have an elusive symmetry, and the summit upon which it rested was curiously flat. I stared for a long time at that glittering enigma, straining my eyes into space, until presently a smell of burning from the galley told me that our breakfast sausage had made their quarter-million mile journey in vain.

All that morning we argued our way across the Mare Crisium while the western mountains reared higher in the sky. Even when we were out prospecting in the space-suits, the discussion would continue over the radio. It was absolutely certain, my companions argued, that there had never been any form of intelligent life on the Moon. The only living things that had ever existed there were a few primitive plants and their slightly less degenerate ancestors. I knew that as well as anyone, but there are times when a scientist must not be afraid to make a fool of himself.

"Listen," I said at last, "I'm going up there, if only for my own peace of mind. That mountain's less than twelve thousand feet high—that's only two thousand under Earth gravity—and I can make the trip in twenty hours at the outside. I've always wanted to go up into those hills, anyway, and this gives me an excellent excuse."

"If you don't break your neck," said Garnett, "you'll be the laughing-stock of the expedition when we get back to Base. That mountain will probably be called Wilson's Folly from now on."

"I won't break my neck," I said firmly. "Who was the first man to climb Pico and Helicon?"

"But weren't you rather younger in those days?" asked Louis gently.

"That," I said with great dignity, "is as good a reason as any for going."

We went to bed early that night, after driving the tractor to within half a mile of the promontory. Garnett was coming with me in the morning; he was a good climber, and had often been with me on such exploits before. Our driver was only too glad to be left in charge of the machine.

At first sight, those cliffs seemed completely unscaleable, but to anyone with a good head for heights, climbing is easy on a world where all weights are only a sixth of their normal value. The real danger in lunar mountaineering lies in over-confidence; a six-hundred-foot drop on the Moon can kill you just as thoroughly as a hundred-foot fall on Earth.

We made our first halt on a wide ledge about four thousand feet above the plain. Climbing had not been very difficult, but my limbs were stiff with the unaccustomed effort, and I was glad of the rest. We could still see the tractor as a tiny metal insect far down at the foot of the cliff, and we reported our progress to the driver before starting on the next ascent.

Inside our suits it was comfortably cool, for the refrigeration units were fighting the fierce sun and carrying away the body-heat of our exertions. We seldom spoke to each other, except to pass climbing instructions and to discuss our best plan of ascent. I do not know what Garnett was thinking, probably that this was the craziest goose-chase he had ever embarked upon. I more than half agreed with him, but the joy of climbing, the knowledge that no man had ever gone this way before and ex-hilaration of the steadily widening landscape gave me all the reward I needed.

I don't think I was particularly excited when I saw in front of us the wall of rock I had first inspected through the tele-scope from thirty miles away. It would level off about fifty feet above our heads, and there on the plateau would be the thing that had lured me over these barren wastes. It was, almost cer-tainly, nothing more than a boulder splintered ages ago by a falling meteor, and with its cleavage planes still fresh and bright in this incorruptible, unchanging silence.

There were no hand-holds on the rock face, and we had to use a grapnel. My tired arms seemed to gain new strength as I swung the three-pronged metal anchor round my head and sent it sailing up toward the stars. The first time it broke loose and came falling slowly back when we pulled the rope. On the third attempt, the prongs gripped firmly and our combined weights could not shift it.

Garnett looked at me anxiously. I could tell that he wanted to go first, but I smiled back at him through the glass of my helmet and shook my head. Slowly, taking my time, I began the final ascent.

Even with my space-suit, I weighed only forty pounds here, so I pulled myself up hand over hand without bothering to use my feet. At the rim I paused and waved to my companion, then I scrambled over the edge and stood upright, staring ahead of me.

You must understand that until this very moment I had been almost completely convinced that there could be nothing strange or unusual for me to find here. Almost, but not quite; it was that haunting doubt that had driven me forward. Well, it was a doubt no longer, but the haunting had scarcely begun.

I was standing on a plateau perhaps a hundred feet across. It had once been smooth—too smooth to be natural—but falling meteors had pitted and scored its surface through immeasurable eons. It had been leveled to support a glittering, roughly pyramidal structure, twice as high as a man, that was set in the rock like a gigantic, many-faceted jewel.

Probably no emotion at all filled my mind in those first few seconds. Then I felt a great lifting of my heart, and a strange, inexpressible joy. For I loved the Moon, and now I knew that the creeping moss of Aristarchus and Eratosthenes was not the only life she had brought forth in her youth. The old, discredited dream of the first explorers was true. There had, after all, been a lunar civilization—and I was the first to find it. That I had come perhaps a hundred million years too late did not distress me; it was enough to have come at all.

My mind was beginning to function normally, to analyze

and to ask questions. Was this a building, a shrine—or something for which my language had no name? If a building, then why was it erected in so uniquely inaccessible a spot? I wondered if it might be a temple, and I could picture the adepts of some strange priesthood calling on their gods to preserve them as the life of the Moon ebbed with the dying oceans, and calling on their gods in vain.

I took a dozen steps forward to examine the thing more closely, but some sense of caution kept me from going too near. I knew a little of archaeology, and tried to guess the cultural level of the civilization that must have smoothed this mountain and raised the glittering mirror surfaces that still dazzled my eyes.

The Egyptians could have done it, I thought, if their workmen had possessed whatever strange materials these far more ancient architects had used. Because of the thing's smallness, it did not occur to me that I might be looking at the handiwork of a race more advanced than my own. The idea that the Moon had possessed intelligence at all was still almost too tremendous to grasp, and my pride would not let me take the final, humiliating plunge.

And then I noticed something that set the scalp crawling at the back of my neck—something so trivial and so innocent that many would never have noticed it at all. I have said that the plateau was scarred by meteors; it was also coated inches-deep with the cosmic dust that is always filtering down upon the surface of any world where there are no winds to disturb it. Yet the dust and the meteor scratches ended quite abruptly in a wide circle enclosing the little pyramid, as though an invisible wall was protecting it from the ravages of time and that slow but ceaseless bombardment from space.

There was someone shouting in my earphones, and I realized that Garnett had been calling me for some time. I walked unsteadily to the edge of the cliff and signaled him to join me, not trusting myself to speak. Then I went back toward that circle in the dust. I picked up a fragment of splintered rock and tossed it gently toward the shining enigma. If the pebble had vanished at that invisible barrier I should not have been surprised, but it seemed to hit a smooth, hemispherical surface and slide gently to the ground.

I knew then that I was looking at nothing that could be matched in the antiquity of my own race. This was not a building, but a machine, protecting itself with forces that had challenged Eternity. Those forces, whatever they might be, were still operating, and perhaps I had already come too close. I thought of all the radiations man had trapped and tamed in the past century. For all I knew, I might be as irrevocably doomed as if I had stepped into the deadly, silent aura of an unshielded atomic pile.

I remember turning then toward Garnett, who had joined me and was now standing motionless at my side. He seemed quite oblivious to me, so I did not disturb him but walked to the edge of the cliff in an effort to marshal my thoughts. There below me lay the Mare Crisium—Sea of Crises, indeed—strange and weird to most men, but reassuringly familiar to me. I lifted my eyes toward the crescent Earth, lying in her cradle of stars, and I wondered what her clouds had covered when these unknown builders had finished their work. Was it the steaming jungle of the Carboniferous, the bleak shoreline over which the first amphibians must crawl to conquer the land—or, earlier still, the long loneliness before the coming of life?

Do not ask me why I did not guess the truth sooner—the truth that seems so obvious now. In the first excitement of my discovery, I had assume without question that this crystalline apparition had been built by some race belonging to the Moon's remote past, but suddenly, and with overwhelming force, the belief came to me that it was as alien to the Moon as I myself.

In twenty years we had found no trace of life but a few degenerate plants. No lunar civilization, whatever its doom, could have left but a single token of its existence.

I looked at the shining pyramid again, and the more remote it seemed from anything that had to do with the Moon. And suddenly I felt myself shaking with a foolish, hysterical laughter, brought on by excitement and overexertion: for I had imagined that the little pyramid was speaking to me and was saying: "Sorry, I'm a stranger here myself."

It has taken us twenty years to crack that invisible shield and to reach the machine inside those crystal walls. What we could not understand, we broke at last with the savage might of atomic power and now I have seen the fragments of the lovely, glittering thing I found up there on the mountain.

They are meaningless. The mechanisms—if indeed they are mechanisms—of the pyramid belong to a technology that lies far beyond our horizon, perhaps to the technology of paraphysical forces.

The mystery haunts us all the more now that the other planets have been reached and we know that only Earth has ever been the home of intelligent life in our Universe. Nor could any lost civilization of our own world have built that machine, for the thickness of the meteoric dust on the plateau has enabled us to measure its age. It was set there upon its mountain before life had emerged from the seas of Earth.

When our world was half its present age, *something* from the stars swept through the Solar System, left this token of its passage, and went again upon its way. Until we destroyed it, that machine was still fulfilling the purpose of its builders; and as to that purpose, here is my guess.

Nearly a hundred thousand million stars are turning in the circle of the Milky Way, and long ago other races on the worlds of other suns must have scaled and passed the heights that we have reached. Think of such civilizations, far back in time against the fading afterglow of Creation, masters of a universe so young that life as yet had come only to a handful of worlds. Theirs would have been a loneliness we cannot imagine, the loneliness of gods looking out across infinity and finding none to share their thoughts.

They must have searched the star-clusters as we have searched the planets. Everywhere there would be worlds, but they would be empty or peopled with crawling, mindless things. Such was our own Earth, the smoke of the great volcanoes still staining the skies, when that first ship of the peoples of the dawn came sliding in from the abyss beyond Pluto. It passed the frozen outer worlds, knowing that life could play no part in their destinies. It came to rest among the inner planets, warming themselves around the fire of the Sun and waiting for their stories to begin.

Those wanderers must have looked on Earth, circling safely in the narrow zone between fire and ice, and must have guessed that it was the favorite of the Sun's children. Here, in the distant future, would be intelligence; but there were countless stars before them still, and they might never come this way again.

So they left a sentinel, one of millions they have scattered throughout the Universe, watching over all worlds with the promise of life. It was a beacon that down the ages has been patiently signaling the fact that no one had discovered it.

Perhaps you understand now why that crystal pyramid was set upon the Moon instead of on the Earth. Its builders were not concerned with races still struggling up from savagery. They would be interested in our civilization only if we proved our fitness to survive—by crossing space and so escaping from the Earth, our cradle. That is the challenge that all intelligent races must meet, sooner or later. It is a double challenge, for it depends in turn upon the conquest of atomic energy and the last choice between life and death.

Once we had passed that crisis, it was only a matter of time before we found the pyramid and forced it open. Now its signals have ceased, and those whose duty it is will be turning their minds upon Earth. Perhaps they wish to help our infant civilization. But they must be very, very old, and the old are often insanely jealous of the young.

I can never look now at the Milky Way without wondering from which of those banked clouds of stars the emissaries are coming. If you will pardon so commonplace a simile, we have set off the fire-alarm and have nothing to do but to wait.

I do not think we will have to wait for long.

Charles Adams

ABOUT THE AUTHOR

ARTHUR C. CLARKE was born in Minehead, England, in 1917 and was made a Freeman of his hometown in 1992. He now lives in Sri Lanka, where he was the first person to be granted "Resident Guest" status. He is a graduate, and Fellow, of King's College, London, and Chancellor of the International Space University and the University of Moratuwa, near which the Government has established the Arthur C. Clarke Institute for Modern Technologies.

Sir Arthur has twice been Chairman of the British Interplanetary Society. While serving as an RAF radar officer in 1945, he published the theory of communications satellites, most of which operate in what is now called the Clarke Orbit. The impact of this invention upon global politics resulted in his nomination for the 1994 Nobel Peace Prize.

He has written over seventy books and shared an Oscar nomination with Stanley Kubrick for the movie based on his novel *2001: A Space Odyssey*. His *Mysterious World*, *Strange Powers*, and *Mysterious Universe* TV series have been shown worldwide.

His many honors include the Marconi and Lindbergh Awards, as well as three Hugos and three Nebulas for his science fiction. In a global satellite ceremony in 1995, he received NASA's highest civilian honor, its Distinguished Public Service Medal.

Sir Arthur's recreations are scuba diving on Indian Ocean wrecks with his company, Underwater Safaris, table tennis (despite Post Polio Syndrome), observing the Moon through his fourteen-inch telescope, and playing with his Chihuahua, "Pepsi," and his six computers.

He received the Vidya Jyothi ("Light of Science") Award from the president of Sri Lanka in 1986, and the CBE (Commander of the British Empire) from H.M. Queen Elizabeth in 1989. And in 1996 he went to Beijing to receive the International Academy of Astronautics' highest honor, the von Karman Award.

Sir Arthur was made a Knight in the Queen's 1998 New Year's Honours List for his "services to literature."

Candy's
Corporate Crush
A Blackstone Family Novel

TINA MARTIN

<u>The Blackstone Family</u>

PARENTS: Theodore (Theo) Blackstone & Elowyn Blackstone

CHILDREN:

Bryson Blackstone [Age 39]
-Married to Kalina Blackstone
-Owns Blackstone Tree Service

Barringer (Barry) Blackstone [Age 37]
-Married to Calista Blackstone
-CEO of Blackstone Financial Services Group (BFSG)
-CHILDREN: Bella Blackstone [Age 3 months old]

Garrison (Gary) Blackstone [Age 35]
-Widowed (Was married to Vivienne Blackstone)
-Director of Finance at Blackstone Financial Services Group (BFSG)
-CHILDREN: Garrison Blackstone, Jr. [Age 1 year old]

Everson Blackstone [Age 33]
-Married to June Blackstone
-Business Management Analyst (Freelance)

Candice (Candy) Blackstone [Age 29]
-Single and looking
-Manager of Customer Relations at Blackstone Financial Services Group (BFSG)

COUSINS:

Rexford Blackstone [Age 38]
-Single and *always* looking
-Police Officer

Colton Blackstone [Age 34]
-Single
-Painter, owns Blackstone Painting, LLC

Chapter 1

That nagging feeling in her gut wouldn't go away. It had occupied her mind on the drive to Asheville and even with the music blaring, she couldn't shake it. It was that sinking feeling she imagined every woman probably experienced in their lifetime – the thought that there was something better out there than the person they were with. She knew it wasn't true – that it didn't get much better than Kurt. He was smart, handsome and had a body out of this world, so where was this feeling of missing out on something coming from? And with a man like him, what exactly was she supposed to be missing out on?

She glanced over at the passenger seat to grab her phone when she heard it ringing. It was him. Her man.

"Hey, you. I'm almost there," she answered.

"Why's it taking so long, or am I *that* anxious?" he asked.

"Yes, you're anxious, Kurt. The drive is five hours. You know this."

"I know, I know but it seems longer and longer every time. We need to do something about that."

"I know," she said. She was coming to visit him from Wilmington and his patience was wearing thin with the distance separating them. They hadn't seen each other in two weeks. Two whole weeks. That was a long time to be without his woman. His wife. They'd been married for a month but their lives were still very much separate and utterly complicated. As newlyweds, they didn't need those problems, especially when they had a huge mushroom cloud of a problem hanging over their heads already. Kurt worked for The Champion Corporation – the very company who wanted to buy Blackstone Financial Services Group – the company Candice's father founded. The company of which she was also currently employed as an executive.

"Okay, I'm about to pull up now," she told him.

"No, you're not. I'm standing at the door. I don't see headlights in my driveway. Where are you?"

She found his impatience amusing. "Give me a few seconds, Mr. Hempstead. I'm pulling up in five...four...three...two..."

"Ah, there you are." A sigh of relief calmed his anxiety and satisfied his soul. "Bring your pretty behind on in here. I got dinner waiting."

"Yeah, like we're *actually* going to eat," she quipped.

"We will. Eventually."

Candice came to a stop in front of the garage door and threw the gear into park before she turned off the engine. She got out and in a full sprint, ran up to the tall, deliciously handsome man who was all hers. She leaped into his arms squeezed the life out of him. He was all too receiving as he held on to his love, kissed her lips and took full possession of her mouth. The hours that had turned into days that irritatingly became weeks had sparked this kind of reuniting, this longing, but their reconnection was proof that no distance could keep them apart. They were committed to making it work. Their love. Their secret marriage. Their rival companies. It *had* to work.

Kurt held her close as they kissed up the front stairs of his home. His tongue tousled with hers when they made it to the porch. When they stepped inside, he closed the door and hungrily devoured her lips again in a way that told her they were *not* going to eat dinner right away. They needed each other for sustenance at the moment in a way that could only be described as uncontrolled recklessness. They were wild again. Panting, in need and careless as they knocked over a lamp and the table it was sitting on.

He snatched her shirt up over her head. She secured her legs around his waist. Anything between the door and bedroom was an obstacle. There had been many times when they hadn't made it. Like now, when they tripped over a rug in his living room. He hit the floor first, breaking her fall with a bed of muscles but still took the opportunity to undo her pants and her self-control, feeling her unravel in his arms.

She giggled playfully between kisses. Pulling his shirt up over his head, she commented, "It smells good in here. What'd you cook?"

"Don't worry about all that right now," he said, tugging her bra loose. Food was the last thing on his mind.

She gasped the moment his cold hands touched her bare skin. "Ah...Kurt."

"Yes?" he said kissing her around her neck.

"We could just go to the bedroom, you know."

"We could, but this is a perfectly good floor," he

told her, feeling the carpet beneath his back. She came down on top of him, kissing him again as she maneuvered her body to merge with his until his length filled her. She gasped, chewed a long moan and let the feeling overtake her.

"I miss you," she panted.

"Hey, let's not worry about that right now, baby," he said staring up into her eyes, his back still on the floor. Their bodies fused together. She rocking, moving, riding slow. "We're here together, making love. Let's just have this moment. Are you with me?"

"Yes," she gasped, closing her eyes temporarily to savor it as she angled her head to the ceiling. "I'm with you." She placed her hands on his face feeling his prickly beard tickle her fingers. She bit down on her lip and closed her eyes when she felt his lips skim across her breasts.

His woman was something special. In a way, she was lost when they'd met, he knew. Behind the strong, independent woman was the shadow of another woman – one who had trust issues. In some ways, she still had those issues. That's why he loved her harder. Why he made her trust him. And when he made love to her, like he was doing now, he made sure he conveyed in action what he'd said to her in words.

He loved her. Loved her soul. Her spirit. Her body. She was his woman and she would always be his.

And he would always be hers.

Her body quivered against his as he held on tight to her, trying to absorb her spasms into his own being. It worked, triggering an explosion that left them both gasping for air while the sounds of their lovemaking filled the living room. She was still panting, still struggling to catch her breath when he whispered, "Welcome home, baby."

She smiled and lowered her mouth to his for more of his lips. He was all she needed. The little voice in her head that threatened her sanity and made her feel like there was something missing needed to keep quiet. But would it?

Chapter 2

In the kitchen, Kurt rewarmed the meal he'd prepared – beef with mushroom gravy, rice and string beans. He even took a stab at making biscuits from scratch. After they'd wrestled on the living room floor, he'd slid into a pair of sweats and a plain, white T-shirt. The chocolate contrast of his skin against the white shirt made Candice's mouth water, and it wasn't for those biscuits. "Ain't nothing sexier than watching a man cook," she told him.

"Correction—ain't nothing sexier than watching *your* man cook," Kurt corrected.

"Right," she smiled. "My man."

Kurt pulled out a chair for her. She'd just come from taking a shower and was wearing a pink pajama set – a spaghetti strap top with shorts. Her complexion was a few shades lighter than his. And she was shorter, five-seven, body bangin' in all the right places – small waist, thick thighs, plump breasts and a round bottom.

"Plant your booty right here in this seat."

"Yes, Sir," she said, sitting at the glass-top table, gathering her damp hair back into a ponytail.

He brought her a glass of red wine, something to keep her occupied while he worked. She sipped and watched him. He'd cooked for her plenty of times before, and every time a smile came to her face. He was hers. She was proud of that, especially after dealing with a guy like Quinton.

After her relationship with Quinton went sour, she took a break from dating – a break so long, it had her brothers thinking they'd won in their quest to keep their little sister single and man-free. Little did they know she had a man. That was one advantage of a long-distance relationship. She didn't have to worry about the family being in her business. Now that they were married, a long-distance husband/wife relationship wasn't feasible any longer – not to her or him. But it wasn't Kurt doing the stalling. He was ready to love life with her the way they should've been living. The hesitation came from her end.

"What are you thinking about?" Kurt asked as he brought her a plate.

She smiled. "Nothing much. Just thinking."

She remembered when she first met Kurt on the boardwalk in Wilmington. She'd been out alone that night, doing that freeing thing single people did called *dating themselves* when he'd approached her, asking if he knew her from somewhere. Candice took it for what it was – a line from a handsome guy to break the ice. He'd given her his business card, wrote his cell phone number on the back and that was that.

It was later she found out he probably *did* know her – well, in passing. He'd gone to high school with her brother, Everson. Still, Candice had no intention of calling him, and she didn't think twice about hanging on to his business card just in case she changed her mind.

It wasn't until Kurt showed up at her job that she would see him again. He worked for the enemy – The Champion Corporation – the company who were now representing a former client of Blackstone Financial – The Blakeney Agency. In fact, the client was the biggest client, in terms of dollars, that Blackstone had. Since they'd lost the company, The Champion Corporation wanted Blackstone to become a subsidiary. Barringer Blackstone, Candice's second oldest brother, nearly had a stroke when he listened to Desmond Champion make him an offer to bring Blackstone Financial Service Group under The Champion Corporation brand.

He wasn't having any of it. He wanted to wait it out to see if the company could bounce back after losing one of its biggest, most important clients. As customer relations manager for the company, Candice was tasked with securing new business and over the last six months, she'd done her job, especially with bringing on Telmark Corporation. Still, with their largest client in the hands of a rival company, they needed more clients to fill the gap and increase their profit margin.

But that was the business side of her relationship with Kurt – the side that caused a lot of strain.

She wanted to enjoy the *personal* time with him. It was a pain to always have the business issues following them, but when you loved someone, you pushed that aside. Dwelling on business wasn't conducive to a healthy, happy marriage – especially a long-distance one like theirs.

"Thank you for cooking."

"You're welcome, baby."

Back at the table with his food, he sat across from her and they began eating.

"Talk to me," he said.

"What?"

"You have something on your mind, so get it off. Come on. Let's hear it."

She smiled. "I don't have anything on my mind."

"You do. I've been watching you daydreaming. Something's got you occupied."

"Yeah, something like *you*."

He narrowed his eyes, then took a spoonful of beef tips to his mouth.

"Dinner is delicious, by the way," she said.

"Thank you." He sipped wine then said, "I have some things on my mind I would like to discuss with you."

"Okay. Let's hear 'em."

Kurt took the white napkin from his lap and wiped his mouth. "Your family."

"What about my family?"

"I'm not a part of it."

"Kurt—"

"I want to feel like I'm a part of your family just as much as I am a part of you."

To him, nothing was more important than family. His parents divorced when he was sixteen. At the time, he didn't understand why they couldn't reconcile, but he knew he didn't want to endure that kind of heartache. He watched his mother suffer for a while then regain her balance again after remarrying. His parent's failed marriage made him realize how important family was. How fragile it was. How easily something that was supposed to last forever could so easily be torn apart if it wasn't maintained properly. He vowed to never let that happen to his family. *She* was his family, and he didn't need any outsiders whether they be flesh and blood or otherwise disturbing their relationship. That's what she feared her family would do –

disrupt their marriage.

"It doesn't work like that all the time, Kurt. Just because *I* like you doesn't mean everyone in my family will automatically fall in line."

"I understand that."

"And I've warned you about my brothers."

"Yes, and I'm willing to accept whatever they have to throw my way to prove how much I love you."

Candice sighed. It was her belief he shouldn't have to prove anything – especially to them. If they didn't like him, they didn't like him. As long as she liked him – loved him – she didn't care what they thought.

"I want you to meet them, Kurt—I do—but I think we should push it back a little."

"Why? You don't think I can handle myself?"

"The company you work for is trying to acquire the company my family owns. The conflict of interest is crystal clear, and trust me when I say this won't go over well with my family."

"Yet, it hasn't stopped you from being with me, so why should we let it stop us from living our lives? You live in Wilmington. I live in Asheville. Every time I bring up the subject of us moving together, you cringe." He cracked a smile looking at her. "See, you did it just now."

"I know, but it's not because I don't want to. I do. I just—I've never been away from my family. My mother will lose her mind if she knew I was considering moving here with you."

"Then I'll move to Wilmington with you. It doesn't matter as long as we're together, baby. That's what I don't think you understand. I'm willing to do whatever it takes."

She blushed. "Stop staring into my eyes like that. Why do you look so serious?"

"Because I *am* serious and I want you to know that. I don't want to be in company meetings with you, watching you pretend you don't know me. Pretending I haven't laid between your thick thighs. I'm your husband. I want to be treated like that."

"Okay. I hear you."

He lifted a brow. "Do you?"

"Yes. Loud and clear." She followed her confirmation with a sip of wine and more thoughts. "When are we scheduled to meet again to discuss the acquisition?"

"I'm not one-hundred percent sure if it's on the calendar yet, but I know it's coming up soon. It's going to be me and Desmond coming over there again."

"Okay, then I'll come up with a plan to tell my brothers about us while you're in Wilmington."

"Good."

"Can you smile now and reduce the tension in the room?"

Kurt flashed a smile, one that always made Candice's heart skip a beat.

"Do we have anything planned tomorrow?"

"You mean after I let you out of the bed?"

Candice giggled. "Yes. After you let me out of the bed."

"No. I don't have anything planned. We'll figure something out. We always do." He said, reaching across the table to hold her hand. "I really miss you when we're not together."

"I know. We'll make it work. We have no choice but to, right?"

"Right."

Chapter 3

The sun poured through the windows of Kurt's second-floor bedroom. Candice could hardly open her eyes as its brightness showered her with the gift of morning, but she welcomed it in little doses. Once she was able to get her eyes all the way open, she saw the fine specimen lying next to her.

He was all man and then some.

His features told the story of his masculinity. He was tall, six-four, with enough muscles – enough stamina – to build structures with his bare hands, yet his job was one of strategies and analytics. He used his intelligence for a living. His eyes were closed, but she always enjoyed staring into their deep, rich brown color while thinking of the untold stories they held. And his lashes – those long lashes of his put him in a special category of handsome when it came to good-looking men – not to mention the carved-to-perfection jawline, trimmed goatee and toasted almond colored skin. He was everything – so much more than just his looks.

He was a man she could trust. Granted that trust came over the course of six months but she was comfortable with him. She didn't have to question his motives or worry he'd do something to hurt her. She came with the baggage of distrust, but with this man, she knew things would be different. They'd dated for five months before getting married, but during that time, she was comfortable with him and his relationship with his divorced parents. He kept in contact with his mother and father.

And he was a true gentleman. The open-doors and get-the-chair-for-a-woman kind of gentleman. He was polite. Kind. A perfect mixture of strength and mildness – the kind of man a girl didn't mind introducing to her parents.

But she hadn't done that. Hadn't introduced the man she loved, the man she married on the low-low to any of her family members. She wanted to put it off for as long as she could but she knew he was getting tired of that approach.

His eyes slowly opened. He released a soft moan like he did whenever he was waking up. He stretched causing his joints to crackle and wake up while the muscles in his arms flexed.

Candice strummed the black hair beneath his arms. "Good morning."

He smiled. "Good morning."

She kissed his chest then propped her chin up on the valley between his pecks. He smelled like the comforting scent of the man she loved. Every time she was with him, she felt guilty for keeping him in hiding until she was ready to answer a million questions from her family. She was afraid of their judgments. What would her father think about her dating a man who worked for a company that wanted to buy the company he'd built with his own hands?

"Did you give any thought to what you wanted to do today?" she asked.

"I think we should stay in bed, get up at noon,

eat a late lunch and get back in bed."

"Kurt, nooo. I'm leaving tomorrow night. We have to take advantage of every moment we have together."

"There are plenty of *moments* we can have on this mattress."

"We had those moments last night. Now, get up. Let's do something."

"What did you have in mind, baby?"

"I don't care what we do as long as I'm with you."

Kurt lifted his head from the pillow to kiss her forehead. He brushed her brown strands away from her face. "You better be glad you're so pretty and sweet."

She smiled. "Let's go get some breakfast. I need more energy after you depleted me of it last night."

* * *

After breakfast at Biscuit Head, they took in two games of bowling and a little shopping at the mall. From there, they went straight to dinner at Bouchon, a French-style restaurant where they both ordered the Carre d'Agneau – a Moroccan spiced lamb topped with preserved lemon gremolata and feta, served over couscous and seasoned vegetables. This was one of their favorite spots because of the delicious food and the romantic atmosphere. It was just what they both needed to round out the day.

They were sharing a crepe – one with Grand Marnier orange butter sauce and whipped cream when Candice said, "I can't believe I beat you in two games of bowling."

"I'm rusty. Bowling isn't necessarily one of my favorite activities."

"Right. I'll have to catch you on the basketball court."

He smirked. "You won't be able to handle me on the court, baby."

"You don't think so? I think that game of bowling is proof I can handle my balls pretty well."

"Trust me when I say I didn't need to see you bowling to know you can handle some balls, baby," Kurt said then grinned slyly.

"You and your gutter mind..."

Kurt laughed more.

"If you say so."

"When I was growing up, my family went bowling all the time. My parents loved it. Dad had his own ball and glove—the works. My brothers were pretty good at it, too. They always beat me."

"Do you still think your brothers are going to give me a hard time once they find out about us?"

"I *know* they will. I have no doubt in my mind about it."

"Okay, so give me an *in* here. Which one am I likely to get along with? I think my strategy is to go from the good to the bad."

"In that case, you should probably talk to Everson first."

"Right. Everson. The only member of your family who actually knew me before we met..."

"He doesn't know you like that. Just because you went to the same high school doesn't mean you know them. Plus, I suggested Everson because he's more reasonable than the rest of them. Him and Garrison."

"What's Garrison's story? You told me his wife died."

"Yeah, a little over a year ago. And she was such a lovable, sweet woman. I miss her."

"What happened to her?"

"She died while giving birth to their son."

"Right. I remember now. Wow. I couldn't fathom what he has to endure on a daily basis."

"Yeah," Candice said, realizing she hadn't had a real, heart-to-heart talk with Garrison in a while. He always presented himself in a way that made it appear all was well with him. She hoped that was the case.

"What about Bryson?" Kurt asked.

Candice shook her head. "Bryson is—he's— Bryson is very protective of me. Well, they all are, but he takes it to a new level. He's like a second father."

"Because he's the oldest?"

She shrugged. "Probably. He's ten years older than I am, and he loves telling stories of how he used to change my diaper, feed me and rock me to sleep and all that. Even when he left for college, he made sure to be home for my winter concerts and school plays. He always made sure I kept up with my homework."

"He sounds like an overall good brother to have."

"Yeah, he's a good guy. He gets on my last nerve, but that's what brothers are supposed to do, I've learned."

Kurt took a sip of his drink.

"Oh, sorry, you don't know anything about that being an only child and all."

"No, I don't, but hey, I've inherited four brothers by marriage, so I need to know these things. Now, tell me about Barringer. I've already had a few run-ins with him as you know, but I don't know him outside of business."

"All you need to understand about Barry is, he's *all* business. It's in his DNA. When dad passed the company down to him, he vowed to make it a success on his own without help from anyone, especially not a company like The Champion Corporation who gobbles up other companies for midday snacks. Barringer will fall dead before he lets that happen. He's always run the company like he has something to prove, and he does. He has some big shoes to fill."

"The shoes of Daddy Blackstone, huh?"

"Yep. Barringer ain't all that bad, though. You should see him with his baby daughter. He's a different man when he's with Bella. But when he's at the office, he's a shark. He thinks about everything in a round-a-bout way and he takes a while to warm up to people. He gets that from dad."

Kurt furrowed a brow. "Is that your way of telling me Daddy Blackstone won't like me either?"

"I wouldn't say that. We're a pretty close family. I believe he'd be more upset with me for keeping you a secret."

"And what about your mother?"

Candice's cheeks flushed. "I'm sure she'll be upset, too, but only because she didn't get to share this experience with me. I feel bad about that."

"I'm sorry."

"It's nothing for you to be sorry about. When I finally tell everyone about us, I'll have a lot of explaining to do. That's all that means."

Kurt got up from his seat, moved the chair around the table and placed it close to her in the dimly lit restaurant. He took her right hand into his left and said, "We'll get through it, and once we do, baby, then our lives can finally begin. No more back-and-forth to see each other. I'll have you right here with me."

"I like the sound of that," Candice said, squeezing his hand. She licked her lips and leaned close to him until their lips touched. She moaned as she tasted liquor on his tongue.

"Mmm," he said with his eyes closed. He opened them and smiled. "Let's get out of here so I can get my last dose of you before you leave me to go back home."

"Yeah. We should totally do that."

Kurt lifted a finger, signaling the waitress for the check, then tossed back the rest of his drink. Her being away from him was a lot harder than he made it seem, but since knowing she had a lot of pressure coming from her family, he didn't want to burden her by pressing the issue. All he wanted to do was love her – to show her he was worthy of the cause. That, if it came down to it, their marriage was worth fighting for.

Chapter 4

Kalina was busy in her office when Candice walked in. She was tearing up her keyboard responding to anonymous relationship questions that people (more often women than men) sent to her blog email. Kalina owned *The Cooper Files*, a blog she'd started before she married Candice's brother Bryson. She was somewhat of a relationship expert and the blog was highly popular in the relationship advice field.

"Goodness, girl. How fast do you type?" Candice asked.

"Fast, especially when I'm answering a question that women should already know the answer to. Plus, Lizette's off today so here I am replying to a question from this woman who wants to know if her boyfriend is *sincere* when he says he'll never cheat on her again."

"Ugh. If she knows like I know, she'll kick him to the curb," Candice said. "Once a cheater, always a cheater."

"I joke about it but that's not necessarily the case," Kalina said.

Candice raised a brow. "It is with me."

"You say that now until you actually find yourself in that situation. It's kind of a difficult question to answer. A lot of factors go into these sorts of conflicts, like how long the couple has been together, if he's cheated on her before, if she's cheated on *him* before—there's never an easy answer."

"So if Bryson cheated on you, you'd keep him around?"

"I wouldn't know unless I was in that situation, but I don't have to worry about that. Bryson knows where it's at."

Kalina laughed as she finished typing then spun around in her chair, crossed her legs and looked at Candice. "You look nice," she said checking her out. She had on black pants and a yellow front-tie blouse.

"Thanks," Candice said.

"And you're glowing," Kalina commented as she stood up, walked over to Candice and hugged her sister-in-law.

"Oh, stop it," Candice said, blushing, making Kalina's point.

"You are!"

"No, I'm not. That's this yellow shirt doing funky things to my makeup. It's the angles—like Drake said. That's all."

Kalina chuckled. "Whatever the case, you look good, girl. Where are you coming from? Work?"

"Yeah, I ducked out early so I could catch you before you left to go home."

"Oh. How's everything going at Blackstone Financial Services? Barringer still seems to be a little flustered about trying to get the company back on track."

"He is, but Bella is keeping him somewhat sane at the moment," she said speaking of Calista and

Barringer's three-month-old daughter – the child they always wanted but thought they'd never have. She was definitely a miracle baby, and boy was she a gorgeous little thing – pretty just like her mother.

"I know she is, and I'm glad somebody can keep him sane. Whew." The woman laughed together. "Have a seat, girl," Kalina told Candice. "Take a load off. You look like you got something on your mind."

"Oh, you know me so well," Candice said, pulling the chair from Lizette's workstation to sit in. She stabbed her elbows in her thighs as she rested her chin on her interlocked hands.

"What's wrong, Candy?"

Candice hesitated and Kalina knew why. It was difficult to confide in someone who was married to her brother – her oldest brother. The strict one. But if she couldn't talk to Kalina about this, who would she talk to? Calista was busy with baby Bella and Junior. June and Everson – well, they had their marital struggles and were trying to get back on track and she definitely wasn't prepared for the backlash of telling Elowyn Blackstone that her only daughter had run off and gotten hitched.

So, Kalina it was...

"Well, I'm just going to say it because I'm tired of hiding it and I have to tell somebody or I'm going to explode."

"O-kay." Kalina looked at her, waiting for Candice's announcement but she appeared to be having a hard time getting it out. "Candy..."

"I got married," Candice blurted out.

Kalina's eyes grew big. "You did what!"

"I got married," Candice said smiling.

Kalina laughed. "Good one, Candy. Everybody knows you ain't got time for no man, so why are you up in here playing with me?"

"I'm serious, Kalina. I'm a married woman."

Kalina scrunched up her face as she analyzed Candice. Then she said, "First of all, you have to date somebody and get to know them to get married."

"Not necessarily. There are such things as marriages of convenience, arranged marriages—"

"Okay, Candice—stop playing with me."

Candice laughed. "I did none of those things so don't worry. I chose to date."

"You chose to date *who* exactly?"

Candice stared at the spot on her left finger where her ring was supposed to go. Every time she left Asheville after visiting Kurt, she took it off and kept it inside her purse. No one in Wilmington – more specifically – no one in her *family* was supposed to know she was married.

"You remember that guy I was telling y'all about named Kurt?"

"The cute guy you met at the boardwalk?"

Candice beamed. "Yes. He's the one. Well—"

"You married him?"

"Yes. We're—"

"You married him!" Kalina said louder.

"Yes. We're married."

"Okay, timeout," Kalina said standing up from her computer desk chair to lie on the sofa – the spot where she usually de-stressed and meditated while working. "When? How?"

"We've been secretly dating for five months. When month six came around, we decided to make it official."

"But why so fast?"

"Fast? How is that fast when you and Bryson dated for like three seconds?"

"Yeah, well that's *Bryson*," Kalina said beaming. "He's everything."

"Ew."

Kalina laughed. "He is."

"And Kurt is everything to me."

"If that's true, why keep him a secret?"

"Because I didn't want the family dynamic to ruin what we have. It's confusing enough as it is."

"Why?"

"Because Kurt works for The Champion Corporation."

"Oh. That's right! *That* guy," Kalina said when she realized The Champion Corporation was the company that wanted to acquire Blackstone Financial. "I remember telling you that dating him would be counter-productive."

"I remember, and I'm sure my brothers will say the same thing. I don't need them ganging up on me about this."

"Then that's going to be a problem for you, girl. You can't keep Kurt a secret forever."

"I know. I want to tell them. I just—I don't know how. Mom's gonna think I've lost it. According to dad, there is no man good enough for his baby girl—"

"Aw, that's so sweet."

"No, it ain't. Do you know what kind of pressure that puts me under? That makes me look for perfection, especially after the screwed-up relationship I had with Quinton." Candice released a heavy sigh.

"Not to overshadow your good news, that still has my head spinning by the way, but what exactly happened between you and Quinton?"

"As a woman, you have a certain intuition about the things going on with your man, you know, but I didn't have any alarms going off in my head. I thought Quinton and I were fine. That *I* was enough. Then things fell apart. He stopped talking to me, wouldn't take my phone calls, didn't answer my text messages and I didn't know what to think, so I assumed he'd found someone else. Then I found out it was Bryson who told Quinton to cease all contact with me. He hated Quinton from the jump and I didn't know why. Anyway, Bryson told Quinton to stop talking to me and later when I pressed him about why he would do something like that, he said it was because he saw Quinton having a cozy dinner with another woman."

"Oh my goodness."

"Yeah, hence my reluctance to tell him about Kurt."

"You need a plan. That's the bottom line. They need to know and they need to find out straight from you. You can't be tiptoeing around them. They need to recognize that you're their little sister, yes, but you're also a grown woman."

"You're right, but I don't have a plan. I was hoping I could bounce some ideas off of you."

"Okay. Let's hear 'em?"

"Um, what if I dropped it all on everybody at the same time during family dinner?"

"Ooh…I don't think you want that. You'll have like eight people screaming at you all at once."

"Then should I tell them all individually?"

"No. I think certain people should know before the whole squad knows. Like your parents. Bryson. The girls."

Candice chuckled. "You're naming everyone."

Kalina sat up and said, "I am, aren't I? Alright, scratch that. First, tell your parents. Then, after that we can have a girl's night and you can tell the ladies. Eventually, the news will get to your brothers without you having to tell them directly."

Candice bowed over with knots in her stomach.

"Look, Candy—it is what it is. If you love this

man, and you must do since you married him, you should want to tell the world about him. I'm sure Kurt doesn't want to remain a hidden husband. He should know the family."

"I know and I want him to know the family and I shouldn't feel so nervous to introduce him. It's killing me...and then there's something else—something I can't quite wrap my mind around."

"What's that?"

"When you married my brother, did you ever feel like something was missing?"

"Not at all, honey. Bryson got everything I need, and trust me when I say it ain't nothing missing. Nuh-thing!"

"Okay, okay. Spare me the visuals," Candice said. "I mean it's this feeling I've been having like what if there's someone else out there, you know."

"But I thought you said Kurt was your everything."

"He is. That's why I can't explain this feeling."

"I'm sure it's just a fluke. It's sort of like cold feet, but women usually get that before they get married. Since you and your lil' corporate crush got married so quickly, maybe the cold-feet-thing is happening."

"Yeah, I guess."

"But it won't last, especially if you know in your heart he's a good man and he's the one you want."

"Yeah. You're right."

"Anyway, stop stressing out and go get dinner, girl. You have a long way to go before this thing is over."

"Yeah, you're right about that."

"Don't make yourself sick, oh and don't worry. I won't mention anything to Bryson or anyone else."

"Okay. Thanks, Kali."

"No problem."

Chapter 5

After talking matters over with Kalina, Candice woke up Tuesday morning more optimistic than she'd been in a while. With her head held high, confidence on fleek, flat-ironed hair hanging around her shoulders, she sashayed into her office, placed her bag next to her desk and sat down taking a bite of the blueberry bagel she picked up from Panera Bread along the bumper-to-bumper morning drive. She logged into her computer and took a sip of coffee, reading emails as she picked up her cell to call Kurt.

FROM: Barringer Blackstone
TO: Candice Blackstone
CC: Garrison Blackstone
SUBJECT: Transition Issues @ Telmark

Candice,

I got a call from the CEO today over at Telmark. It seems they are having some issues integrating their system with ours. Follow up with IT and let's get this resolved quickly. We don't need any issues with this new client.

Thanks,

--

Barringer Blackstone | CEO
Blackstone Financial Services Group (BFSG)
Ext. 200

———

"Hello?"

"Oh, hey. Sorry 'bout that, babe. I was in the middle of reading an email Barringer sent me this morning."

"I tried to call you last night," he said.

"Well, good morning to you, too," she replied.

"Where were you?" he asked.

Candice was immediately taken aback by his tone. "What do you mean? I was home."

"Then why didn't you hit me back?"

"Because I had a pretty rough day, Kurt, and all I wanted to do was go to bed."

"So if I'm hearing this correctly, when my wife has a rough day, instead of talking to her husband about it, her solution is to go to bed. Or is that what this distance does to us? You're comfortable going to bed and not confiding in me because I'm not there."

"That's not it at all, Kurt—"

"I'm sure it is. When you're in Wilmington, you revert back to *single* Candice. When you're in Asheville, you're *married* Candice."

"Nope. Not at all. I didn't call you because I was thinking—more like doing some strategizing. My stomach was in knots. I was thinking about you.

About us. About how I'm going to relay the news about us to my family. It sounds easy to you, I know, but it's not so easy for me. So yes, I had a rough night of trying to process all of this—trying to think about how I was going to let my parents know I'm married and possibly moving from the east side of the state clear to the west side."

"Wow. *Possibly*, you say."

"Kurt, why does it seem like everything I say is offending you this morning. That's not what I'm trying to do."

"I know. I'm just frustrated by it all. Every morning I wake up in bed without you frustrates me."

"I know, but it won't be that way for long."

"I hope not. Anyway, I have to get to work. I'll check in with you later."

Candice placed her phone on the desk and sipped coffee, keying a reply to Barringer's email.

"Ay, are you coming?" Garrison asked, standing at the door.

"Oh. The meeting. Yes. And, good morning."

"Good morning."

"Tell Barry I'll be there in a moment. I need to get my files."

"Yep. Okay."

Candice took a moment to get herself together. She grabbed a few folders and her tablet. Barringer would want to know about the new clients she'd been working on, especially since he was back on the prowl, trying to increase Blackstone's revenue after losing The Blakeney Agency. She'd been working diligently to not only keep the current clients they had happy but also to get others to sign on with them.

She took her coffee cup and headed down the hallway to the conference room.

"Well, well, well, look who decided to show up," Barringer said.

"Don't start with me, Barry."

"How are you doing this morning, Candice?" Garrison asked.

"I'm doing okay, Gary. Thanks for being polite and asking me."

Barringer rolled his eyes. "Anyway, let's get down to business. First off, did you see that email I sent you this morning regarding Telmark?"

"Yes. I replied to you. I'll work on it today."

"Good. We need to keep our clients happy as well as secure new clients to get The Champion Corporation off of our backs. Have you had any luck in that arena?"

Candice opened a folder and flipped through some papers while saying, "Not really. I have some prospects, but they're with other companies right now and not ready to budge."

"Continue working on them," Barringer said. "I may have something for you to look into as well."

"Did you send me an email?"

"No. I'll just let you know now. Mom and Pops were out having dinner a few nights ago when he ran into an old business partner of his. He owns a company called CheckMate and it's just as big as The Blakeney Agency. Granted it doesn't have the same revenue stream Blakeney had, but it's a good prospect. Plus, the CEO knows dad already so it's pretty much a done deal. However, to seal the deal, he wants to break bread over it."

"When and where?" Garrison asked.

"Ribeye's, the restaurant over on Cantle Court. They want to meet on Monday around 5:30. Is that good?"

"They?" Candice questioned.

"Yes. The big boss is sending two of his

executives."

"Are we all going to meet them?" Candice asked.

"No. I figured you and Gary could handle this."

"Yeah. No problem," Garrison said. He was just now getting back into the swing of things at work. It had been hard on him for a while after losing Vivienne. Work gave him the distraction he needed until he could get back home to his son.

"Is that good with you, Candice?"

"Yes. That's fine," she said. Anything to help the company, she was willing to do.

"Beautiful," Barringer said, dramatically closing his laptop. "Well, that's all I had to discuss. Do you have anything further?"

"What's the latest on that Champion Corporation deal?" Garrison asked.

Candice cringed at the mention of The Champion Corporation.

"As far as I'm concerned there *is* no deal. There will *never* be a deal. They can't walk in here and take everything we worked so hard for. Everything dad built. I won't let that happen. What kind of businessman would I be if I folded and handed over everything without putting up a fight?"

Candice stayed quiet on the subject as she made the habit of doing with all discussions pertaining to The Champion Corporation. She'd already had a not so ideal conversation with Kurt early this morning and right now, she wanted to go call him and at least see where his head was at.

"Alright, guys, I need to get back to the office," Candice stood up and said.

"Me, too," Garrison added.

"Hey, Candy, let me holla at you for a minute," Barringer said.

Crap, she thought. *I almost made it out...*

Garrison proceeded toward the door and after he

exited, Barringer looked at Candice and asked, "You good?"

"Yeah. I'm *good*. Why are you asking me if I'm good?"

Barringer narrowed his eyes. "I have a hunch about these things."

"What *things*?"

He shrugged. "Don't know. I just feel like something is off with you. I haven't quite put my finger on it yet."

"That's because nothing's *off*. I'm working and minding my own business like always."

"Is that right?"

"Yeah, that's right. Now, tell me how my princess is doing," she said, a slick way to change subjects.

Barringer took the bait. He instantly smiled thinking of his daughter. "She's good, and that's another reason I asked you how you were. You used to come by to spend some time with Bella and hang out with Calista. Now, you keep to yourself."

"I'm not *keeping* to myself, Barry." To be honest, she was – spending her time with her new husband, but he couldn't know that. "I'm just busy. I have a life too, you know."

"Doing what? Running in and out of nail salons and beauty supply stores?"

She rolled her eyes. "I'm going back to my desk. Call me if you need assistance with something *job*-related."

"Yeah, ah'ight, sis. I catch your drift."

Candice took her folder and walked back to her office. She dialed Kurt from her cell and waited for him to answer. She wasn't sure if he would since he was at work.

"Hey," he said in a much softer, caring tone than before.

"Hi."

"I'm sorry about earlier," he said. "Sometimes I sit here and get so worked up with this situation, Candy."

"I know, and if it's any consolation, it's equally irritating for me. I want to be with you, too. That's why I'm going to talk to my parents tonight."

"Tonight? I thought you wanted me to be there so we could break the news to them together?"

"It'll probably be better this way. I don't want to wait anymore. I'm tired of waiting. I want to go ahead and do this right now."

"Okay. Do you need me to be on speakerphone?"

Candice chuckled. "No, I don't need you on speakerphone to talk to my parents. I got it. I'll call you later on tonight after I've dropped the news on them. I love you."

"I love you, too, girl. Now, get some work done."

"You get some work done and put a smile on your face before Desmond realizes something's wrong."

"Will do, baby. I'll talk to you later."

"Okay. Bye."

Chapter 6

She was a ball of nerves when she stepped on the first few steps of her parent's house. She knew they were home. They were always home. She could smell the aroma of food as soon as she pulled up in the driveway. Several times she considered turning back, putting it off yet again, but the time had come for her to finally get this off of her shoulders and tell them.

She pushed the doorbell and her father opened the door immediately almost like he'd been standing there. Waiting.

"Hey, daughter. What are you doing here, girl?"

"I can't just pop up to see my daddy?" she asked, then hugged her father. "I brought you some soda." She held up the bottle of root beer.

"I see. Come on in. Your mother's doing her thang in the kitchen."

"I know she is. I could smell it from the car. I hope you have enough for me, Ma."

Elowyn took a napkin and wiped her hands. She walked over to Candice and embraced her. "Of course I got some for you. How you doing, baby girl? I ain't seen you since the last family dinner about four weeks ago."

"I know. I've been busy."

"Barringer hasn't been working you too hard has he?" her father asked.

"No, not at all. It's just—"

"Did he tell you about CheckMate?" he cut in to ask.

"He did. Me and Gary are going to meet with them on Monday."

"Good. Like I told Barringer, it's as good as ours."

"*Ours*?" her mother said. "You hear that, Candy? The man doesn't know how to stop working to save his life. You may as well go back to Blackstone Financial honey," she told him.

Theodore smiled. "I'm not going back, dear, but if I see where I can assist, I don't mind throwing in my two cents every once in a while."

Candice walked over to the table where her mother had prepared her a plate. Elowyn then made one for herself and her husband before they joined her at the table.

A few bites into their meal, Candice said, "So, mom, dad, I have something I want to discuss with you two. Now, before I say this, I want you to keep an open mind."

"What's going on, sweetie?" Elowyn asked. "You know I don't like being kept in suspense. I'm too old to be waiting around for stuff."

"You're not old."

"Tell my knees that," she said chuckling.

Candice smiled. "Dad, make her stop."

"I will not," he said. "I'm glad she's complaining to somebody else about those knees for a change. I hear it every night, and every night she got me under the covers rubbing this and that. I don't mind it, though," he said then winked.

"Oh, jeez, please stop," Candice said.

"Ain't no need in hiding nothing," Theodore said. "We have five children—"

"Yep. Un, huh. I get it. I understand. Moving right along," Candice said. She cleared her throat. "So, as you're both aware, I took a break from relationships for a while—"

"You know, I meant to talk to you about that," Elowyn said interrupting. "Is it because of your brothers, because you know I can set them boys straight for you?"

"No, Ma," she replied, even though she had her reservations about introducing Kurt to her brothers. Kurt wanted nothing more than to feel a part of her family so he'd do whatever necessary – like endure countless interrogations from her brothers to win their favor if that would prove his love.

"What's the news you want to discuss?" her mother asked.

"Okay. Um—I've been seeing someone."

Theodore and Elowyn's forks hit the plates, giving Candice their full attention.

"His—his name is Kurt. Kurt Hempstead."

"And how long have you been seeing this *Kurt*? He must mean something to you if you're telling us about him now," her father said.

"Yeah, telling us after the fact," her mother added on.

She could already detect the impatience in their voices. Now was a good time to just let it all out. She said, "In answer to your question, Dad, we've been together for six months. Married for one of those months."

The frown in her father's forehead was deeper than the ditch beside a lonely country road. "You say what, now, because I *know* I didn't hear you correctly? I *couldn't* have."

"I said we've been married for a month."

Her mother crossed her arms and used the backrest of the chair to lean against. "You eloped, Candy?"

"Yes. I'm married."

"I—I don't know what to say," Elowyn said. "This is not how I expected my *only* daughter to get married."

Candice could see the hurt in her mother's eyes. That's what she didn't want – to hurt someone else by her actions.

"Did you not want me to be a part of your special day?"

"Mom—"

"And what do you want me to say now?" Elowyn probed further. "I don't even know the guy. And what about the things a mother and daughter do together when they're preparing for a wedding? The parties, bridal showers, the fun of looking for a dress together, cake tastings, picking out venues and setting up registries—we didn't get to do any of that. And where did you get married? Please don't say Vegas for goodness sakes..."

"Okay, first of all, please calm down. Of course I wanted you to be a part of my day. The decision to get married without all the family being around wasn't about you, Mother. And no, I didn't get married in Vegas—it was a small ceremony in Asheville."

Her father frowned and dipped his head back. "Asheville? So that's where this guy—a guy we don't know—is from, I take it."

"Yes, Dad. Kurt lives in Asheville."

"Which means, you're going to be moving there—leaving your family behind for a man you've known for six short months..."

"Dad—"

"How can a man prove himself in six months? How can you trust somebody after six months?"

"Wow...such a double standard. Did you ask Bryson the same thing when he married Kalina? They didn't know each other all that long."

"Bryson is my son. I know *him*."

"And you know *me*, but since I'm a woman I'm held to a different set of standards?"

"That's not what I'm saying at all and I'm sorry if you think it's coming across that way. As your father, I want to make sure you're well taken care of. I think it's my right and I don't know this man. He didn't come to me and ask for your hand in marriage. Back in my day, a man didn't marry a woman without asking for her father's blessing. It's a sign of respect."

"You assume that's his fault when it's not. He wanted to do all that. He wanted to talk to you. He wanted to have a traditional wedding. I'm the one who didn't want those things. Look, all you need to know at this point is I love Kurt and I know he's a good man."

"Then if you love him so much, why don't we know anything about him?" Elowyn asked.

"I want you to know him, Ma. In fact, the next time he comes to Wilmington, I would like to introduce him to both of you. Maybe we can sit down and have dinner and talk about this."

"What's there to talk about? You already married the boy now," her father said, then stood up and walked away from the table, leaving the rest of his food. Apparently, news of his daughter getting married made him lose his otherwise ferocious appetite.

All the life drained from Candice's face when she looked at her mother.

"What can I say, dear? We're worried about you. And you know he is. You're his only daughter."

Candice's face warmed over with irritation. "Why does everyone keep saying that? I'm aware I'm the only girl in this family. Trust me. It's been stamped into my head so many years of how I'm supposed to follow a different code of conduct than my brothers."

"Not necessarily."

"There's no need to deny it because it's true, mother. That's why I married Kurt without talking about it with anyone. I needed to do what was right for me without seeking anyone's approval."

Elowyn pushed her plate aside. She was done with her meal, too. "Okay, so at this point, it's already happened so there's no use in dwelling on what's already been done. So tell me about him."

Nervous and all, Candice still couldn't hide the smile that glowed on her face or the slight wetness in her eyes. "He's amazing, mom. You know I wouldn't just marry any old guy."

"What makes him amazing?"

And so the interrogation begins...

She pinched the small tear from her eyes and said, "He's an overall good man."

"Has he ever been married?"

"No, he's never been married."

"Does he have kids?"

"Definitely not! I couldn't handle a man with kids."

"Does he work?"

"Yes. He works. He's a marketing manager at a major corporation in Asheville," she said, hoping to leave it at that.

"What corporation?" Elowyn pressed.

Candice turned around to see if her father was any where in sight or earshot of them and when she saw that he wasn't, she looked at her mother again and responded, "He works for The Champion Corporation."

"The Champion Corporation...why does that name sound familiar?"

"Because it's—" She hesitated to tell her for obvious reasons, then decided she was going to be transparent about her relationship with Kurt. She didn't want to hide anything that could come back to look suspicious at a later time when her family finally did find out. And they *would* find out. "The Champion Corporation is the company who wants Blackstone to merge with them."

"Wow. And you're dating a man from that company?"

"No. I'm married, mom."

"Right. Married..." Elowyn shook her head. She didn't have to verbalize her displeasure. Candice could read through the lines, but at least her mother didn't get up from the table and give up on the conversation like her father had done. She was surprised by that. She was a daddy's girl. They could usually talk about anything and being the youngest, she always felt the closest to her parents, but the news of her marriage sent him over the edge.

"When your father finds out about this, he's going to hit the roof."

"Why?"

"Why do you think, Candy? Your *new* husband works for a company that wants to basically dissolve Blackstone Financial. And besides all that I—I still can't believe you're married. It all happened so fast."

"It wasn't fast. It just seems that way to you because I'm just now telling you about this. What I need from you and dad is to trust my judgment.

Trust that you raised a daughter who followed her heart and is doing what she thinks is right for herself without anyone else making her decisions for her. Isn't that what you want?"

"Of course that's what I want, but I have to be honest with you. I feel like you've gone about this all wrong—well, not *wrong* but, you know—not the way these things are typically done. It could've been handled a lot better."

"I know and—" Candice sighed. "I know it's going to take some getting used to but what's done is done. Kurt is my husband and he's always going to be my husband."

"When are we going to meet him?"

"Soon. I'll talk it over with him to see when we could make it happen."

"Good. In the meantime, I'll try to calm your father down a little."

"Thanks, Mom. I appreciate it. I'm sorry I came here and ruined your dinner."

Elowyn stood up and walked around the table to hug her daughter. "You didn't ruin anything. You just shook us up. That's all. What I do know is, this Kurt fellow better live up to the hype."

"You'll love him. Trust me."

Chapter 7

Kurt loved his job. Working for The Champion Corporation brought him financial stability and afforded him to live comfortably in Asheville. He had a nice, four-bedroom house with a two-car garage. He lived in a gated community that came with a pool, playground and tennis courts and whenever he wasn't home, he had the financial freedom to access all the city had to offer. But now, things were different.

Loyalty to his wife took precedence over the job. That's why when Dante Champion, CEO of the company, called a meeting this morning, he didn't want to attend but knew he had to. No one turns down Dante Champion's meeting requests, plus, as a manager, he needed to be kept in the loop of what was going on with the company. Still, Kurt found himself checking out. He'd especially checked out when he heard Dante say, "I'm calling Tennyson and Savannah off the investigation into Forsyth and Blakeney. I don't want any parts of it. Quite frankly, I'm getting tired of dealing with it."

Tennyson Tillman and Savannah Champion were the two lawyers who worked for the corporation.

"Wait—what investigation?" Kurt asked.

Desmond spoke up to say, "Dante wanted Tennyson and Savannah to look into the details of Forsyth's acquisition of Blakeney. If you recall, shortly after they acquired them, they dropped them. That's when we picked up Blakeney."

Kurt nodded.

"Ay, have you already made them aware of this?" Dimitrius Champion asked his brother. He handled the accounts for the company.

"No, but I will immediately after this meeting is over," Dante answered.

"I know there are certain things around here that are well over my pay grade," Kurt said, "But me and Desmond have been working to acquire Blackstone for a while. How did I not know about this Blakeney investigation?"

"It was probably just an oversight, Kurt," Dante replied. "Besides, I'm calling it off before it ever started, so no harm, no foul."

Desmond spoke up to ask, "Then what direction are we going with Blackstone because I'll be honest—this is getting out of hand. Maybe we should let them be."

"I agree that it's getting out of hand," Dante responded, "But as for letting them be, no. I say we take another crack at them. I don't want to hear any more talks of merging. Let's change the dialogue to buying them out. We have their biggest client. Why can't we buy them as well?"

Kurt had to literally bite his tongue to keep quiet. If he said he thought it was a bad idea and they found out he was married to Candice, they would know right away that his answer was based on personal reasons and not the best interest of the company. If he said he thought it was a good idea, he would be doing harm to Blackstone Financial and he couldn't do that to Candice. He was stuck in the middle of all of this.

Desmond looked at Dimitrius before they both returned their gazes to Dante.

"Why the change of heart?" Desmond asked.

"I need this to be over so we can focus our energy on other pursuits."

"They're plenty of finance companies around, though, Dante," Dimitrius said. "Why are you zeroing in on this one?"

"For the reason I just stated. We already have their biggest client and while there are plenty of other finance companies we could go after, Blackstone is fairly large in size and has a massive potential for growth. Plus, I get the feeling Blakeney would rather do business with Blackstone."

"If that's the case, why'd they leave them in the first place?" Kurt asked.

Dimitrius chimed in to answer, "Because Blackstone doesn't have the new technologies that most of their competition offers."

"That would leave a lot of people out of work, wouldn't it?" Kurt asked.

"Not necessarily," Dante replied. "We can bring them all on board. They can still work out of Wilmington and after brainstorming earlier, I don't think it would be a bad idea to open up an office in the Raleigh-Durham area."

"I don't know about this," Desmond said. "It sounds like a huge undertaking."

"Then what do you suggest."

"I think we may need to back off and let Blackstone be. We go our way and they go theirs. Me and Kurt have already been down this road. Barringer Blackstone isn't letting go of his company."

"Desmond's right," Kurt said. "He'll never go for it. It'll probably be a waste of time going over there again." He said he would stay quiet on the matter, but he saw a way in and he took it. If he could convince the team to back off of Blackstone, it would alleviate some pressure in his marriage. No one from the company knew he was married to her. Had they known, they'd certainly made sure he stayed away from anything pertaining to the company. Business with pleasure mixed just as well as oil and water, and when it came to business, Dante, Desmond and Dimitrius didn't play around with their money.

Kurt knew that all too well. He'd thought about asking Desmond for permission to take a step back from anything Blackstone-related, but then Desmond would want to know why. Even more importantly, if he removed himself from Blackstone discussions, he would lose the advantage of knowing in advance what was going on with his wife's company. He'd be completely in the dark.

Dante thought for a moment and after tapping his pen on his desktop, he said, "I think we should proceed. We got a pretty good shot at taking them. Giving up now isn't the way to go. What I need you to do, Desmond and Kurt, is convince them that this is the way to go. Show them the numbers. If they turn you down this time, we'll let them be."

"Alright. Got it," Desmond said. "I'm booked for the rest of the week, but I can be out that way on Tuesday. Is that good with you, Kurt?"

"Yes. That's fine."

"Good," Dante said. "Stay a few days if you need to. Let's see if we can finally get some traction on this."

"Yep. We'll take care of it."

Chapter 8

Kurt went home after the workday and fell across the couch. He was still dressed in the black suit he wore and had on his shoes and all. He just laid there exhausted from the meeting that had him feeling like he was being pulled in two different directions and at the moment, he wasn't sure what to do about it.

He'd dozed off when the ringing of his cell phone woke him up again. He took it from the coffee table and answered in a groggy voice, "Hello?"

"Hey. Were you sleep?"

"I dozed off. I had a rough day."

"Aw...wish I was there to give you a back rub or something."

"I need a lot more than a back rub, baby."

Candice smiled.

"You must've had a hard time last night, huh?"

"Oh, you mean with my parents. My goodness, Kurt—I knew this would be difficult for them, but I didn't know how much."

"What happened?"

"Well, my dad walked out of the room. In the middle of dinner, actually..."

"Oh, no."

"He didn't like the fact that they didn't meet you first, I suppose. And he said he felt like you should've asked him for my hand in marriage. I told him you wanted to, but I didn't want you to."

"You should've left that blame on me."

"I can't do that when it wasn't your fault."

"I don't care—whatever would take the pressure off of you, I'll take responsibility for."

"I appreciate that, Kurt, but taking the blame for things that aren't your fault wouldn't do anything to help my family dynamic. It's almost as if they think I'm not capable of making a good decision when it comes down to men. Who did they think I would bring home? Tyrone Biggums? Somebody scratching their neck with white lips, begging for crack rocks?"

Kurt laughed.

"Oh, and my mother went so far as to ask where you worked. Guess she wanted to make sure you weren't a bum."

"Did you tell her?"

"I had to. I can't lie to my mama."

"Okay, so now, your family knows I work for their worst enemy."

Candice chuckled. "You sound paranoid. The Champion Corporation is not Blackstone Financial's worst enemy."

"You thought so before you fell for me."

"Well, yeah, but let's get one thing straight, Mr. Hempstead. As far as I'm concerned, *you* are not The Champion Corporation. You just so happen to *work* for them."

"If you think your brothers will understand that logic, you're wrong."

"My brother's won't understand any logic. I'm just telling you where I stand. You don't own that company. Ultimately, whatever's going on between the two companies is up to the CEOs to decide."

"Right," Kurt said, feeling awful. He'd already decided not to tell her about Dante's new buyout plan – at least not yet. That was sure to upset her.

"I can't help but think that maybe we should've waited to get married," Candice said.

"You didn't want that."

"No, I didn't, but seeing how upset my parents were last night had me rethinking everything."

"Even us?"

"No. Not us. Just the way we did everything. Had we done this the traditional way from the jump, we'd be living together right now. Instead, we're pedaling backward while trying to move forward...going up the down escalator trying to get to the second floor."

"Who's to say we didn't do this right? Okay so we didn't have a traditional wedding—that's not a big deal. Look, all I want is for us to be together so whatever we have to do to get there, let's just keep taking it one step at a time."

"You're right." Candice sighed. "Anyway, how was your day?"

"It was rough," he said, still hearing the words, *buy them out* echoing in his mind. How was he going to break that news to her? She was stressed out enough as it was.

"What happened?"

"Oh, just normal work stuff, baby. Just know I'm laying over here on the sofa, still in my work clothes missing you right now."

"I'm missing you, too. This long-distance thing is a lot harder than I thought it would be."

"Well, we're on the home stretch now. You've talked to your parents so you can check that off the list. Now, you just need to break the news to your brothers. Do you have a plan on how you're going to do that?"

"Um...somewhat, I guess. I figure if I tell the girls, they can relay the news to their husbands. Kalina knows already so she's putting together a girl's night out on Friday and I'm going to break the news to the rest of them."

"I didn't know you told Kalina."

"Yeah, I told her on Monday."

"And she didn't have any crazy reactions, I take it?"

"No, well she was a little shocked that I was married. That's the bit of news that will throw everybody off—the fact that I'm married. If we were dating, they probably wouldn't have much to say, but since we're married, everybody wants to know how it happened so soon."

"Just tell them your boy spit that game in your ear and you had no choice but to marry me."

Candice laughed. "Hush, Kurt."

"What? That ain't true? I didn't get you by my handsome good looks and charm."

"Okay, that had something to do with it, but—"

"But what?"

"You're an overall good person and I respected and admired you before I fell in love with you," she replied.

"See, you can't be talking like that when we're this far apart. My hands are twitching to get a hold of your body."

"Is that right?"

"Yeah, that's right."

"No worries. That'll make it that much more special when you can finally touch me, huh?"

"Yes, it will."

Candice smiled, closed her eyes and could swear she could feel his warmth touch her even though he was five hours away in another city. Then she said, "Listen, Kurt, go take a shower, get comfortable and have a good night's rest. We'll talk tomorrow."

"Okay. I love you."

"Love you, too."

Chapter 9

Candice passed on alcohol for the second time during girl's night. She needed to have a clear head when she broke the news of her marriage but Kalina, the organizer of tonight's girl's night thought the opposite. She just knew Candice would need a drink to ease into the conversation and so the ladies met at one of their favorite spots on the boardwalk. Candice had been overcome with a feeling of serendipity from the moment she arrived. This place – the Wilmington downtown boardwalk – was the exact place where she'd met Kurt and right now, she couldn't stop thinking about him. It was almost like he was here with her. But when you love a man as much as she loved Kurt, he was always there, even though he wasn't.

"Earth to Candice," Kalina said, then brightened her eyes at Candice, trying to snap her out of her reverie.

"Oh, sorry y'all. My mind is in a million different places right now."

"We've noticed," Calista said, "But I can't talk about you. My mind is in a million places too, thinking about Bella—not that Barry doesn't know what to do, but I still worry."

"Aw," Kalina said placing a hand on her heart. "Wait—this is your first girl's night out since the baby isn't it?"

"It is," Calista answered. "I'm so in love with her I didn't want to come. I never knew motherhood would zap the partying right out of me."

"Oh, is that how it works?" Candice asked, amused.

"For me it is."

"Then we better party all we can, ladies," June said, knowing she didn't have a partying bone in her body.

"Bella is so sweet, Cali," Candice said. "And by the way, let me know whenever you need me to babysit."

"Really, Candice? How are you going to babysit when you've been MIA, taking trips and whatnot? You don't have time to babysit."

"Who told you I've been MIA?"

"Barry said you've been hightailing it out of the office early most Fridays."

"Did he really say that?" Candice asked.

"Yep, and inquiring minds want to know why," Calista said.

Candice looked up at the girls to see all eyes beaming back at her. Kalina smiled and lifted her brows, subtly telling Candice to proceed with the news she wanted to tell them.

"Okay, well I've been seeing someone."

June giggled. "We already know there's a man involved. What I want to know is who is he and how long has this secret rendezvous been going on?"

Candice was all smiles when she said, "His name is Kurt."

"I told you!" Calista said to June. "Didn't I tell you?"

"Yeah, you told me," June said.

"Wait, you already knew?" Candice asked.

"Yeah. I knew the moment you told us about how Kurt had approached you with his business card. Something about the way you told the story made me realize you liked him more than what you led on."

"I think it was the fact that she was blushing," Kalina said.

"I was not blushing, Kalina."

"Oh yeah you were," June said.

The women laughed.

"Anyway, how long have you been seeing him?" Calista asked.

"Six months."

"Wow," June said. "Kudos to you for managing to keep this quiet for six months."

"Yes, and before I lose the nerve to tell you, there's more."

"Are you pregnant?" June asked. "Elowyn is always on the prowl for more grandbabies and I noticed you didn't order a cocktail."

"Oh my God! Are you pregnant, Candy?" Calista asked all excited, hoping Bella was due to have a new little cousin soon.

"No, I'm not pregnant."

"Are you sure? You're wolfing down those nachos like you're eating for two."

"I'm just hungry. Trust me. There's no baby in this stomach." Candice finished chewing then said, "I'm married." She dug around in her purse to find the ring she was tired of hiding. When a person married their soulmate, what use was there in hiding it? It shouldn't matter what anyone thought as long as they were happy.

"Wait, you say what now?" June asked, sitting straight up in her chair.

"I said, I'm married," Candice repeated, sliding her ring onto her finger as she did so.

"You're married!" Calista said.

"Yes, and keep your voice down, girl. You're causing a scene," Candice said.

Calista jumped out of her seat, ran around the table and wrapped her arms around her.

"Congratulations," June said leaving her chair to hug her as well.

"Yes. Congratulations," Kalina said, glad that Candice had finally let the cat out of the bag.

"So how did it happen?" Calista asked.

"Well, we were dating for five months. When the sixth month came around, we both knew we only wanted to be with each other. He gets me. I get him. We *got* married."

"Where?"

"We went to this cute, quaint little venue in Asheville."

June set her martini glass on the table. "Asheville? He lives in Asheville?"

"Yes, and I'll be living there soon."

"No! Ut-uh. Ain't gon' happen," Calista said. "Tell Kurt he has to move here."

Candice smiled. "See, that's why I had to date my man in private. I knew how difficult this would be for everyone."

"Did you tell your parents yet?" Kalina asked.

"I did. I went over there for dinner last night. Dad got up and walked out of the room. Mom wasn't too thrilled either. I mean, I get it. They were blindsided, but at some point, they have to come to the realization that I have to live my own life and stop living behind the shadow of other people."

"Yeah, that's true," June said. "I still don't want you to leave, though."

"I know. Anyway, it's no longer a secret, so I

don't care if my brothers know. They're going to have a stroke when they find out."

"They'll get over it," Kalina said. "I honestly don't think Bryson is going to have a hard time with it."

"Please," Candice said. "He's the ringleader. Then Barringer gon' add his freakin' two cents. Everson and Gary haven't really been on my back with the overprotective crap but you watch—as soon as they find out it's gon' be a problem, especially when they find out who the guy is."

"Why's that a factor?"

"Because Kurt works for The Champion Corporation—the company who now has Blackstone's largest client. The company who also wants Blackstone to merge with them."

"Oh. Wow," Calista said. "When Barringer hears that, he's going to flip."

"I know, but I'm not hiding him anymore. I won't do it, so however he reacts is just how he'll react."

"So how has it been working out?" Calista asked, "Is he here right now, or—?"

"No. He's still in Asheville. Still working."

"When is he due back this way? We definitely have to have a little get-together."

"I'm not sure. I'll find out when I talk to him tonight."

"Too bad he won't be here for the family dinner on Sunday," Kalina said. "That would've been perfect."

"Nah. I think it's still too early, especially for dad. I'm telling you—he was livid. He walked out in the middle of dinner. I ain't never seen him do that."

"He'll be okay," Kalina said. "I think it's sweet that he and your brothers care about you as much

54

as they do."

"I guess so, but at the same time, it can be overbearing."

June nodded. "I can see that. That's why I think you need to set some boundaries. There are certain things they can do when it comes to looking out for you. Completely controlling your life shouldn't be one of those things."

"I wouldn't worry too much about it," Kalina said.

"I'm not," Candice said even though she knew that wasn't true. "Anyway, how's everybody else?"

"Oh my goodness—life is so good to me right now," Calista said. "Me and Barry have been through it but we came out victorious with a beautiful baby girl. And our marriage is stronger than ever. He still gets on my nerves, though."

"Then all is well."

The women erupted in laughter.

"Everything is fine on my end," she added. "Bryson and I are fine. He's all that and a few bags of chips. Y'all know how he rolls."

"Has Everson been behaving himself, June?" Candice asked, especially since June and Everson had been going through a rough patch.

"Girl, yes. He's home more and it actually feels like we're a new couple again. Like you and Kurt."

Candice smiled asking, "What is the new couple feeling?"

"You know—when you can't wait to talk to that person on the phone. You kiss all day long. Whenever you see each other, body parts start to tingle just being in close proximity. *That* new feeling. When that feeling is lost, that's when a marriage is in trouble, I think."

Kalina nodded. "Not necessarily. You can't expect everything will always be that way.

Unfortunately, life is going to happen and cut right into those rosy moments and test your faithfulness to each other. That's how it works. I see it all the time."

"Have you and Bryson been through some of those times, Kalina?" Candice asked.

"Most definitely. There are so many factors that go into marriage. It won't just be marital bliss all the time. No one should expect that."

"Amen," Calista said, throwing up her hand.

June raised her glass and said, "I second that."

"I think that's why a lot of people end up getting divorced," Kalina said, "Because they think marriage is supposed to be all celebratory like the wedding and reception was. Then when problems come up, they don't know how to handle it. I'm not saying this to scare you, Candice. I'm just being real."

"Oh, I'm not scared at all. I didn't get married to turn around and get divorced when things don't go as planned. As it is, me and Kurt are starting out rocky only because of this long-distance between us. Then the family...ugh..."

"Well, it's *your* marriage," Kalina told her. "Don't get me wrong, I don't want you to leave us girl, but you have to live your life. We can't live your life for you."

"I wish my brothers understood that."

"I'll talk to Bryson," Kalina said.

"And you know I'll talk to Barringer," Calista added. "I'm not sure if he'll listen. Knowing him, he won't, but I'll make an effort."

"Okay. That's better than nothing."

"So how does it feel being married?" June asked. "Like do you still get butterflies in your stomach when you see him?"

"I do, but lately, I've been having this feeling like

I'm sort of questioning myself if he's the one when I know he's the one. I don't know why I'm so uneasy about this now."

"It's probably the distance," June said. "Long-distance relationships will have you thinking all kinds of stuff."

"Yeah. If you're sure he's the one, then I'm sure that uneasy feeling will go away," Calista added. "Like June said, it's probably the long-distance."

"Yeah. You're probably right. I'm so glad I get to have these discussions with y'all."

"Yeah, so what are you going to do when you leave?" Kalina asked.

"Hey, there's always the phone. Video chat. I'll find a way."

"It won't be the same without you here, though," June said fanning her eyes.

"Stop before you make me cry," Candice told her. "Let's have some fun."

"Now you're talking," Calista said.

* * *

Later when she was back at her apartment after a couple of drinks and too many laughs to count, she kicked off her heels, relieved that she'd made another step in the saga that was the current state of her life. It was unnerving thinking about what was to come and all the heat she was sure her brothers would bring, so to ease her mind of the drama, she called Kurt.

"I didn't expect you to call me," he said.

"I told you I would."

"Yeah, but I figured you'd be a lil' tipsy after girl's night."

"Nah. I had two martinis and they weren't strong at all."

"You told them about us and you only had two drinks?"

She smiled. "Yes, and those came *after* I told them. I wanted to have a clear head when I told them about this man I married who's stealing me away from them."

Kurt grinned. "How did they take it?"

"They were surprised, but it was a good conversation. Kalina already knew, of course. Calista and June were shocked about the marriage, but they claimed they already knew I was seeing you."

"How would they know that?"

"I don't know. I think they were just pulling my leg."

"Refresh my memory—which one is married to Barringer?"

"Calista. June is married to Everson."

"Okay. I'm anxious to meet your family."

"In due time, babe. In due time. Anyway, I'm exhausted. I need to take a shower and hop in the bed."

"I'm already in bed, wishing you were here."

"Kurt..."

"I don't have on any clothes. No shirt, no boxers—nothing."

"Oh my goodness...I can't believe you're doing this to me."

"I thought I'd give you a little motivation to get here faster. So tell me, love—how long before this is over?"

"I'm not sure at the moment."

"Have you begun packing?" he asked.

"Not yet. I'm waiting to get over the hurdle of telling everyone about us first."

"Well, now that you've told the women, I'm sure your brothers know."

"Yes, I'm sure they do."

"You haven't had any phone calls from them yet?"

"No. I literally just got home. If anybody calls me tonight, trust me—I ain't answering."

"Well, get some sleep and call me tomorrow."

"I will."

"In the meantime, just know I'm over here naked and wishing you were over here naked, too."

"You're such a tease, Mr. Hempstead. Put that thang away and go to bed. Goodnight."

"Goodnight, baby."

Chapter 10

"Hey beautiful," Kurt said stepping into his mother's house. She no longer lived in his childhood home since she'd remarried. He doubted if she wanted to stay there simply because of the memories between those walls. They weren't all bad. There were some good ones. Still, she needed to move on and so she did – moved right into her new husband's house.

"Oh, hi there son. I didn't think you'd be over here so fast."

"I wasn't doing anything," he said then pressed his lips to her cheeks. "Now where's this cabinet you need me to move?"

"We'll get to that in a minute. Sit down and talk to your mother."

He smirked and sat on the couch next to her. He wondered why she would ask him to come over to move something when she had a perfectly capable husband. Now he knew why. She wanted to talk. "What's up, Ma? Where's Carl, by the way?"

"He went out with a few of the guys."

"Oh, so you conveniently call me over here to move something or is this about something else?"

"I just want to talk to my son. Is there any harm in that?"

"No, Ma."

"Good." She looked at him from head to toe and asked, "So, what's going on with you? How's everything?"

He smirked. "By everything, I assume you're talking about Candice."

"Of course. How is she doing? I haven't seen her since you two told me you had gotten married."

"She's doing good. She was just here this past weekend."

"Then y'all ain't living together yet I take it?"

"Not quite. We're getting close."

"But, son, aren't you tired of all the back and forth?"

"Ma, it's fine. We'll be fine."

"That may be true, but still—you need some stability in your life. Unfortunately, me and your father couldn't provide that for you all the time, but I at least want to see you happy in your own life, son."

"I am happy, mother. What makes you think I'm not happy?"

"Well, for one, you're married to a girl who's not here."

"She's not here at the moment, but she will be."

"When?"

"Soon. I don't have an exact date but we're working on it."

"Are you sure about that? Looks like you're the only one working on it."

"Okay, Ma, I'm going to stop you right there. Candice is going through a lot in Wilmington, trying to talk to her parents about us and make sure they're okay and all that. It's been stressful on her."

"Look—all a mother wants for her son is for him

to be with a woman who'll love and care for him just as well as she does."

"Candice *does* love me. I have no doubt about that."

"I don't doubt it either, but why isn't she here? Something doesn't feel right about the whole ordeal."

"Mother, trust me. I know what I'm doing and I also know there's no other woman for me. Candice is my wife. We're making this work no matter how difficult it is at the moment."

"Just tell me if my only son is moving away. Can you tell me that?"

"I'm not one-hundred percent sure what's going to happen right now. One thing I do know is, I don't want you over here worried to death about what's going on in my life when you have your own life to live. I'll be just fine," he said, taking her hand into his. "You have to trust that the man you raised is capable of handling his own."

"I know. I just love you so much, son."

"And I love you. Now stop worrying about me and show me where this cabinet is."

"It's the one right over there in the corner. It needs to go over there near the front door."

"Okay," Kurt said, standing up. "Let me take care of this so I can treat you to breakfast this morning."

"Alright, son."

* * *

Candice got out of bed, snacked on a bowl of Cinnamon Toast Crunch for breakfast and just as she was done with her quick morning meal, the doorbell rang. She didn't question who was at her door. It was probably one of her neighbors. One had a habit of borrowing things and the other she considered somewhat of a friend. She even watched her five-year-old daughter occasionally.

Candice took a glance through the peephole and saw neither neighbor. What she saw made her stomach curl. She opened the door and there stood Barringer, Bryson, Everson and Garrison.

Before she could say anything, Everson said, "I'm only here because Barringer said it was an emergency."

"There's no emergency," Candice said.

"Oh, I beg to differ," Barringer said stepping into her apartment.

The other brothers followed him inside like a clique of gangsters.

"And you *know* why we're here," Barringer said.

"Then somebody enlighten me," Garrison spoke up to say. "When you first said to meet over here, I thought Candice was in trouble or something."

"She *is* in trouble," Barringer said.

Candice rolled her eyes.

Bryson sat on the armrest of the sofa and didn't say a word.

Barringer looked at Candice and asked, "On what planet did you think it would be a good idea to marry some cat from the company that's trying to tear Blackstone Financial to shreds?"

"What?" Garrison asked.

"Yeah, Gary," Barringer said. "Let me *enlighten* you of what's going on here. Our sister done ran off and got hitched to the enemy."

"He's not the enemy, Barringer," Candice said. "Why don't you just calm down and stop making everything about you."

"How am I making this about me? It's *way* bigger than me. It's about our father's legacy. His company—something you obviously care nothing about."

"Of course I care about dad's company. I work there. It's my job!"

"Not for long, especially now that you're moving to Asheville to be with the enemy."

The enemy. She could just choke him.

"You're moving to Asheville, Candy?" Bryson asked.

"Ye-yes. I'm moving."

"Okay, timeout," Garrison said. "Candy, did you get married?"

"Yeah, she got married," Barringer said before Candice could answer. "Look at her hand."

The brother's eyes all settled on the diamond sparkling on her left ring finger.

Candice sat on the sofa, buried her face in her hands and released a heavy sigh. She knew her brothers wouldn't take it easy on her when they found out about Kurt, but she didn't think it would be this frustrating. She could already feel a headache coming on as she held her head in her hands. This was the story of her life – well what little life she had that wasn't controlled by her brothers. All throughout high school, she had to deal with their constant over-protection. Even in college they kept tabs on her. Why was she allowing this to continue as a twenty-nine-year-old woman?

"Yes, I'm married, Gary."

"When did this happen?" Garrison and Everson asked in sync.

"We got married a month ago."

"*We*, who?" Garrison asked.

"I'll tell you who he is," Barringer said. "He's an executive who works for The Champion Corporation. He came down here with Desmond Champion trying to convince Blackstone to merge with them. I guess since we didn't take the offer, they found a new *in*." He gestured toward Candice.

"That's not true."

"It *is* true. You really think this guy is interested in you?"

"He is—"

"Then why was the marriage so quick and secret?" Barringer asked. "Tell me that. None of us knew about it. Found out from mom and dad that you didn't tell them either. Was that Kurt's plan or yours? I bet any money it was his."

Candice stood up and said. "Okay, stop! What is this? You're interrogating me for living my life? I don't stalk y'all and tell you what to do. I'm grown, okay, and I don't need anyone's permission for my decisions. If you don't like it, fine, don't like it, but you *will not* tell me what to do with my life. And you definitely *will* not tell me who I can and can't love."

"Whoa, okay, calm down, Candice," Garrison said.

"You need to tell your crazy brother to calm down," Candice shot back, gesturing toward Barringer.

"*Everybody* calm down," Bryson said to diffuse the situation. "Let's talk this through. Candy, do you love this man?"

"His name is Kurt, and yes I love him. I never would've married him if I didn't love him."

"I think the frustration surrounding us is, we don't know this guy," Bryson said. He'd even thought about asking their cousin, Rexford – a police officer – to do a background check on him. "As your brothers, we love you and we've always protected you—"

"And I appreciate that, Bryson, but you have to see how overwhelming this is for me to always feel like I have to constantly meet your standards."

"That's the thing, sis—it's not about meeting *our*

standards. It's making sure the man who's captured your heart meets our standards. I don't want you to get hurt."

"I'm entitled to make my own mistakes. If I end up getting hurt in the end, it's my mistake to make."

"Okay," Bryson said. He couldn't argue with that. For once he understood her position. He was married to a woman before Kalina came along. The woman had cheated on him, left him and subsequently, he ended up filing for divorce. It was an experience he had to go through and he eventually saw the woman for what she was. She wasn't right for him. Candice deserved to have her own experiences but if he could spare her...

"I don't like the fact that he works for The Champion Corporation," Barringer said.

"Yeah," Everson added. "I don't even work at Blackstone and that smells fishy."

"I'm telling you it's not like that," Candice said coming to her man's defense yet again. "Besides, Blackstone will be okay, right? I have a meeting with the new client dad was telling us about. I'm expecting that to go over well. We don't need any support from The Champion Corporation, we certainly don't need a bailout and I thought you'd already told them all negotiations were off the table anyway, Barry."

"I did, so why are they coming here on Tuesday for a follow-up meeting."

Candice frowned and looked shocked for a moment. "What?"

"Oh, your lil' boyfriend didn't tell you he was coming to town, huh? Eleanor confirmed it— Desmond Champion and Kurt Hempstead will be here to discuss more *options* they said. If this *Kurt* guy truly had your best interests at heart, why didn't you know about this meeting?"

That's a good question, Candice thought. "It was probably just an oversight."

"Or maybe it was intentional," Barringer said.

"Look, before we jump to conclusions about Kurt, we should at least talk with the man and feel him out to see what his motives are," Garrison said.

"That should've happened before Candy ran off and married him," Barringer said.

"Alright, Barry. Enough," Bryson said. "Gary is right. Since we know he'll be here on Tuesday, let's take him out and see what he's really up to."

"Um, hello—I'm right here in case y'all forgot I was in the room," Candice said.

Everson chuckled.

"Let's go," Barringer said heading for the front door. Everson and Garrison gave Candice a half hug before they left.

Bryson stayed back to chat one-on-one with his sister. He perched up on the armrest of the couch and asked, "How could you run off and marry this guy? Do our parents know?"

"Yes. I told them already."

"And?"

"And what?"

"How did they react?"

"Well, dad was upset. Mom was too, but at least she heard me out and didn't leave the room."

Bryson raised a brow. "Dad left the room?"

"Yeah. We were having dinner. He got up and left his food right there on the table."

"Listen—I'm not going to pretend like this isn't a shock. When Kalina told me last night, I was completely blindsided."

"I know."

"All I'm saying is, you could have at least introduced him to us first."

"Why? So y'all could interrogate him and make

him run for the hills to get away?"

"One day you'll appreciate how much we care about you, sis."

"I'm sure," she said, "But in the meantime, can you make sure Barringer keeps a level head? He's always barking about something and I can't have him acting a fool in this meeting on Tuesday."

"Yeah, I'll talk to him. He'll be fine. You know it takes him a minute."

"That's what I'm worried about. I never know when he's going to explode."

"Well, I hope Kurt has a backbone. That's all I can say."

"He can handle his own. Trust me. I just don't want to deal with Barringer's ranting. If he has a problem with him, business or otherwise, things can be talked out grown-man-style instead of blaming people and accusing Kurt of marrying me for professional gain. That's absurd. Who would do something like that?"

"People have done worse."

"So you agree with him?"

"No, I don't. I'm a little surprised that you'd make this move knowing how close of a family we are. I'm not surprised at dad's reaction. I feel the same way. But, hey, I'm open to having a one-on-one with this guy...see what he's made of."

"Well, I appreciate that, Bryson. I'm surprised you're open to doing that considering how much you hated Quinton."

Bryson smirked then stood up. "I'm not barking up that tree. I'll see you tomorrow night."

"Tomorrow night?"

"Yes. Sunday dinner. Mom and Dad's."

"Oh, jeez. With so much going on, I almost forgot. Okay. Yes. I'll see you tomorrow night."

Chapter 11

"Hello everybody," Candice said when she walked into her parent's home. She'd been the last to arrive only because she wasn't sure if she wanted to come. She didn't want the dinner conversation to revolve around her and Kurt. She wanted the family to get along. To enjoy good food and good conversation with her mother's coconut cake and cherry pies as a dessert to top it all off. She could get through one night without being in defense mode about her decision to marry Kurt, couldn't she?

"Hey, Candy," Calista said bouncing Gary Jr. in her lap. She still kept him a few times a week when Garrison went to work, in addition to taking care of her own child. She always felt a connection to little Gary. He was the child she never thought she'd have, then little Bella came along.

"Hey, Cali. And who do we have here?" Candice asked, touching Junior's little cheeks.

He smiled and stretched his arms up high, reaching for her. She took him from Calista's grasp and held him up on her hip after kissing his cheek. "Hey, you. How's my favorite little man? Huh?"

Lil' Gary giggled.

She returned her attention to Calista and said, "Bella must be sleeping."

"Yeah. She's in mom's room."

Candice returned her attention back to Lil' Gary and said, "He looks so cute in these little Levi's and this green Polo."

"You can thank Cali for that," Garrison said. "She buys all of his clothes." Garrison winked at Calista.

She smiled. She did whatever she needed to do to make sure Lil' Gary was taken care of. She owed that much to Vivienne. She promised her she'd take care of him, and in doing so, she helped Garrison out a great deal.

Candice pulled out a chair and sat next to Kalina.

"Aw, look how he's looking at you," Kalina said, watching Lil' Gary. "He misses his Aunt Candy."

Candice smiled, then glanced around the table at all the inquisitive eyes beaming back at her. There was Barringer who'd flipped his lid yesterday. He looked like he was ready to do more *flipping*.

Bryson was buttering a piece of bread like he didn't have a care in the world.

Garrison was talking to Daddy Blackstone who had yet to acknowledge Candice was there.

Everson was whispering something in June's ear.

And Mama Blackstone – she was in the kitchen working.

"Let me see if mom needs any help," Candice said.

"You know she's going to send you right back in here," Kalina warned.

"Oh, well..."

She walked into the kitchen, feeling the temperature rise a few degrees. Elowyn had the kitchen blazing. "Hey, Ma."

"Hey, lil' girl. I didn't think you would make it."

"I'm here. I had to handle some last-minute business, but I'm here."

Last-minute business...

She cracked herself up with that one. She had considered calling Kurt last night to ask him about the *surprise* meeting Barringer told her about but not wanting to react off emotion alone, she took a step back and reconsidered. Kurt had tried to call her, but she didn't answer. She'd call him tonight.

She adjusted Junior on her hip then said, "Tell me what can I help you with?"

"You can grab that salad over there."

"Okay," she said walking toward the counter. "What's in the oven?"

"I made lasagna and barbecue chicken. I kept it simple this time."

"Na-na," Junior said, smiling, showing the two little teeth at the bottom of his mouth.

"Hey, handsome," Elowyn said, smiling at her grandson. She opened the oven and removed two pans of lasagna and a large tray of chicken.

"Jeez. You cooked enough for an army, didn't you?"

"You know I need a lot for the men in this family."

"Yes, that's true."

"Your father and I had a chance to talk about you and Kurt—is that his name? Kurt?"

"Yes. Did dad calm down any? He didn't say anything to me when I came in."

"Well, he's worried, dear. Men worry more about their daughters than they do their sons. That just the way it goes."

"I know. I'll talk to him at some point. I just need a breather."

"I'm sure you do, especially after yesterday. I heard your brothers ambushed you."

Candice glanced back into the dining room to make sure everyone was occupied and no one was listening to their conversation.

"They did, and Barringer was the ringleader. He was heated."

"When is Barringer *not* heated about something," Elowyn said and chuckled.

"I know. He thinks Kurt is using me as a pawn to gain control of Blackstone Financial."

"Has that thought ever crossed your mind?"

"No. Not at all. When I'm with Kurt, it's like everything is right. Like, nothing exists but me and him. I know he wouldn't do anything to hurt me." She said those words while trying to rationalize why he failed to tell her about his meeting coming up on Tuesday...

"Go ahead and take the salad in there for me," Elowyn said.

"Yes, ma'am."

Candice took the bowl to the dining room and all conversation immediately ceased in a way that would make a person think they were the main topic.

"What?" she asked.

Kalina smiled. "Ooh, that looks good."

Bryson threw a piece of bread in his mouth and glanced over at Barringer who'd promised him earlier he'd keep his mouth in check at dinner.

Candice walked back to the kitchen. It was an uneasy feeling to know the family was gossiping about her but she couldn't do anything about it if she wanted to. People – family – talked and everyone had an opinion on things that didn't concern them. *Especially* family. That's just the way it was.

"Anything else I can take, Ma?"

"No. Go get your seat, hun."

Candice walked back to the dining room, pulled out her chair and sat down. Lil' Gary reached for Calista again.

Elowyn brought out the rest of the food. Theodore prayed and then they took turns adding servings to their plates.

"So, what's new?" Theodore asked.

What's new? Everyone knew what was *new*. She and Kurt were *new*.

"Umm..." Kalina said. "Nothing new on my end."

"Me either," June said.

"This lasagna is really good, Ma," Candice said to divert the conversation.

"Thank you, dear."

"So, Candice surprised us with some news this week," Theodore said.

Candice smiled. Her diversion didn't work. "Yes, Dad. I did. I'm glad it's out and everyone knows now."

"And when did you say we would meet this fella again? What's his name?" Theodore asked.

"Kurt," Candice replied. "And he's—"

"He'll be in town on Tuesday, Pop," Barringer broke in to say.

"Oh, yeah?"

"Yep. He'll be at Blackstone Financial to discuss more options about taking over our company."

Candice took a sip of water. She wasn't about to start up with Barringer again and she definitely wasn't going to interrupt dinner with an argument about her personal business. Keeping it light, she said, "I know you all don't know much about Kurt and you will meet him soon, but just so you're not completely in the dark, let me tell you a little about him. He's smart. Handsome. He went to college to study marketing and he's good at his job. He works as marketing manager for The Champion Corporation—"

"And he *managed* to wrap you around his thumb so he can have an *in* when it comes to attempting to acquire Blackstone Financial, but it ain't happening," Barringer said.

"That's not—" Candice sighed and collected herself. "Look, Barry, we're adding new clients to Blackstone Financial, so there's no use in worrying about The Champion Corporation trying to acquire us. And you know what—I want to keep business out of this conversation. Let me tell you who Kurt is as a person."

"I don't *care* who this buster is as a person," Barringer blurted out.

"Barry, will you let her talk, please?" Calista stepped in to say.

Candice wiped her mouth and said, "It's okay, Calista. I expected this much from him. I don't know why you're beside yourself, Barry, but you need to get a handle on your emotions. As I was saying—Kurt is one of the kindest, sweetest men you'll ever meet. He's an only child. He collects rocks. You should see his rock collection—looks like it belongs in a museum. He's an outdoorsy person—loves hikes and connecting with nature."

"He sounds like an all-around good guy," Kalina said.

"He is."

Everyone was quietly eating for a moment. All you could hear were forks and knives clanking against ceramic plates.

Everson spoke up and said, "Well, even though it seems like the marriage was done a little quick and backwards, I would still like to say congratulations, baby sis. As long as you're happy, I'm happy."

"That's right," June said. "Congratulations, Candy."

And then more congratulations followed except Barringer and their father.

BY THE TIME dessert was being served, Candice opted to take hers to-go. She survived enough tension throughout dinner and she couldn't take any more indirect stares for one night while wondering what everyone was *really* thinking about her decision to marry Kurt, so she bolted, kissed her mother on the cheek, hugged her father and now she was sitting in the car, taking breaths of relief like she'd survived something. In a way she had.

She started the car and as she was preparing to back out a call came through from Kurt.

"Hey," she answered.

"Hey. What you up to?"

"I'm just leaving dinner at my parents."

"Oh. It was just you and them?"

"No. It was one of our family dinners—you know—the ones I told you about that we have once a month," she said.

"Yes, only you neglected to tell me you had one coming up. One I could've very easily attended."

"Um, do I detect some base in your voice?"

"Come on, Candy—I've been dying to get to know your family and here you are with them having a family dinner and look who's not invited. Me."

"I can't invite you in the middle of a bunch of chaos, so don't make it seem like I was trying to hide it from you."

"That's exactly what you did."

"Oh, well, let's talk about hiding stuff—like the

fact that you neglected to tell me you and Desmond Champion are sneaking over here for a meeting at Blackstone on Tuesday. Why wouldn't you tell me that, Kurt? I had to hear it from my crazy brother Barringer of all people! And he was seething with madness, like a volcano about to erupt. Said I didn't know who I was marrying and for the first time, I had to question your motives. Why didn't you tell me?"

"I *wanted* to tell you—"

"But you didn't. You may have *wanted* to, but the words never left your mouth. Do you know how that made me look in front of my brothers, especially Barringer who already thinks you're the devil."

Kurt chuckled.

"This is serious, Kurt."

"I know, baby. I know. Okay, first, I apologize for not telling you. I wanted to, but I didn't know how to tell you because of the nature of the meeting."

"Meaning what?"

"I'm not at liberty to discuss that with you. Desmond will present the offer to you and your brothers in the meeting."

"So you can't tell me anything?"

"No, I'm sorry, Candy. I can't. And you know what? We need to keep work out of our relationship. My love for you is personal. My job is business. I work for a company and I'm doing my job."

"You're right," Candice thought. She had to do her job, too. She didn't know what The Champion Corporation had up their sleeve and the man who could tell her couldn't break his silence. She couldn't control anything on their end, but she could make sure she covered all of her bases.

On Monday, she had a meeting with executives

from CheckMate. She intended to make the most of it. Bringing on new clients was her job – not worrying about decisions that fell under Barringer's umbrella of responsibilities.

"I have to get some sleep, Kurt," she said, completely drained. "I have a long day ahead of me."

"Work?"

"Yes. Work."

"Alright. I'll talk to you later. Love you."

"Love you, too."

Chapter 12

"How much longer do we have to wait, Gary?" Candice asked her brother. She'd been excited, looking forward to this meeting with the CheckMate executives since this client would help stabilize Blackstone Financial. However, they were already fifteen minutes late.

"They'll be here. They confirmed...probably just ran into some traffic. Why don't you get a drink or something?"

"I'm too nervous to drink. We really need to lock down this client."

Gary shrugged. "I'm not worried. Barringer pretty much told us we have the contract. All we have to do is play this right and show them who we are as a business. They're ready to sign."

"I know. I just really need this to work out so I can get Barringer off my back."

"I wouldn't worry too much about Barringer, Candy."

"But I am worried. I do actually want my family to like my husband."

Garrison took a sip of water. He placed the glass on the table and said, "In that case, maybe you should've told us about your relationship with him upfront."

"I wanted to, but something told me *not* to. I didn't want to make a decision about Kurt based on all of y'all's negative opinions."

"Why would you assume our opinion of the man would've been negative?"

"Because of who he works for. I knew that once you knew that he'd be a target."

"Let's be clear—he's not a target to me. I trust your judgment."

"Whatever, Gary."

"I do. However, I would be lying if I said I didn't feel leery about this guy. I mean, surely you've met other men who didn't work for a rival company."

"Yes, but what's the fun in that?" Candice joked.

Gary shook his head. "You always know how to get yourself in some trouble, don't you?"

"Hush." She elbowed him. "Anyway, how have you been doing?"

"I'm doing fine."

"Don't give me the standard *I'm doing fine*. Tell me—how are you?"

He shrugged and said, "Okay. I'm doing terrible. I'm trying to learn how to be a single dad, have no clue what I'm doing and every day I miss my wife. Every day I miss her."

Candice touched and squeezed his hand. "What can I do to help?"

"There's nothing you can do, sis. It's just something I have to work through."

"How are you working through it?" she asked at the same time two gentlemen walked up to their table.

"Mr. Blackstone?" one of the men said.

Candice looked over at them. One was Hispanic. The other...

The pit of her stomach fell to her shoes. She knew the other man. Bernard Baptiste – her ex-boyfriend's brother.

He was a spitting image of Quinton. Same chocolate skin. Same tall, athletic body. Same bald head and black eyes. What were the odds he would work for a company that Blackstone needed to stay afloat?

"I'm Romero Cruz," the Hispanic guy said to Garrison.

"Romero, I'm Garrison and this is my sister, Candice."

Romero reached to shake Candice's hand, then Bernard stepped forward and said, "I'm. Bernard Baptiste."

"Nice to meet you."

"Likewise. And it's good to see you again as well, Candice."

"Oh. You two know each other?" Garrison asked.

"Yes," Candice replied with an uneasy chuckle. "It's a long story."

Garrison glanced at Bernard then back at Candice trying to read the two.

"Theodore tells me we'll be in good hands with BFSG," Bernard said, looking directly at Candice. Then he smiled.

Candice narrowed her eyes slightly, probably reading too much into it, but why was he smiling at her almost like he'd somehow had the upper hand in this deal?

Garrison stood up and said, "Excuse us for a moment. I need to have a word with my sister."

"Sure," Bernard said.

"Take your time," Romero told him.

Candice got up and followed Garrison to the front entrance of the restaurant.

"What's going on with you and this Bernard

guy?" he asked her.

"He's Quinton's brother."

"Your *ex* Quinton?"

"Yes. I can't believe it either."

Garrison sighed deeply. This reeked of trouble, something he didn't want any of. "So what are you going to do?"

Candice shrugged. "What do you think I should do?"

"I don't know. I'm at a loss right now. On one end, you got Kurt causing problems and on the other, your ex's brother pops up out of nowhere."

"He didn't pop up out of nowhere. He popped up from CheckMate."

"You didn't know he worked there?"

"No. I didn't date Quinton long enough to know the intricate details of his family. But don't worry—I don't see this being a problem. What does Bernard have to do with my failed relationship with his brother? If this is truly business, that shouldn't be a factor in any of their decision making."

"Yeah, it shouldn't but you know how these things work, Candy. Personal always finds a way to creep into business, and you already know if Barringer finds out about your connection to this guy, he's going to spaz out. You know that."

Candice rolled her eyes. "Barringer would spaz out if I looked at him wrong."

Garrison chuckled.

"But, I'm a team player, so here's what I suggest. You continue the meeting. I'll take a step back from this. If Bernard and Romero ask you what happened, just tell them I had an emergency and had to leave. I don't want to interfere in the family business with yet *another* conflict of interest."

"Candy, you don't have to—"

"It's fine, Gary. You handle it. That way, I don't

have to worry about being in the way of anything. I'm so ready to move to Asheville. I can't take any more of this."

"Candy—" Garrison called out to her, but she kept on walking until she cleared the exit.

* * *

"I don't know how much more I can take, Kalina," Candice said, stretching out on the couch in Kalina's office again like she was at a therapy session. "Family dinner was awful for me. Just plain awful. There's no other way to describe it. I feel like everybody is against me. The tension in the air literally gave me a headache."

"Well, everybody's not against you. I'm not against you. The girls aren't either. Elowyn even seems to be coming around. So do Everson, Bryson and Gary. This will take time for everyone to grasp."

"It's not just that, Kalina. It's affecting my work, too. Me and Gary had a dinner meeting with a new client this evening. Guess who's one of the representatives for this company?"

"Who?"

"Quinton's brother."

"Your ex Quinton?"

"Yes. And he had this smirk on his face like he had me where he wanted me."

"But you were in a relationship with his brother. Not him."

"Doesn't matter, I guess, or maybe I read into it wrong, but that's what it felt like. So, I thought it would be a good idea if I left the meeting due to yet *another* conflict of interest. I can't win."

"You *can* win," Kalina said. She took a long look at Candice lying on her couch, staring up at the ceiling like she was in distress. "What happened to the fun, playful Candy who had a smart comeback for anything her brothers said? Where's *that* Candy?"

"She's tired of being *that* Candy and looking forward to being *wife* Candy. I'm actually at the stage in my life where I would be comfortable having a baby. I want a family life. I want my husband in bed beside me at night. Single, playful Candy no longer exists."

"Then it sounds like it's time for you to make your move. You're stressing out because you're still holding on to the past and haven't grabbed on to the future. Kurt is your future. Asheville is your new home."

"I know."

"And trust me, I don't want you to move. Nobody wants you to leave, but you have to do what you have to do for the sake of your marriage. Have you ever thought that maybe it's the reason everything seems to be falling apart here? Because you're supposed to be over there, but you're still fighting battles you can't win over here."

"You're absolutely right," Candice said. "I hadn't thought about it like that. It makes perfect sense." She stood up, gave Kalina a side hug and said, "I know what I need to do now. Thanks so much, Kalina."

"Yep. No problem."

Candice drove to the nearest home improvement store to buy boxes. Thanks to her conversation with Kalina, she realized that was part of her problem – she didn't have a timeline for anything. When Kurt asked if she was packing or when she expected to move, she'd put it off. For a woman who was excited about starting a new life in Asheville, she hadn't packed a thing. She wanted to change that.

AT HOME, SHE assembled a box and was already taking down pictures in the living room. Then she assembled another box in the kitchen and packed up some dinnerware and a few other kitchen utensils.

After eating a small salad for dinner, she called Kurt before she stepped in the shower. She didn't get a response. When she was out of the shower, she was sure she'd have a return call from him, but there were no missed calls. Only a text from Garrison that said:

The meeting went okay. I'll tell you more about it at the office tomorrow.

She placed her phone on the nightstand, turned off the lamp and closed her eyes. Sleep couldn't come fast enough after the day she had, but at least the day provided her with clarity on what she needed to do. She needed to pack up. Her new life was waiting and she was tired of putting it off. It was time to make a move.

Chapter 13

Kurt let himself inside of Candice's apartment eleven-thirty at night, surprised to see she'd already been packing. He smiled, appreciating the effort. The last time he was here, she'd made no changes – her life was carrying on as normal. This time, she had boxes and had already started packing, confirming in his mind she was ready to move. To start a life with him in Asheville. It gave him a sense of relief. He was beginning to think she didn't want to move.

He took quiet steps to her bedroom to see her lying there beneath the covers, asleep. He walked closer, eased down on the bed next to her. The brown tone of her skin looked like milk chocolate in a sea of white sheets. She looked relaxed, peaceful an undisturbed. So beautiful. He didn't want to wake her but knew he had to. He wanted her and his need couldn't wait until the morning.

He pulled his shirt up over his head, took off his jeans and crept closer to her, his five o'clock shadow brushing against her soft skin. She smelled good – like that berry-scented lotion he'd come to love.

"Candy," he whispered against her ear.

She stirred a little.

"Candy," he said again and left kisses along her jaw. He basked in her warmness. In her scent. In being this close to the woman he loved again.

Her eyes opened slowly. She caught glimpses of him and they opened wider. "Kurt!" she said sitting up and wrapping her arms around his neck. "You're here. I've missed you so much." She pelted kisses all over his face – his nose, his lips, his jaw and then she came back and kissed those lips of his that she missed so much.

"I knew you would be happy to see me, but I didn't think you would eat my face."

Candice laughed. "Hush, and kiss me," she told him.

And kiss her he did, wasting no time parting her lips with his tongue and delivering stroke after delicious stroke, causing her entire body to shudder just off the kiss alone.

Then she took a break only to look at his face, touching and familiarizing herself with it – enjoying the company of her king. She smiled and said softly, "You're here."

"I am, baby. I figured I'd come up early since I got that meeting tomorrow. I wanted to spend the night with my lady."

He kissed her lips then covered her body with his like one of the sheets tousled on her, feeling her hardened buds through the thin material of her nightgown – a fabric so flimsy, she may as well had gone to bed naked. Then he sank his tongue inside her mouth reacquainting himself with her taste – one he was sure he could never get used to. Any amount of time they were apart made him want her much more and tonight wasn't the exception as he savored the taste of her mouth while listening to her soft moans fill the air. Her warm body immediately took the slight chill of his skin away – made her shiver for a moment while their legs were intertwined. As he kissed her, he pulled up the thin fabric of her gown and took his lips away from her mouth for a moment to pull it completely over her head. Then she continued on kissing her with intention and passion on his mind, loving the woman he missed.

Parting her thighs, he sank into the very heat of her, sensations tearing through him as he concealed his length in her cave. Only minutes into this madness, her body writhed beneath him. Shuddered. She was already losing control of herself.

"Kurt," she moaned as she ran her fingertips up and down his back then wrapped her arms around him tight as her body crumbled beneath him. She closed her eyes and arched her neck as he kissed her there. As he steadily moved on top of her as his own need set him ablaze. Like he'd never had her before. Like he'd never have her again.

"Kurt!" she said again, exploding beneath him for a second time. This explosion triggered one in him that built and built and built until the passion overwhelmed him. Until he was grinding his hips against hers so fast, he felt like he was in auto-drive. Until he bucked, shattered and flooded her with his release.

"Candy!" he exclaimed in the thick of it, throwing his head back while spasms locked up his body, drained him and had him pinching his eyes closed while groaning, moaning, keeping all kinds of noises.

He gasped for air.

She fought to maintain a steady, normal breath again.

After a few minutes of cool-down time, he pulled her close to him and laid there looking into her eyes. She watched him back, but her eyelids were slowly bouncing closed toward sleep. He touched the tip of her nose with his and left a kiss on her lips.

"I love you, Candy."

"Love you, too."

"I can't tell you how happy I was to see you've been packing boxes."

"I figured it was time for me to make some moves. I already pissed off my entire family. I may as well, right?"

"No. You should be ready to leave because you want to be with me—not because you're running away from them. I don't want you to feel like that."

"And yet, that's exactly how I feel. I want to be with you *and* I'm running away."

"I'll be here for the rest of the week. I don't have a problem meeting your family, having a one-on-one with your parents or your brothers. I want them to know how much I love you."

"That'll be nice."

"You're cool with that?"

"Yes. It would certainly help to ease some of my stress."

"And I'm all about alleviating your stress, baby," he told her. Too bad she was going to be stressed all over again when they had their meeting tomorrow.

Chapter 14

Candice walked into the office this morning all smiles. Her man was here. Well, he was still at her apartment at the moment since his meeting wasn't scheduled until ten, but still, he was here. In her city. That alone was enough to give her a good feeling. And this morning...

Goodness, this morning....

They'd made love again – love so good it made her want to stay in bed and sleep the rest of the day away. She had to drag herself to the shower and as she got dressed, Kurt was in the kitchen making coffee, eggs and toast.

She went to the break room for another cup of coffee when she ran into Garrison.

"Mornin' Gary."

"Hey, girl. You look especially awake this morning."

"I am. I already had a cup of coffee at home...coming in here for a second." She took one of the paper cups and filled it. "You said you were going to update me on how the meeting went yesterday."

"It was productive. I think they're ready to move

forward. Bernard seems to be running things in that respect. I think once we win him over, we're pretty much in."

"I'm sure you've done that already with your charming personality."

"I did the best I could, but I think he wants to talk to you, and I hope it has nothing to do with Quinton."

"Why would it?" Candice asked frowning. "That's history."

"I know, but like I said before—you know how these things can be." Garrison took a sip of coffee. "I gave him your office number."

"Good. I wouldn't want him to have my cell."

"Anyway, what time does this meeting jump off with your boyfriend?"

"Husband."

"Oh, yeah. My bad. *Husband.*"

"It starts at ten."

"Have you heard from him at all this morning?"

Candice smiled, thinking about the lovely morning she had with Kurt. Oh, she'd heard from him all right...

And touched him.

Kissed him.

Made love to him.

Squeezed his tight, lil' butt...

"Candy?"

"Oh," she blinked out of her daydream. "Yes. I heard from him." And she left it at that. "I'll be in my office if you need me."

She strutted down the hallway to her office in her red heels, navy blue pants and white blouse. When she arrived, sat in her chair, spun around just for the heck of it and then checked her messages. There were a few calls from potential clients, a return call from Telmark and the last call was from

Bernard. He didn't state the nature of his call – only that he wanted her to call him back.

She did so immediately.

"Hi, Candice. This is a surprise," he answered.

"Why is it a surprise? You called me. I'm returning your call."

"That's the surprise. I didn't think you would."

"Well, here I am. Oh, and I'm sorry I had to bolt yesterday."

"No worries. Garrison told us you had an emergency. I hope everything is okay."

"It is. Now, what can I do for you?"

He paused for a moment and then said, "This isn't work-related—"

"Then we probably shouldn't be discussing it," she said.

"We should because my brother hasn't been the same without you and I think you'd like to hear what he has to say."

Candice was already shaking her head when she said, "I'm sure I wouldn't. Look, Bernard, I'm trying to do a job here."

"And so am I, Candice, and I see an opportunity to give my brother some closure so I'm going to take it."

Livid, Candice got up from her desk, hurried to close her door and said, "Closure? He wants closure after what he did to me?"

"I don't know who did what to who, and I won't even begin to try and figure it out. You two were in the relationship...had nothing to do with me. I'm just relaying a message."

"And if I don't meet with him..."

"Let's just say I won't confirm yay or nay when it comes to signing with your company. There are a few other options on the table, and you know what, Candice? The deal is as good as done. We *want*

Blackstone. No question. But I'ma need you to do this for me, first."

"Unbelievable."

"He only wants to talk. I think it'll be good for you both."

"Why? I'm married now."

"And he's in a relationship, too."

"So what's the point of talking to me? I don't understand."

"Look, you two will have to hash that out. He wants to meet you Thursday night at the spot where y'all used to hang out at 6:30. He said you'll know the place."

Candice closed her eyes, fully disgusted by the idea of sitting at a table with her ex-boyfriend. But how could she not do it and risk losing CheckMate as a client? "Okay. Fine."

"Should I take that as a confirmation?"

Candice slammed the phone down and dropped her head. On one end, she had The Champion Corporation to contend with, not to mention the drama surrounding Kurt, but now she was being blackmailed into having dinner with her ex-boyfriend to land another deal. Suddenly, the success or failure of the company rested on her shoulders.

What was a girl to do?

A tap at the door had her glancing up to see Barringer stepping into her office.

Great. Another headache...

Barringer was such a boss at work and even though he was her brother, she could feel his authority at the office almost like they weren't related at all.

"How can I help you, Barry?"

He took a seat. Crossed one leg over the other and asked, "What's up with you?"

"Nothing." She rolled her wrist to glance at her watch. "Just waiting for this meeting to start."

"Gary told me y'all ran into a little problem yesterday evening."

"There's no problem. I just had to leave. That's all."

"Why?"

Since he was asking, she concluded Gary hadn't told him about Bernard's request.

"It's nothing I can't handle," she responded.

He didn't look convinced.

"So did your *husband* give you any inside information about this meeting?"

"No. We decided to keep business dealings out of our relationship."

"Good move, but how does that help Blackstone Financial?"

Candice shrugged. "Here's the thing, Barry—it's not up to Kurt, CheckMate, The Blakeney Agency or anybody else to make sure this company stays afloat. You're the CEO. That's *your* job."

"And that's why I'm sitting here in your office. I'm *doing* my job—trying to get information from you, but you don't have any to share, huh?"

"Nope. Sorry."

He went quiet for a moment then said, "I'll soon have to fill your position with someone—some *outside* person who doesn't know a thing about this company or how it operates."

"Is that your way of saying you'll miss me when I'm gone?"

"That's my way of saying I *know* it's my job to run this company, but I've never been the only one calling the shots. I value and appreciate your efforts and work ethic. I couldn't do this without you and Garrison."

"I appreciate you saying that, Barry, and I'm

sure whoever you hire as my replacement will be just as good as I am."

"Yeah, but it won't be the same without family."

"Aw, he does love me," Candice said, walking around her desk to where Barringer was sitting. She wrapped her arms around him and said, "I love you, too, Barry."

"Yeah, yeah, yeah...get off me and get ready for this meeting."

Candice released him. "I'm ready, I think."

"And while you're at it, be thinking of some replacements for your job."

"You're kicking me out already?"

"Well, I imagine you'll be moving soon. Ain't no man in his right mind going to allow his new wife to live this far apart from him."

"Yeah, you're right. I'll be moving soon. I don't have a date yet, but I will definitely give you notice."

"Good." Barringer stood and stretched. "Alright. I'll see you in a few."

"Okay, and Barry?"

"Yes?"

"Try to keep a level head in this meeting, okay?"

"No worries. After meeting with CheckMate last night, Garrison was pretty confident we'll get them onboard real soon."

Yeah, after I meet with Quinton...

"Ay, did you hear me?"

"Yeah, I heard you," she said.

"Alright. I'll see you shortly."

Barringer exited the office and Candice hung her head. Amid everything, she'd forgotten about assisting her brother in finding a replacement. No matter how much of a pain-in-the-butt he was, she couldn't leave him high and dry.

WHEN TEN O'CLOCK rolled around and she got word that Kurt and Desmond Champion had arrived, Candice emerged from her office with her iPad in hand along with a cup of coffee and walked to the conference room. Barringer and Garrison were already there and waiting.

"It's that time, huh?" she asked, taking a seat between her brothers.

"Yep. It's that time," Garrison responded.

Eleanor walked into the room and escorted Kurt and Desmond inside.

Candice looked at Kurt and smiled big inwardly but on the outside, she only showed a small one – a pleasant greeting before business ensued.

"Gentlemen," Desmond said. He reached to shake hands with Barringer and Garrison.

"And I can't forget you, Ms. Blackstone," Desmond said.

"Yeah, we can't forget you," Kurt said, taking her hand, feeling it tremble in his grasp. "It's good to see you again, Candice."

"It's good to see you again as well, Kurt."

Barringer frowned and leaned forward to look at Garrison. Why was Candice acting like this man wasn't her husband when she told them he was?

After Kurt exchanged handshakes with Barringer and Garrison, they all sat down.

Candice glanced up at Kurt again. He had his game face on as he removed a folder from his briefcase. Her eyes traced his lips. Her mind drifted to them tangling in the sheets this morning.

"Let me start off by saying I know we've had pretty rocky dealings in the past," Desmond said. "And I'm sure the offer we're bringing you today probably won't change that."

"So, you came here to make it worse," Garrison said.

Barringer chuckled.

"I'm sure you will think so," Desmond responded. "We want to buy Blackstone Financial."

Barringer laughed.

Candice frowned and looked at Kurt who couldn't lift his head to look at her. He was staring down at a document in a folder he'd just opened.

Garrison cleared his voice and said, "I'm sorry, I don't think I heard you correctly."

"We would like to buy Blackstone Financial," Kurt said, looking directly at Garrison. He then focused his attention to Barringer, handed him a folder and said, "Here's the official offer and it's only good for two weeks."

Barringer rubbed his head. Candice told him not to fly off the handle but he wanted to. Boy did he want to give these men a piece of his mind, but instead, he said, "If this is the only thing you want to discuss, this meeting is going to be over real early."

"Not so fast," Desmond said. "That's quite a generous offer if you take the time to look it over. Don't be too quick to pass on it."

"What's *generous* about trying to take something that doesn't belong to you?" Candice asked, directing the question more toward Kurt than Desmond.

Kurt looked at her. He didn't want to be a part of this no more than she wanted to, but he was and he hoped she would stay focused on the fact that business should've had nothing to do with their marriage. Somehow, staring into the shock and disappointment on her face, he knew that it had.

He responded, "We're not taking anything. As Desmond has stated, the offer is a very generous one—one we wouldn't necessarily give to anyone else—"

"Oh, so you're doing us a favor? Is that what this is?" Candice asked, taking her iPad from the table, leaving the room in a hurry.

Kurt glanced at her, was ready to run after her but he couldn't. He had to remind himself of that. Desmond knew nothing of his relationship with Candice. He couldn't taint business with his personal problems, so he stayed at the table. Stayed in business mode.

After entering her office, Candice slammed the door and paced the floor in front of her desk while one hand rested on her stomach.

"This isn't happening," she chanted. "This isn't happening. This isn't happening."

How could Kurt blindside her like this? He couldn't give her a warning that The Champion Corporation was going to hit them with this kind of offer? An offer to take over their family's business?

She continued pacing thinking about the ideas her brothers put in her head. That she was being used. That Kurt saw an opportunity to use their marriage as a way to convince her to follow along with his plans. But she gave him the benefit of the doubt. Plus, she loved the man. Was she *that* blinded by love, so much so that she was willing to fall for a man whose sole aim was to gain control of Blackstone Financial? Had she been duped, yet again, by a man who claimed to love her?

A tap on the door took her out of her thoughts but didn't do a thing to make her steady. She placed a hand on her desk, took a moment to breathe then walked to the door, snatching it open, thinking it was Kurt.

It wasn't. It was Garrison.

"What the heck was that?" he asked, stepping inside and closing the door. "Kurt didn't tell you about this? Why was he acting like he didn't know you?"

"He hasn't told Desmond about us yet and no, he didn't tell me anything about this. He said he wanted to keep business out of our relationship. Now, I see why. I can't believe I fell for it."

"Look, maybe he *is* trying to keep the two separate, Candy. What do you expect when you fall in love with the competition?"

"I didn't expect *this*!"

"Okay, first of all, you need to calm down before you have a stroke in here. Sit down for a minute."

Candice sat in the chair behind her desk and sighed heavily.

"You already know we're not taking a deal. I don't care how good it is. We're not selling Blackstone Financial. You know that, right?"

"Yes."

"So, negotiations are pretty much over. There's nothing else for us to talk about with The Champion Corporation. This is it. We never have to meet with them again."

"Yeah, I get that but I feel like I've been stabbed in the back and that's not a good feeling to get from a man who's supposed to be my husband. Who's supposed to love me and protect me. Instead, he does something like this."

She held her head in frustration.

"I get it but you can always talk to him about it to see where his head is at."

"That's my only option at this point. Are they still here?"

"No. They were headed for the elevators when I left the conference room. I'm sure Kurt doesn't want to have the conversation here, anyway. He knows how upset you are. Anyway, look, why don't you take an early lunch and just chill out for a minute, sis."

"I would, but I'm too pissed to eat."

"And that's why you should be eating. I'll run pick up something for you. What are you in the mood for?"

"Revenge," she said through gritted teeth.

Garrison chuckled. "Okay. I'll be right back with a revenge sandwich and fries."

Candice dropped her head and rested on her desk. This was too much. It was all getting to be too much for her to handle.

Chapter 15

She hung around the office as long as she could, not ready to go home and face Kurt. He'd called her cell phone. Called her desk phone. Texted her. She didn't respond. Something about his behavior in the meeting didn't sit well with her. He was Kurt the businessman and not her husband. He had to have known an offer like this would hurt her and her family. Maybe he didn't care.

His car was parked out front. He was there, waiting. Waiting to talk after the nonsense of the day. She still didn't know what to say to him.

When she opened the door, he was standing in the living room with his arm crossed. Smelled like he'd cooked.

"Hi," he said.

"Hi," she replied dryly.

"I made a roast."

Candice placed her keys on the counter and set her bag down.

"Look, Candice, I know the offer caught you by surprise. It caught *me* by surprise when I first learned about it."

"And exactly when was that, Kurt?"

"It doesn't matter when. I told you I couldn't discuss it."

"Right—you couldn't tell me your main objective was to take my father's company."

"That's not *my* objective, Candy. That's the objective of the company I work for—"

"You know what—I've had enough," she said cutting him off. "I can't tell you how humiliated I was to have to sit there between my brothers and listen to you and Desmond spew this nonsense about buying Blackstone Financial. Have you lost your freaking mind? This is my family we're talking about! My brothers, who I've tried my best to defend you against. My brothers who think the only reason you came after me was strictly for business reasons and after this crap you pulled today, I'm beginning to think they're right."

"They're not right—"

"How could you *not* tell me about this, Kurt?"

"I wanted to, Candy, but I told you, my hands are tied in these kinds of decisions."

"Yeah. Sure. Your hands are tied," she said in a way that told him she didn't believe a word he said. "I want you to leave."

"Are you kidding me?"

"No, I'm not kidding. I want you to leave. Now. I'm not sure how to handle this and I don't want to say something I'll regret. I need some time to think. Please leave."

Kurt frowned then said, "Sure. I'll leave. I'll do anything for you, Candy, like I've always done."

"Yeah, except for having my back when your goons come looking for my father's company. How am I supposed to introduce you to him after this? Ain't no way."

"Candice—"

"Just leave, Kurt," she told him. "I don't have

anything else to say to you tonight."

"Alright. You want me to leave. I'm leaving. Have a good night."

When he walked out, Candice locked the door and pressed her forehead to it in angst. Then she walked over to the stove, turned it off. She saw the dishes on the kitchen table. Ones he'd placed there for their dinner. She saw the candles. The roses in the vase on the counter. These were all signs that Kurt was a good man. Still, she needed time to figure out what his true motives were.

Chapter 16

Kurt sat in the parking lot at a hotel ten miles away from Candice's apartment. He was so close to Candice yet so far away. He may as well had been back in Asheville. He wanted to tell her about the proposal before he arrived, but at the same time, he couldn't allow himself to get that involved.

Looking back, he realized he could've handled this a lot differently. He should've had a talk with Desmond and told him the state of his relationship with Candice. Desmond would've probably taken him off the project but hindsight being twenty-twenty, that was the best option for this scenario. He'd have the conversation with Desmond tomorrow, but too little too late. The damage had already been done.

Right now, he had to check into a hotel. He was in town for a week. He'd planned on staying with Candice but that didn't work out too well. And now he was in limbo. Again. It was bad enough they lived in different cities. Now they were in the same city and were still apart. They'd never had a disagreement like this and it was only because of the job.

He got out of the car, took a duffle bag from the backseat and walked toward the hotel to check into a room for the night. After he did so, he took a shower and sat on the bed.

The look on her face when she realized what Desmond was offering...

He sighed heavily and hung his head. He instantly hated himself for not telling her in advance what the meeting was about. For her to feel like he was a liar and she couldn't trust him were all signs he wasn't doing his job as a man. And he didn't want his woman to feel that way. Didn't want her to suffer the same way his mother had to suffer when his father moved out. Yes, they'd had a mutual divorce, but after being with someone for so long, it took a toll on you when they were no longer around. She'd kept quiet about it, probably for his sake, but he knew how much the divorce had damaged her.

Candice felt like he had betrayed her. That was enough to eat at him and there was nothing that could comfort him at the moment to make him feel contrary to what he'd caused. He knew he couldn't allow this disagreement to fester. That would only make matters worse.

He took his phone, considering calling her but an unknown number appeared on his display. A number with a Wilmington area code.

"Hello?" he answered.

"Hey. Is this Kurt?"

"Who's calling?"

"This is Bryson Blackstone. My name probably clues you in on who I am."

"You're one of Candy's brothers."

"I am. I apologize for introducing myself to you over the phone. I'd much rather talk to you in person."

"Give me the time and place and I'm there."

"Good. There's a steakhouse at the Riverwalk."

"Yeah, I know the place."

"Can you meet me there tomorrow at six?"

"I can. I'll be there."

Chapter 17

On Wednesday, Candice couldn't bring herself to go to work. She woke up after ten and even then she didn't get out of bed. She just laid there, thinking – thinking things she didn't want to think. Things she didn't want to believe. Things like maybe her quick marriage to Kurt had been a mistake – one she never saw coming but one her family could predict. Leave it up to them and she should make a clean break while the marriage could still be annulled. Of course, that's not what she wanted. She wanted him, but she couldn't allow herself to be with a man she didn't trust.

She walked to the kitchen in her robe and made coffee. She took a sip and sat down when a call from Calista came through.

"Girl, where are you?" Calista asked.

"I'm home. I didn't go to work."

"I know. Barringer said he tried to call you a few times. He sounded worried. Are you ignoring him again?"

Candice chuckled a bit. "You make it sound like I ignore your husband on a regular basis."

"Well, let's be honest—you do. I know Barringer

gets on your nerves, but he means well."

"I know, and I'm not ignoring him. I just needed to take a moment for myself. If you haven't noticed, I've been pretty stressed out over the last few weeks."

"I've noticed."

"And it doesn't help that Kurt is in the mix. It was hard enough without him being here but he adds to my frustration so much, you just don't understand, especially after that lil' stunt he pulled last night."

"Honey, welcome to marriage. That's all I can tell you."

"Is that right?"

"You doggone right that's right. That man will get on your nerves, twist your gut, make you want to slap him over the head and have you asking why you got married in the first place. They say that's how you know it's real."

Candice laughed. "If that's the gauge for determining if a marriage is real, I must've hit the jackpot."

"Think about it. You see those couple who always look like they got it together in public. Like the woman being all prissy while the man follows her like he's her personal assistant instead of her man—those people ain't happy. They'll be the main ones hollering for a divorce. But people like us—people who have to struggle to hang on to our marriages, I think that's where the beauty lies. It's hard, but after every dispute, it's a win."

"Sounds like something Kalina would say."

"Yep. I'm sure it is. So, don't let frustration ruin your new marriage. If Kurt gets on your nerves, trust me, you're on the right path and you got the *right* man."

Candice chuckled. "Thanks for that, Cali."

"No problem."

"How's Bella this morning?"

"She's good. I just fed her."

"You have Junior today, too?"

"Yeah, he's playing with his toys. I'm so glad they get to spend time together."

"They are the only Blackstone children for right now."

"Yeah, that is until you and Kurt have a few."

"A *few*?" Candice laughed.

"Girl, as much as you love kids, you know you're going to have some babies."

"Yeah, but the only thing I want right now is a shot of Tequila."

"Maybe you can get that since you're not working today."

I'll definitely need it tomorrow when I meet with Quinton...

"You know what, Cali...I think I will," Candice replied.

"Good. Hey, I have to go. Junior is trying to take the phone out of my hand."

"Aw, he wants to say hi to his Aunt Candy. Hey, Junior."

She heard his sweet laughter. Sounded like music to her ears.

"Okay, Candy. I'll let you go."

"Alright. Later."

Chapter 18

Kurt wasn't sure what he was walking into. Was he meeting with Bryson alone or Bryson and all the brothers? He didn't mind meeting with them. He already met Garrison and Barringer. He could plan better had he known what he was walking into.

He parked then took the Riverwalk toward the restaurant. He spotted who he thought was Bryson waiting near the entrance. He was tall, a little taller than him and he favored Barringer and Garrison.

"Bryson?" he said, just to be sure.

"You must be Kurt, the man Barringer put a hit out on," Bryson said as he shook his hand.

Kurt chuckled. "It can't be that bad, can it?"

"This is Barringer we're talking about. Of course."

Bryson opened the door and Kurt followed him inside.

After they were seated and drink orders were placed, Bryson said, "I'll get straight to the point and hopefully we can talk like men and be open and honest about this."

"Sure."

The waitress placed two beers on the table and

the men both ordered steaks, then Bryson took a long swig of his beer and looked at Kurt. "I have to admit, when I first learned about your relationship with my sister, the first thought that came to my mind was that this was a business move for you."

"How so?"

"Well, by getting my sister to fall for you, you're basically putting her in a precarious position to take sides with you over the welfare of her family."

"I can understand how you might think that way, but that was in no way a part of my thought process."

"How could it not be? You're a businessman—you're the marketing manager for The Champion Corporation. You know how to play your cards. I just hope my sister wasn't one of them."

"She wasn't. I wouldn't do that to the woman I love."

Bryson squinted, trying to accept those words. He asked, "Is she the only woman you've ever loved?"

"Besides my mother, yes."

"How old are you?"

"I'm thirty-three."

"Thirty-three and the only woman you've been in a relationship with that you actually loved is my sister."

"That would be correct."

"Sounds a little suspect to me."

"There's nothing suspicious about it. I waited until I found the right one. Candy is the right one."

"So why are you staying at a hotel right now?"

"How'd you know I was staying at a hotel?"

Bryson shrugged and didn't give up his source.

Kurt sighed and shook his head. "Well, after the business meeting with your brothers, things went sour. She was upset with the offer presented—

actually, I think she was more upset with me that I didn't tell her in advance about The Champion Corporation wanting to buy Blackstone Financial. Look, Bryson, I tried to warn her about keeping business out of our marriage."

"Yeah, and how did that work out?"

"It didn't. Didn't work at all."

"Exactly. Look, I'm going to be honest with you, Kurt. I have an uneasy feeling about this. I've had one from the start. I realize Candice is a grown woman, but she's my little sister and I will do anything to protect her, especially if I think she's caught up with someone who isn't right for her."

"You don't think your sister is free to make her own choices?"

"Of course. We all have that right, but with us Blackstone brothers comes an extra obligation to protect Candice."

"Why?"

"She's the youngest. Most vulnerable."

"You don't have to protect her from me."

"I have to protect her from everyone, *especially* you."

"Wow. Now I understand why she didn't want to tell you all about our marriage. Leave it up to you and she'd die single."

Kurt took another sip of beer. He wasn't about to let Bryson or anyone else tell him what he felt for Candice. He knew the truth and after telling him his position, if he wasn't buying it then that was on him.

"So why her?" Bryson asked. "What is it about Candice that made you want to put a ring on her finger?'

"She's a good woman. She's fun. I love being around her."

"That's it?"

Kurt sighed again. "What more do you want me to say because whatever I say won't be good enough to satisfy you. I don't think there's a man on the planet good enough for Candice in your eyes."

"There's not."

"So why call this meeting with me? It seems like a waste of time on your end and mine."

"Because I'm making an attempt to like you. For Candice's sake."

"Now I feel like I'm on an interview."

"That's how you *should* feel. Look, man—if you had a sister, you'd be the same way."

"How do you know I don't have a sister?"

"I've done my homework. You're an only child. Your parents are divorced."

"That's right."

"I made it my business to know things about you in advance, but I asked you here to get to know you on a more personal level."

Kurt took a drink of beer, then asked, "What do you want to know?"

"Candy told us you collect rocks."

He nodded. "Yes, I do. I love nature. Hiking, you know—being outdoors."

"She told us that, too, which I thought was odd. Candice is the complete opposite. She likes makeup and glitter."

Kurt smiled. "They say opposites attract."

"That's true." Bryson drank more beer. "How'd you get into marketing?"

"It was my father's line of work. It wasn't something I enjoyed, necessarily—just something I was good at so I stuck with it."

Bryson nodded.

When the food arrived, the conversation continued. This time it was Kurt with the questions. "So why are you the only brother who decided not to work for the family business?"

"It's not what I wanted. Don't get me wrong—I respect my father and all he's accomplished over the years, but I wanted something that was my own."

"And what did you come up with?"

"What do you mean what did I come up with? You didn't do your homework on me, man?"

"I didn't want to investigate any of you. I wanted to get to know you organically, so no, I didn't do any homework."

Bryson wiped his mouth and said, "I own Blackstone Tree Service."

"What do you do? Tree removal?"

"Planting, pruning and removal. I also do landscaping."

"Hmm. Interesting."

"What's interesting?"

"Oh, nothing. I'm just doing what I do. I always go into work mode when I shouldn't."

"Okay, then marketing manager—let's hear it. I saw the lightbulb go off. What are you thinking?"

"I was thinking about how your business name is geared only toward one service. That could be hindering your company's growth."

"I'm going to tell you the same thing I told my wife when she told me that. My website lists all the services that Blackstone Tree Service offers."

"Yes, but that's for those people who make it that far. Most will have already moved on to another company."

Bryson grinned. "Are you trying to sell me your services?"

"No. I'm not an independent contractor. I'm simply giving you free marketing advice."

"And that advice would be...?"

"To change your business name to Blackstone

Tree Service & Landscaping."

Bryson smirked. "Not bad."

Kurt continued with his meal and then said, "I love your sister. I'm not playing games. I'm not doing this for any financial gain. I'm not trying to steal your father's company. I truly, genuinely love your sister. I don't know if you believe that or not. In fact, I don't care if you don't believe it. I love her and that's that."

Bryson nodded. He appreciated the man's straightforwardness, even after he'd given him a hard time about being with Candice. He noted a couple of things about Kurt that he liked already – he was confident and poised. Whatever he threw at him, he didn't fly off the handle. He stayed in control and at ease. That was a good quality for a man to have when dealing with his sister. At times, she could be hard to understand. No one knew that better than him. They got into disputes on a regular, but he knew how to handle her. From the looks of things, so did Kurt.

"Okay," Bryson said. "I want you to present that argument to Barringer."

Kurt smiled. "I'm sure Barringer doesn't want to hear anything I have to say. Every time I see him, there's a deep ridge in his forehead."

Bryson chuckled. "That's Barringer, alright." He finished his beer. "No but seriously, Barringer called me after that lil' stunt your company pulled."

"I'm sure he did, and let me just say that I work for that company. I get paid—I'm not an owner but at the same time, what Barringer doesn't realize is, I need this job to be able to support Candy in whatever she wants to do when she moves to Asheville."

"So she's moving there?"

"Yes." Kurt wiped his mouth and continued,

"Her choice. I offered to move here. She didn't want that."

"What if she changes her mind?"

"Then I would have no other choice but to move here."

Bryson cleared his throat, laid the fork down in his plate and said, "I think I'm starting to like you, man."

"That's a relief."

"Yeah, now you have to convince the others."

"How much work is that going to be?"

"To be honest with you, Garrison and Everson are pretty easygoing. Barringer is going to give you the most problems and then there's pops. Candice is a daddy's girl and you're taking his only daughter. You definitely have some ground to make up with him. But hey, that's the price you have to pay for taking our sister away."

Kurt nodded. "I'll pay whatever price I have to if that's the case."

"Alright. Let me get the check so we can get out of here," Bryson said.

"No, I got it. That's the least I can do for you taking the time to meet me out here like this."

"Okay. I appreciate it, man. I think we've made some progress."

"Yes. Definitely."

Chapter 19

On Thursday, Kurt met Desmond for breakfast to discuss how they would move forward after finding out the deal was a no-go. Kurt walked into the restaurant and joined Desmond at the table. Since Desmond was on the phone, Kurt took a moment to check his cell for messages, hoping he'd see a text from Candice. There were none. He hadn't spoken to her since Tuesday night when she asked him to leave her apartment. He wondered how she was doing and if he'd hear from her soon. Was what he'd done unforgivable?

"Hey, man. Sorry 'bout that," Desmond said. That was Dante. I told him Barringer turned down the offer, so we're done here. We can wrap it up and head home."

"Yeah, that's what I wanted to talk to you about. I can't leave just yet."

"No?"

"No. Look, there's something I need to make you aware of. It's something I've been hiding for about six months and, well, you need to know."

"What's that, man?"

"I've been seeing Candice Blackstone and—"

"I knew it! I knew something was going on between you two."

"How'd you know?"

"I could feel the energy in the conference room, especially when you two shook hands. And when we told them about the offer, I saw the way she looked at you. When there's an issue with a woman brewing, shrew—that's a can you don't want to open."

"Tell me about it."

"So you and Candice, huh?" Desmond said.

"I'll be honest—I thought you'd be upset about this news."

"Upset? Why? Because she works for Blackstone?"

"Yeah. Exactly."

"Who am I to decide who you can and can't love? I can't make that call."

"I know, but there's clearly a conflict of interest..."

Desmond cracked a smile. "So what. I know you. I know how you work. I'm sure you've had a talk with her about not mixing business with pleasure."

"I have, several times, but after that offer we presented Tuesday, it put our relationship in a bind. She hasn't said a word to me since."

"What's the problem, exactly?"

"She says I should've told her about the proposal. Said she felt blindsided."

"That wouldn't be separating business from pleasure."

"In this particular case, she feels this was so important, I should've told her, and I can't say I disagree. I probably should've told her."

"That's a tough one, man. I don't know what I would've done if I was in your position."

Kurt sipped coffee. "What do you think Dante

will do about my job? He's not going to fire me, is he?"

"Nah. He wouldn't go that far and being that you've asked the question I take it you're not leaving Asheville to move to Wilmington."

"No. Candice wants to move to Asheville. Well, let me rephrase—she *wanted* to move there. Now, she probably wants a divorce."

Desmond grinned. "A conversation will cure all of this, man."

"Yeah. Maybe."

After finishing his breakfast, Desmond said, "Anyway, I'm going to head home. I need to see my family. The twins are driving Sherita nuts."

Kurt chuckled. "Hey, tell Sherita I said hi."

"I will."

"I'll talk to Dante when I'm back," Kurt told him.

"Yeah, man. Hey, look—when Candice is all moved in, me and Sherita would love to have y'all over for dinner."

"I'll keep that in mind."

As Desmond exited the restaurant, Kurt dialed Candice's number. He didn't expect her to answer so when he heard her voice on the other end, he was pleasantly surprised.

"Hello?" she said again.

"Hi, Candy. How are you?"

"I'm doing okay. How are you, Kurt?"

"I'll be a lot better if we could have this conversation face-to-face."

"We will."

"Are you working today?"

"I am, and I'm about to jump on a conference call, so I'll have to call you back."

"Will you?"

"Will I what?"

"Will you call me back?" he asked, not caring the

least about the desperation in his voice.

"Yes, I'll call, but I have to go right now."

"Okay. I'll talk to you later, then."

"Okay."

* * *

Her heart fluttered when she walked into the bar. She tried to make it stop, but it was something she couldn't control. A part of her warned her not to meet up with Quinton – probably the same part that reminded her she was married to a wonderful man – a man who was hers. And he was a good man. Top-of-the-line. That's why it felt odd meeting with her ex. If Blackstone Financial didn't need CheckMate's business, she wouldn't be here meeting with a person she intended to leave in the past. The past was the past for a reason. So why did the sight of him sitting alone at a booth with the hanging table light above illuminating his rich, chocolate face cause her to skip a breath? He was still the same gorgeous man he always was.

What are you doing here, Candy? Leave while you still can. You should be talking to Kurt rather than entertaining this loser. The man who cheated on you. What's there to say?

She was seriously considering turning around until he looked up and saw her.

Quinton's eyes settled on her and he didn't think about turning away or whether he thought the stare made her uncomfortable. His eyes feasted on her frame – enough to make her walk a little unsteady. She adjusted the purse strap on her shoulder, remembered why she was there, put on her game face and cleared her throat as she approached the table.

Quinton rose to his feet like a gentleman – all

six-feet-four of him. Candice wasn't buying any of his act. She plastered a smile on her face and slid into the booth. He sat down again and took in her familiar face up close. It had been years since they'd last spoken. She would have liked to keep it that way, but thanks to him, here they were. *He* wanted to talk.

"So, it's been a long time," he said.

"Yep," she replied, tight-lipped and completely disinterested.

"You're still beautiful."

Apparently not beautiful enough if you still cheated on me...

"Quinton, it was a struggle for me to come here so let's not waste time. What do you want?"

"This. Just to talk to you." He glanced at the ring on her finger. "I realize you're married now. I'm with someone as well, but I can't fully be with her until I close the door on us."

"Oh, you closed the door, alright. You slammed that sucker shut...made the hinges fall right off. You don't remember?"

"I remember your brother threa—"

"You cheated on me, Quinton. At first, I thought it was my fault that you stopped talking to me. Maybe you found other women interesting. I mean, what did you think I was going to do? Be your little puppet while you went on a cheating spree? Is that what you thought?"

"I asked you here to clear up some things about me, Candy. First and foremost, I *never* cheated on you."

"Now you're just going to lie to my face."

"No, I'm not lying. I never cheated on you. Never."

"So all the rumors were false? And you stopped talking to me, wouldn't answer my text messages—

nothing. Even my brother saw you with a woman."

"Yes, he did, and I don't know what he told you, but the minute I saw him that night, I told him it was a business meeting so he didn't get the wrong idea."

"Then why were you holding the woman's hand? Why'd you kiss her?"

"I did neither of those things. That's an outright lie."

"Okay, then why were you there to begin with?"

"I was having a meeting. A few minutes after Bryson saw me, four other people had joined us. I tried to explain this to you back then, but your brother ordered me to stay away from you and issued a bunch of other threats I don't care to mention. Anyway, I stayed away from you. I gave him what he wanted. I cut off all communication with you but it wasn't because I was cheating. It was because I had enough. Your brothers never liked me from jump so I figured I'd stay away. At that point, I asked myself why I was fighting for something no one wanted us to have. I didn't want that fight for the rest of my life. But, they've eased up a bit, I see since you're married now. I guess I should've hung in there a little longer."

"Are you done?"

He gestured for her to have the floor.

"You're a liar, I shouldn't have come here and I'm not going to sit here and listen to you lie about my brother."

Candice reached for her purse.

"Why would I lie? It's not like I have anything to gain from you. I can't get you back. You belong to another man. I just wanted you to know I'm not who Bryson made me out to be."

"Sure you're not. Goodbye, Quinton."

She'd heard enough. She took her purse and

focused her attention on the front exit. She couldn't get away from Quinton fast enough.

It wasn't until she looked up at her car that her already rapid pulse became faster because standing there was her husband. She'd been busted.

Chapter 20

"Kurt, what are you doing here?" Candice asked. His sharp gaze told her he'd witnessed her meeting with Quinton.

"What am *I* doing here? That's what you're asking me after you come out of a bar seven o'clock in the evening with another man."

"It's not what you think."

"Not what I think? I never *thought* you'd put me in this kind of position. Not you, Candice. What have I done to you to deserve this?"

"He's my ex—"

"I know who he is," he said loudly. "I made it my business to know. What I don't know is why my wife is having drinks and appetizers with her ex."

"I didn't have anything to eat or drink. I told you it's not what you think, so calm—"

"It's not? Because you're leaving a bar and you weren't with me. Is that not a bar?"

"It is, but—"

"Then what were you doing in there with him?"

Candice held her temples. If they were keeping business out of their marriage as he suggested, then she couldn't tell him what she was doing here, just like he couldn't tell her about The Champion Corporation's plans to buy Blackstone Financial. So she said nothing – not the smartest thing to do in the world when your man caught you having dinner with your ex-boyfriend.

"Candice?"

"I—I can't tell you why. It's business. I'm sorry."

"You know what? I'm sorry, too. This—us—I think this was one big mistake, Candice."

"Mistake—?"

"Yes. There's no way a relationship between us will work with all of these outside forces constantly working against us. I can't tell you things. You can't tell me things. You're having secret meetups with your ex-boyfriend...this doesn't feel right. Us not being able to discuss our work doesn't feel right and then on top of an already confusing situation, your brothers don't want you with anyone. I've never seen anything like it and quite frankly, I find it disturbing. Why wouldn't your brothers want you to be happy?"

"They do."

"No, they don't. How did you think I found out about you being here? Do you think I was driving around and saw your car in the parking lot? Your brother, Barringer, told me you wanted to talk to me here. He must've known I'd see you and Quinton together, his way of plotting to break us up. Why? Because it's what's best for Blackstone Financial if we cut ties. And he's right."

"No, he's not right Kurt."

"He is, and until we figure out another way, I'm going back home."

"So your solution is to leave me here to handle this all on my own."

"It's time you stood up to your brothers. Until then, there's not much I can do. And I *will not* stick around and watch you have dinner with your ex-boyfriend. That's for sure."

"Kurt—"

"When you fix this dysfunction, talk to me," he said as he continued walking away from her.

"Kurt, just wait a minute," she said, but he kept on to his car.

Candice was so hurt, so angry, her hands were shaking. Did Barringer really do this? She'd only told Garrison about this *blackmail* dinner-meeting with Quinton. How did Barringer find out?

She got in the car, swallowed her emotions and called Garrison.

"Hey, how'd it go?"

"Not good. Gary, did you tell Barry about this?"

"Yeah, I told him."

"Why? Why would you do that?"

"He said he wanted to know what was going on with you—something about you making wrong decisions for the company and I wanted to prove to him you'd do whatever it takes for this company, even if it meant meeting an ex-boyfriend you despised."

"Wow. That's—wow. I gotta go."

Candice hung up the phone and drove straight to Barringer's house. She pushed the doorbell too many times to count. Calista answered with baby Bella in her hands.

"Candy, what's wrong?" she asked upon seeing the distress on her sister-in-law's face.

"Where's Barry?" she asked, stepping inside. Her face was red with agitation. Her eyes glistened over with tears anger had caused.

"What's going on?" Calista asked.

"Where is he, Cali?"

"What's all the noise about?" Barringer asked, coming out of the kitchen with a drink in his hand wearing sweats.

"How could you do that to me, Barry?"

"What are you talking about?"

"You *know* what I'm talking about! You knew I was meeting up with Quinton—"

"You met up with Quinton?" Calista asked, frowning.

Candice continued, "So you sent Kurt there so he'd see me and Quinton together, all in an effort to break us up."

"Unlike you, I'm doing what's best for the company."

"So it doesn't matter if I'm unhappy or if you ruin my marriage...just so as long as the *company* is fine."

"Listen—you should not have been meeting up with Quinton, anyway. If you would've told me what CheckMate was trying to do, I'd stopped it then and there."

"Yeah, sure you would. I'm outta here."

"Candy, wait," Calista said.

"I can't take this anymore, Calista. And you can find somebody else for my job, Barry because there's no way I'm stepping a foot back in that building."

Candice was already out the door when Calista looked at Barringer and said, "Why would you do that to her?"

Barry left the question up in the air as Calista hurried out the door to catch Candice as she was backing out of the driveway. Candice stopped and rolled down the window.

"Where are you going?" Calista asked.

"Anywhere but here."

"Candy, you know how your brother is—"

"Yes, I know how he is and that's why I'm done making excuses for him. I'm not doing it anymore.

Not doing it for him, Gary, Everson, Bryson or my parents. I'm done! I'm tired of this. I'm out."

"Where are you going?"

"I don't know where I'm going. I just need to go. Bye."

She backed out of the driveway and hit the gas.

Chapter 21

Kurt arrived home early in the morning which was fine since he didn't have to go back to work until Monday. Still, after waking up around eleven and having lunch, he went to The Champion Corporation to meet with Dante. He was sure Dante had questions for him and he wanted to clear everything up without having to worry about it over the weekend.

Phyllis, the receptionist in the lobby, smiled at him and said, "Hey, I thought you weren't going to be back until Monday."

"That was the plan, but I came in to talk to Dante. Is he free?"

"It looks like he's on the phone at the moment but you can go on up. I'll ping him and let him know you're on your way."

When Kurt got off of the elevator, he slid his hands into his pockets not sure of what he would say. Before he could ponder any further on it, Dante waved him inside.

"Kurt, how are you, man? You're not bruised and battered are you?" he joked. "Desmond told me the meeting wasn't any better than the last. Said

Barringer Blackstone wasn't down to play ball."

"If you ask me, that was to be expected. Listen...before we get too deep into that, I need to bring something to your attention. I don't know if Desmond has mentioned anything to you already or—"

"About what? All Desmond talked about was the meeting."

"Well, I'm in a relationship with Candice Blackstone."

Dante's brows went up. "You are?"

"Yes, and full disclosure, she's Candice Hempstead now."

"She's your wife?"

"Yes."

Dante got up from his desk and walked over to slap hands with Kurt. "You sneaky dog. Congratulations, man."

"Thanks," Kurt said, baffled. He thought the news would have Dante in a different mood than the joyful one he was currently displaying.

"How long have you been married?"

"A month. We dated for five months and decided to make it official."

"You must be on some real top-secret stuff because I didn't know anything about it."

"That's the way we wanted it. We didn't want anyone from either side telling us what we should and shouldn't do so she kept it quiet and so did I."

"Until now, that is."

"Yeah, until now."

"Why'd you choose to break your silence?" Dante inquired.

"I told Desmond. I figured it would only be right to let you know what was going on. That way, everything's out in the open. And I also wanted to let you know that I've always told Candice I would keep our business life separate from our personal life."

"That's easier said than done. How's that working out?"

Kurt shook his head remembering his last conversation with Candice. He was too upset to look at her when he walked away, something he regretted now.

"Not so good. It was working at first, and then she told her brothers about us and they disapproved—well, I think I'm working on gaining the oldest one's trust at least. The others, I'm not so sure about just yet. Then she told her parents and I know for a fact she's not getting any support from her father."

"So you brought her back here with you?"

"No. She's still there."

Dante frowned. "Still where?"

"In Wilmington."

"Then why are you here?"

"My home is here. My job is here."

"But your *wife* isn't here. All the other stuff doesn't matter. You need your wife here to make the home and the job mean something. Right?"

"Of course, man, but it's not that easy."

Dante grinned. "It's never easy when it's the right one. Trust me. I know. I had to pretend to be some dude online to get to know Emily because she didn't like me. Don't know what it was—but in the beginning, she just didn't like me. I used to go by her shop and buy stuff just for the heck of it—just to have an opportunity to see her. I did what I had to do to get the girl I wanted to get. And now I got her, and she's mine. What you need to do is go get your woman. If her family is giving her a hard time, who better for her to lean on than you?"

"You don't have an issue with me and Candice

being together?"

"No. Not at all. Why would I have an issue with that?"

"Come on, Dante...there's clearly a conflict of interest here. That's why I kept my relationship with her hidden for so long."

"The only conflict I see is this disagreement going on between you and your wife. And, let me give you some advice, man. It's only going to get worse if you let it fester. Go handle your business. Desmond will be just fine a few days without you. Family is more important."

"You're right. Thanks, man."

"Oh, and Kurt."

"Yep."

"The job is yours for as long as you want it. It'll be here when you get back."

Kurt nodded. "Hey, why did you want to buy Blackstone, anyway? I thought you were more interested in bringing them on as a subsidiary."

"I only wanted something to happen and quickly. Since now I know where they stand, I can close the door on that and move to other options for the company."

"I see."

"Now, you go handle your business."

"Yep."

Kurt left the meeting with the assurance that his job, his livelihood, would be intact when he smoothed things over with Candice. That's if he was able to do so. If the way they left each other that night in the parking lot of the restaurant was any indicator, he was in trouble. And it was his fault. But how else is a man supposed to react when he saw his wife having dinner with her ex-boyfriend?

He went home, repacked and called Candice as he began the drive back to Wilmington. It was a long, boring drive, but it would give him some time to process their relationship. He shouldn't have left in the first place. He realized that now. Exhausted and all, he realized that.

He dialed Candice's number and when it went to voicemail after the fifth ring, he left a message:

Hey, Candice. It's me. We need to talk. I want to talk to you in person but I just have to say I'm sorry how I left things between us. I take full responsibility for that. I'm on the way back right now. I'll see you soon. I love you.

Chapter 22

Candice arrived at Seashell Island Resort and could already smell the scent of relaxation – lavender, chamomile and rosemary – wafting through the lobby from the resort's spa. That's what she needed – to relax – to let her mind drift and be free of the constant drama of her family.

And then there was Kurt...

He didn't know what he was getting himself into when he became her husband and subsequently a member of her family. Her brothers, even her father, wasn't willing to welcome him with open arms. Instead, he was being judged and talked about – the subject of ridicule as to why he wasn't good enough for her.

She'd gotten a call from Kurt last night. She didn't answer. She listened to his voicemail, but she didn't want to talk to him or anyone else. She just wanted to take the time to process what she was feeling and determine at this stage in her life how she would move forward. A woman shouldn't have to choose between her family and her man, but here she was at a fork in the road.

At breakfast, she bit into a croissant and glanced

at her phone when she saw Bryson's number on the display – a call she let go to voicemail. This was her day of peace. No one would ruin that.

After breakfast, she went to the fitness room to workout followed by a hot shower then a trip to the spa. She laid there, closed her eyes and relaxed, breathing deeply as the masseuse had suggested and while she did, she tried to think of reasons her family were so opinionated when it came to her decisions. They loved her. And weren't they supposed to care that much? She appreciated that about her family. No matter how much they got on her nerves, that was a constant that always remained true – they cared about her. Her issue was navigating around their judgments.

* * *

Saturday evening had come quickly and Kurt was starting to worry when he couldn't get in touch with Candice. He pulled up at her apartment and right away noticed her car was missing. He decided to go inside since he was already there. The place was just like he'd last seen it – half-packed boxes in the living room and kitchen.

"Candice, are you here?" he asked, walking to the bedroom but she wasn't there. The bed was made, curtains open. He knew she wasn't at work, so where was she?

He called Bryson, the *one* brother he'd established a rapport with.

"Hello."

"Hey, Bryson. It's Kurt."

"Oh. Hey, man. What's up?"

"I'm looking for Candice. Have you seen her?"

"Wait—what do you mean you're *looking* for Candice."

"We got into an argument yesterday and I went back to Asheville. I drove all the way back here to talk to her and she's not at her apartment, she's not at work and she's not answering her phone."

"Where are you now?"

"I'm at the apartment."

"Okay. Meet me at my house. I'll text you the address."

"Alright. I'll be right there."

Chapter 23

The massage was so good, she didn't want it to be over. Her body was so relaxed, she didn't want to get dressed. As she made herself put on clothes, a call came through from Kalina. She almost answered it. Almost, but something told her to let it be. She'd had a beautiful, uninterrupted day so far. She wanted to continue that streak.

She ate a late lunch and then slid into a bikini and reclined by the pool. The thing that bothered her the most about this whole situation was probably the fact that her family didn't take the time to get to know Kurt. They were so busy trying to sabotage the relationship that they didn't bother getting to know who Kurt was as a person. And then there was the devious plan Barringer had set up so Kurt would catch her with Quinton. And what about Quinton's allegations that Bryson was the cause of their failed relationship?

She couldn't believe they would stoop so low. Was Blackstone Financial so important to Barringer that he'd intentionally ruin her marriage to save the company? And was Quinton so bad of a person that Bryson had to threaten him to stay away from her?

When her phone beeped, she rolled her eyes behind her shades and looked at it. There was a text message from Kalina:

> Hey, where are you? Kurt is on the way here and he's worried since he hasn't been able to reach you. Please text me back when you get this. We're all worried at this point.

And now another call was coming through – from Bryson. Then Kurt, again. Moments later one came from Calista. Next, June.

Annoyed, Candice responded to Kalina's message only hoping it would calm everyone down so they'd stop calling back-to-back.

> **Candice**: I'm fine. Taking some time for myself to figure some things out. Tell everyone I'm fine so they can stop calling and texting me.
> **Kalina**: You're not taking calls from Kurt either?

Candice rolled her eyes. She could hear the insinuation in her question. Like, who wouldn't take a phone call from their husband?

> **Candice**: I'll call him later, too.

He wasn't getting off the hook so easily. He'd turned his back and walked away from her, drove all the way back home just to turn around and come back. Would this be a pattern for him? When things got tough, he'd bail? She wanted a man who would fight for her. Who'd make it work no matter what happened – not someone who walked away from an already stressful situation, making it much worse.

Chapter 24

When Kurt pulled up at his house, Bryson was outside digging holes for the evergreen trees that would separate his yard from the neighbors. Kalina thought trees would look much nicer than a fence. He agreed.

"So what happened?" he asked Kurt.

Not knowing where to start, Kurt rubbed his chin.

"You told me you'd fight for my sister. Said you'd do anything for her. So what could possibly make you run back to Asheville?"

"A bunch of nonsense. I got a call from Barringer telling me to meet Garrison and Candy at a bar. I'm thinking it's going to be something business-related so I show up and Garrison wasn't there. Candy was there. With her ex-boyfriend."

Bryson stopped digging but left his right foot on the metal part of the shovel. "What?"

"Candice was sitting with a guy who I figured out was her ex-boyfriend, Quinton. So here I am caught off guard and dumbfounded that my wife is, for some reason, having dinner with her ex. She leaves the restaurant and I see her in the parking lot. First of all, she looked shocked to see me like she knew she was doing something she had no business. That bothered me because if it was innocent why would she be shocked to see me."

"Maybe she didn't expect you to be lurking in the parking lot."

Kurt shrugged. "That still doesn't explain why she was there with him. I asked her what the conversation was about and she couldn't tell me."

"What you *should* do is ask Barringer why he sent you there in the first place. Sounds like a setup because if it's one thing I know about my sister is, she's loyal. She's not a cheater. And if you claim to love her, you wouldn't jump to conclusions."

"I *do* love your sister."

"Then why'd you leave town?"

"What would your reaction be if you saw your wife having dinner with her ex?"

"I would ask her about it, of course, but I wouldn't make assumptions because I know my wife loves me—this from a man who's been cheated on. I was married before Kalina. That relationship ended because my wife at the time cheated on me."

"Wow."

"Yeah, and for a while, I dealt with trust issues until Kalina came along, but let's get back to Candy. I told you before and I'll tell you again, man. We've all done things to protect her from men we see as threats. Maybe this was Barringer's way of protecting her from you."

"More like protecting his company..."

Bryson resumed digging when he said, "Barry doesn't live far. I'll call him up so he can come over here and straighten this thing out. You cool with that?"

"Yeah. Call him."

Bryson stopped digging again, wiped sweat from

his face with his forearm then dialed Barringer. They spoke briefly before he returned his attention back to Kurt. "He'll be here in a few minutes. I guess I'll take a break."

The men walked to the house and on to the kitchen where Kalina looked up and saw Kurt.

"Hey, Kurt. I'm Kalina."

"Nice to meet you, Kalina."

"Oh, I'm sorry, baby," Bryson said. "It completely escaped me that Kurt hasn't really met the family."

"Yeah, we should do something about that, shouldn't we?" Kalina asked.

"We should," Kurt said. "I would love to meet everyone."

"You would?" Kalina asked. "After the way everybody's been treating you, I'm surprised."

"Well, I'm trying to be understanding. I know everyone doesn't know me and people fear what they don't know. If everyone would just take a moment and get to know me, I think Candy will feel a lot better about us. It shouldn't be this way."

"You're absolutely right. It shouldn't."

"Did Candy tell you where she was, by the way?"

"No. She just said she'd call you later."

Kurt nodded.

"Can I get you something to drink? Water or tea?"

"Tea would be nice."

"Okay. I'll bring you some, too, Bryson."

"Thanks, baby."

When the doorbell rang, Bryson said, "Come in," guessing it was Barringer. It was.

"Yo," Barringer said.

"Hey, man. We're in the kitchen," Bryson said.

Barringer walked in, surprised to see Kurt standing there with a drink in his hand. "You didn't tell me *he* was here," he told Bryson.

"That's because I actually wanted you to show up."

Kurt looked at Barringer and instantly felt anger seep through his pores.

"What's up? Why am I here?" Barringer asked.

Kurt said, "I have some questions for you. I—"

"About what?" Barringer asked, cutting him off.

"Thursday, you called me and told me to meet with Garrison and Candy at that bar. When I got there, Garrison was nowhere to be found. I did, however, see my wife having dinner with her ex-boyfriend. So my question to you is, was that intentional? A stunt to break us up?"

"What if it was?" Barringer asked. "My sister can do better."

"You're right. She can do better than a brother like you. What kind of man would do something like that to his own sister?" Kurt asked, heated.

"What kind of man would pretend to like my sister only so he can steal my company?"

Kurt balled his fists and closed his eyes to channel his frustration. Then he said in an eerily calm voice, "That's not what I did. I've always told Candy we'd leave business out of our relationship. That's what I've done. But maybe I was focused on leaving business out when I should've been more concerned with her leaving you out and anybody else who has a problem with me. I'm a good man and I love your sister. I couldn't care less about taking your company. All I want is her. Now, I understand why she was so leery about introducing me to her family. I didn't get it back then, but it's clear to me now. So, here's what I'm going to do— I'm going to take my wife and we're going to get out of here as fast as we can. I'm tired of the games and I'm not playing them anymore."

"Wait," Bryson said. "Come on, man."

"No. I will not allow her to go through this anymore. I'm done with it." With that, he was out the door, dialing Candice on his way to the car. When she didn't answer he left yet another voicemail:

Come home. I'm going to go to your place to do some packing. I understand things better now. Call me.

Chapter 25

Candice woke up refreshed the next morning. Taking a day to relax was just what the doctor ordered. Even while knowing she still had to go back to her life, she was glad she took this time to escape from it.

She'd come down early to the restaurant to have breakfast – biscuits and gravy. Eating alone reminded her of how much she missed Kurt. She knew she had to call him. Knew he was worried, so she picked up the phone and called.

"Baby, where are you?" he asked.

The frantic tone in his voice gave her goosebumps. "I went to a resort for the weekend. I'm not far...still in Wilmington."

"Come home."

"I am. I'm just finishing up breakfast. I got your messages. Are you still packing boxes?"

"Yes. I'm getting you out of here. The way your family is behaving is not healthy for you or our relationship."

"I know."

"And I'm sorry about the restaurant incident. Turns out, your brother Barringer set the whole thing up. He wanted me to see you with Quinton so we'd break up."

"How'd you find out?"

"I confronted him about it. Listen, I don't know what the solution is to this. All I know is, we have a life waiting for us in Asheville and until they can come to terms with that and with the fact that you're not a child, then I don't know what else to tell them."

"Yeah," Candice said, surprised that her stomach was no longer in knots. She'd come to the same conclusion as Kurt. That's how she knew they were on the same page. "I'll be there in about an hour."

"Okay. Are you doing okay otherwise?"

"Yes, I'm fine."

"Good. Then, I'll see you soon. I love you."

"I love you, too, Kurt."

* * *

The *what ifs* that goes through a woman's mind when she found out she'd been lied to...

She didn't want to think about it. She wanted to brush it aside and forget Quinton had ever told her what Bryson had done. Besides, she still didn't know if it was true. She had to either confront Bryson about it or ignore Quinton's confession like it was nothing.

Sunday afternoon before she went to her apartment to see Kurt, she went to see Kalina.

Kalina opened the door. Her face brightened when she saw her sister-in-law standing there, but nothing glowed on Candice's face. She was stoic. Expressionless.

"Hey, Candy," Kalina said, embracing her. "Come on in."

Candice shook her head. "That's okay. Is Bryson here?"

"Yeah. Is everything okay?"

"I just need to talk to Bryson."

Kalina looked confused. "And you don't want to come in?"

"No. I'll stand here and trust me when I say it's taking a lot just to do that."

"Okay. Let me go get him."

Candice twiddled her thumbs waiting anxiously for Bryson to appear. She saw him walking through the foyer toward her. She stepped back, allowing him room to step out onto the porch.

"What's up, girl?" he asked. "You had everybody worried disappearing like that. Then Kurt came over here and—"

"I need to ask you something, Bryson, and please don't lie to me."

"What is it?"

"When I was dating Quinton, you told me you saw him cozied up with another woman. Said they were holding hands and kissing like they were a couple. You said he was cheating on me. Is that true?"

"I saw him with another woman. Yes."

"But were they a couple? Did you see him kiss her?"

Bryson sighed and finally responded, "No."

"No?" Candice repeated.

"No."

"So you lied and *then* you threatened him not to come near me. Told him to cease all communication with me. You intentionally broke us up for nothing."

"I did," Bryson confessed.

"Why would you do something like that?"

"Because I didn't think he was good enough for my sister."

"You don't get to make these kinds of judgment

calls, Bryson."

"I realize that now, Candy, and I'm sorry."

"You're sorry? That's all you have to say to me?"

"Yes. What do you expect me to do about it now? I can't go back and change the past."

"Right, because it's too late for that now. I really liked Quinton. We were good together and because you did what you did, our relationship fell apart and I grew to hate men for a long time, probably exactly what you wanted, right? Your little sister to die alone."

"Okay, okay, stop with the ranting and listen, Candy. I'm sorry. I lied to you. I did. I thought I was doing the right thing, but maybe I wasn't. At the time, I thought I was."

"Yeah, well, I'm over it. You and everything else," she said heading down the steps.

"Candy, just—"

"I don't want to hear anything else you have to say. I'm done. You win. Okay. You all win. Goodbye."

Chapter 26

Candice pinched tears away from her eyes as she began the drive to her apartment. She didn't live far from Bryson – only five miles or so – and she didn't want Kurt to think she'd been crying. She unlocked the door and walked into her apartment. Kurt told her he'd packed more boxes. He had the entire living room packed up. He'd even taped and labeled boxes. But where was he?

She'd been so busy trying to fix her face that she didn't check to see if his car was out in the parking lot. She walked to the kitchen, saw more boxes packed there. She continued to the bedroom. It's where she found him, laid out on the bed in a pair of shorts. He was on top of the covers, face up with his head resting on a pillow.

She stood there and observed him from head to toe. His long, muscular legs leading down to a pair of sturdy feet. He had nice feet. She liked that about him. And his chest – it was firm and expansive, even as she watched him. Ogled him. Never in a million years did she think she'd have to make a choice between her man and her family. Right now, she was choosing him. Her husband.

She walked to the bed, sat next to him and ran her index finger down the center of his chest. His eyes opened. He smiled immediately upon setting his sights on her.

"You packed up the whole house," she said softly.

"I'm ready to get you out of here."

"I'm ready to *get* out of here." She leaned down and pressed her lips to his.

"I'm sorry for leaving you."

She smiled – first time she'd smiled in days. "I'm sorry, too."

"Why are you sorry when you did nothing wrong?"

"Because I could've told you what was going on with Quinton and all that."

"What *was* going on? I still don't know that part."

"My father had spoken to Barringer about a business that wanted to sign with Blackstone Financial. Barringer said if we secured their business, it would put us in a better position so we wouldn't need to entertain any offers from The Champion Corporation about merging. So, he assigned me and Garrison to meet with the representatives from the company. Only problem was, when Garrison and I arrived, I discovered that one the representatives from that company was my ex-boyfriend's brother who basically told me if I wanted the deal to go through, I had to meet with Quinton for *closure.*"

"Closure? What kind of closure? The man who cheated on you wants closure?"

"Turns out, he didn't cheat on me. It was a lie orchestrated by one of my brothers to break us up, and it worked."

"Which brother? Barringer?"

"No. Bryson."

"Wow. Unbelievable. That's why we have to get out of here. All that underhanded stuff they're doing ain't going to work this time."

"No, it's not," she said, straddling him, lowering her mouth to his. She kissed his lips and parted his lips with her tongue, savoring the taste of him she'd missed. He sat up, pulled her shirt up over her head and took full control over their kiss with his strong tongue and lips. He threaded his fingers through her hair and tightened their closeness, kissing her with all the feeling of a man who knew he'd wronged the woman he loved. Who knew how much she needed him. That, at this stage in her life, he was her only real support. She wasn't getting the support she needed from her family. All she had was him.

"IT SHOULDN'T BE this way," Kurt said, strumming her back while she rested in his arms, their legs intertwined. "I never wanted it to be this way for you."

Candice inhaled a deep, satisfying breath of him. His skin. His essence. She was thoroughly relaxed after making love and didn't care to entertain the topic of her family. She wanted to talk about them. Their family.

"Candy, are you asleep?"

"No. Just thinking about my life with you."

"Oh, yeah?"

"Yes."

"And what'd you come up with?"

A soft grin escaped. "It's not that I've come up with anything. I was just thinking about how things would go, you know, with us living together. You at work. Me looking for a job. Taking care of the house. Cooking."

"Honestly, you don't need to work—not saying I don't want you to work because I want you to do whatever makes you happy."

"I know you do."

"So, if you want to take a break for a few months and hang around the house until you figure out what you want to do, that's fine with me. Even beyond three months is fine with me. You can get into doing something you want to do. Like, what did you want to do before you started working for Blackstone Financial?"

"I don't know. I've never had a thing. I just went with the flow."

"Well, now you have time to think about that."

"And kids?"

He smiled. "Yes. And kids. I think we should wait a few years on that, though. It'll give us time to learn, travel and grow together."

"I have no objections to that."

He squeezed her in another tight hug and left a kiss on her temple. "Goodnight, sweetheart."

"Goodnight, Kurt."

Chapter 27

On Monday, a truck from the moving company arrived. Kurt made sure the workers loaded all the boxes and some of the furniture she wanted to bring. Everything else would be donated.

Before they left for Asheville, Candice requested they go by her parent's house. Kurt still hadn't met them and she just couldn't move without them meeting first whether they liked him or not. And so she drove them there and parked in the driveway. After a deep breath, she looked at him. Her nerves were all to pieces.

"Are you sure it's safe if I go in?" Kurt asked.

"It'll be okay. Come on. Let's go."

He got out of the car. So did she, holding his hand tight and walked to the front door.

Her mother opened the door, stepped out on the porch and embraced her daughter.

"You must be Kurt," she said.

"Yes, Ma'am."

She embraced him, too, then said, "Come on in."

Her mother was coming around and being more receptive of Candice's decisions before this visit, so Candice wasn't at all surprised with her reaction. It was her father she was concerned about.

"So, you're the man who has stolen Candice's heart."

"That would be accurate," Kurt said. He smiled.

Elowyn smiled at Candice, "Come on back here and let's sit down and eat."

"Mom, you cooked already? It's only three o'clock."

"I made a lil' something-something when you told me y'all were coming. Have a seat."

After they got comfortable at the table, Candice asked, "Where's Dad?"

"He'll be down in a minute."

"Is he okay?"

"I'm okay, lil' girl," Theodore said walking into the kitchen. He leaned down and kissed her on the cheek.

Kurt stood up and reached to shake his father-in-law's hand saying, "Mr. Blackstone. Hi, I'm Kurt Hempstead."

Theodore accepted his hand and asked, "How are you doing, Kurt?"

"I'm okay, Sir."

"You know we need to have a chat, don't you?"

"Yes. I agree."

"Come on. Let's step out back for a minute."

Candice couldn't believe what she was witnessing. Once they were completely outside, she looked at her mother and asked, "What was that about?"

Elowyn smiled. "I had to talk to your father. He's as stubborn as the boys. You know that's where they get it from."

"I don't doubt that one bit."

"Have you spoken with any of them recently?"

"I just spoke with Bryson yesterday and it didn't go well."

"No?"

"No, and my problem with Bryson has nothing to do with Kurt."

"There's always been a rift between you and Bryson."

"Well, now you can add Barry to the list. Everson and Garrison are okay. They don't seem to mind that I have a brain and can think for myself."

"You know I don't like this division between y'all. You're flesh and blood. This is not how family is supposed to treat each other."

"I know Mother, but at the same time, I can't let them dictate my life."

"You're absolutely right. I can't argue with you there. Maybe it's time I gave them my two cents like I had to do with your father."

"What'd you tell him?"

"I told him to give Kurt a chance. How can you determine in your mind that you don't like someone when you haven't taken the time to get to know that person?"

"Oh, that reminds me," Candice said, getting up. She peeped out the window to judge how the conversation with her father and Kurt was going. They seemed to be okay.

"Everything good?" Elowyn asked, preparing plates.

"Yeah...looks like they're heading back in now."

"Good. All this food ain't going to eat itself."

Kurt walked in first. He glanced over at Candice and flashed a smile. She took that to mean his conversation with her father went okay. At least it was a start.

They all gathered around the table. Candice sat next to Kurt. Her parents sat opposite of them. Theodore prayed over the food and the part that touched Candice the most was how he also prayed that their marriage get off on a good start. She smiled, glad her father had finally come around.

"Compliments to the chef," Kurt said after wasting no time digging into his meal.

"Thank you," Elowyn replied, all smiles.

"This is my first time trying country-fried steak. It's phenomenal."

"I'm glad you like it. You know Candice knows how to make it, too," Elowyn said, then winked at Candice.

She smiled. "Don't be telling him all my secrets, Ma."

"No, tell me everything, Mrs. Blackstone. I'm loving this."

Elowyn laughed, then said, "The only thing you need to know about Candice is that she's loyal."

"And she's very determined," Theodore added. "Has a mind of her own. That's why she ran off and married you."

"Dad!"

"It's true. Look, Kurt—you must be something special if she was willing to go through such drastic measures to make sure you two were together, so like I told you outside a moment ago—you have my blessing."

Candice placed a hand over her heart, touched by her father's words.

"Mine, too," Elowyn said. "I just wish we could get to watch you two grow as a couple right here in Wilmington."

"I know, Mother, but we're going to live in Asheville."

"Well, I only have one request of you before you leave, baby girl," Theodore said.

"What's that, Dad?"

"Please fix whatever issues you have with your brothers before you go."

"Dad, I tried—"

"Try a little harder. Tomorrow's not promised. You never want to live your life with regrets, wishing you had made amends with someone who's no longer around."

"You're right. I suppose we can stay a few more days."

Kurt shook his head. "I'm leery about this only because I know what one of them tried to do to us."

"Who?"

"I don't want to drop names, but I will support Candice if she wants to fix things with them. If they don't like me, I can't worry about that, can I?"

"It's not that they don't like you, Kurt. They don't *know* you and they love their sister," Theodore explained. "Your brothers have always looked out for you and had your back. Sure they've overstepped a time or two."

"Or ten," Candice said.

Theodore chuckled. "Yes, or ten, but they love you. I have no doubt in my mind about that and deep down, I know you don't either."

She knew how much her brothers loved and cared for her and if it took her to be the bigger person, she was willing to obey her father's request and take a stab at it making peace.

Chapter 28

Candice stopped by Calista's Monday morning. Barringer was at the office so she didn't have to worry about running into him just yet.

Calista opened the door as she gently bounced baby Bella to sleep. "Hey, Candy. Come on in."

"Aw, the princess is sleeping."

"Yes. Let me put her down. I'll be right back."

Calista returned to the family room and joined Candice on the sofa.

"You look like you need a break," Candice told her. Her hair was tossed about. Some strands made it into the ponytail, others didn't and she seemed completely unfazed by it. She still had on her robe and was steadily yawning.

"Girl, Bella kept me up all last night."

"Why? Is she okay?"

"Yes. I think she got her days and nights mixed up. Barringer had to work today, so I figured I'd stay up." She yawned again. "Anyway, how's packing going? I was trying to call you yesterday to see if you needed some help, but—"

"Girl, you already got your hands full over here. Plus, I got Kurt there to help. He packed most of the stuff by himself and the movers have boxes and furniture on the truck already."

"Kurt is ready to go! I ain't mad at him."

"Yeah, he's ready, especially after what Barringer did."

"What did he do because I asked him what was going on but in pure, Barringer fashion, he didn't want to talk about it."

"Girl..." Candice shook her head. "I don't want to talk about it either, but after discussing some of it with Dad, he wants me to make peace with all of my brothers before I leave, so I have to talk to him at some point."

"What did Barringer do, Candy?"

"It's complicated, but putting it in a nutshell I had to meet with my ex, Quinton, for business. Barringer made sure Kurt saw us together, hoping me and Kurt would get into an argument and eventually break up."

Calista's mouth fell open. "Did Barry really do that?"

"He did. And I think it was more so because the company Kurt worked for made an offer to buy Blackstone Financial."

"Okay, so I can't tell you why Barry did that but I can tell you what his aim is. Barry will stop at nothing to protect Blackstone Financial."

"I know that."

"And it's not for him. He's doing it for his father."

"I understand that. I get it, but I'm his sister. It's almost like he's lost that connection to me. I'm the enemy now. And then there's Bryson...don't get me started on him."

"I know. Kalina told me."

"So, she knows what Bryson did?"

"Yeah. She said she heard you two arguing on

the porch."

"Crap...so that's why she's been calling me nonstop. Now, I have to deal with that situation. You know what—I'ma go talk to her now. Then, it's Bryson and your worrisome husband."

Calista chuckled. "You know how Barringer is. He's been your brother longer than he's been my husband."

* * *

After leaving Calista's house, Candice went straight to Blackstone Financial. She was supposed to stop by Kalina's first but decided she'd clean out her office last minute. That would also give her time to talk to Barringer.

She managed to sneak in without him noticing, surprised that her badge still worked. In her office, she gathered up her pen holder and some pictures on her desk – her college graduation picture, pictures of her niece and nephew and a family picture with her brothers. She opened the desk drawers and took out an almost empty lotion bottle and tossed it in the trash. Then her eyes focused on the red light on her phone. Loose ends. Things she'd leave behind for Barringer to deal with. There were voicemails from new clients but the voicemail from Quinton was the one that gave her pause. She listened intently to his message, reading his breaths. His tone. Remembering how sad his features were when she met him at the restaurant:

Hi, Candice. I just wanted to call to say thank you for meeting with me, even though it ended abruptly. Uh...*releases a loud sigh* I just wanted to let you know that I was being truthful. I hope one day, you will find out the truth. Anyway, *thanks again. I'll tell Bernard to proceed with signing on with Blackstone Financial. He was going to do that no matter what happened. Bye.*

It wasn't right. The sour feeling she felt in her gut wasn't right. This was the feeling she'd been fighting all along – the feeling that there was something better out there – not to say anyone could ever be better than Kurt, but what if? Had Bryson not interfered in their relationship, she didn't know how her relationship with Quinton would've ended up. The least she could do was provide closure for the both of them and let Quinton know she had found out the truth. It wouldn't serve any other purpose except closure because what was done was done. She couldn't do anything to change that.

"I thought you were supposed to be leaving."

Candice looked up at the sound of her brother's voice. "I am eventually. I had a lil' chat with dad. He thinks it's best if we talk before I leave town."

"What's there to talk about?"

Her eyes narrowed. "Is it possible that you can come out of business mode for a one minute and see me as your sister and not your employee?"

"Well, you're not my employee any longer since you're skipping town."

"Okay, then can I be your sister?"

Barringer closed the door and took a seat. "What is it, Candice?"

"What you did was foul, Barry—just plain wrong. There's no way around it."

"It wasn't wrong. It was business, and I still don't trust that man."

"Who cares! *I* trust him. He's *my* husband."

"Okay. Is that all you have to say?"

"No. That's not all I have to say. I have always

been there to support you, Barry. Even when you and Calista were going through hard times, I was always there. I had your back. I was worried sick about you. Thought you were going to lose it. I was talking to Calista, making excuses—saying anything for her to not give up on you—telling her how stressed out you were about the company. But here you are, once again, not having my back on anything because everything is always about what Barringer wants. Do you even care about me?"

"Don't ask me no stupid question like that. You know I care about you."

"Then why don't you show it? And why would my brother try to intentionally wreck my marriage."

"Because I don't know Kurt outside of business. I know he came to my company with some bogus proposals. That's all I know about him. How am I supposed to see him in a good light if, when I look at him, all I see is a man who's trying to take my father's company?"

"Get to know him outside of business because your little plan to break us up, it didn't work so stop being a jerk and be my brother for once!"

Barringer leaned back in the chair. The stubbornness in him didn't want anything to do with Kurt Hempstead, but for the sake of family unity, he said, "Fine. I'll hit him up. We'll go out for beers or something, but after that, if I don't like him, I'm not forcing any more interaction."

Candice smiled. Pleased. "It's really sad how stubborn you are."

Barringer stood up and walked over to the desk where Candice was sitting and said, "No, what's sad is how you still don't get me after all these years." He opened his arms and said, "Bring it in."

"Get away from me, Barry. I'm still mad at you."

"I said bring it in, girl," he said leaning toward

her and wrapping her in a big, brotherly bear hug. "You know I love you."

"I love you too, Barry."

"That's why you're leaving me high and dry, huh? Because you love me."

"Oh, stop it. You'll be just fine without me, especially once you find somebody to take my place here. Have you started looking yet?"

"Nah. Not yet, but I will. You leave me no choice."

"I'll still help you. I told you I would, so—"

"No, don't worry about it. You need to focus on your new life. I'll handle finding a replacement."

"Thank you, Barry. I appreciate that."

* * *

After leaving the office, Candice went to see Kalina at her office. She was making her rounds, tackling issues one by one, but visiting Kalina had to do with a different issue. The Quinton issue.

"Oh my God, girl! Where have you been?" Kalina asked throwing her arms around Candice. "I've been blowing you up, trying to make sure you were okay. Then I thought you were mad at me because of Bryson and—"

"Kalina, I'm not mad at you, girl. Bryson, on the other hand...the revelation from Bryson is really messing with my head."

"Come on in. Let me get you some coffee."

Candice stepped inside and sat on the couch.

"Here you go," Kalina said. "Now what did my husband do?"

"You know what he did. Calista said you told her."

"Yes, I told her what I heard, but Bryson didn't want to talk about it. I ain't never seen him so worked up in my life."

"He lied to me—lied straight to my face."

"About Quinton..."

"Yes...told me Quinton was cheating on me."

"But wasn't he? You said he stopped talking to you."

"He did, but only because Bryson threatened him. And if that wasn't bad enough, he proceeded to tell me that Quinton was cheating on me. It was all a lie. The only reason things didn't work out between me and Quinton is because Bryson didn't like him and didn't want me with him. In his eyes he wasn't good enough for me, so therefore, he had to go. Now, I'm left with questions of what could've been."

Kalina shook her head. "Don't do that to yourself. I'm not endorsing what Bryson did. That was totally wrong on so many levels. I'm sure he has his reasons, but it was wrong. As for you questioning yourself—it's over and done with, Candy. You're married now. You've moved on."

"I have and the way I feel is nothing against Kurt, but what if I wasn't *supposed* to move on? What if Quinton was supposed to be the man in my life? Since Bryson interfered, I'll never know. Unless..."

"Unless what?"

"Unless maybe I talk to Quinton. He called me. Left a message."

"Candy, please don't tell me you gave him your cell phone number."

"No. He has my office number and when I went by the office to clean out my desk drawers, I listened to my voicemails and there was one from him. I owe him an apology, Kalina."

"Bryson's the one who owes him an apology."

"I was the one in the relationship with him. I

should've trusted him."

"So, what are you going to do?"

"I'm going to talk to him. I at least want him to know that *I* know he's not a liar. I owe him that much."

"You don't *owe* him anything."

"But I feel like I do. I think I should say something, close it out and leave it off like that."

"Do you think it'll be that simple?"

"Yes. Why wouldn't it be?"

"Because you're vulnerable right now. Your emotions are involved. You're mad at Bryson and you're pondering over how your life with Quinton would've turned out."

"Listen, Kalina—I know you're the relationship expert but I think I'm making the right call here. I have to do what's best for me in this situation. Quinton isn't the only one who needs closure from all of this."

"Candy, Candy, Candy," Kalina sighed. "Just be careful. You're a newlywed. These situations can be tricky. If you're not careful, you'll find yourself in a predicament you don't want to be in."

"I'll be careful. I'll talk to him and then this will be all over."

* * *

And now it was Bryson's turn...

Candice walked into Bryson's office the next morning feeling completely opposite of the way she thought she'd feel. She wasn't angry. Wasn't there to chew him out or talk about how wrong he was for interfering in her life. All she wanted to know was why. And that's what she asked him. The one word. Why?

Bryson tapped a pen on his desk as he thought

about it and responded, "I told you I didn't think he was right for you."

"You never thought *anyone* was right for me."

"In my mind, no one is. I told you that, too. I had no right to interfere in your life. I didn't. You wouldn't have done that to me, I shouldn't have done that to you. I realize that now. So, how do we squash this and move forward?"

"It's squashed. I'll just leave it at that, but for future reference, I won't tolerate it so don't even try to pull that stunt with Kurt. Understand?"

Bryson smirked. "No worries. I like Kurt. He's a cool guy."

She narrowed her eyes. He just said no one was right for her but now, he was saying Kurt was a cool guy.

"I'm serious. He is. We're meeting him for drinks later."

"We, who?"

"Me, Barry, Gary and Everson. Barry set it all up."

"Is this a *setup* to get him drunk, then beat him up in the alley or something?"

Bryson shrugged. "Let your man handle his own battles."

"Alright. Fine. I'm just happy to see you're making an effort." Candice walked around the desk and wrapped her arms around her brother.

"Forgive me," he said. "Everything I've done I thought was for your best interest. I wouldn't intentionally hurt you."

"I know, and I forgive you. Just make sure you return my husband in one piece."

"No worries. I got you."

Chapter 29

Bryson slapped hands with Kurt as he walked into the bar. "You made it."

"Wouldn't have missed it," Kurt said. He spoke to Garrison, Everson and mumbled a greeting to Barringer. He didn't want to say anything to him at all.

"Let's grab a table," Bryson said since they'd all been sitting at the bar. When they settled at a table, Bryson ordered a round of beers.

"I guess this is the bachelor party that never was, huh?" Barringer joked.

The brothers chuckled.

Kurt clenched his jaw and ignored the comment. How do you find common ground with a man who tried to sabotage your marriage?

"I think, before we have drinks and break bread, we should acknowledge the elephant in the room," Bryson said.

Kurt grinned. "First, I'm the man who stole your sister. Now, I'm the elephant."

Garrison chuckled. "Look, as long as my sister is happy, I'm good."

"I second that," Everson said right before he took a swig of beer.

"And you know we're cool," Bryson told him.

All eyes then went to Barringer. He was holding his beer when he said, "Look, man—you know my reason for the animosity between us, but now that I know you weren't in this to take advantage of my sister for business reasons, I can get behind this...whole...marriage...*thing*."

Kurt took a sip of beer, not acknowledging anything Barringer had said.

"Okay," Barringer said. "I get it. I did something I shouldn't have."

"Something like what?" Garrison asked. He was out of the loop on Barringer's plan.

"When you told me about Quinton's meeting with Candice, I sent Kurt to the bar so he'd see Candice talking to her ex-boyfriend."

"Yeah," Kurt said, looking directly at Barringer. "He tried to break us up."

"Wow. That's a new level of shady, Barry," Garrison said.

"It was, but I thought I was doing what was right at the time, so—"

"So you think *lying* to your sister is right?" Kurt asked.

"No, not at all, and I've since made peace with my sister. I came here tonight to attempt to do that with you."

"I honestly don't need peace with you, man, and I don't need you to be okay with me. All I ask of you is that you respect my wife."

"I guess you heard that," Everson said.

Barringer leaned back in his chair. "Yeah, I heard it."

"Then I guess we're on the same page for once," Kurt said.

"Yeah, man. We're good. Just keep those Champions away from my company and we'll be even better."

"No, we'll be better if we keep business out of this."

Garrison nodded. "He has a point there. There's no sense in destroying family ties over business dealings."

"Agreed," Bryson said.

"Alright. The issues are out of the way, now let's have some fun," Everson said.

"Sounds good to me," Kurt said. "I'm sure the women are having their fair share of fun tonight."

Bryson raised a brow, confused. "They are? Kalina told me she was about to soak in a hot bubble bath which made me immediately regret coming out here with y'all."

"June said she was going to bed early tonight," Everson said.

"Yeah and Calista has Bella and Junior, of course," Garrison added.

"Oh, then I probably misunderstood her," Kurt said to save face, but he was sure Candice said she was going out with Kalina and the girls tonight. If she wasn't with them, where was she?

"Kurt, you play pool or does collecting *rocks* consume most of your time?" Everson quipped.

Kurt laughed. "I play pool."

Everson stood up and said, "Then, let's see what you got."

Chapter 30

Candice sat in the car for a moment rationalizing in her mind that if she walked up to the door of Quinton's house, spoke her peace, apologized for her brother's actions and then left, all would be right with her world. She would be given a clean slate and so would Quinton. This would give him the closure he needed.

That they *both* needed.

She got out of the car and walked to the door. She didn't have to ring the bell to alert him of her presence. As she got closer, he stepped out onto the porch.

"I was wondering if you were ever going to get out of the car," he said. "For a moment there, I thought you would drive off."

"How'd you know I was out here?"

"I was watching TV...saw you pull up."

"I know I should've called first," she said stepping up on the porch.

"Nonsense. A surprise visit from you is never a disturbance," he said, then smiled. "Come on in."

"Oh, no. I'm not going to stay long. I just thought I should come by and—"

"Candy, come in," he said opening the door.

She reluctantly stepped inside and said, "Wow. I see you've redecorated the place."

"Yeah. Thought I'd switch it up a bit."

"It looks nice."

"Thank you. Um...can I get you something to drink?"

"No. Like I said, I won't stay long. I just wanted to apologize."

"For what?" he asked, walking over to sit on the armrest of a chair in the living room.

She followed, sitting on the couch opposite of him. "Well, I thought about what you told me at the bar and figured I'd ask my brother and he finally told me the truth. All this time I thought you were a jerk, a liar and a cheater and it turns out my brother is the liar. You didn't do anything wrong. I'm sorry about everything. Sorry I didn't trust you enough to stand up to him."

"Well, we can't do anything about that now, can we?"

"Nope. All I can do is offer you my apology."

Quinton nodded. "That's too bad, though."

"What is?"

"This. These circumstances. Things could've been so different. Now, you're married to someone else."

"And you're seeing someone too, aren't you?"

"Yes, *seeing* someone. I'm not married. I—" he paused. "I hope he's good to you."

"He is."

"Good, then let me offer you a bit of advice."

"What's that?"

"Don't let your brothers ruin that for you."

Candice smiled. "I won't. I've learned my lesson." She stood up, extended her hand to him and said, "I wish you nothing but happiness."

"Same to you," he said taking her hand, but the handshake wasn't good enough. He wanted a full hug. Needed to feel her in his arms again. And he did. He wrapped his arms around her. Held her. Squeezed her, embraced her warmly by holding her snug against his chest with his chin resting on her hair.

Feelings she thought she shouldn't feel crept back into her mind. She was married – happily married – so why was she *feeling* anything?

"I should go," she said attempting to break the hug.

"I don't want to let go of you just yet." He took a final, farewell squeeze then loosened his grip on her. Without even thinking about it, he leaned down, aiming for her lips.

Candice darted her head away from him and asked, "What are you doing?"

"I'm sorry, I—"

"I gotta go," she said, nearly tripping over her own feet as she plowed her way to the front door.

"Candy..."

"I said what I had to say, Quinton, but me and you, we could never be. I'm married, and I love my husband. I hope you can move on now and be happy with whoever you're with. Goodbye Quinton."

"Goodbye, Candy."

Chapter 31

Kurt said his goodbyes to the fellas and on the drive home, he called Candice. He wanted to know where she was or where she'd been all night but when she didn't answer, that only made him anxious. She'd lied to him. That wasn't like Candice. She wasn't a liar.

When he pulled up at the apartment, he saw her car in the parking lot. He shut off his engine and walked in the nearly empty living room toward the bathroom with a towel wrapped around her body. Upon setting his eyes on her, she looked like she'd been upset about something. Her eyes were puffy which told him something opposite to the smile on her face. Something wasn't right with her.

"Hey."

"Hey. How'd it go with my brothers?"

"It was fine. How did it go with the women?"

She smiled and said, "Oh, I never have a problem with the women."

"I know, but how did it go tonight?"

"Um—" She couldn't tell him another lie. She shouldn't have told the first one. So she said, "Um...I didn't go out with the girls tonight. I'm sure you figured that out."

"I did. What's bothering me is, why you felt the need to lie. If you didn't go out with the girls, where'd you go?"

She sniffled. "I went...um..."

"You went where?" he asked.

"I went to see Quinton."

Kurt considered himself to be a pretty level-headed person – that is until now. "You—you went to see Quinton?"

"Yes."

"Went to see him where?"

"I was at his house, but—"

"So, you're telling me, you went to see your ex-boyfriend at *his* house tonight."

"Yes, Kurt, and I know how this looks, but—"

"You know how this looks!" he repeated, fuming. "You know how this looks? Why'd you go see him, Candy? And how long were you there? Were you there all this time? What were you doing over there? Huh?"

"Will you calm down?" she asked. She'd never seen him so amped up. So angry. But until she answered his questions, she knew all he had was assumptions.

"I wasn't there long and nothing happened, so just relax."

He stepped out of the bathroom and into the bedroom, pacing the floor saying, "My wife wants me to *relax* after telling me she spent the evening with her ex."

"I didn't spend the evening with him. I just went by there."

"Why? Why do you feel the need to go by there? And why did you lie and tell me you were going to be with the girls?"

"I went over there to apologize."

"Apologize for what?"

"For what Bryson did. I apologized for not believing him when I should have. For not—"

"For not what, Candy?"

"For not giving our relationship a chance. For letting my brothers control things."

"So, you want Quinton? Is that what you're telling me?"

"No, Kurt, that's not what I'm saying."

"Then if you could go back and change things, who would you be with? Me or him?"

"That's not a fair question."

"Oh, it's not, because if you ask me that question about any of my exes, the answer is you. I'll choose *you* every time, but you can't choose me because you still want your ex. After all these years..."

"That's not true!"

"If it's not true, then speak your truth!" he yelled. "Tell me what the truth is."

"The truth is, we, Quinton and I—never got the chance to find out what we could've been and that's my fault."

He was still fuming when he asked, "And you'd like that chance, right so go take it, Candy. I'm out."

"No," she said running up to him. "Kurt, I don't want him. I want you."

"You want me?"

"Yes."

"Then why when I got here, you looked like you'd been crying? What happened over at his house, huh?"

"Nothing happened."

"*Something* happened. What was it? You two had a good ol' time reminiscing about the past? Huh? Did you sleep with him?"

"No!"

"Then what happened?" he pressed.

"He tried to kiss me, but I pushed him away."

Kurt shook his head and peeled her hands off of him before walking out the front door.

Chapter 32

Ashamed. Embarrassed. That's how she felt walking up to Bryson and Kalina's house a few days later, hoping to talk to her sister-in-law about what she'd done and seeking to rectify it. Bryson opened the door and invited her in.

"What's wrong, Candy?"

"Nothing. Where's Kalina?" she asked, not answering his question. This wasn't the kind of discussion a girl was supposed to have with her brother.

"She's upstairs." He called for her then asked Candice for a second time, "Are you sure nothing's wrong?"

"I didn't say anything wasn't wrong, Bryson. It's a girl thing. I need to talk to Kalina about it."

"Hey, Candy. What's up?" Kalina said coming downstairs.

"Hey, I need to talk to you for a minute."

"Oh, okay. Sure. Come on upstairs."

Candice went up and when she stepped into Kalina's bedroom, she said, "I messed up big time."

"What happened?"

"I told you I was going to see Quinton and I

should've listened to you when you told me not to. Anyway, he tried to kiss me."

"You kissed him!"

"Shh...keep your voice down. I don't want Bryson to overhear this."

"You kissed him, Candy?" she asked softer.

"No. He *tried* to kiss me and I got out of there. I told Kurt everything, but he was furious because I lied and told him I was going to be hanging out with you and the girls but I was at Quinton's house."

Kalina's eyes nearly bulged out of her head when she said, "You went to his house!"

Candice could only drop her head.

"If you put yourself in Kurt's position, you'd be furious, too!"

"I would, definitely. So how do I fix this?"

"First you need to ask yourself who you want?"

Candice frowned. "You know who I want."

"Yes, I know who you want, but there was something about Quinton that made you lie to your husband and sneak around behind his back."

"I thought I could handle being alone with him and I felt the need to apologize—"

"Apologize for what? I told you before you went you had nothing to apologize for. I think you wanted to go over there because you *wanted* to and honestly, if you still have feelings for him, Candy—"

"I don't. It's not feelings. It's more like I'm at a loss because I'll never know how good me and Quinton could've been together. Just because I have those feelings doesn't mean I don't love Kurt."

"No, but it does mean you're getting dangerously close to ruining your marriage."

"What should I do now? I think I really hurt him, Kalina. Kurt didn't deserve that."

"He needs to know that you love him. That you'll choose him over all the others. That he doesn't have to worry about anyone stepping in between you two and causing a disruption."

Candice nodded. "You're right. Now, I need to figure out a way to do that."

Chapter 33

Candice went back to her empty apartment and walked in circles, strategizing. She wanted to make sure she was as clear, concise and as upfront as she could be before she called Kurt. She needed to have her story together. Needed for him to hear the sincerity in her words when she told him there was no other man for her.

Of all the drama that had encircled them in the last few weeks, it was her own actions that ultimately drove him away. That told her something – that it didn't matter who didn't like who or what anybody else thought about their marriage. The determination for how well their marriage would work was based on the way they treated each other. Trusted and loved each other. Everything else was futile.

Leaning up on the sink in the kitchen, she dialed his number and as the phone rang, she heard keys at the front door. She watched the knob twist and open. She slowly lowered the phone when Kurt stepped around the door, then closed it.

Candice swallowed the lump in her throat that had almost restricted her breathing. She forced out,

"I was just trying to call you."

He didn't respond. He walked in and leaned against the counter opposite of her.

"Kurt, I'm sorry."

"Do you love him?" he asked.

"No."

"Are you in love with him?"

"No," she said shaking her head, feeling awful that he felt the need to ask her the questions.

"Do you want to be with him?"

"No."

"Do you love *me*?" he asked.

Tears came to Candice's eyes. After everything he endured with her family – her parents, her brothers, their company disputes – he had to ask her if she loved him. "Yes, I love you."

He frowned, took a few steps closer to her and said, "Then if you love me, no man, and I mean *no man* touches these lips." He brushed his thumb across them as he spoke.

"He didn't—"

"I'm just letting you know. No man touches you, period. Do you understand me?"

"Yes. I understand. I'm sorry. It will never happen again, Kurt. Please forgive me."

"I've already forgiven you," he said, attacking her lips with a kiss that made her gasp for air. "That's why I came back. Why I'm here. I love you."

"I love you too, Kurt," she replied, a tear sliding down her face. "I'm so sorry."

He scooped her up, took her to the bedroom and stripped her naked in seconds before flattening her to the mattress with his body. He parted her legs and entered her, feeling pure satisfaction when he settled inside of her. He groaned, savored the feeling before delivering potent stroke after potent stroke, listening and enjoying her moans and screams. She was his. She'd always be his. Nothing or no one would ever take her away or disturb that.

He took her mouth while buried to her depths, grinding, stroking and making love to her the only way he knew how – with a passionate fervor that let her know, without any doubts that he loved her. This was real. No man would love her this way. No man could have her this way. And then she screamed, belted out his name while he owned her quivering body even more. While he told her she was his. While he claimed her. Loved her. Stroked her.

And he screamed – screamed for the way she clenched him and took all he had to give. Screamed for all the love he felt for this woman. For the fight in him to keep what they had together. Screamed for her to realize that this love was real. There was nothing better for her out there, nor would there ever be. He was it. By the way she was panting, he was sure she got the message.

"Did I make myself clear?" he asked, staring down at her, kissing her lips again before she had a chance to answer him.

"Yes."

"I love you, Candice."

"I love you, Kurt," she said, steadily panting. "I'm so sorry," she cried.

He disconnected his body from hers and pulled her into his arms. "Don't cry. Everything's okay. We're back on track. Everything's going to be okay. Do you believe that?"

"Yes." She sniffled.

"Good. Now, stop crying, baby. Tomorrow, we're going home."

"Okay."

"And we finally get to live our lives the way we want to with no interference," he said, rubbing her back, but deep down he knew how much she needed her family.

Epilogue

A Month Later

Candice smiled as she stood at the door, watching Bryson, Kalina and her parents get out of the car. This was the first time her family came to visit – the first time she'd seen any of them since moving to Asheville to begin her new life with Kurt. She'd settled in comfortably in her new role as wife, taking care of the house while Kurt worked. She was a natural at it, found her new life rewarding and exciting, but she missed her family.

Now, they were here. Well, some of them...

She couldn't wait for them to walk up to the house. She pushed open the storm door and ran out to the driveway, hugging her parents in a full I-miss-you embrace. She wrapped her arms around Kalina, then hugged Bryson.

"I'm so glad y'all made it," she said as she held on to them.

"Yes, we made it, now let me go so I can breathe, girl," Bryson said.

Her parents chuckled.

"Come on in, y'all. We almost have dinner ready."

"We?" Theodore asked.

"Yes. Kurt can cook. It's one of his many talents."

"Alright," Elowyn said. "I'm looking forward to this."

"Me, too," Theodore said.

When they stepped inside, Elowyn looked around and said, "Isn't this nice?"

Kurt came out of the kitchen wearing an apron and said, "Welcome family."

"Good to see you again, man," Bryson said slapping hands with him.

"Same here. Hi, Kalina. Mr. and Mrs. Blackstone. I'm glad you were able to make it."

"We wouldn't have missed it," Elowyn said. "You have a lovely home."

"Thank you. Your daughter made it a home," Kurt said then smiled at Candice.

She smiled back.

"Anyway, get comfortable," Kurt said. "Our home is your home."

"Yes, get comfortable, guys," Candice said. "I'll get you something to drink."

Candice walked to the kitchen while the family sat in the living room. She walked up to Kurt, embraced him and said, "This is going to be nice. I'm so happy."

"I love seeing you happy," he told her.

"Yeah, I just wish everyone could've made it."

"Do you?" All that time you spent complaining about your brothers and now you want them here, huh?"

"I know. They get on my nerves but I still love them. And I haven't seen Lil' Gary or my sweet little Bella."

"They'll make it here next time."

"Or maybe we'll make it here this time," Calista said, making a surprise entrance in the kitchen.

Candice turned around in disbelief.

"Calista, Barry—what are y'all doing here!" she asked, beyond excited.

"Well, your husband called and told us how

much you wanted us to be here so we're here, sis," Barringer said. He hugged his sister tight and left a kiss on her temple.

Tears glistened in Candice's eyes as she embraced Calista and then she took baby Bella, held her in her arms and stared. "I'm so glad y'all are here."

"Me, too," Calista said. "Barringer did ninety miles an hour all the way here. I think he misses you, but he'll never say it."

"Oh, definitely not," Candice said smiling.

When Candice heard Garrison's voice in the living room, she nearly screamed but quickly realized she couldn't do that while holding a baby. Instead, she walked there and brushed tears from her face. She handed Bella to her mother and squeezed Garrison like she hadn't seen him in ages.

"Why are you crying, girl?"

"I missed you guys so much," she said. Then she picked up Junior and pelted his face with kisses saying, "Do you miss your Aunt Candy? Do you miss your Aunt Candy?"

Junior shied away from her questions and with a smile on his face, he rested in the cradle of her neck.

And then June and Everson came walking in.

More tears sprang from Candice's eyes. "Oh, my heart can't take this," she said, wrapping her arms around Everson's neck. And then she hugged June.

"Everyone's here. My family is all here," she said.

"Yeah, when Kurt called me, I knew I had to be here," Everson said.

Candice looked across the room at Kurt feeling her heart explode with love.

"I knew how much you missed them, so—" Kurt walked over to her, planted a kiss on her lips. "I want nothing more than to see you happy and I know you love me, baby. I know you do, but I feel like I've taken you away from your family and so I wanted the entire family here when I make this proposal to you."

"What proposal, Kurt? What are you talking about?"

"I want you to know I'd be willing to move to Wilmington so you can be with all the people you love. All these people—people who sometimes drive you crazy but can't live without."

"Kurt—"

"I'll be just fine with the move. Listen, sweetie—I know your family is a huge part of your life—a huge part of who you are. For years, it's been you with your brothers and your new in-laws—women you call your sisters. And your niece and nephew—baby I'm perfectly okay with moving. Asheville's a hot market. It won't take long to sell this house and there are plenty of comparable properties in Wilmington."

Candice sniffled and asked, "But what about your job?"

"Ay, we could find a spot for a man with your talent at Blackstone Financial," Barringer said.

Kurt grinned. "No offense, bruh, but it's a strong *no* to that."

The family laughed.

"I was thinking of going solo, starting my own consulting business for companies who need marketing and branding help."

"I'd be your first client," Bryson said. "I think it's about time I gave Blackstone Tree Service a new name and an updated logo."

"And I can use some rebranding," Everson said of his business management company, "And I'm sure Colton could use some structure in his painting business."

"Colton?" Kurt asked.

"He's our cousin, the painter," Everson told him.

"See—I already have customers," Kurt said.

"Oh, and by the way, Candy, I still haven't filled your position," Barringer said. "So if you move back, it's yours."

"Wow. This is—wow. I'm speechless." Candice turned to Kurt and said, "I don't know what to say."

"Say the answer that'll make you the happiest. Whatever it is, I'm okay with it."

"Okay. Um...I guess I'm coming home," she said.

"Yes!" Kalina said.

Elowyn was so happy, tears welled up in her eyes.

"You really do love my daughter, don't you?" Theodore asked.

"Yes, Sir. I do."

"Then you've just inherited yourself four brothers," Everson said.

"And three sisters," Calista added.

Candice looked at Kurt, kissed him and closed her arms around him. She had no more jitters. No *what ifs*. No more questions about whether there was something better out there. Kurt was a man who'd do anything to see her happy – one who'd uproot his life for her to be with her family. He was definitely the man for her. The man she loved and adored. The man who'd do anything for her happiness. It didn't get any better than that.

* ~ *

Enjoyed *Candy's Corporate Crush*? Please take a moment to leave a review on Amazon. And if you want more of The Blackstone Family, check out the following books, available now!

EVENINGS WITH BRYSON
(A Blackstone Family Novel, Book 1)

What happens when a woman who doesn't believe in love meets a man who's given up on love?

Kalina Cooper has been hiding her loneliness by drowning herself in work at her home office and continuing on until the late evenings at her Aunt Edith's café. Her 'happily ever after' doesn't involve a husband. Having seen her father walk out on her mother when she was a teenager, she doesn't believe in love.

After a bad divorce from a cheating woman, Bryson Blackstone vows to never marry again. But he never expected to cross paths with a woman like Kalina Cooper. She's different. She's special. From what he has learned about her, he knows she doesn't believe in love, but he doesn't know why. Now he plans to weasel his way into her life to find out, because Kalina Cooper is just the woman he'd consider if he was crazy enough to fall in love again.

LEAVING BARRINGER
(A Blackstone Family Novel, Book 2)

Calista Blackstone has no problem playing her position as the supportive, dutiful wife of Barringer Blackstone. All she wants is a family, but after five years, she's given up hope of actually becoming a mother - at least to Barringer's children.

Barringer (Barry) Blackstone is too busy making money to make babies. CEO of Blackstone Financial Services Group, he's actively working on taking his father's company to the next level and avoids the subject of children. He's no longer certain that he wants the added stress of trying to raise a family while growing the business. But the workaholic will learn the hard way that money should never precede family.

FOREVER US: BARRINGER AND CALISTA BLACKSTONE
(Book 2.5, A Short Story follow-up to *Leaving Barringer*)

Barringer Blackstone is rough around the edges. That's no surprise to Calista. His demeanor is a gift and a curse – a gift because his strong-willed character makes him a great business leader. A curse because that same no-nonsense, merciless attitude doesn't make for a loving, passionate husband at times – the very reason Calista left him for four months.

They've been back together for two months and while their marriage and communication has improved, a weekend away reveals that their issues haven't been fully resolved. Is another separation in the works for this Blackstone couple?

THE THINGS EVERSON LOST
(A Blackstone Family Novel, Book 3)

When a past love throws a marriage off balance...

Everson is one of those men. Those sexy, chocolate Blackstone men. He has the perfect house. In June, he's found a wonderful wife, and marriage has been doing his body good. But the past has a way of finding its way to the present.

The past in the form of an old flame. Eliana Simmons. Everson's high school sweetheart.

Eliana moved away when they were younger. Seniors in high school. Now, work has made them cross paths, and those old feelings easily resurface, especially since Eliana was his first love – and she's not shy about confessing that she hasn't been able to get over him after all those years have passed.

When Everson finds himself lying to June, he knows he's in trouble. But this is just the beginning of what's to come for a man who gives another woman the attention he should be giving his wife.

Discover other books by Tina Martin:

St. Claire Series
*All books in this series are standalone novels and are full, complete stories. Read them in any order.

Royal
Ramsey
Romulus
Regal
Magnus

Seasons of Love Novelettes
Hot Chocolate: A Winter Novelette

The Boardwalk Bakery Romance
*This is a continuation series that must be read in order.

Baked With Love
Baked With Love 2
Baked With Love 3

The Marriage Chronicles
*This is a continuation series that must be read in order.

Life's A Beach
Falling Out
War, Then Love

The Blackstone Family Series
*All books in this series are standalone novels and are full, complete stories. Read them in any order.

Evenings With Bryson
Leaving Barringer
Forever Us: Barringer and Calista Blackstone (A short story follow-up to *Leaving Barringer*. You must read *Leaving Barringer* before reading this short story)
The Things Everson Lost

A Lennox in Love Series
*All books in this series are standalone novellas and are full, complete stories. Read them in any order.

Claiming You
Making You My Business
Wishing That I Was Yours
Caught in the Storm with a Lennox (A Short Story Prequel to Claiming You)
Before You Say I Do

Mine By Default Mini-Series:
*This is a continuation series that must be read in order.

Been In Love With You, Book 1
When Hearts Cry, Book 2
You Belong To Me, Book 3
When I Call You Mine, Book 4
Who Do You Love?, Book 5
Forever Mine, Book 6

The Champion Brothers Series:
*All books in this series are standalone novels and are full, complete stories. Read them in any order.

His Paradise Wife
When A Champion Wants You
The Best Thing He Never Knew He Needed
Wives And Champions
The Way Champions Love
His By Spring

The Accidental Series:
*This is a continuation series that must be read in order.

Accidental Deception, Book 1
Accidental Heartbreak, Book 2
Accidental Lovers, Book 3
What Donovan Wants, Book 4

Dying To Love Her Series:
*This is a continuation series that must be read in order.

Dying To Love Her
Dying To Love Her 2
Dying To Love Her 3

The Alexander Series:
*Books 1-4 must be read in order. Books 5, 6,7 and can be read in any order as a standalone books.

The Millionaire's Arranged Marriage, Book 1
Watch Me Take Your Girl, Book 2
Her Premarital Ex, Book 3
The Object of His Obsession, Book 4
Dilvan's Redemption, Book 5
His Charity Challenge, Book 6 (Heshan Alexander and Charity Eason)
Different Tastes, Book 7 (An Alexander Spin-off novel. Tamera Alexander's Story)
As Long As We Got Love, Book 8 (Family Novel)

Non-Series Titles:
*Individual standalone books that are not part of a series.
Secrets On Lake Drive
Can't Just Be His Friend
The Baby Daddy Interviews
Might As Well Be Single
Just Like New to the Next Man
Falling Again
Vacation Interrupted
The Crush
Wasn't Supposed To Love Her
What Wifey Wants
Man of Her Dreams
Bae Watch

ABOUT THE AUTHOR

TINA MARTIN is the author of over 60 romance, romantic suspense and women's fiction titles including the Amazon #1 New Release, Magnus (A St. Claire Novel). Tina lives in Charlotte, North Carolina.

You can reach Tina by email at tinamartinbooks@gmail.com, Facebook at https://www.facebook.com/tinamartinauthor/ or visit her website for more information at www.tinamartin.net.

55623159R00119

Made in the USA
Columbia, SC
16 April 2019